RIDERS
OF THE PURPLE SAGE

RIDERS
OF THE PURPLE SAGE

A NOVEL

By

ZANE GREY

With Illustrations by

W. HERBERT DUNTON

GYAN

Published by

Gyan Publishing House
5, Ansari Road
Daryaganj, New Delhi-110002
Phone: 011-47034999, 9811692060
E-mail: books@gyanbooks.com

Distribution Network
gyanbooks.com
India, USA, Canada, UK, Australia

ISBN: 978-81-212-9775-2 (PB)
First Published, 1912

2nd Impression 2024

Printed at: Gyan Press, Delhi.

RIDERS OF THE PURPLE SAGE
Author: ZANE GREY

RIDERS OF THE PURPLE SAGE

"HE HAS BROUGHT YOU FAR TO-DAY?"

RIDERS OF THE PURPLE SAGE

A NOVEL

By

ZANE GREY

Author of

"The Mysterious Rider" "The Man of the Forest"
"Desert Gold" "The U. P. Trail" "Tales of Fishes" "Wildfire"
"The Desert of Wheat" "The Lone Star Ranger" etc.

With Illustrations by
W. Herbert Dunton

HARPER & BROTHERS PUBLISHERS
NEW YORK AND LONDON

CONTENTS

RIDERS OF THE PURPLE SAGE

ILLUSTRATIONS

CHAPTER I

LASSITER

A SHARP clip-clop of iron-shod hoofs deadened and died away, and clouds of yellow dust drifted from under the cottonwoods out over the sage.

Jane Withersteen gazed down the wide purple slope with dreamy and troubled eyes. A rider had just left her and it was his message that held her thoughtful and almost sad, awaiting the churchmen who were coming to resent and attack her right to befriend a Gentile.

She wondered if the unrest and strife that had lately come to the little village of Cottonwoods was to involve her. And then she sighed, remembering that her father had founded this remotest border settlement of southern Utah and that he had left it to her. She owned all the ground and many of the cottages. Withersteen House was hers, and the great ranch, with its thousands of cattle, and the swiftest horses of the sage. To her belonged Amber Spring, the water which gave verdure and beauty to the village and made living possible on that wild purple upland waste. She could not escape being involved by whatever befell Cottonwoods.

That year, 1871, had marked a change which had

been gradually coming in the lives of the peace-loving Mormons of the border. Glaze—Stone Bridge—Sterling, villages to the north, had risen against the invasion of Gentile settlers and the forays of rustlers. There had been opposition to the one and fighting with the other. And now Cottonwoods had begun to wake and bestir itself and grow hard.

Jane prayed that the tranquillity and sweetness of her life would not be permanently disrupted. She meant to do so much more for her people than she had done. She wanted the sleepy quiet pastoral days to last always. Trouble between the Mormons and the Gentiles of the community would make her unhappy. She was Mormon-born, and she was a friend to poor and unfortunate Gentiles. She wished only to go on doing good and being happy. And she thought of what that great ranch meant to her. She loved it all—the grove of cottonwoods, the old stone house, the amber-tinted water, and the droves of shaggy, dusty horses and mustangs, the sleek, clean-limbed, blooded racers, and the browsing herds of cattle and the lean, sun-browned riders of the sage.

While she waited there she forgot the prospect of untoward change. The bray of a lazy burro broke the afternoon quiet, and it was comfortingly suggestive of the drowsy farmyard, and the open corrals, and the green alfalfa fields. Her clear sight intensified the purple sage-slope as it rolled before her. Low swells of prairie-like ground sloped up to the west. Dark, lonely cedar-trees, few and far between, stood out strikingly, and at long distances ruins of red rocks. Farther on, up the gradual slope, rose a broken wall, a huge monument, looming dark purple and stretching its solitary, mystic way, a wavering line that faded in the north. Here to the westward was the light and color and beauty. Northward the slope descended to a dim line of cañons from which rose an up-flinging of the earth, not mountainous, but a vast heave of purple uplands, with ribbed and fan-shaped walls, castle-crowned cliffs, and gray escarpments. Over it all crept the lengthening, waning afternoon shadows.

The rapid beat of hoofs recalled Jane Withersteen to the question at hand. A group of riders cantered up the lane, dismounted, and threw their bridles. They were seven in number, and Tull, the leader, a tall, dark man, was an elder of Jane's church.

"Did you get my message?" he asked, curtly.

"Yes," replied Jane.

"I sent word I'd give that rider Venters half an hour to come down to the village. He didn't come."

"He knows nothing of it," said Jane. "I didn't tell him. I've been waiting here for you."

"Where is Venters?"

"I left him in the courtyard."

"Here, Jerry," called Tull, turning to his men, "take the gang and fetch Venters out here if you have to rope him."

The dusty-booted and long-spurred riders clanked noisily into the grove of cottonwoods and disappeared in the shade.

"Elder Tull, what do you mean by this?" demanded Jane. "If you must arrest Venters you might have the courtesy to wait till he leaves my home. And if you do arrest him it will be adding insult to injury. It's absurd to accuse Venters of being mixed up in that shooting fray in the village last night. He was with me at the time. Besides, he let me take charge of his guns. You're only using this as a pretext. What do you mean to do to Venters?"

"I'll tell you presently," replied Tull. "But first tell me why you defend this worthless rider?"

"Worthless!" exclaimed Jane, indignantly. "He's nothing of the kind. He was the best rider I ever had. There's not a reason why I shouldn't champion him and every reason why I should. It's no little shame to me, Elder Tull, that through my friendship he has roused the enmity of my people and become an outcast. Besides, I owe him eternal gratitude for saving the life of little Fay."

"I've heard of your love for Fay Larkin and that you intend to adopt her. But—Jane Withersteen, the child is a Gentile!"

"Yes. But, Elder, I don't love the Mormon children any less because I love a Gentile child. I shall adopt Fay if her mother will give her to me."

"I'm not so much against that. You can give the child Mormon teaching," said Tull. "But I'm sick of seeing this fellow Venters hang around you. I'm going to put a stop to it. You've so much love to throw away on these beggars of Gentiles that I've an idea you might love Venters."

Tull spoke with the arrogance of a Mormon whose power could not be brooked and with the passion of a man in whom jealousy had kindled a consuming fire.

"Maybe I do love him," said Jane. She felt both fear and anger stir her heart. "I'd never thought of that. Poor fellow! he certainly needs some one to love him."

"This 'll be a bad day for Venters unless you deny that," returned Tull, grimly.

Tull's men appeared under the cottonwoods and led a young man out into the lane. His ragged clothes were those of an outcast. But he stood tall and straight, his wide shoulders flung back, with the muscles of his bound arms rippling and a blue flame of defiance in the gaze he bent on Tull.

For the first time Jane Withersteen felt Venters's real spirit. She wondered if she would love this splendid youth. Then her emotion cooled to the sobering sense of the issue at stake.

"Venters, will you leave Cottonwoods at once and forever?" asked Tull, tensely.

"Why?" rejoined the rider.

"Because I order it."

Venters laughed in cool disdain.

The red leaped to Tull's dark cheek.

"If you don't go it means your ruin," he said, sharply.

"Ruin!" exclaimed Venters, passionately. "Haven't you already ruined me? What do you call ruin? A year ago I was a rider. I had horses and cattle of my own. I had a good name in Cottonwoods. And now when I come into the village to see this woman you set your men on me. You hound me. You trail me as if I were a rustler. I've no more to lose—except my life."

"Will you leave Utah?"

"Oh! I know," went on Venters, tauntingly, "it galls you, the idea of beautiful Jane Withersteen being friendly to a poor Gentile. You want her all yourself. You're a wiving Mormon. You have use for her—and Withersteen House and Amber Spring and seven thousand head of cattle!"

Tull's hard jaw protruded, and rioting blood corded the veins of his neck.

"Once more. Will you go?"

"*No!*"

"Then I'll have you whipped within an inch of your life," replied Tull, harshly. "I'll turn you out in the sage. And if you ever come back you'll get worse."

Venters's agitated face grew coldly set and the bronze changed to gray.

Jane impulsively stepped forward. "Oh! Elder Tull!" she cried. "You won't do that!"

Tull lifted a shaking finger toward her.

"That 'll do from you. Understand, you'll not be allowed to hold this boy to a friendship that's offensive to your Bishop. Jane Withersteen, your father left you wealth and power. It has turned your head. You haven't yet come to see the place of Mormon women. We've reasoned with you, borne with you. We've patiently waited. We've let you have your fling, which is more than I ever saw granted to a Mormon woman. But you haven't come to your senses. Now, once for all, you can't have any further friendship with Venters. He's going to be whipped, and he's got to leave Utah!"

"Oh! Don't whip him! It would be dastardly!" implored Jane, with slow certainty of her failing courage.

Tull always blunted her spirit, and she grew conscious that she had feigned a boldness which she did not possess. He loomed up now in different guise, not as a jealous suitor, but embodying the mysterious despotism she had known from childhood—the power of her creed.

"Venters, will you take your whipping here or would you rather go out in the sage?" asked Tull. He smiled a flinty smile that was more than inhuman, yet seemed to give out of its dark aloofness a gleam of righteousness.

"I'll take it here—if I must," said Venters. "But by God!—Tull, you'd better kill me outright. That 'll be a dear whipping for you and your praying Mormons. You'll make me another Lassiter!"

The strange glow, the austere light which radiated from Tull's face, might have been a holy joy at the spiritual conception of exalted duty. But there was something more in him, barely hidden, a something personal and sinister, a deep of himself, an engulfing abyss. As his religious mood was fanatical and inexorable, so would his physical hate be merciless.

"Elder, I—I repent my words," Jane faltered. The religion in her, the long habit of obedience, of humility, as well as agony of fear, spoke in her voice. "Spare the boy!" she whispered.

"You can't save him now," replied Tull, stridently.

Her head was bowing to the inevitable. She was grasping the truth, when suddenly there came, in inward constriction, a hardening of gentle forces within her breast. Like a steel bar it was, stiffening all that had been soft and weak in her. She felt a birth in her of something new and unintelligible. Once more her strained gaze sought the sage-slopes. Jane Withersteen loved that wild and purple wilderness. In times of sorrow it had been her strength, in happiness its beauty was her continual delight. In her extremity she found herself murmuring, "Whence cometh my help!" It was a prayer, as if forth from those lonely purple reaches and walls of red and clefts of blue might ride a fearless man, neither creed-bound nor creed-mad, who would hold up a restraining hand in the faces of her ruthless people.

The restless movements of Tull's men suddenly quieted down. Then followed a low whisper, a rustle, a sharp exclamation.

"Look!" said one, pointing to the west.

"A rider!"

Jane Withersteen wheeled and saw a horseman, silhouetted against the western sky, coming riding out of the sage. He had ridden down from the left, in the golden glare of the sun, and had been unobserved till close at hand. An answer to her prayer!

"Do you know him? Does any one know him?" questioned Tull, hurriedly.

His men looked and looked, and one by one shook their heads.

"He's come from far," said one.

"Thet's a fine hoss," said another.

"A strange rider."

"Huh! he wears black leather," added a fourth.

With a wave of his hand, enjoining silence, Tull stepped forward in such a way that he concealed Venters.

The rider reined in his mount, and with a lithe forward-slipping action appeared to reach the ground in one long step. It was a peculiar movement in its quickness and inasmuch that while performing it the rider did not swerve in the slightest from a square front to the group before him.

"Look!" hoarsely whispered one of Tull's companions. "He packs two black-butted guns—low down—they're hard to see—black agin them black chaps."

"A gun-man!" whispered another. "Fellers, careful now about movin' your hands."

The stranger's slow approach might have been a mere leisurely manner of gait or the cramped short steps of a rider unused to walking; yet, as well, it could have been the guarded advance of one who took no chances with men.

"Hello, stranger!" called Tull. No welcome was in this greeting, only a gruff curiosity.

The rider responded with a curt nod. The wide brim of a black sombrero cast a dark shade over his face. For a moment he closely regarded Tull and his comrades, and then, halting in his slow walk, he seemed to relax.

"Evenin', ma'am," he said to Jane, and removed his sombrero with quaint grace.

Jane, greeting him, looked up into a face that she trusted instinctively and which riveted her attention. It had all the characteristics of the range rider's—the leanness, the red burn of the sun, and the set changelessness that came from years of silence and solitude. But it was not these which held her; rather the intensity of his gaze, a strained wearinesss, a piercing wistfulness of keen, gray sight, as if the man was forever looking for that which he never found. Jane's subtle woman's intuition, even in that brief instant, felt a sadness, a hungering, a secret.

"Jane Withersteen, ma'am?" he inquired.

"Yes," she replied.

"The water here is yours?"

"Yes."

"May I water my horse?"

"Certainly. There's the trough."

"But mebbe if you knew who I was—" He hesitated, with his glance on the listening men. "Mebbe you wouldn't let me water him—though I ain't askin' none for myself."

"Stranger, it doesn't matter who you are. Water your horse. And if you are thirsty and hungry come into my house."

"Thanks, ma'am. I can't accept for myself—but for my tired horse—"

Trampling of hoofs interrupted the rider. More restless movements on the part of Tull's men broke up the little circle, exposing the prisoner Venters.

"Mebbe I've kind of hindered somethin'—for a few moments, perhaps?" inquired the rider.

"Yes," replied Jane Withersteen, with a throb in her voice.

She felt the drawing power of his eyes; and then she saw him look at the bound Venters, and at the men who held him, and their leader.

"In this here country all the rustlers an' thieves an' cut-throats an' gun-throwers an' all-round no-good men jest happen to be Gentiles. Ma'am, which of the no-good class does that young feller belong to?"

"He belongs to none of them. He's an honest boy."

"You *know* that, ma'am?"

"Yes—yes."

"Then what has he done to get tied up that way?"

His clear and distinct question, meant for Tull as well as for Jane Withersteen, stilled the restlessness and brought a momentary silence.

"Ask him," replied Jane, her voice rising high.

The rider stepped away from her, moving out with the same slow, measured stride in which he had approached; and the fact that his action placed her wholly to one side, and him no nearer to Tull and his men, had a penetrating significance.

"Young feller, speak up," he said to Venters.

"Here, stranger, this 's none of your mix," began Tull. "Don't try any interference. You've been asked to drink and eat. That's more than you'd have got in any other village on the Utah border. Water your horse and be on your way."

"Easy—easy—I ain't interferin' yet," replied the rider. The tone of his voice had undergone a change. A different man had spoken. Where, in addressing Jane, he had been mild and gentle, now, with his first speech to Tull, he was dry, cool, biting. "I've jest stumbled onto a queer deal. Seven Mormons all packin' guns, an' a Gentile tied with a rope, an' a woman who swears by his honesty! Queer, ain't that?"

"Queer or not, it's none of your business," retorted Tull.

"Where I was raised a woman's word was law. I 'ain't quite outgrowed that yet."

Tull fumed between amaze and anger.

"Meddler, we have a law here something different from woman's whim—Mormon law! . . . Take care you don't transgress it."

"To hell with your Mormon law!"

The deliberate speech marked the rider's further change, this time from kindly interest to an awakening menace. It produced a transformation in Tull and his companions. The leader gasped and staggered backward at a blasphemous affront to an institution he held most sacred. The man Jerry, holding the horses, dropped the bridles and froze in his tracks. Like posts the other men stood, watchful-eyed, arms hanging rigid, all waiting.

"Speak up now, young man. What have you done to be roped that way?"

"It's a damned outrage!" burst out Venters. "I've done no wrong. I've offended this Mormon Elder by being a friend to that woman."

"Ma'am, is it true—what he says?" asked the rider of Jane; but his quiveringly alert eyes never left the little knot of quiet men.

"True? Yes, perfectly true," she answered.

"Well, young man, it seems to me that bein' a friend to such a woman would be what you wouldn't want to help an' couldn't help. . . . What's to be done to you for it?"

"They intend to whip me. You know what that means—in Utah!"

"I reckon," replied the rider, slowly.

With his gray glance cold on the Mormons, with the restive bit-champing of the horses, with Jane failing to repress her mounting agitation, with Venters standing pale and still, the tension of the moment tightened. Tull broke the spell with a laugh, a laugh without mirth, a laugh that was only a sound betraying fear.

"Come on, men!" he called.

Jane Withersteen turned again to the rider.

"Stranger, can you do nothing to save Venters?"

"Ma'am, you ask me to save him—from your own people?"

"Ask you? I beg of you!"

"But you don't dream who you're askin'."

"Oh, sir, I pray you—save him!"

"These are Mormons, an' I . . ."

"At—at any cost—save him. For I—I care for him!"

Tull snarled. "You love-sick fool! Tell your secrets. There'll be a way to teach you what you've never learned. . . . Come men, out of here!"

"Mormon, the young man stays," said the rider.

Like a shot his voice halted Tull.

"What!"

"He stays."

"Who'll keep him? He's my prisoner!" cried Tull, hotly. "Stranger, again I tell you—don't mix here. You've meddled enough. Go your way now or—"

"Listen! . . . He stays."

Absolute certainty, beyond any shadow of doubt, breathed in the rider's low voice.

"Who are you? We are seven here."

The rider dropped his sombrero and made a rapid movement, singular in that it left him somewhat crouched, arms bent and stiff, with the big black gun-sheaths swung round to the fore.

"*Lassiter!*"

It was Venters's wondering, thrilling cry that bridged the fateful connection between the rider's singular position and the dreaded name.

Tull put out a groping hand. The life of his eyes dulled to the gloom with which men of his fear saw the approach of death. But death, while it hovered over him, did not descend, for the rider waited for the twitching fingers, the downward flash of hand that did not come. Tull, gathering himself together, turned to the horses, attended by his pale comrades.

CHAPTER II

COTTONWOODS

VENTERS appeared too deeply moved to speak the gratitude his face expressed. And Jane turned upon the rescuer and gripped his hands. Her smiles and tears seemingly dazed him. Presently, as something like calmness returned, she went to Lassiter's weary horse.

"I will water him myself," she said, and she led the horse to a trough under a huge old cottonwood. With nimble fingers she loosened the bridle and removed the bit. The horse snorted and bent his head. The trough was of solid stone, hollowed out, moss-covered and green and wet and cool, and the clear brown water that fed it spouted and splashed from a wooden pipe.

"He has brought you far to-day?"

"Yes, ma'am, a matter of over sixty miles, mebbe seventy."

"A long ride—a ride that— Ah, he is blind!"

"Yes, ma'am," replied Lassiter.

"What blinded him?"

"Some men once roped an' tied him, an' then held white-iron close to his eyes."

"Oh! Men? You mean devils. . . . Were they your enemies—Mormons?"

"Yes, ma'am."

"To take revenge on a horse! Lassiter, the men of my creed are unnaturally cruel. To my everlasting sorrow I confess it. They have been driven, hated, scourged till their hearts have hardened. But we women hope and pray for the time when our men will soften."

"Beggin' your pardon, ma'am—that time will never come."

"Oh, it will! . . . Lassiter, do you think Mormon women wicked? Has your hand been against them, too?"

"No. I believe Mormon women are the best and noblest, the most long-sufferin', and the blindest, unhappiest women on earth."

"Ah!" She gave him a grave, thoughtful look. "Then you will break bread with me?"

Lassiter had no ready response, and he uneasily shifted his weight from one leg to another, and turned his sombrero round and round in his hands. "Ma'am," he began, presently, "I reckon your kindness of heart makes you overlook things. Perhaps I ain't well known hereabouts, but back up North there's Mormons who'd rest oneasy in their graves at the idea of me sittin' to table with you."

"I dare say. But—will you do it, anyway?" she asked.

"Mebbe you have a brother or relative who might drop in an' be offended, an' I wouldn't want to—"

"I've not a relative in Utah that I know of. There's no one with a right to question my actions." She turned smilingly to Venters. "You will come in, Bern, and Lassiter will come in. We'll eat and be merry while we may."

"I'm only wonderin' if Tull an' his men 'll raise a storm down in the village," said Lassiter, in his last weakening stand.

"Yes, he'll raise the storm—after he has prayed," replied Jane. "Come."

She led the way, with the bridle of Lassiter's horse over her arm. They entered a grove and walked down a wide path shaded by great low-branching cottonwoods. The last rays of the setting sun sent golden bars through the leaves. The grass was deep and rich, welcome contrast to sage-tired eyes. Twittering quail darted across the path, and from a tree-top somewhere a robin sang its evening song, and on the still air floated the freshness and murmur of flowing water.

The home of Jane Withersteen stood in a circle of cottonwoods, and was a flat, long, red-stone structure with a covered court in the center through which flowed a lively stream of amber-colored water. In the massive blocks of stone and heavy timbers and solid doors and shutters showed the hand of a man who had builded against pillage and time; and in the flowers and mosses lining the stone-bedded stream, in the bright colors of rugs and blankets on the court floor, and the cozy corner with hammock and books, and the clean-linened table, showed the grace of a daughter who lived for happiness and the day at hand.

Jane turned Lassiter's horse loose in the thick grass. "You will want him to be near you," she said, "or I'd have him taken to the alfalfa fields." At her call appeared women who began at once to bustle about, hurrying to and fro, setting the table. Then Jane, excusing herself, went within.

She passed through a huge low-ceiled chamber, like the inside of a fort, and into a smaller one where a bright wood-fire blazed in an old open fireplace, and from this into her own room. It had the same comfort as was manifested in the home-like outer court; moreover, it was warm and rich in soft hues.

Seldom did Jane Withersteen enter her room without looking into her mirror. She knew she loved the reflection of that beauty which since early childhood she had never been allowed to forget. Her relatives and friends, and later a horde of Mormon and Gentile suitors, had fanned the flame of natural vanity in her. So that at twenty-eight she scarcely thought at all of her wonderful influence for good in the little community where her father had left her practically its beneficent landlord; but cared most for the dream and the assurance and the allurement of her beauty. This time, however, she gazed into her glass with more than the usual happy motive, without the usual slight conscious smile. For she was thinking of more than the desire to be fair in her own eyes, in those of her friend; she wondered if she were to seem fair in the eyes of this Lassiter, this man whose name had crossed the long, wild brakes of stone and plains of sage, this gentle-voiced, sad-faced man who was a hater and a killer of Mormons. It was not now her usual half-conscious vain obsession that actuated her as she hurriedly changed her riding-dress to one of white, and then looked long at the stately form with its gracious contours, at the fair face with its strong chin and full firm lips, at the dark-blue, proud, and passionate eyes.

"If by some means I can keep him here a few days, a week—he will never kill another Mormon," she mused. "Lassiter! . . . I shudder when I think of that name, of him. But when I look at the man I forget who he is—I almost like him. I remember only that he saved Bern. He has suffered. I wonder what it was—did he love a Mormon woman once? How splendidly he championed us poor misunderstood souls! Somehow he knows—much."

Jane Withersteen joined her guests and bade them to her board. Dismissing her woman, she waited upon them with her own hands. It was a bountiful supper and a strange company. On her right sat the ragged and half-starved Venters; and though blind eyes could have seen what he counted for in the sum of her happiness, yet he looked the gloomy outcast his allegiance had made him, and about him there was the shadow of the ruin presaged by Tull. On her left sat the black-leather-garbed Lassiter looking like a man in a dream. Hunger was not with him, nor composure, nor speech, and when he twisted in frequent unquiet movements the heavy guns that he had not removed knocked against the table-legs. If it had been otherwise possible to forget the presence of Lassiter those telling little jars would have rendered it unlikely. And Jane Witherseen talked and smiled and laughed with all the dazzling play of lips and eyes that a beautiful, daring woman could summon to her purpose.

When the meal ended, and the men pushed back their chairs, she leaned closer to Lassiter and looked square into his eyes.

"Why did you come to Cottonwoods?"

Her question seemed to break a spell. The rider arose as if he had just remembered himself and had tarried longer than his wont.

"Ma'am, I have hunted all over southern Utah and Nevada for—somethin'. An' through your name I learned where to find it—here in Cottonwoods."

"My name! Oh, I remember. You did know my name when you spoke first. Well, tell me where you heard it and from whom?"

"At the little village—Glaze, I think it's called—some fifty miles or more west of here. An' I heard it from a Gentile, a rider who said you'd know where to tell me to find—"

"What?" she demanded, imperiously, as Lassiter broke off.

"Milly Erne's grave," he answered low, and the words came with a wrench.

Venters wheeled in his chair to regard Lassiter in amazement, and Jane slowly raised herself in white, still wonder.

"Milly Erne's grave?" she echoed, in a whisper. "What do you know of Milly Erne, my best-beloved friend—who died in my arms? What were you to her?"

"Did I claim to be anythin'?" he inquired. "I know

people—relatives—who have long wanted to know where she's buried. That's all."

"Relatives? She never spoke of relatives, except a brother who was shot in Texas. Lassiter, Milly Erne's grave is in a secret burying-ground on my property."

"Will you take me there? . . . You'll be offendin' Mormons worse than by breakin' bread with me."

"Indeed yes, but I'll do it. Only we must go unseen. To-morrow, perhaps."

"Thank you, Jane Withersteen," replied the rider, and he bowed to her and stepped backward out of the court.

"Will you not stay—sleep under my roof?" she asked.

"No, ma'am, an' thanks again. I never sleep indoors. An' even if I did there's that gatherin' storm in the village below. No, no. I'll go to the sage. I hope you won't suffer none for your kindness to me."

"Lassiter," said Venters, with a half-bitter laugh, "my bed, too, is the sage. Perhaps we may meet out there."

"Mebbe so. But the sage is wide an' I won't be near. Good night."

At Lassiter's low whistle the black horse whinnied, and carefully picked his blind way out of the grove. The rider did not bridle him, but walked beside him, leading him by touch of hand, and together they passed slowly into the shade of the cottonwoods.

"Jane, I must be off soon," said Venters. "Give me my guns. If I'd had my guns—"

"Either my friend or the Elder of my church would be lying dead," she interposed.

"Tull would be—surely."

"Oh, you fierce-blooded, savage youth! Can't I teach you forbearance, mercy? Bern, it's divine to forgive your enemies. 'Let not the sun go down upon thy wrath.'"

"Hush! Talk to me no more of mercy or religion—after to-day. To-day this strange coming of Lassiter left me still a man, and now I'll die a man! . . . Give me my guns."

Silently she went into the house, to return with a heavy cartridge-belt and gun-filled sheath and a long rifle; these she handed to him, and as he buckled on the belt she stood before him in silent eloquence.

"Jane," he said, in gentler voice, "don't look so. I'm not going out to murder your churchman. I'll try to avoid him and all his men. But can't you see I've reached the end of my rope? Jane, you're a wonderful woman. Never was there a woman so unselfish and good. Only you're blind in one way. . . . Listen!"

From behind the grove came the clicking sound of horses in a rapid trot.

"Some of your riders," he continued. "It's getting time for the night shift. Let us go out to the bench in the grove and talk there."

It was still daylight in the open, but under the spreading cottonwoods shadows were obscuring the lanes. Venters drew Jane off from one of these into a shrub-lined trail, just wide enough for the two to walk abreast, and in a roundabout way led her far from the house to a knoll on the edge of the grove. Here in a secluded nook was a bench from which, through an opening in the tree-tops, could be seen the sage-slope and the wall of rock and the dim lines of canoñs. Jane had not spoken since Venters had shocked her with his first harsh speech; but all the way she had clung to his arm, and now, as he stopped and laid his rifle against the bench, she still clung to him.

"Jane, I'm afraid I must leave you."

"Bern!" she cried.

"Yes, it looks that way. My position is not a happy one—I can't feel right—I've lost all—"

"I'll give you anything you—"

"Listen, please. When I say loss I don't mean what you think. I mean loss of good-will, good name—that which would have enabled me to stand up in this village without bitterness. Well, it's too late. . . . Now, as to the future, I think you'd do best to give me up. Tull is implacable. You ought to see from his intention today that— But you can't see. Your blindness—your damned religion! . . . Jane, forgive me—I'm sore within and something rankles. Well, I fear that invisible hand will turn its hidden work to your ruin."

"Invisible hand? Bern!"

"I mean your Bishop." Venters said it deliberately and would not release her as she started back. "He's the law. The edict went forth to ruin me. Well, look at me! It 'll now go forth to compel you to the will of the Church."

"You wrong Bishop Dyer. Tull is hard, I know. But then he has been in love with me for years."

"Oh, your faith and your excuses! You can't see what I know—and if you did see it you'd not admit it to save your life. That's the Mormon of you. These elders and bishops will do absolutely any deed to go on building up the power and wealth of their church, their empire. Think of what they've done to the Gentiles here, to me—think of Milly Erne's fate!"

"What do you know of her story?"

"I know enough—all, perhaps, except the name of the Mormon who brought her here. But I must stop this kind of talk."

She pressed his hand in response. He helped her to a seat beside him on the bench. And he respected a silence that he divined was full of woman's deep emotion, beyond his understanding.

It was the moment when the last ruddy rays of the sunset brightened momentarily before yielding to twilight. And for Venters the outlook before him was in some sense similar to a feeling of his future, and with searching eyes he studied the beautiful purple, barren waste of sage. Here was the unknown and the perilous. The whole scene impressed Venters as a wild, austere, and mighty manifestation of nature. And as it somehow reminded him of his prospect in life, so it suddenly resembled the woman near him, only in her there were greater beauty and peril, a mystery more unsolvable, and something nameless that numbed his heart and dimmed his eye.

"Look! A rider!" exclaimed Jane, breaking the silence. "Can that be Lassiter?"

Venters moved his glance once more to the west. A horseman showed dark on the sky-line, then merged into the color of the sage.

"It might be. But I think not—that fellow was coming in. One of your riders, more likely. Yes, I see him clearly now. And there's another."

"I see them, too."

"Jane, your riders seem as many as the bunches of sage. I ran into five yesterday 'way down near the trail to Deception Pass. They were with the white herd."

"You still go to that cañon? Bern, I wish you wouldn't. Oldring and his rustlers live somewhere down there."

"Well, what of that?"

"Tull has already hinted of your frequent trips into Deception Pass."

"I know." Venters uttered a short laugh. "He'll make a rustler of me next. But, Jane, there's no water for fifty miles after I leave here, and that nearest is in the cañon. I must drink and water my horse. There! I see more riders. They are going out."

"The red herd is on the slopo, toward the Pass."

Twilight was fast falling. A group of horsemen crossed the dark line of low ground to become more distinct as they climbed the slope. The silence broke to a clear call from an incoming rider, and, almost like the peal of a hunting-horn, floated back the answer. The outgoing riders moved swiftly, came sharply into sight as they topped a ridge to show wild and black above the horizon, and then passed down, dimming into the purple of the sage.

"I hope they don't meet Lassiter," said Jane.

"So do I," replied Venters. "By this time the riders of the night shift know what happened to-day. But Lassiter will likely keep out of their way."

"Bern, who is Lassiter? He's only a name to me—a terrible name."

"Who is he? I don't know, Jane. Nobody I ever met knows him. He talks a little like a Texan, like Milly Erne. Did you note that?"

"Yes. How strange of him to know of her! And she lived here ten years and has been dead two. Bern, what do you know of Lassiter? Tell me what he has done—why you spoke of him to Tull—threatening to become another Lassiter yourself?"

"Jane, I only heard things, rumors, stories, most of which I disbelieved. At Glaze his name was known, but none of the riders or ranchers I knew there ever met him. At Stone Bridge I never heard him mentioned. But at Sterling and villages north of there he was spoken of often. I've never been in a village which he had been known to visit. There were many conflicting stories about him and his doings. Some said he had shot up this and that Mormon village, and others denied it. I'm inclined to believe he has, and you know how Mormons hide the truth. But there was one feature about Lassiter upon which all agree—that he was what riders in this country call a gun-man. He's a man with marvelous quickness and accuracy in the use of a Colt. And now that I've seen him I know more. Lassiter was born without fear. I watched him with eyes which saw him my friend. I'll never forget the moment I recognized him from what had been told me of his crouch before the draw. It was then I yelled his name. I believe that yell saved Tull's life. At any rate, I know this, between Tull and death then there was not the breadth of the littlest hair. If he or any of his men had moved a finger downward . . . ."

Venters left his meaning unspoken, but at the suggestion Jane shuddered.

The pale afterglow in the west darkened with the merging of twilight into night. The sage now spread out black and gloomy. One dim star glimmered in the southwest sky. The sound of trotting horses had ceased, and there was silence broken only by a faint, dry pattering of cottonwood leaves in the soft night wind.

Into this peace and calm suddenly broke the high-keyed yelp of a coyote, and from far off in the darkness came the faint answering note of a trailing mate.

"Hello! the sage-dogs are barking," said Venters.

"I don't like to hear them," replied Jane. "At night, sometimes, when I lie awake, listening to the long mourn or breaking bark or wild howl, I think of you asleep somewhere in the sage, and my heart aches."

"Jane, you couldn't listen to sweeter music, nor could I have a better bed."

"Just think! Men like Lassiter and you have no home, no comfort, no rest, no place to lay your weary heads. Well! . . . Let us be patient. Tull's anger may cool, and time may help us. You might do some service to the village—who can tell? Suppose you discovered the long-unknown hiding-place of Oldring and his band, and told it to my riders? That would disarm Tull's ugly hints and put you in favor. For years my riders have trailed the tracks of stolen cattle. You know as well as I how dearly we've paid for our ranges in this wild country. Oldring drives our cattle down into that network of deceiving cañons, and somewhere far to the north or east he drives them up and out to

Utah markets. If you will spend time in Deception Pass try to find the trails."

"Jane, I've thought of that. I'll try."

"I must go now. And it hurts, for now I'll never be sure of seeing you again. But to-morrow, Bern?"

"To-morrow surely. I'll watch for Lassiter and ride in with him."

"Good night."

Then she left him and moved away, a white, gliding shape that soon vanished in the shadows.

Venters waited until the faint slam of a door assured him she had reached the house; and then, taking up his rifle, he noiselessly slipped through the bushes, down the knoll, and on under the dark trees to the edge of the grove. The sky was now turning from gray to blue; stars had begun to lighten the earlier blackness; and from the wide flat sweep before him blew a cool wind, fragrant with the breath of sage. Keeping close to the edge of the cottonwoods, he went swiftly and silently westward. The grove was long, and he had not reached the end when he heard something that brought him to a halt. Low padded thuds told him horses were coming his way. He sank down in the gloom, waiting, listening. Much before he had expected, judging from sound, to his amazement he descried horsemen near at hand. They were riding along the border of the sage, and instantly he knew the hoofs of the horses were muffled. Then the pale starlight afforded him indistinct sight of the riders. But his eyes were keen and used to the dark, and by peering closely he recognized the huge bulk and black-bearded visage of Oldring and the lithe, supple form of the rustler's lieutenant, a masked rider. They passed on; the darkness swallowed them. Then, farther out on the sage, a dark, compact body of horsemen went by, almost without sound, almost like specters, and they, too, melted into the night.

CHAPTER III

AMBER SPRING

NO unusual circumstance was it for Oldring and some of his men to visit Cottonwoods in the broad light of day, but for him to prowl about in the dark with the hoofs of his horses muffled meant that mischief was brewing. Moreover, to Venters the presence of the masked rider with Oldring seemed especially ominous. For about this man there was mystery; he seldom rode through the village, and when he did ride through it was swiftly; riders seldom met him by day on the sage; but wherever he rode there always followed deeds as dark and mysterious as the mask he wore. Oldring's band did not confine themselves to the rustling of cattle.

Venters lay low in the shade of the cottonwoods, pondering this chance meeting, and not for many moments did he consider it safe to move on. Then, with sudden impulse, he turned the other way and went back along the grove. When he reached the path leading to Jane's home he decided to go down to the village. So he hurried onward, with quick soft steps. Once beyond the grove he entered the one and only street. It was wide, lined with tall poplars, and under each row of trees, inside the foot-path, were ditches where ran the water from Jane Withersteen's spring.

Between the trees twinkled lights of cottage candles, and far down flared bright windows of the village stores. When Venters got closer to these he saw knots of men standing together in earnest conversation. The usual lounging on the corners and benches and steps was not in evidence. Keeping in the shadow, Venters went closer and closer until he could hear voices. But he could not distinguish what was said. He recognized many Mormons, and looked hard for Tull and his men, but looked in vain. Venters concluded that the rustlers had not passed along the village street. No doubt these earnest men were discussing Lassiter's coming. But Venters felt positive that Tull's intention toward himself that day had not been and would not be revealed.

So Venters, seeing there was little for him to learn, began retracing his steps. The church was dark, Bishop Dyer's home next to it was also dark, and likewise Tull's cottage. Upon almost any night at this hour there would be lights here, and Venters marked the unusual omission.

As he was about to pass out of the street to skirt the grove, he once more slunk down at the sound of trotting horses. Presently he descried two mounted men riding toward him. He hugged the shadow of a tree. Again the starlight, brighter now, aided him, and he made out Tull's stalwart figure, and beside him the short, frog-like shape of the rider Jerry. They were silent, and they rode on to disappear.

Venters went his way with busy, gloomy mind, revolving events of the day, trying to reckon those brooding in the night. His thoughts overwhelmed him. Up in that dark grove dwelt a woman who had been his friend. And he skulked about her home, gripping a gun stealthily as an Indian, a man without place or people or purpose. Above her hovered the shadow of grim, hidden, secret power. No queen could have given more royally out of a bounteous store than Jane Withersteen gave her people, and likewise to those unfortunates whom her people hated. She asked only the divine right of all women—freedom; to love and to live as her heart willed. And yet prayer and her hope were vain.

"For years I've seen a storm clouding over her and

the village of Cottonwoods," muttered Venters, as he strode on. "Soon it 'll burst. I don't like the prospect." That night the villagers whispered in the street —and night-riding rustlers muffled horses—and Tull was at work in secret—and out there in the sage hid a man who meant something terrible—Lassiter!

Venters passed the black cottonwoods, and, entering the sage, climbed the gradual slope. He kept his direction in line with a western star. From time to time he stopped to listen and heard only the usual familiar bark of coyote and sweep of wind and rustle of sage. Presently a low jumble of rocks loomed up darkly somewhat to his right, and, turning that way, he whistled softly. Out of the rocks glided a dog that leaped and whined about him. He climbed over rough, broken rock, picking his way carefully, and then went down. Here it was darker, and sheltered from the wind. A white object guided him. It was another dog, and this one was asleep, curled up between a saddle and a pack. The animal awoke and thumped his tail in greeting. Venters placed the saddle for a pillow, rolled in his blankets, with his face upward to the stars. The white dog snuggled close to him. The other whined and pattered a few yards to the rise of ground and there crouched on guard. And in that wild covert Venters shut his eyes under the great white stars and intense vaulted blue, bitterly comparing their loneliness to his own, and fell asleep.

When he awoke, day had dawned and all about him was bright steel-gray. The air had a cold tang. Arising, he greeted the fawning dogs and stretched his cramped body, and then, gathering together bunches of dead sage sticks, he lighted a fire. Strips of dried beef held to the blaze for a moment served him and the dogs. He drank from a canteen. There was nothing else in his outfit; he had grown used to a scant fare. Then he sat over the fire, palms outspread, and waited. Waiting had been his chief occupation for months, and he scarcely knew what he waited for, unless it was the passing of the hours. But now he sensed action in the immediate present; the day promised another meeting with Lassiter and Jane, perhaps news of the rustlers; on the morrow he meant to take the trail to Deception Pass.

And while he waited he talked to his dogs. He called them Ring and Whitie; they were sheep-dogs, half collie, half deer-hound, superb in build, perfectly trained. It seemed that in his fallen fortunes these dogs understood the nature of their value to him, and governed their affection and faithfulness accordingly. Whitie watched him with somber eyes of love, and Ring, crouched on the little rise of ground above, kept tireless guard. When the sun rose, the white dog took the place of the other, and Ring went to sleep at his master's feet.

By and by Venters rolled up his blankets and tied them and his meager pack together, then climbed out to look for his horse. He saw him, presently, a little way off in the sage, and went to fetch him. In that country, where every rider boasted of a fine mount and was eager for a race, where thoroughbreds dotted the wonderful grazing ranges, Venters rode a horse that was sad proof of his misfortunes.

Then, with his back against a stone, Venters faced the east, and, stick in hand and idle blade, he waited. The glorious sunlight filled the valley with purple fire. Before him, to left, to right, waving, rolling, sinking, rising, like low swells of a purple sea, stretched the sage. Out of the grove of cottonwoods, a green patch on the purple, gleamed the dull red of Jane Withe steen's old stone house. And from there extended the wide green of the village gardens and orchards marked by the graceful poplars; and farther down shone the deep, dark richness of the alfalfa fields. Numberless red and black and white dots speckled the sage, and these were cattle and horses.

So, watching and waiting, Venters let the time wear

away. At length he saw a horse rise above a ridge, and he knew it to be Lassiter's black. Climbing to the highest rock, so that he would show against the sky-line, he stood and waved his hat. The almost instant turning of Lassiter's horse attested to the quickness of that rider's eye. Then Venters climbed down, saddled his horse, tied on his pack, and, with a word to his dogs, was about to ride out to meet Lassiter, when he concluded to wait for him there, on higher ground, where the outlook was commanding.

It had been long since Venters had experienced friendly greeting from a man. Lassiter's warmed in him something that had grown cold from neglect. And when he had returned it, with a strong grip of the iron hand that held his, and met the gray eyes, he knew that Lassiter and he were to be friends.

"Venters, let's talk awhile before we go down there," said Lassiter, slipping his bridle. "I ain't in no hurry. Them's sure fine dogs you've got." With a rider's eye he took in the points of Venters's horse, but did not speak his thought. "Well, did anythin' come off after I left you last night?"

Venters told him about the rustlers.

"I was snug hid in the sage," replied Lassiter, "an' didn't see or hear no one. Oldrin's got a high hand here, I reckon. It's no news up in Utah how he holes in cañons an' leaves no track." Lassiter was silent a moment. "Me an' Oldrin' wasn't exactly strangers some years back when he drove cattle into Bostil's Ford, at the head of the Rio Virgin. But he got harassed there an' now he drives some place else."

"Lassiter, you knew him? Tell me, is he Mormon or Gentile?"

"I can't say. I've knowed Mormons who pretended to be Gentiles."

"No Mormon ever pretended that unless he was a rustler," declared Venters.

"Mebbe so."

"It's a hard country for any one, but hardest for Gentiles. Did you ever know or hear of a Gentile prospering in a Mormon community?"

"I never did."

"Well, I want to get out of Utah. I've a mother living in Illinois. I want to go home. It's eight years now."

The older man's sympathy moved Venters to tell his story. He had left Quincy, run off to seek his fortune in the gold fields, had never gotten any farther than Salt Lake City, wandered here and there as helper, teamster, shepherd, and drifted southwa d over the divide and across the barrens and up the rugged plateau through the passes to the last border settlements. Here he became a rider of the sage, had stock of his own, and for a time prospered, until chance threw him in the employ of Jane Withersteen.

"Lassiter, I needn't tell you the rest."

"Well, it 'd be no news to me. I know Mormons. I've seen their women's strange love an' patience an' sacrifice an' silence an' what I call madness for their idea of God. An' over against that I've seen the tricks of the men. They work hand in hand, all together, an' in the dark. No man can hold out against them, unless he takes to packin' guns. For Mormons are slow to kill. That's the only good I ever seen in their religion. Venters, take this from me, these Mormons ain't just right in their minds. Else could a Mormon marry one woman when he already had a wife, an' call it duty?"

"Lassiter, you think as I think," returned Venters.

"How'd it come then that you never throwed a gun on Tull or some of them?" inquired the rider, curiously.

"Jane pleaded with me, begged me to be patient, to overlook. She even took my guns from me. I lost all before I knew it," replied Venters, with the red color in his face. "But, Lassiter, listen. Out of the wreck I saved a Winchester, two Colts, and plenty of shells. I packed these down into Deception Pass. There, almost every day for six months, I have practised with my rifle till the barrel burnt my hands. Practised the draw—the firing of a Colt, hour after hour!"

"Now that's interestin' to me," said Lassiter, with a quick uplift of his head and a concentration of his gray gaze on Venters. "Could you throw a gun before you began that practisin'?"

"Yes. And now . . ." Venters made a lightning-swift movement.

Lassiter smiled, and then his bronzed eyelids narrowed till his eyes seemed mere gray slits. "You'll kill Tull!" He did not question; he affirmed.

"I promised Jane Withersteen I'd try to avoid Tull. I'll keep my word. But sooner or later Tull and I will meet. As I feel now, if he even looks at me I'll draw!"

"I reckon so. There'll be hell down there, presently." He paused a moment and flicked a sage-brush with his quirt. "Venters, seein' as you're considerable worked up, tell me Milly Erne's story."

Venters's agitation stilled to the trace of suppressed eagerness in Lassiter's query.

"Milly Erne's story? Well, Lassiter, I'll tell you what I know. Milly Erne had been in Cottonwoods years when I first arrived there, and most of what I tell you happened before my arrival. I got to know her pretty well. She was a slip of a woman, and crazy on religion. I conceived an idea that I never mentioned—I thought she was at heart more Gentile than Mormon. But she passed as a Mormon, and certainly she had the Mormon woman's locked lips. You know, in every Mormon village there are women who seem mysterious to us, but about Milly there was more than the ordinary mystery. When she came to Cottonwoods she had a beautiful little girl whom she loved passionately. Milly was not known openly in Cottonwoods as a Mormon wife. That she really was a Mormon wife I have no doubt. Perhaps the Mormon's other wife or wives would not acknowledge Milly. Such things happen in these villages. Mormon wives wear yokes, but they get jealous. Well, whatever had brought Milly to this country—love or madness of religion—she repented of it. She gave up teaching the village school. She quit the church. And she began to fight Mormon upbringing for her baby girl. Then the Mormons put on the screws—slowly, as is their way. At last the child disappeared. Lost, was the report. The child was stolen, I know that. So do you. That wrecked Milly Erne. But she lived on in hope. She became a slave. She worked her heart and soul and life out to get back her child. She never heard of it again. Then she sank. . . . I can see her now, a frail thing, so transparent you could almost look through her—white like ashes—and her eyes! . . . Her eyes have always haunted me. She had one real friend—Jane Withersteen. But Jane couldn't mend a broken heart, and Milly died."

For moments Lassiter did not speak, or turn his head.

"The man!" he exclaimed, presently, in husky accents.

"I haven't the slightest idea who the Mormon was," replied Venters; "nor has any Gentile in Cottonwoods."

"Does Jane Withersteen know?"

"Yes. But a red-hot running-iron couldn't burn that name out of her!"

Without further speech Lassiter started off, walking his horse, and Venters followed with his dogs. Half a mile down the slope they entered a luxuriant growth of willows, and soon came into an open space carpeted with grass like deep green velvet. The rushing of water and singing of birds filled their ears. Venters led his comrade to a shady bower and showed him Amber Spring. It was a magnificent outburst of clear, amber water pouring from a dark, stone-lined hole. Lassiter knelt and drank, lingered there to drink again. He made no comment, but Venters did not need words. Next to his horse a rider of the sage loved a spring. And this spring was the most beautiful and remarkable known to the upland riders of southern Utah. It was the spring that made old Withersteen a feudal lord and now enabled his daughter to return the toll which her father had exacted from the toilers of the sage.

The spring gushed forth in a swirling torrent, and leaped down joyously to make its swift way along a willow-skirted channel. Moss and ferns and lilies overhung its green banks. Except for the rough-hewn stones that held and directed the water, this willow thicket and glade had been left as nature had made it.

Below were artificial lakes, three in number, one above the other in banks of raised earth; and round about them rose the lofty green-foliaged shafts of poplar trees. Ducks dotted the glassy surface of the lakes; a blue heron stood motionless on a water-gate; kingfishers darted with shrieking flight along the shady banks; a white hawk sailed above; and from the trees and shrubs came the song of robins and cat-birds. It was all in strange contrast to the endless slopes of lonely sage and the wild rock environs beyond. Venters thought of the woman who loved the birds and the green of the leaves and the murmur of water.

Next on the slope, just below the third and largest lake, were corrals and a wide stone barn and open sheds and coops and pens. Here were clouds of dust, and cracking sounds of hoofs, and romping colts and hee-hawing burros. Neighing horses trampled to the corral fences. And from the little windows of the barn projected bobbing heads of bays and blacks and sorrels. When the two men entered the immense barnyard, from all around the din increased. This welcome, however, was not seconded by the several men and boys who vanished on sight.

Venters and Lassiter were turning toward the house when Jane appeared in the lane leading a horse. In riding-skirt and blouse she seemed to have lost some of her statuesque proportions, and looked more like a girl-rider than the mistress of Withersteen. She was bright, smiling, and her greeting was warmly cordial.

"Good news," she announced. "I've been to the village. All is quiet. I expected—I don't know what. But there's no excitement. And Tull has ridden out on his way to Glaze."

"Tull gone?" inquired Venters, with surprise. He was wondering what could have taken Tull away. Was it to avoid another meeting with Lassiter that he went? Could it have any connection with the probable nearness of Oldring and his gang?

"Gone, yes, thank goodness," replied Jane. "Now I'll have peace for a while. Lassiter, I want you to see my horses. You are a rider, and you must be a judge of horseflesh. Some of mine have Arabian blood. My father got his best strain in Nevada from Indians who claimed their horses were bred down from the original stock left by the Spaniards."

"Well, ma'am, the one you've been ridin' takes my eye," said Lassiter, as he walked round the racy, clean-limbed, and fine-pointed roan.

"Where are the boys?" she asked, looking about. "Jerd, Paul, where are you? Here, bring out the horses."

The sound of dropping bars inside the barn was the signal for the horses to jerk their heads in the windows, to snort and stamp. Then they came pounding out of the door, a file of thoroughbreds, to plunge about the barnyard, heads and tails up, manes flying. They halted afar off, squared away to look, came slowly forward with whinnies for their mistress, and doubtful snorts for the strangers and their horses.

"Come—come—come," called Jane, holding out her

hands. "Why Bells—Wrangle, where are your manners? Come, Black Star—come, Night. Ah, you beauties! My racers of the sage!"

Only two came up to her; those she called Night and Black Star. Venters never looked at them without delight. The first was soft dead black, the other glittering black, and they were perfectly matched in size, both being high and long-bodied, wide through the shoulders, with lithe, powerful legs. That they were a woman's pets showed in the gloss of skin, the fineness of mane. It showed, too, in the light of big eyes and the gentle reach of eagerness.

"I never seen their like," was Lassiter's encomium, "an' in my day I've seen a sight of horses. Now, ma'am, if you was wantin' to make a long an' fast ride across the sage—say to elope—"

Lassiter ended there with dry humor, yet behind that was meaning. Jane blushed and made arch eyes at him.

"Take care, Lassiter, I might think that a proposal," she replied, gaily. "It's dangerous to propose elopement to a Mormon woman. Well, I was expecting you. Now will be a good hour to show you Milly Erne's grave. The day-riders have gone, and the night-riders haven't come in. Bern, what do you make of that? Need I worry? You know I have to be made worry."

"Well, it's not usual for the night shift to ride in so late," replied Venters, slowly, and his glance sought Lassiter's. "Cattle are usually quiet after dark. Still, I've known even a coyote to stampede your white herd."

"I refuse to borrow trouble. Come," said Jane.

They mounted, and, with Jane in the lead, rode down the lane, and, turning off into a cattle trail, proceeded westward. Venters's dogs trotted behind them. On this side of the ranch the outlook was different from that on the other; the immediate foreground was rough and the sage more rugged and less colorful; there were no dark-blue lines of cañons to hold the eye, nor any uprearing rock walls. It was a long roll and slope into gray obscurity. Soon Jane left the trail and rode into the sage, and presently she dismounted and threw her bridle. The men did likewise. Then, on foot, they followed her, coming out at length on the rim of a low escarpment. She passed by several little ridges of earth to halt before a faintly defined mound. It lay in the shade of a sweeping sage-brush close to the edge of the promontory; and a rider could have jumped his horse over it without recognizing a grave.

"Here!"

She looked sad as she spoke, but she offered no explanation for the neglect of an unmarked, uncared-for grave. There was a little bunch of pale, sweet lavender daisies, doubtless planted there by Jane.

"I only come here to remember and to pray," she said. "But I leave no trail!"

A grave in the sage! How lonely this resting-place of Milly Erne! The cottonwoods or the alfalfa fields were not in sight, nor was there any rock or ridge or cedar to lend contrast to the monotony. Gray slopes, tinging the purple, barren and wild, with the wind waving the sage, swept away to the dim horizon.

Lassiter looked at the grave and then out into space. At that moment he seemed a figure of bronze.

Jane touched Venters's arm and led him back to the horses.

"Bern!" cried Jane, when they were out of hearing. "Suppose Lassiter were Milly's husband—the father of that little girl lost so long ago!"

"It might be, Jane. Let us ride on. If he wants to see us again he'll come."

So they mounted and rode out to the cattle trail and began to climb. From the height of the ridge, where they had started down, Venters looked back. He did not see Lassiter, but his glance, drawn irresistibly farther out on the gradual slope, caught sight of a moving cloud of dust.

"Hello, a rider!"

"Yes, I see," said Jane.

"That fellow's riding hard. Jane, there's something wrong."

"Oh yes, there must be. . . . How he rides!"

The horse disappeared in the sage, and then puffs of dust marked his course.

"He's short-cut on us—he's making straight for the corrals."

Venters and Jane galloped their steeds and reined in at the turning of the lane. This lane led down to the right of the grove. Suddenly into its lower entrance flashed a bay horse. Then Venters caught the fast rhythmic beat of pounding hoofs. Soon his keen eye recognized the swing of the rider in his saddle.

"It's Judkins, your Gentile rider!" he cried. "Jane, when Judkins rides like that it means hell!"

CHAPTER IV

DECEPTION PASS

THE rider thundered up and almost threw his foam-flecked horse in the sudden stop. He was of giant form, and with fearless eyes.

"Judkins, you're all bloody!" cried Jane, in affright. "Oh, you've been shot!"

"Nothin' much, Miss Withersteen. I got a nick in the shoulder. I'm some wet an' the hoss's been throwin' lather, so all this ain't blood."

"What's up?" queried Venters, sharply.

"Rustlers sloped off with the red herd."

"Where are my riders?" demanded Jane.

"Miss Withersteen, I was alone all night with the herd. At daylight this mornin' the rustlers rode down. They began to shoot at me on sight. They chased me hard an' far, burnin' powder all the time, but I got away."

"Jud, they meant to kill you," declared Venters.

'Now I wonder," returned Judkins. "They wanted me bad. An' it ain't regular for rustlers to waste time chasin' one rider."

"Thank Heaven you got away," said Jane. "But my riders—where are they?"

"I don't know. The night-riders weren't there last night when I rode down, an' this mornin' I met no day-riders."

"Judkins! Bern, they've been set upon—killed by Oldring's men!"

"I don't think so," replied Venters, decidedly. "Jane, your riders haven't gone out in the sage."

"Bern, what do you mean?" Jane Withersteen turned deathly pale.

"You remember what I said about the unseen hand?"

"Oh! . . . Impossible!"

"I hope so. But I fear—" Venters finished, with a shake of his head.

"Bern, you're bitter; but that's only natural. We'll wait to see what's happened to my riders. Judkins, come to the house with me. Your wound must be attended to."

"Jane, I'll find out where Oldring drives the herd," vowed Venters.

"No, no! Bern, don't risk it now—when the rustlers are in such shooting mood."

"I'm going. Jud, how many cattle in that red herd?"

"Twenty-five hundred head."

"Whew! What on earth can Oldring do with so many cattle? Why, a hundred head is a big steal. I've got to find out."

"Don't go," implored Jane.

"Bern, you want a hoss thet can run. Miss Withersteen, if it's not too bold of me to advise, make him take a fast hoss or don't let him go."

"Yes, yes, Judkins. He must ride a horse that can't be caught. Which one—Black Star—Night?"

"Jane, I won't take either," said Venters, emphatically. "I wouldn't risk losing one of your favorites."

"Wrangle, then?"

"Thet's the hoss," replied Judkins. "Wrangle can outrun Black Star an' Night. You'd never believe it, Miss Withersteen, but I know. Wrangle's the biggest an' fastest hoss on the sage."

"Oh no, Wrangle can't beat Black Star. But, Bern, take Wrangle, if you will go. Ask Jerd for anything you need. Oh, be watchful, careful. . . . God speed you!"

She clasped his hand, turned quickly away, and went down the lane with the rider.

Venters rode to the barn, and, leaping off, shouted for Jerd. The boy came running. Venters sent him for meat, bread, and dried fruits, to be packed in saddle-bags. His own horse he turned loose into the nearest corral. Then he went for Wrangle. The giant sorrel had earned his name for a trait the opposite of amiability. He came readily out of the barn, but once in the yard he broke from Venters, and plunged about with ears laid back. Venters had to rope him, and then he kicked down a section of fence, stood on his hind legs, crashed down and fought the rope. Jerd returned to lend a hand.

"Wrangle don't git enough work," said Jerd, as the big saddle went on. "He's unruly when he's corralled, an' wants to run. Wait till he smells the sage!"

"Jerd, this horse is an iron-jawed devil. I never straddled him but once. Run? Say, he's swift as wind!"

When Venters's boot touched the stirrup the sorrel bolted, giving him the rider's flying mount. The swing of this fiery horse recalled to Venters days that were not really long past, when he rode into the sage as the leader of Jane Withersteen's riders. Wrangle pulled hard on a tight rein. He galloped out of the lane, down the shady border of the grove, and hauled up at the watering-trough, where he pranced and champed his bit. Venters got off and filled his canteen while the horse drank. The dogs, Ring and Whitie, came trotting up for their drink. Then Venters remounted and turned Wrangle toward the sage.

A wide, white trail wound away down the slope. One keen, sweeping glance told Venters that there was neither man nor horse nor steer within the limit of his vision, unless they were lying down in the sage. Ring loped in the lead and Whitie loped in the rear. Wrangle settled gradually into an easy swinging canter, and Venters's thoughts, now that the rush and flurry of the start were past, and the long miles stretched before him, reverted to a calm reckoning of late singular coincidences.

There was the night ride of Tull's, which, viewed in the light of subsequent events, had a look of his covert machinations; Oldring and his Masked Rider and his rustlers riding muffled horses; the report that Tull had ridden out that morning with his man Jerry on the trail to Glaze, the strange disappearance of Jane Withersteen's riders, the unusually determined attempt to kill the one Gentile still in her employ, an intention frustrated, no doubt, only by Judkins's magnificent riding of her racer, and lastly the driving of the red herd. These events, to Venters's color of mind, had a dark relationship. Remembering Jane's accusation of bitterness, he tried hard to put aside his rancor in judging Tull. But it was bitter knowledge that made him see the truth. He had felt the shadow of an unseen hand; he had watched till he saw its dim outline, and then he had traced it to a man's hate, to the rivalry of a Mormon Elder, to the power of a Bishop, to the long, far-reaching arm of a terrible creed. That unseen hand had made its first move against Jane Withersteen. Her riders had been called in, leaving her without help to drive seven thousand head of cattle. But to Venters it seemed extraordinary that the power which had called in these riders had left so many cattle to be driven by rustlers and harried by wolves. For hand in glove with that power was an insatiate greed; they were one and the same.

"What can Oldring do with twenty-five hundred head of cattle?" muttered Venters. "Is he a Mormon? Did he meet Tull last night? It looks like a black plot to me. But Tull and his churchmen wouldn't ruin Jane Withersteen unless the Church was to profit by that ruin. Where does Oldring come in? I'm going to find out about these things."

Wrangle did twenty-five miles in three hours and walked little of the way. When he had gotten warmed up he had been allowed to choose his own gait. The afternoon had well advanced when Venters struck the trail of the red herd and found where it had grazed the night before. Then Venters rested the horse and used his eyes. Near at hand were a cow and a calf and several yearlings, and farther out in the sage some straggling steers. He caught a glimpse of coyotes skulking near the cattle. The slow, sweeping gaze of the rider failed to find other living things within the field of sight. The sage about him was breast-high to his horse, oversweet with its warm, fragrant breath, gray where it waved to the light, darker where the wind left it still, and beyond the wonderful haze-purple lent by distance. Far across that wide waste began the slow lift of uplands through which Deception Pass cut its tortuous many-cañoned way.

Venters raised the bridle of his horse and followed the broad cattle trail. The crushed sage resembled the path of a monster snake. In a few miles of travel he passed several cows and calves that had escaped the drive. Then he stood on the last high bench of the slope with the floor of the valley beneath. The opening of the cañon showed in a break of the sage, and the cattle trail paralleled it as far as he could see. That trail led to an undiscovered point where Oldring drove cattle into the pass, and many a rider who had followed it had never returned. Venters satisfied himself that the rustlers had not deviated from their usual course, and then he turned at right angles off the cattle trail and made for the head of the pass.

The sun lost its heat and wore down to the western horizon, where it changed from white to gold and rested like a huge ball about to roll on its golden shadows down the slope. Venters watched the lengthening of the rays and bars, and marveled at his own league-long shadow. The sun sank. There was instant shading of brightness about him, and he saw a kind of cold purple bloom creep ahead of him to cross the cañon, to mount the opposite slope and chase and darken and bury the last golden flare of sunlight.

Venters rode into a trail that he always took to get down into the cañon. He dismounted and found no tracks but his own made several days previous. Nevertheless he sent the dog Ring ahead and waited. In a little while Ring returned. Whereupon Venters led his horse on to the break in the ground.

The opening into Deception Pass was one of the remarkable natural phenomena in a country remarkable for vast slopes of sage, uplands insulated by gigantic red walls, and deep cañons of mysterious source and outlet. Here the valley floor was level, and here opened a narrow chasm, a ragged vent in yellow walls of stone. The trail down the five hundred feet of sheer depth always tested Venters's nerve. It was bad going for even a burro. But Wrangle, as Venters led him, snorted defiance or disgust rather than fear, and, like a hobbled horse on the jump, lifted his ponderous iron-shod fore hoofs and crashed down over the first rough step. Venters warmed to greater admiration of the sorrel; and, giving him a loose bridle, he stepped down foot by foot. Oftentimes the stones and shale started by Wrangle buried Venters to his knees; again he was hard put to it to dodge a rolling boulder; there were times when he could not see Wrangle for dust, and once he and the horse rode a sliding shelf of yellow, weathered cliff. It was a trail on which there could be no stops, and, therefore, if perilous, it was at least one that did not take long in the descent.

Venters breathed lighter when that was over, and felt a sudden assurance in the success of his enterprise. For at first it had been a reckless determination to achieve something at any cost, and now it resolved itself into an adventure worthy of all his reason and cunning, and keenness of eye and ear.

Piñon pines clustered in little clumps along the level floor of the pass. Twilight had gathered under the walls. Venters rode into the trail and up the cañon. Gradually the trees and caves and objects low down turned black, and this blackness moved up the walls till night enfolded the pass, while day still lingered above. The sky darkened; and stars began to show, at first pale and then bright. Sharp notches of the rim-wall, biting like teeth into the blue, were landmarks by which Venters knew where his camping site lay. He had to feel his way through a thicket of slender oaks to a spring where he watered Wrangle and drank himself. Here he unsaddled and turned Wrangle loose, having no fear that the horse would leave the thick, cool grass adjacent to the spring. Next he satisfied his own hunger, fed Ring and Whitie, and, with them curled beside him, composed himself to await sleep.

There had been a time when night in the high altitude of these Utah uplands had been satisfying to Venters. But that was before the oppression of enemies had made the change in his mind. As a rider guarding the herd he had never thought of the night's wildness and loneliness; as an outcast, now when the full silence set in, and the deep darkness, and trains of radiant stars shone cold and calm, he lay with an ache in his heart. For a year he had lived as a black fox, driven from his kind. He longed for the sound of a voice, the touch of a hand. In the daytime there was riding from place to place, and the gun practice to which something drove him, and other tasks that at least necessitated action; at night, before he won sleep, there was strife in his soul. He yearned to leave the endless sage slopes, the wilderness of cañons; and it was in the lonely night that this yearning grew unbearable. It was then that he reached forth to feel Ring or Whitie, immeasurably grateful for the love and companionship of two dogs.

On this night the same old loneliness beset Venters,

the old habit of sad thought and burning unquiet had its way. But from it evolved a conviction that his useless life had undergone a subtle change. He had sensed it first when Wrangle swung him up to the high saddle, he knew it now when he lay in the gateway of Deception Pass. He had no thrill of adventure, rather a gloomy perception of great hazard, perhaps death. He meant to find Oldring's retreat. The rustlers had fast horses, but none that could catch Wrangle. Venters know no rustler could creep upon him at night when Ring and Whitie guarded his hiding-place. For the rest, he had eyes and ears, and a long rifle and an unerring aim, which he meant to use. Strangely his foreshadowing of change did not hold a thought of the killing of Tull. It related only to what was to happen to him in Deception Pass; and he could no more lift the veil of that mystery than tell where the trails led to in that unexplored cañon. Moreover, he did not care. And at length, tired out by stress of thought, he fell asleep.

When his eyes unclosed, day had come again, and he saw the rim of the opposite wall tipped with the gold of sunrise. A few moments sufficed for the morning's simple camp duties. Near at hand he found Wrangle, and to his surprise the horse came to him. Wrangle was one of the horses that left his viciousness in the home corral. What he wanted was to be free of mules and burros and steers, to roll in dust-patches, and then to run down the wide, open, windy sage-plains, and at night browse and sleep in the cool wet grass of a spring-hole. Jerd knew the sorrel when he said of him, "Wait till he smells the sage!"

Venters saddled and led him out of the oak thicket, and, leaping astride, rode up the cañon, with Ring and Whitie trotting behind. An old grass-grown trail followed the course of a shallow wash where flowed a thin stream of water. The cañon was a hundred rods wide; its yellow walls were perpendicular; it had abundant sage and a scant growth of oak and piñon. For five miles it held to a comparatively straight bearing, and then began a heightening of rugged walls and a deepening of the floor. Beyond this point of sudden change in the character of the cañon Venters had never explored, and here was the real door to the intricacies of Deception Pass.

He reined Wrangle to a walk, halted now and then to listen, and then proceeded cautiously with shifting and alert gaze. The cañon assumed proportions that dwarfed those of its first ten miles. Venters rode on and on, not losing in the interest of his wide surroundings any of his caution or keen search for tracks or sight of living thing. If there ever had been a trail here, he could not find it. He rode through sage and clumps of piñon trees and grassy plots where long-petaled purple lilies bloomed. He rode through a dark constriction of the pass no wider than the lane in the grove at Cottonwoods. And he came out into a great amphitheater into which jutted huge towering corners of a confluence of intersecting cañons.

Venters sat his horse, and, with a rider's eye, studied this wild cross-cut of huge stone gullies. Then he went on, guided by the course of running water. If it had not been for the main stream of water flowing north he would never have been able to tell which of those many openings was a continuation of the pass. In crossing this amphitheater he went by the mouths of five cañons, fording little streams that flowed into the larger one. Gaining the outlet which he took to be the pass, he rode on again under overhanging walls. One side was dark in shade, the other light in sun. This narrow passageway turned and twisted and opened into a valley that amazed Venters.

Here again was a sweep of purple sage, richer than upon the higher levels. The valley was miles long, several wide, and inclosed by unscalable walls. But it was the background of this valley that so forcibly struck him. Across the sage-flat rose a strange up-flinging of yellow rocks. He could not tell which were close and which were distant. Scrawled mounds of stone, like mountain waves, seemed to roll up to steep bare slopes and towers.

In this plain of sage Venters flushed birds and rabbits, and when he had proceeded about a mile he caught sight of the bobbing white tails of a herd of running antelope. He rode along the edge of the stream which wound toward the western end of the slowly looming mounds of stone. The high slope retreated out of sight behind the nearer projection. To Venters the valley appeared to have been filled in by a mountain of melted stone that had hardened in strange shapes of rounded outline. He followed the stream till he lost it in a deep cut. Therefore Venters quit the dark slit which baffled further search in that direction, and rode out along the curved edge of stone where it met the sage. It was not long before he came to a low place, and here Wrangle readily climbed up.

All about him was ridgy roll of wind-smoothed, rain-washed rock. Not a tuft of grass or a bunch of sage colored the dull rust-yellow. He saw where, to the right, this uneven flow of stone ended in a blunt wall. Leftward, from the hollow that lay at his feet, mounted a gradual slow-swelling slope to a great height topped by leaning, cracked, and ruined crags. Not for some time did he grasp the wonder of that acclivity. It was no less than a mountain-side, glistening in the sun like polished granite, with cedar-trees springing as if by magic out of the denuded surface. Winds had swept it clear of weathered shale, and rains had washed it free of dust. Far up the curved slope its beautiful lines broke to meet the vertical rim-wall, to lose its grace in a different order and color of rock, a stained yellow cliff of cracks and caves and seamed crags. And straight before Venters was a scene less striking but more significant to his keen survey. For beyond a mile of the bare, hummocky rock began the valley of sage, and the mouths of cañons, one of which surely was another gateway into the pass.

He got off his horse, and, giving the bridle to Ring to hold, he commenced a search for the cleft where the stream ran. He was not successful and concluded the water dropped into an underground passage. Then he returned to where he had left Wrangle, and led him down off the stone to the sage. It was a short ride to the opening cañons. There was no reason for a choice of which one to enter. The one he rode into was a clear, sharp shaft in yellow stone a thousand feet deep, with wonderful wind-worn caves low down and high above buttressed and turreted ramparts. Farther on Venters came into a region where deep indentations marked the line of cañon walls. These were huge, cove-like blind pockets extending back to a sharp corner with a dense growth of underbrush and trees.

Venters penetrated into one of these offshoots, and, as he had hoped, he found abundant grass. He had to bend the oak saplings to get his horse through. Deciding to make this a hiding-place if he could find water, he worked back to the limit of the shelving walls. In a little cluster of silver spruces he found a spring. This inclosed nook seemed an ideal place to leave his horse and to camp at night, and from which to make stealthy trips on foot. The thick grass hid his trail; the dense growth of oaks in the opening would serve as a barrier to keep Wrangle in, if, indeed, the luxuriant browse would not suffice for that. So Venters, leaving Whitie with the horse, called Ring to his side, and, rifle in hand, worked his way out to the open. A careful photographing in mind of the formation of the bold outlines of rimrock assured him he would be able to return to his retreat, even in the dark.

Bunches of scattered sage covered the center of the cañon, and among these Venters threaded his way with the step of an Indian. At intervals he put his hand on the dog and stopped to listen. There was a drowsy hum of insects, but no other sound disturbed the warm midday stillness. Venters saw ahead a turn, more abrupt than any yet. Warily he rounded this corner, once again to halt bewildered.

The cañon opened fan-shaped into a great oval of green and gray growths. It was the hub of an oblong wheel, and from it, at regular distances, like spokes, ran the outgoing cañons. Here a dull red color predominated over the fading yellow. The corners of wall bluntly rose, scarred and scrawled, to taper into towers and serrated peaks and pinnacled domes.

Venters pushed on more heedfully than ever. Toward the center of this circle the sage-brush grew smaller and farther apart. He was about to sheer off to the right, where thickets and jumbles of fallen rock would afford him cover, when he ran right upon a broad cattle trail. Like a road it was, more than a trail; and the cattle tracks were fresh. What surprised him more, they were wet! He pondered over this feature. It had not rained. The only solution to this puzzle was that the cattle had been driven through water, and water deep enough to wet their legs.

Suddenly Ring growled low. Venters rose cautiously and looked over the sage. A band of straggling horsemen were riding across the oval. He sank down, startled and trembling. "Rustlers!" he muttered. Hurriedly he glanced about for a place to hide. Near at hand there was nothing but sage-brush. He dared not risk crossing the open patches to reach the rocks. Again he peeped over the sage. The rustlers—four—five—seven—eight in all, were approaching, but not directly in line with him. That was relief for a cold deadness which seemed to be creeping inward along his veins.

He crouched down with bated breath and held the bristling dog.

He heard the click of iron-shod hoofs on stone, the coarse laughter of men, and then voices gradually dying away. Long moments passed. Then he rose. The rustlers were riding into a cañon. Their horses were tired, and they had several pack animals; evidently they had traveled far. Venters doubted that they were the rustlers who had driven the red herd. Oldring's band had split. Venters watched these horsemen disappear under a bold cañon wall.

The rustlers had come from the northwest side of the oval. Venters kept a steady gaze in that direction, hoping, if there were more, to see from what cañon they rode. A quarter of an hour went by. Reward for his vigilance came when he descried three more mounted men, far over to the north. But out of what cañon they had ridden it was too late to tell. He watched the three ride across the oval and round the jutting red corner where the others had gone.

"Up that cañon!" exclaimed Venters. "Oldring's den! I've found it!"

A knotty point for Venters was the fact that the cattle tracks all pointed west. The broad trail came from the direction of the cañon into which the rustlers had ridden, and undoubtedly the cattle had been driven out of it across the oval. There were no tracks pointing the other way. It had been in his mind that Oldring had driven the red herd toward the rendezvous, and not from it. Where did that broad trail come down into the pass, and where did it lead? Venters knew he wasted time in pondering the question, but it held a fascination not easily dispelled. For many years Oldring's mysterious entrance and exit to Deception Pass had been all-absorbing topics to sage-riders.

All at once the dog put an end to Venters's pondering. Ring sniffed the air, turned slowly in his tracks with a

LIKE A FLASH THE BLUE BARREL OF HIS RIFLE GLEAMED LEVEL AND HE SHOT ONCE—TWICE

whine, and then growled. Venters wheeled. Two horsemen were within a hundred yards, coming straight at him. One, lagging behind the other, was Oldring's Masked Rider.

Venters cunningly sank, slowly trying to merge into sage-brush. But, guarded as his action was, the first horse detected it. He stopped short, snorted, and shot up his ears. The rustler bent forward, as if keenly peering ahead. Then, with a swift sweep, he jerked a gun from its sheath and fired.

The bullet zipped through the sage-brush. Flying bits of wood struck Venters, and the hot, stinging pain seemed to lift him in one leap. Like a flash the blue barrel of his rifle gleamed level and he shot once—twice.

The foremost rustler dropped his weapon and toppled from his saddle, to fall with his foot catching in a stirrup. The horse snorted wildly and plunged away, dragging the rustler through the sage.

The Masked Rider huddled over his pommel, slowly swaying to one side, and then, with a faint, strange cry, slipped out of the saddle.

CHAPTER V

THE MASKED RIDER

VENTERS looked quickly from the fallen rustlers to the cañon where the others had disappeared. He calculated on the time needed for running horses to return to the open, if their riders heard shots. He waited breathlessly. But the estimated time dragged by and no riders appeared. Venters began presently to believe that the rifle reports had not penetrated into the recesses of the cañon, and felt safe for the immediate present.

He hurried to the spot where the first rustler had been dragged by his horse. The man lay in deep grass, dead, jaw fallen, eyes protruding—a sight that sickened Venters. The first man at whom he had ever aimed a weapon he had shot through the heart. With the clammy sweat oozing from every pore Venters dragged the rustler in among some boulders and covered him with slabs of rock. Then he smoothed out the crushed trail in grass and sage. The rustler's horse had stopped a quarter of a mile off and was grazing.

When Venters rapidly strode toward the Masked Rider not even the cold nausea that gripped him could wholly banish curiosity. For he had shot Oldring's infamous lieutenant, whose face had never been seen. Venters experienced a grim pride in the feat. What would Tull say to this achievement of the outcast who rode too often to Deception Pass?

Venters's curious eagerness and expectation had not prepared him for the shock he received when he stood over a slight, dark figure. The rustler wore the black mask that had given him his name, but he had no weapons. Venters glanced at the drooping horse; there were no gun-sheaths on the saddle.

"A rustler who didn't pack guns!" muttered Venters. "He wears no belt. He couldn't pack guns in that rig. . . . Strange!"

A low, gasping intake of breath and a sudden twitching of body told Venters the rider still lived.

"He's alive! . . . I've got to stand here and watch him die. And I shot an unarmed man."

Shrinkingly Venters removed the rider's wide sombrero and the black cloth mask. This action disclosed bright chestnut hair, inclined to curl, and a white, youthful face. Along the lower line of cheek and jaw was a clear demarcation, where the brown of tanned skin met the white that had been hidden from the sun.

"Oh, he's only a boy! . . . What! Can he be Oldring's Masked Rider?"

The boy showed signs of returning consciousness. He stirred; his lips moved; a small brown hand clenched in his blouse.

Venters knelt with a gathering horror of his deed. His bullet had entered the rider's right breast, high up to the shoulder. With hands that shook, Venters untied a black scarf and ripped open the blood-wet blouse.

First he saw a gaping hole, dark red against a whiteness of skin, from which welled a slender red stream. Then the graceful, beautiful swell of a woman's breast!

"A woman!" he cried. "A girl! . . . I've killed a girl!"

She suddenly opened eyes that transfixed Venters. They were fathomless blue. Consciousness of death was there, a blended terror and pain, but no consciousness of sight. She did not see Venters. She stared into the unknown.

Then came a spasm of vitality. She writhed in a

torture of reviving strength, and in her convulsions she almost tore from Venters's grasp. Slowly she relaxed and sank partly back. The ungloved hand sought the wound, and pressed so hard that her wrist half buried itself in her bosom. Blood trickled between her spread fingers. And she looked at Venters with eyes that saw him.

He cursed himself and the unerring aim of which he had been so proud. He had seen that look in the eyes of a crippled antelope which he was about to finish with his knife. But in her it had infinitely more—a revelation of mortal spirit. The instinctive clinging to life was there, and the divining helplessness and the terrible accusation of the stricken.

"Forgive me! I didn't know!" burst out Venters.

"You shot me—you've killed me!" she whispered, in panting gasps. Upon her lips appeared a fluttering, bloody froth. By that Venters knew the air in her lungs was mixing with blood. "Oh, I knew—it would—come—some day! . . . Oh, the burn! . . . Hold me—I'm sinking—it's all dark. . . . Ah, God! . . . Mercy—"

Her rigidity loosened in one long quiver and she lay back limp, still, white as snow, with closed eyes.

Venters thought then that she died. But the faint pulsation of her breast assured him that life yet lingered. Death seemed only a matter of moments, for the bullet had gone clear through her. Nevertheless, he tore sage-leaves from a bush, and, pressing them tightly over her wounds, he bound the black scarf round her shoulder, tying it securely under her arm. Then he closed the blouse, hiding from his sight that blood-stained, accusing breast.

"What—now?" he questioned, with flying mind. "I must get out of here. She's dying—but I can't leave her."

He rapidly surveyed the sage to the north and made out no animate object. Then he picked up the girl's

"OH, HE'S ONLY A BOY! . . . WHAT! CAN HE BE OLDRING'S MASKED RIDER?"

sombrero and the mask. This time the mask gave him as great a shock as when he first removed it from her face: For in the woman he had forgotten the rustler, and this black strip of felt-cloth established the identity of Oldring's Masked Rider. Venters had solved the mystery. He slipped his rifle under her, and, lifting her carefully upon it, he began to retrace his steps. The dog trailed in his shadow. And the horse, that had stood drooping by, followed without a call. Venters chose the deepest tufts of grass and clumps of sage on his return. From time to time he glanced over his shoulder. He did not rest. His concern was to avoid jarring the girl and to hide his trail. Gaining the narrow cañon, he turned and held close to the wall till he reached his hiding-place. When he entered the dense thicket of oaks he was hard put to it to force a way through. But he held his burden almost upright, and by slipping sidewise and bending the saplings he got in. Through sage and grass he hurried to the grove of silver spruces.

He laid the girl down, almost fearing to look at her. Though marble pale and cold, she was living. Venters then appreciated the tax that long carry had been to his strength. He sat down to rest. Whitie sniffed at the pale girl and whined and crept to Venters's feet. Ring lapped the water in the runway of the spring.

Presently Venters went out to the opening, caught the horse, and, leading him through the thicket, unsaddled him and tied him with a long halter. Wrangle left his browsing long enough to whinny and toss his head. Venters felt that he could not rest easily till he had secured the other rustler's horse; so, taking his rifle and calling for Ring, he set out. Swiftly yet watchfully he made his way through the cañon to the oval and out to the cattle trail. What few tracks might have betrayed him he obliterated, so only an expert tracker could have trailed him. Then, with many a wary backward glance across the sage, he started to round up the rustler's horse. This was unexpectedly easy. He led the horse to lower ground, out of sight from the opposite side of the oval, along the shadowy western wall, and so on into his cañon and secluded camp.

The girl's eyes were open; a feverish spot burned in her cheeks; she moaned something unintelligible to Venters, but he took the movement of her lips to mean that she wanted water. Lifting her head, he tipped the canteen to her lips. After that she again lapsed into unconsciousness or a weakness which was its counterpart. Venters noted, however, that the burning flush had faded into the former pallor.

The sun set behind the high cañon rim, and a cool shade darkened the walls. Venters fed the dogs and put a halter on the dead rustler's horse. He allowed Wrangle to browse free. This done, he cut spruce boughs and made a lean-to for the girl. Then, gently lifting her upon a blanket, he folded the sides over her. The other blanket he wrapped about his shoulders and found a comfortable seat against a spruce-tree that upheld the little shack. Ring and Whitie lay near at hand, one asleep, the other watchful.

Venters dreaded the night's vigil. At night his mind was active, and this time he had to watch and think and feel beside a dying girl whom he had all but murdered. A thousand excuses he invented for himself, yet not one made any difference in his act or his self-reproach.

It seemed to him that when night fell black he could see her white face so much more plainly.

"She'll go, presently," he said, "and be out of agony—thank God!"

Every little while certainty of her death came to him with a shock; and then he would bend over and lay his ear on her breast. Her heart still beat.

The early night blackness cleared to the cold starlight. The horses were not moving, and no sound disturbed the deathly silence of the cañon.

"I'll bury her here," thought Venters, "and let her grave be as much a mystery as her life was."

For the girl's few words, the look of her eyes, the prayer, had strangely touched Venters.

"She was only a girl," he soliloquized. "What was she to Oldring? Rustlers don't have wives nor sisters nor daughters. She was bad—that's all. But somehow . . . well, she may not have willingly become the companion of rustlers. That prayer of hers to God for mercy! . . . Life is strange and cruel. I wonder if other members of Oldring's gang are women? Likely enough. But what was his game? Oldring's Masked Rider! A name to make villagers hide and lock their doors. A name credited with a dozen murders, a hundred forays, and a thousand stealings of cattle. What part did the girl have in this? It may have served Oldring to create mystery."

Hours passed. The white stars moved across the narrow strip of dark-blue sky above. The silence awoke to the low hum of insects. Venters watched the immovable white face, and as he watched, hour by hour waiting for death, the infamy of her passed from his mind. He thought only of the sadness, the truth of the moment. Whoever she was—whatever she had done—she was young and she was dying.

The after-part of the night wore on interminably. The starlight failed and the gloom blackened to the darkest hour. "She'll die at the gray of dawn," muttered Venters, remembering some old woman's fancy. The blackness paled to gray, and the gray lightened and day peeped over the eastern rim. Venters listened at the breast of the girl. She still lived. Did he only imagine that her heart beat stronger, ever so slightly, but stronger? He pressed his ear closer to her breast. And he rose with his own pulse quickening.

"If she doesn't die soon—she's got a chance—the barest chance—to live," he said.

He wondered if the internal bleeding had ceased. There was no more film of blood upon her lips. But no corpse could have been whiter. Opening her blouse, he untied the scarf, and carefully picked away the sage-leaves from the wound in her shoulder. It had closed. Lifting her lightly, he ascertained that the same was true of the hole where the bullet had come out. He reflected on the fact that clean wounds closed quickly in the healing upland air. He recalled instances of riders who had been cut and shot, apparently to fatal issues; yet the blood had clotted, the wounds closed, and they had recovered. He had no way to tell if internal hemorrhage still went on, but he believed that it had stopped. Otherwise she would surely not have lived so long. He marked the entrance of the bullet, and concluded that it had just touched the upper lobe of her lung. Perhaps the wound in the lung had also closed. As he began to wash the blood stains from her breast and carefully rebandage the wound, he was vaguely conscious of a strange, grave happiness in the thought that she might live.

Broad daylight and a hint of sunshine high on the cliff-rim to the west brought him to consideration of what he had better do. And while busy with his few camp tasks he revolved the thing in his mind. It would not be wise for him to remain long in his present hiding-place. And if he intended to follow the cattle trail and try to find the rustlers he had better make a move at once. For he knew that rustlers, being riders, would not make much of a day's or night's absence from camp for one or two of their number; but when the missing ones failed to show up in reasonable time there would be a search. And Venters was afraid of that.

"A good tracker could trail me," he muttered. "And I'd be cornered here. Let's see. Rustlers are a lazy set when they're not on the ride. I'll risk it. Then I'll change my hiding-place.

He carefully cleaned and reloaded his guns. When he rose to go he bent a long glance down upon the unconscious girl. Then, ordering Whitie and Ring to keep guard, he left the camp.

The safest cover lay close under the wall of the cañon, and here through the dense thickets Venters made his slow, listening advance toward the oval. Upon gaining the wide opening he decided to cross it and follow the left wall till he came to the cattle trail. He scanned the oval as keenly as if hunting for antelope. Then, stooping, he stole from one cover to another, taking advantage of rocks and bunches of sage, until he had reached the thickets under the opposite wall. Once there, he exercised extreme caution in his surveys of the ground ahead, but increased his speed when moving. Dodging from bush to bush, he passed the mouths of two cañons, and in the entrance of a third cañon he crossed a wash of swift, clear water, to come abruptly upon the cattle trail.

It followed the low bank of the wash, and, keeping it in sight, Venters hugged the line of sage and thicket. Like the curves of a serpent the cañon wound for a mile or more and then opened into a valley. Patches of red showed clear against the purple of sage, and farther out on the level dotted strings of red led away to the wall of rock.

"Ha, the red herd!" exclaimed Venters.

Then dots of white and black told him there were cattle of other colors in this inclosed valley. Oldring, the rustler, was also a rancher. Venters's calculating eye took count of stock that outnumbered the red herd.

"What a range!" went on Venters. "Water and grass enough for fifty thousand head, and no riders needed!"

After his first burst of surprise and rapid calculation Venters lost no time there, but slunk again into the sage on his back trail. With the discovery of Oldring's hidden cattle-range had come enlightenment on several problems. Here the rustler kept his stock; here was Jane Withersteen's red herd; here were the few cattle that had disappeared from the Cottonwoods slopes during the last two years. Until Oldring had driven the red herd his thefts of cattle for that time had not been more than enough to supply meat for his men. Of late no drives had been reported from Sterling or the villages north. And Venters knew that the riders had wondered at Oldring's inactivity in that particular field. He and his band had been active enough in their visits to Glaze and Cottonwoods; they always had gold; but of late the amount gambled away and drunk and thrown away in the villages had given rise to much conjecture. Oldring's more frequent visits had resulted in new saloons, and where there had formerly been one raid or shooting fray in the little hamlets there were now many. Perhaps Oldring had another range farther on up the pass, and from there drove the cattle to distant Utah towns where he was little known. But Venters came finally to doubt this. And, from what he had learned in the last few days, a belief began to form in Venters's mind that Oldring's intimidations of the villages and the mystery of the Masked Rider, with his alleged evil deeds, and the fierce resistance offered any trailing riders, and the rustling of cattle—these things were only the craft of the rustler-chief to conceal his real life and purpose and work in Deception Pass.

And like a scouting Indian Venters crawled through the sage of the oval valley, crossed trail after trail on the north side, and at last entered the cañon out of which headed the cattle trail, and into which he had watched the rustlers disappear.

If he had used caution before, now he strained every nerve to force himself to creeping stealth and to sensitiveness of ear. He crawled along so hidden that he could not use his eyes except to aid himself in the toilsome progress through the brakes and ruins of cliff-wall. Yet from time to time, as he rested, he saw the massive red walls growing higher and wilder, more looming and broken. He made note of the fact that he was turning and climbing. The sage and thickets of oak and brakes of alder gave place to piñon pine growing out of rocky soil. Suddenly a low, dull murmur assailed his ears. At first he thought it was thunder, then the slipping of a weathered slope of rock. But it was incessant, and as he progressed it filled out deeper and from a murmur changed into a soft roar.

"Falling water," he said. "There's volume to that. I wonder if it's the stream I lost."

The roar bothered him, for he could hear nothing else. Likewise, however, no rustlers could hear him. Emboldened by this, and sure that nothing but a bird could see him, he arose from his hands and knees to hurry on. An opening in the piñons warned him that he was nearing the height of slope.

He gained it, and dropped low with a burst of astonishment. Before him stretched a short cañon with rounded stone floor bare of grass or sage or tree, and with curved, shelving walls. A broad rippling stream flowed toward him, and at the back of the cañon a waterfall burst from a wide rent in the cliff, and, bounding down in two green steps, spread into a long white sheet.

If Venters had not been indubitably certain that he had entered the right cañon his astonishment would not have been so great. There had been no breaks in the walls, no side cañons entering this one where the rustlers' tracks and the cattle trail had guided him, and, therefore, he could not be wrong. But here the cañon ended, and presumably the trails also.

"That cattle trail headed out of here," Venters kept saying to himself. "It headed out. Now what I want to know is how on earth did cattle ever get in here?"

If he could be sure of anything it was of the careful

scrutiny he had given that cattle track, every hoof-mark of which headed straight west. He was now looking east at an immense round boxed corner of cañon down which tumbled a thin, white veil of water, scarcely twenty yards wide. Somehow, somewhere, his calculations had gone wrong. For the first time in years he found himself doubting his rider's skill in finding tracks, and his memory of what he had actually seen. In his anxiety to keep under cover he must have lost himself in this offshoot of Deception Pass, and thereby, in some unaccountable manner, missed the cañon with the trails. There was nothing else for him to think. Rustlers could not fly, nor cattle jump down thousand-foot precipices. He was only proving what the sage-riders had long said of this labyrinthine system of deceitful cañons and valleys—trails led down into Deception Pass, but no rider had ever followed them.

On a sudden he heard above the soft roar of the waterfall an unusual sound that he could not define. He dropped flat behind a stone and listened. From the direction he had come swelled something that resembled a strange muffled pounding and splashing and ringing. Despite his nerve the chill sweat began to dampen his forehead. What might not be possible in this stone-walled maze of mystery? The unnatural sound passed beyond him as he lay gripping his rifle and fighting for coolness. Then from the open came the sound, now distinct and different. Venters recognized a hobble-bell of a horse, and the cracking of iron on submerged stones, and the hollow splash of hoofs in water.

Relief surged over him. His mind caught again at realities, and curiosity prompted him to peep from behind the rock.

In the middle of the stream waded a long string of packed burros driven by three superbly mounted men. Had Venters met these dark-clothed, dark-visaged, heavily armed men anywhere in Utah, let alone in this robbers' retreat, he would have recognized them as rustlers. The discerning eye of a rider saw the signs of a long, arduous trip. These men were packing in supplies from one of the northern villages. They were tired, and their horses were almost played out, and the burros plodded on, after the manner of their kind when exhausted, faithful and patient, but as if every weary, splashing, slipping step would be their last.

All this Venters noted in one glance. After that he watched with a thrilling eagerness. Straight at the waterfall the rustlers drove the burros, and straight through the middle, where the water spread into a fleecy, thin film like dissolving smoke. Following closely, the rustlers rode into this white mist, showing in bold black relief for an instant, and then they vanished.

Venters drew a full breath that rushed out in brief and sudden utterance.

"Good Heaven! Of all the holes for a rustler! . . . There's a cavern under that waterfall, and a passageway leading out to a cañon beyond. Oldring hides in there. He needs only to guard a trail leading down from the sage-flat above. Little danger of this outlet to the pass being discovered. I stumbled on it by luck, after I had given up. And now I know the truth of what puzzled me most—why that cattle trail was wet!"

He wheeled and ran down the slope, and out to the level of the sage-brush. Returning, he had no time to spare, only now and then, between dashes, a moment when he stopped to cast sharp eyes ahead. The abundant grass left no trace of his trail. Short work he made of the distance to the circle of cañons. He doubted that he would ever see it again; he knew he never wanted to; yet he looked at the red corners and towers with the eyes of a rider picturing landmarks never to be forgotten.

Here he spent a panting moment in a slow-circling gaze of the sage-oval and the gaps between the bluffs. Nothing stirred except the gentle wave of the tips of the brush. Then he pressed on past the mouths of several cañons and over ground new to him, now close under the eastern wall. This latter part proved to be easy traveling, well screened from possible observation from the north and west, and he soon covered it and felt safer in the deepening shade of his own cañon. Then the huge, notched bulge of red rim loomed over him, a mark by which he knew again the deep cove where his camp lay hidden. As he penetrated the thicket, safe again for the present, his thoughts reverted to the girl he had left there. The afternoon had far advanced. How would he find her? He ran into camp, frightening the dogs.

The girl lay with wide-open, dark eyes, and they dilated when he knelt beside her. The flush of fever shone in her cheeks. He lifted her and held water to her dry lips, and felt an inexplicable sense of lightness as he saw her swallow in a slow, choking gulp. Gently he laid her back.

"Who—are—you?" she whispered, haltingly.

"I'm the man who shot you," he replied.

"You'll—not—kill me—now?"

"No, no."

"What—will—you—do—with me?"

"When you get better—strong enough—I'll take you back to the cañon where the rustlers ride through the waterfall."

As with a faint shadow from a flitting wing overhead, the marble whiteness of her face seemed to change.

"Don't—take—me—back—there!"

CHAPTER VI

THE MILL-WHEEL OF STEERS

MEANTIME, at the ranch, when Judkins's news had sent Venters on the trail of the rustlers, Jane Withersteen led the injured man to her house and with skilled fingers dressed the gunshot wound in his arm.

"Judkins, what do you think happened to my riders?"

"I—I'd rather not say," he replied.

"Tell me. Whatever you'll tell me I'll keep to myself. I'm beginning to worry about more than the loss of a herd of cattle. Venters hinted of—but tell me, Judkins."

"Well, Miss Withersteen, I think as Venters thinks—your riders have been called in."

"Judkins! . . . By whom?"

"You know who handles the reins of your Mormon riders."

"Do you dare insinuate that my churchmen have ordered in my riders?"

"I ain't insinuatin' nothin', Miss Withersteen," answered Judkins, with spirit. "I know what I'm talking about. I didn't want to tell you."

"Oh, I can't believe that! I'll not believe it! Would Tull leave my herds at the mercy of rustlers and wolves just because—because—? No, no! It's unbelievable."

"Yes, thet particular thing's onheard of around Cottonwoods. But, beggin' pardon, Miss Withersteen, there never was any other rich Mormon woman here on the border, let alone one thet's taken the bit between her teeth."

That was a bold thing for the reserved Judkins to say, but it did not anger her. This rider's crude hint of her spirit gave her a glimpse of what others might think. Humility and obedience had been hers always. But had she taken the bit between her teeth? Still she wavered. And then, with a quick spurt of warm blood along her veins, she thought of Black Star when he got the bit fast between his iron jaws and ran wild in the sage. If she ever started to run! Jane smothered the glow and burn within her, ashamed of a passion for freedom that opposed her duty.

"Judkins, go to the village," she said, "and when you have learned anything definite about my riders please come to me at once."

When he had gone Jane resolutely applied her mind to a number of tasks that of late had been neglected. Her father had trained her in the management of a hundred employees and the working of gardens and fields; and to keep record of the movements of cattle and riders. And beside the many duties she had added to this work was one of extreme delicacy, such as required all her tact and ingenuity. It was an unobtrusive, almost secret aid which she rendered to the Gentile families of the village. Though Jane Withersteen never admitted so to herself, it amounted to no less than a system of charity. But for her invention of numberless kinds of employment, for which there was no actual need, these families of Gentiles, who had failed in a Mormon community, would have starved.

In aiding these poor people Jane thought she deceived her keen churchmen, but it was a kind of deceit for which she did not pray to be forgiven. Equally as difficult was the task of deceiving the Gentiles, for they were as proud as they were poor. It had been a great grief to her to discover how these people hated her people; and it had been a source of great joy that through her they had come to soften in hatred. At any time this work called for a clearness of mind that precluded anxiety and worry; but under the present circumstances it required all her vigor and obstinate tenacity to pin her attention upon her task.

Sunset came, bringing with the end of her labor a patient calmness and power to wait that had not been hers earlier in the day. She expected Judkins, but he did not appear. Her house was always quiet; to-night, however, it seemed unusually so. At supper her women served her with a silent assiduity; it spoke what their sealed lips could not utter—the sympathy of Mormon women. Jerd came to her with the key of the great door of the stone stable, and to make his daily report about the horses. One of his daily duties was to give Black Star and Night and the other racers a ten-mile run. This day it had been omitted, and the boy grew confused in explanations that she had not asked for. She did inquire if he would return on the morrow, and Jerd, in mingled surprise and relief, assured her he would always work for her. Jane missed the rattle and trot, canter and gallop of the incoming riders on the hard trails. Dusk shaded the grove where she walked; the birds ceased singing; the wind sighed through the leaves of the cottonwoods, and the running water murmured down its stone-bedded channel. The glimmering of the first star was like the peace and beauty of the night. Her faith welled up in her heart and said that all would soon be right in her little world. She pictured Venters about his lonely camp-fire sitting between his faithful dogs. She prayed for his safety, for the success of his undertaking

Early the next morning one of Jane's women brought in word that Judkins wished to speak to her. She hurried out, and in her surprise to see him armed with rifle and revolver, she forgot her intention to inquire about his wound.

"Judkins! Those guns? You never carried guns."

"It's high time, Miss Withersteen," he replied. "Will you come into the grove? It ain't jest exactly safe for me to be seen here."

She walked with him into the shade of the cottonwoods.

"What do you mean?"

"Miss Withersteen, I went to my mother's house last night. While there, some one knocked, an' a man asked for me. I went to the door. He wore a mask. He said I'd better not ride any more for Jane Withersteen. His voice was hoarse an' strange, disguised, I reckon, like his face. He said no more, an' ran off in the dark."

"Did you know who he was?" asked Jane, in a low voice.

"Yes."

Jane did not ask to know; she did not want to know; she feared to know. All her calmness fled at a single thought.

"Thet's why I'm packin' guns," went on Judkins. "For I'll never quit ridin' for you, Miss Withersteen, till you let me go."

"Judkins, do you want to leave me?"

"Do I look thet way? Give me a hoss—a fast hoss, an' send me out on the sage."

"Oh, thank you, Judkins! You're more faithful than my own people. I ought not accept your loyalty—you might suffer more through it. But what in the world can I do? My head whirls. The wrong to Venters—the stolen herd—these masks, threats, this coil in the dark! I can't understand! But I feel something dark and terrible closing in around me."

"Miss Withersteen, it's all simple enough," said Judkins, earnestly. "Now please listen—an' beggin' your pardon—jest turn thet deaf Mormon ear aside, an' let me talk clear an' plain in the other. I went around to the saloons an' the stores an' the loafin' places yesterday. All your riders are in. There's talk of a vigilance band organized to hunt down rustlers. They call themselves 'The Riders.' Thet's the report—thet's the reason given for your riders leavin' you. Strange thet only a few riders of other ranchers joined the band! An' Tull's man, Jerry Card—he's the leader. I seen him an' his hoss. He 'ain't been to Glaze. I'm not easy to fool on the looks of a hoss thet's traveled the sage. Tull an' Jerry didn't ride to Glaze! . . . Well, I met Blake an' Dorn, both good friends of mine, usually, as far as their Mormon lights will let 'em go. But these fellers couldn't fool me, an' they didn't try very hard. I asked them, straight out like a man, why they left you like thet. I didn't forget to mention how you nursed Blake's poor old mother when she was sick, an' how good you was to Dorn's kids. They looked ashamed, Miss Withersteen. An' they jest froze up—thet dark set look thet makes them strange an' different to me. But I could tell the difference between thet first natural twinge of conscience an' the later look of some secret thing. An' the difference I caught was thet they couldn't help themselves. They hadn't no say in the matter. They looked as if their bein' unfaithful to you was bein' faithful to a higher duty. An' there's the secret. Why, it's as plain as—as sight of my gun here."

"Plain! . . . My herds to wander in the sage—to be stolen! Jane Withersteen a poor woman! Her head to be brought low and her spirit broken! . . . Why, Judkins, it's plain enough."

"Miss Withersteen, let me get what boys I can gather, an' hold the white herd. It's on the slope now, not ten miles out—three thousand head, an' all steers. They're wild, an' likely to stampede at the pop of a jack-rabbit's ears. We'll camp right with them, an' try to hold them."

"Judkins, I'll reward you some day for your service, unless all is taken from me. Get the boys and tell Jerd to give you pick of my horses, except Black Star and

Night. But—do not shed blood for my cattle nor heedlessly risk your lives."

Jane Withersteen rushed to the silence and seclusion of her room, and there could not longer hold back the bursting of her wrath. She went stone-blind in the fury of a passion that had never before showed its power. Lying upon her bed, sightless, voiceless, she was a writhing, living flame. And she tossed there while her fury burned and burned, and finally burned itself out.

Then, weak and spent, she lay thinking, not of the oppression that would break her, but of this new revelation of self. Until the last few days there had been little in her life to rouse passions. Her forefathers had been Vikings, savage chieftains who bore no cross and brooked no hindrance to their will. Her father had inherited that temper; and at times, like antelope fleeing before fire on the slope, his people fled from his red rages. Jane Withersteen realized that the spirit of wrath and war had lain dormant in her. She shrank from black depths hitherto unsuspected. The one thing in man or woman that she scorned above all scorn, and which she could not forgive, was hate. Hate headed a flaming pathway straight to hell. All in a flash, beyond her control there had been in her a birth of fiery hate. And the man who had dragged her peaceful and loving spirit to this degradation was a minister of God's word, an Elder of her church, the counselor of her beloved Bishop.

The loss of herds and ranges, even of Amber Spring and the Old Stone House, no longer concerned Jane Withersteen; she faced the foremost thought of her life, what she now considered the mightiest problem—the salvation of her soul.

She knelt by her bedside and prayed; she prayed as she had never prayed in all her life—prayed to be forgiven for her sin; to be immune from that dark, hot hate; to love Tull as her minister, though she could not love him as a man; to do her duty by her church and people and those dependent upon her bounty; to hold reverence of God and womanhood inviolate.

When Jane Withersteen rose from that storm of wrath and prayer for help she was serene, calm, sure—a changed woman. She would do her duty as she saw it, live her life as her own truth guided her. She might never be able to marry a man of her choice, but she certainly never would become the wife of Tull. Her churchmen might take her cattle and horses, ranges and fields, her corrals and stables, the house of Withersteen and the water that nourished the village of Cottonwoods; but they could not force her to marry Tull, they could not change her decision or break her spirit. Once resigned to further loss, and sure of herself, Jane Withersteen attained a peace of mind that had not been hers for a year. She forgave Tull, and felt a melancholy regret over what she knew he considered duty, irrespective of his personal feeling for her. First of all, Tull, as he was a man, wanted her for himself; and secondly, he hoped to save her and her riches for his church. She did not believe that Tull had been actuated solely by his minister's zeal to save her soul. She doubted her interpretation of one of his dark sayings—that if she were lost to him she might as well be lost to heaven. Jane Withersteen's common sense took arms against the binding limits of her religion; and she doubted that her Bishop, whom she had been taught had direct communication with God—would damn her soul for refusing to marry a Mormon. As for Tull and his churchmen, when they had harassed her, perhaps made her poor, they would find her unchangeable, and then she would get back most of what she had lost. So she reasoned, true at last to her faith in all men, and in their ultimate goodness.

The clank of iron hoofs upon the stone courtyard drew her hurriedly from her retirement. There, beside his horse, stood Lassiter, his dark apparel and the great black gun-sheaths contrasting singularly with his gentle smile. Jane's active mind took up her interest in him and her half-determined desire to use what charm she had to foil his evident design in visiting Cottonwoods. If she could mitigate his hatred of Mormons, or at least keep him from killing more of them, not only would she be saving her people, but also be leading back this blood-spiller to some semblance of the human.

"Mornin', ma'am," he said, black sombrero in hand.

"Lassiter, I'm not an old woman, or even a madam," she replied, with her bright smile. "If you can't say Miss Withersteen—call me Jane."

"I reckon Jane would be easier. First names are always handy for me."

"Well, use mine, then. Lassiter, I'm glad to see you. I'm in trouble."

Then she told him of Judkins's return, of the driving of the red herd, of Venters's departure on Wrangle, and the calling-in of her riders.

"'Pears to me you're some smilin' an' pretty for a woman with so much trouble," he remarked.

"Lassiter! Are you paying me compliments? But, seriously, I've made up my mind not to be miserable. I've lost much, and I'll lose more. Nevertheless, I won't be sour, and I hope I'll never be unhappy—again."

Lassiter twisted his hat round and round, as was his way, and took his time in replying.

"Women are strange to me. I got to back-trailin' myself from them long ago. But I'd like a game woman. Might I ask, seein' as how you take this trouble, if you're goin' to fight?"

"Fight! How? Even if I would, I haven't a friend except that boy who doesn't dare stay in the village."

"I make bold to say, ma'am—Jane—that there's another, if you want him."

"Lassiter! . . . Thank you. But how can I accept you

as a friend? Think! Why, you'd ride down into the village with those terrible guns and kill my enemies—who are also my churchmen."

"I reckon I might be riled up to jest about that," he replied, dryly.

She held out both hands to him.

"Lassiter! I'll accept your friendship—be proud of it—return it—if I may keep you from killing another Mormon."

"I'll tell you one thing," he said, bluntly, as the gray lightning formed in his eyes. "You're too good a woman to be sacrificed as you're goin' to be. . . . No, I reckon you an' me can't be friends on such terms."

In her earnestness she stepped closer to him, repelled yet fascinated by the sudden transition of his moods. That he would fight for her was at once horrible and wonderful.

"You came here to kill a man—the man whom Milly Erne—"

"The man who dragged Milly Erne to hell—put it that way! . . . Jane Withersteen, yes, that's why I came here. I'd tell so much to no other livin' soul. . . . There 're things such a woman as you'd never dream of—so don't mention her again. Not till you tell me the name of the man!"

"Tell you! I? Never!"

"I reckon you will. An' I'll never ask you. I'm a man of strange beliefs an' ways of thinkin', an' I seem to see into the future an' feel things hard to explain. The trail I've been followin' for so many years was twisted an' tangled, but it's straightenin' out now. An', Jane Withersteen, you crossed it long ago to ease poor Milly's agony. That, whether you want or not, makes Lassiter your friend. But you cross it now strangely to mean somethin' to me—God knows what!—unless by your noble blindness to incite me to greater hatred of Mormon men."

Jane felt swayed by a strength that far exceeded her own. In a clash of wills with this man she would go to the wall. If she were to influence him it must be wholly through womanly allurement. There was that about Lassiter which commanded her respect; she had abhorred his name; face to face with him, she found she feared only his deeds. His mystic suggestion, his foreshadowing of something that she was to mean to him, pierced deep into her mind. She believed fate had thrown in her way the lover or husband of Milly Erne. She believed that through her an evil man might be reclaimed. His allusion to what he called her blindness terrified her. Such a mistaken idea of his might unleash the bitter, fatal mood she sensed in him. At any cost she must placate this man; she knew the die was cast, and that if Lassiter did not soften to a woman's grace and beauty and wiles, then it would be because she could not make him.

"I reckon you'll hear no more such talk from me," Lassiter went on, presently. "Now, Miss Jane, I rode in to tell you that your herd of white steers is down on the slope behind them big ridges. An' I seen somethin' goin' on that 'd be mighty interestin' to you, if you, could see it. Have you a field-glass?"

"Yes, I have two glasses. I'll get them and ride out with you. Wait, Lassiter, please," she said, and hurried within. Sending word to Jerd to saddle Black Star and fetch him to the court, she then went to her room and changed to the riding-clothes she always donned when going into the sage. In this male attire her mirror showed her a jaunty, handsome rider. If she expected some little meed of admiration from Lassiter, she had no cause for disappointment. The gentle smile that she liked, which made of him another person, slowly overspread his face.

"If I didn't take you for a boy!" he exclaimed. "It's powerful queer what difference clothes make. Now

I've been some scared of your dignity, like when the other night you was all in white, but in this rig—"

Black Star came pounding into the court, dragging Jerd half off his feet, and he whistled at Lassiter's black. But at sight of Jane all his defiant lines seemed to soften, and with tosses of his beautiful head he whipped his bridle.

"Down, Black Star, down," said Jane.

He dropped his head, and, slowly lengthening, he bent one foreleg, then the other, and sank to his knees. Jane slipped her left foot in the stirrup, swung lightly into the saddle, and Black Star rose with a ringing stamp. It was not easy for Jane to hold him to a canter through the grove, and like the wind he broke when he saw the sage. Jane let him have a couple of miles of free running on the open trail, and then she coaxed him in and waited for her companion. Lassiter was not long in catching up, and presently they were riding side by side. It reminded her how she used to ride with Venters. Where was he now? She gazed far down the slope to the curved purple lines of Deception Pass, and involuntarily shut her eyes with a trembling stir of nameless fear.

"We'll turn off here," Lassiter said, "an' take to the sage a mile or so. The white herd is behind them big ridges."

"What are you going to show me?" asked Jane. "I'm prepared—don't be afraid."

He smiled as if he meant that bad news came swiftly enough without being presaged by speech.

When they reached the lee of a rolling ridge Lassiter dismounted, motioning to her to do likewise. They left the horses standing, bridles down. Then Lassiter, carrying the field-glasses, began to lead the way up the slow rise of ground. Upon nearing the summit he halted her with a gesture.

"I reckon we'd see more if we didn't show ourselves

against the sky," he said. "I was here less than a hour ago. Then the herd was seven or eight miles south, an' if they 'ain't bolted yet—"

"Lassiter! . . . Bolted?"

"That's what I said. Now let's see."

Jane climbed a few more paces behind him and then peeped over the ridge. Just beyond began a shallow swale that deepened and widened into a valley and then swung to the left. Following the undulating sweep of sage, Jane saw the straggling lines and then the great body of the white herd. She knew enough about steers, even at a distance of four or five miles, to realize that something was in the wind. Bringing her field-glass into use, she moved it slowly from left to right, which action swept the whole herd into range. The stragglers were restless; the more compactly massed steers were browsing. Jane brought the glass back to the big sentinels of the herd, and she saw them trot with quick steps, stop short and toss wide horns, look everywhere, and then trot in another direction.

"Judkins hasn't been able to get his boys together yet," said Jane. "But he'll be there soon. I hope not too late. Lassiter, what's frightening those big leaders?"

"Nothin' jest on the minute," replied Lassiter. "Them steers are quietin' down. They've been scared, but not bad yet. I reckon the whole herd has moved a few miles this way since I was here."

"They didn't browse that distance—not in less than an hour. Cattle aren't sheep."

"No, they jest run it, an' that looks bad."

"Lassiter, what frightened them?" repeated Jane, impatiently.

"Put down your glass. You'll see at first better with a naked eye. Now look along them ridges on the other side of the herd, the ridges where the sun shines bright on the sage. . . . That's right. Now look an' look hard an' wait."

THE MILL-WHEEL OF STEERS

Long-drawn moments of straining sight rewarded Jane with nothing save the low, purple rim of ridge and the shimmering sage.

"It's begun again!" whispered Lassiter, and he gripped her arm. "Watch. . . . There, did you see that?"

"No, no. Tell me what to look for?"

"A white flash—a kind of pin-point of quick light—a gleam as from sun shinin' on somethin' white."

Suddenly Jane's concentrated gaze caught a fleeting glint. Quickly she brought her glass to bear on the spot. Again the purple sage, magnified in color and size and wave, for long moments irritated her with its monotony. Then from out of the sage on the ridge flew up a broad, white object, flashed in the sunlight, and vanished. Like magic it was, and bewildered Jane.

"What on earth is that?"

"I reckon there's some one behind that ridge throwin' up a sheet or a white blanket to reflect the sunshine."

"Why?" queried Jane, more bewildered than ever.

"To stampede the herd," replied Lassiter, and his teeth clicked.

"Ah!" She made a fierce, passionate movement, clutched the glass tightly, shook as with the passing of a spasm, and then dropped her head. Presently she raised it to greet Lassiter with something like a smile. "My righteous brethren are at work again," she said, in scorn. She had stifled the leap of her wrath, but for perhaps the first time in her life a bitter derision curled her lips. Lassiter's cool gray eyes seemed to pierce her. "I said I was prepared for anything; but that was hardly true. But why would they—anybody stampede my cattle?"

"That's a Mormon's godly way of bringin' a woman to her knees."

"Lassiter, I'll die before I ever bend my knees. I might be led; I won't be driven. Do you expect the herd to bolt?"

"I don't like the looks of them big steers. But you can never tell. Cattle sometimes stampede as easily as buffalo. Any little flash or move will start them. A rider gettin' down an' walkin' toward them sometimes will make them jump an' fly. Then again nothin' seems to scare them. But I reckon that white flare will do the biz. It's a new one on me, an' I've seen some ridin' an' rustlin'. It jest takes one of them God-fearin' Mormons to think of devilish tricks."

"Lassiter, might not this trick be done by Oldring's men?" asked Jane, ever grasping at straws.

"It might be, but it ain't," replied Lassiter. "Oldrin's an honest thief. He don't skulk behind ridges to scatter your cattle to the four winds. He rides down on you, an' if you don't like it you can throw a gun."

Jane bit her tongue to refrain from championing men who at the very moment were proving to her that they were little and mean compared even with rustlers.

"Look! . . . Jane, them leadin' steers have bolted! They're drawin' the stragglers, an' that 'll pull the whole herd."

Jane was not quick enough to catch the details called out by Lassiter, but she saw the line of cattle lengthening. Then, like a stream of white bees pouring from a huge swarm, the steers stretched out from the main body. In a few moments, with astonishing rapidity, the whole herd got into motion. A faint roar of trampling hoofs came to Jane's ears, and gradually swelled; low, rolling clouds of dust began to rise above the sage.

"It's a stampede, an' a hummer," said Lassiter.

"Oh, Lassiter! The herd's running with the valley! It leads into the cañon! There's a straight jump-off!"

"I reckon they'll run into it, too. But that's a good many miles yet. An' Jane, this valley swings round almost north before it goes east. That stampede will pass within a mile of us."

The long, white, bobbing line of steers streaked swiftly

"WHAT ON EARTH IS THAT?"

through the sage, and a funnel-shaped dust-cloud arose at a low angle. A dull rumbling filled Jane's ears.

"I'm thinkin' of millin' that herd," said Lassiter. His gray glance swept up the slope to the west. "There's some specks an' dust way off toward the village. Mebbe that's Judkins an' his boys. It ain't likely he'll get here in time to help. You'd better hold Black Star here on this high ridge."

He ran to his horse and, throwing off saddle-bags and tightening the cinches, he leaped astride and galloped straight down across the valley.

Jane went for Black Star and, leading him to the summit of the ridge, she mounted and faced the valley with excitement and expectancy. She had heard of milling stampeded cattle, and knew it was a feat accomplished by only the most daring riders.

The white herd was now strung out in a line two miles long. The dull rumble of thousands of hoofs deepened into continuous low thunder, and as the steers swept swiftly closer the thunder became a heavy roll. Lassiter crossed in a few moments the level of the valley to the eastern rise of ground and there waited the coming of the herd. Presently, as the head of the white line reached a point opposite to where Jane stood, Lassiter spurred his black into a run.

Jane saw him take a position on the off side of the leaders of the stampede, and there he rode. It was like a race. They swept on down the valley, and when the end of the white line neared Lassiter's first stand the head had begun to swing round to the west. It swung slowly and stubbornly, yet surely, and gradually assumed a long, beautiful curve of moving white. To Jane's amaze she saw the leaders swinging, turning till they headed back toward her and up the valley. Out to the right of these wild, plunging steers ran Lassiter's black, and Jane's keen eye appreciated the fleet stride and sure-footedness of the blind horse. Then it seemed that the herd moved in a great curve, a huge half-moon, with the points of head and tail almost opposite, and a mile apart. But Lassiter relentlessly crowded the leaders, sheering them to the left, turning them little by little. And the dust-blinded wild followers plunged on madly in the tracks of their leaders. This ever-moving, ever-changing curve of steers rolled toward Jane, and when below her, scarce half a mile, it began to narrow and close into a circle. Lassiter had ridden parallel with her position, turned toward her, then aside, and now he was riding directly away from her, all the time pushing the head of that bobbing line inward.

It was then that Jane, suddenly understanding Lassiter's feat, stared and gasped at the riding of this intrepid man. His horse was fleet and tireless, but blind. He had pushed the leaders around and around till they were about to turn in on the inner side of the end of that line of steers. The leaders were already running in a circle; the end of the herd was still running almost straight. But soon they would be wheeling. Then, when Lassiter had the circle formed, how would he escape? With Jane Withersteen prayer was as ready as praise; and she prayed for this man's safety. A circle of dust began to collect. Dimly, as through a yellow veil, Jane saw Lassiter press the leaders inward to close the gap in the sage. She lost sight of him in the dust; again she thought she saw the black, riderless now, rear and drag himself and fall. Lassiter had been thrown—lost! Then he reappeared running out of the dust into the sage. He had escaped, and she breathed again.

Spellbound, Jane Withersteen watched this stupendous millwheel of steers. Here was the milling of the herd. The white running circle closed in upon the open space of sage. And the dust circles closed above into a pall. The ground quaked and the incessant thunder of pounding hoofs rolled on. Jane felt deafened, yet she thrilled to a new sound. As the circle of sage lessened the steers began to bawl, and when it closed entirely there came a great upheaval in the center, and a terrible thumping of heads and clicking of horns. Bawling, climbing, goring, the great mass of steers on the inside wrestled in a crashing din, heaved and groaned under the pressure. Then came a deadlock. The inner strife ceased, and the hideous roar and crash. Movement went on in the outer circle, and that, too, gradually stilled. The white herd had come to a stop, and the pall of yellow dust began to drift away on the wind.

Jane Withersteen waited on the ridge with full and grateful heart. Lassiter appeared, making his weary way toward her through the sage. And up on the slope Judkins rode into sight with his troop of boys. For the present, at least, the white herd would be looked after.

When Lassiter reached her and laid his hand on Black Star's mane, Jane could not find speech.

"Killed—my—hoss," he panted.

"Oh! I'm sorry," cried Jane. "Lassiter! I know you can't replace him, but I'll give you any one of my racers—Bells, or Night, even Black Star."

"I'll take a fast hoss, Jane, but not one of your favorites," he replied. "Only—will you let me have Black Star now an' ride him over there an' head off them fellers who stampeded the herd?"

He pointed to several moving specks of black and puffs of dust in the purple sage.

"I can head them off with this hoss, an' then—"

"Then, Lassiter?"

"They'll never stampede no more cattle."

"Oh! No! No! . . . Lassiter, I won't let you go!"

But a flush of fire flamed in her cheeks, and her trembling hands shook Black Star's bridle, and her eyes fell before Lassiter's.

CHAPTER VII

THE DAUGHTER OF WITHERSTEEN

"LASSITER, will you be my rider?" Jane had asked him.

"I reckon so," he had replied.

Few as the words were, Jane knew how infinitely much they implied. She wanted him to take charge of her cattle and horses and ranges, and save them if that were possible. Yet, though she could not have spoken aloud all she meant, she was perfectly honest with herself. Whatever the price to be paid, she must keep Lassiter close to her; she must shield from him the man who had lured Milly Erne to Cottonwoods. In her fear she so controlled her mind that she did not whisper this Mormon's name to her own soul, she did not even think it. Besides, beyond this thing she regarded as a sacred obligation thrust upon her, was the need of a helper, of a friend, of a champion in this critical time. If she could rule this gun-man, as Venters had called him, if she could even keep him from shedding blood, what strategy to play his name and his presence against the game of oppression her churchmen were waging against her? Never would she forget the effect upon Tull and his men when Venters shouted Lassiter's name. If she could not wholly control Lassiter, then what she could do might put off the fatal day.

One of her safe racers was a dark bay, and she called him Bells because of the way he struck his iron shoes on the stones. When Jerd led out this slender, beautifully built horse Lassiter suddenly became all eyes.

A rider's love of a thoroughbred shone in them. Round and round Bells he walked, plainly weakening all the time in his determination not to take one of Jane's favorite racers.

"Lassiter, you're half horse, and Bells sees it already," said Jane, laughing. "Look at his eyes. He likes you. He'll love you, too. How can you resist him? Oh, Lassiter, but Bells can run! It's nip and tuck between him and Wrangle, and only Black Star can beat him. He's too spirited a horse for a woman. Take him. He's yours."

"I jest am weak where a hoss 's concerned," said Lassiter. "I'll take him, an' I'll take your orders, ma'am."

"Well, I'm glad, but never mind the ma'am. Let it still be Jane."

From that hour, it seemed, Lassiter was always in the saddle, riding early and late; and coincident with his part in Jane's affairs the days assumed their old tranquillity. Her intelligence told her this was only the lull before the storm, but her faith would not have it so.

She resumed her visits to the village, and upon one of these she encountered Tull. He greeted her as he had before any trouble came between them, and she, responsive to peace if not quick to forget, met him halfway with manner almost cheerful. He regretted the loss of her cattle; he assured her that the vigilantes which had been organized would soon rout the rustlers; when that had been accomplished her riders would likely return to her.

"You've done a headstrong thing to hire this man Lassiter," Tull went on, severely. "He came to Cottonwoods with evil intent."

"I had to have somebody. And perhaps making him my rider may turn out best in the end for the Mormons of Cottonwoods."

"You mean to stay his hand?"

"I do—if I can."

"A woman like you can do anything with a man. That would be well, and would atone in some measure for the errors you have made."

He bowed and passed on. Jane resumed her walk with conflicting thoughts. She resented Elder Tull's cold, impassive manner that looked down upon her as one who had incurred his just displeasure. Otherwise he would have been the same calm, dark-browed, impenetrable man she had known for ten years. In fact, except when he had revealed his passion in the matter of the seizing of Venters, she had never dreamed he could be other than the grave, reproving preacher. He stood out now a strange, secretive man. She would have thought better of him if he had picked up the threads of their quarrel where they had parted. Was Tull what he appeared to be? The question flung itself involuntarily over Jane Withersteen's inhibitive habit of faith without question. And she refused to answer it. Tull could not fight in the open. Venters had said, Lassiter had said, that her Elder shirked fight and worked in the dark. Just now in this meeting Tull had ignored the fact that he had sued, exhorted, demanded that she marry him. He made no mention of Venters. His manner was that of the minister who had been outraged, but who overlooked the frailties of a woman. Beyond question he seemed unutterably aloof from all knowledge of pressure being brought to bear upon her, absolutely guiltless of any connection with secret power over riders, with night journeys, with rustlers and stampedes of cattle. And that convinced her again of unjust suspicions. But it was convincement through an obstinate faith. She shuddered as she accepted it, and that shudder was the nucleus of a terrible revolt.

Jane turned into one of the wide lanes leading from the main street and entered a huge, shady yard. Here were sweet-smelling clover, alfalfa, flowers, and vegetables, all growing in happy confusion. And like these fresh green things were the dozens of babies, tots, toddlers, noisy urchins, laughing girls, a whole multitude of children of one family. For Collier Brandt, the father of all this numerous progeny, was a Mormon with four wives.

The big house where they lived was old, solid, picturesque, the lower part built of logs, the upper of rough clapboards, with vines growing up the outside stone chimneys. There were many wooden-shuttered windows, and one pretentious window of glass, proudly curtained in white. As this house had four mistresses, it likewise had four separate sections, not one of which communicated with another, and all had to be entered from the outside.

In the shade of a wide, low, vine-roofed porch Jane found Brandt's wives entertaining Bishop Dyer. They were motherly women, of comparatively similar ages, and plain-featured, and just at this moment anything but grave. The Bishop was rather tall, of stout build, with iron-gray hair and beard, and eyes of light blue. They were merry now; but Jane had seen them when they were not, and then she feared him as she had feared her father.

The woman flocked around her in welcome.

"Daughter of Withersteen," said the Bishop, gaily, as he took her hand, "you have not been prodigal of your gracious self of late. A Sabbath without you at service! I shall reprove Elder Tull."

"Bishop, the guilt is mine. I'll come to you and confess," Jane replied, lightly; but she felt the undercurrent of her words.

"Mormon love-making!" exclaimed the Bishop, rubbing his hands. "Tull keeps you all to himself."

"No. He is not courting me."

"What? The laggard! If he does not make haste I'll go a-courting myself up to Withersteen House."

There was laughter and further bantering by the Bishop, and then mild talk of village affairs, after which he took his leave, and Jane was left with her friend, Mary Brandt.

"Jane, you're not yourself. Are you sad about the rustling of the cattle? But you have so many, you are so rich."

Then Jane confided in her, telling much, yet holding back her doubts and fears.

"Oh, why don't you marry Tull and be one of us?"

"But, Mary, I don't love Tull," said Jane, stubbornly.

"I don't blame you for that. But, Jane Withersteen, you've got to choose between the love of man and love of God. Often we Mormon women have to do that. It's not easy. The kind of happiness you want I wanted once. I never got it, nor will you, unless you throw away your soul. We've all watched your affair with Venters in fear and trembling. Some dreadful thing will come of it. You don't want him hanged or shot—or treated worse, as that Gentile boy was treated in Glaze for fooling round a Mormon woman. Marry Tull. It's your duty as a Mormon. You'll feel no rapture as his wife—but think of Heaven! Mormon women don't marry for what they expect on earth. Take up the cross, Jane. Remember your father found Amber Spring, built these old houses, brought Mormons here, and fathered them. You are the daughter of Withersteen!"

Jane left Mary Brandt and went to call upon other friends. They received her with the same glad welcome as had Mary, lavished upon her the pent-up affection of Mormon women, and let her go with her ears ringing of Tull, Venters, Lassiter, of duty to God and glory in Heaven.

"Verily," murmured Jane, "I don't know myself when, through all this, I remain unchanged—nay, more fixed of purpose."

She returned to the main street and bent her thoughtful steps toward the center of the village. A string of wagons drawn by oxen was lumbering along. These "sage-freighters," as they were called, hauled grain and flour and merchandise from Sterling; and Jane laughed suddenly in the midst of her humility at the thought that they were her property, as was one of the three stores for which they freighted goods. The water that flowed along the path at her feet, and turned into each cottage-yard to nourish garden and orchard, also was hers, no less her private property because she chose to give it free. Yet in this village of Cottonwoods, which her father had founded and which she maintained, she was not her own mistress; she was not to abide by her own choice of a husband. She was the daughter of Withersteen. Suppose she proved it, imperiously! But she quelled that proud temptation at its birth.

Nothing could have replaced the affection which the village people had for her; no power could have made her happy as the pleasure her presence gave. As she went on down the street, past the stores with their rude platform entrances, and the saloons, where tired horses stood with bridles dragging, she was again assured of what was the bread and wine of life to her—that she was loved. Dirty boys playing in the ditch, clerks, teamsters, riders, loungers on the corners, ranchers on dusty horses, little girls running errands, and women hurrying to the stores all looked up at her coming with glad eyes.

Jane's various calls and wandering steps at length led her to the Gentile quarter of the village. This was at the extreme southern end, and here some thirty Gentile families lived in huts and shacks and log-cabins and several dilapidated cottages. The fortunes of these inhabitants of Cottonwoods could be read in their abodes. Water they had in abundance, and therefore grass and fruit-trees and patches of alfalfa and vegetable gardens. Some of the men and boys had a few stray cattle, others obtained such intermittent employment as the Mormons reluctantly tendered them. But none of the families was prosperous, many were very poor, and some lived only by Jane Withersteen's beneficence.

As it made Jane happy to go among her own people, so it saddened her to come in contact with these Gentiles. Yet that was not because she was unwelcome; here she was gratefully received by the women, passionately by the children. But poverty and idleness, with their attendant wretchedness and sorrow, always hurt her. That she could alleviate this distress more now than ever before proved the adage that it was an ill wind that blew nobody good. While her Mormon riders were in her employ she had found few Gentiles who could stay with her, and now she was able to find employment for all the men and boys. No little shock was it to have man after man tell her that he dare not accept her kind offer.

"It won't do," said one Carson, an intelligent man who had seen better days. "We've had our warning. Plain and to the point! Now there's Judkins, he packs guns, and he can use them, and so can the daredevil boys he's hired. But they've little responsibility. Can we risk having our homes burned in our absence?"

Jane felt the stretching and chilling of the skin of her face as the blood left it.

"Carson, you and the others rent these houses?" she asked.

"You ought to know, Miss Withersteen. Some of them are yours."

"I know? . . . Carson, I never in my life took a day's labor for rent or a yearling calf or a bunch of grass, let alone gold."

"Bivens, your store-keeper, sees to that."

"Look here, Carson," went on Jane, hurriedly, and now her cheeks were burning. "You and Black and Willet pack your goods and move your families up to my cabins in the grove. They're far more comfortable than these. Then go to work for me. And if aught happens to you there I'll give you money—gold enough to leave Utah!"

The man choked and stammered, and then, as tears welled into his eyes, he found the use of his tongue and cursed. No gentle speech could ever have equaled that curse in eloquent expression of what he felt for Jane Withersteen. How strangely his look and tone reminded her of Lassiter!

"No, it won't do," he said, when he had somewhat recovered himself. "Miss Withersteen, there are things that you don't know, and there's not a soul among us who can tell you."

"I seem to be learning many things, Carson. Well, then, will you let me aid you—say till better times?"

"Yes, I will," he replied, with his face lighting up. "I see what it means to you, and you know what it means to me. Thank you! And if better times ever come I'll be only too happy to work for you."

"Better times will come. I trust God and have faith in man. Good day, Carson."

The lane opened out upon the sage-inclosed alfalfa fields, and the last habitation, at the end of that lane of hovels, was the meanest. Formerly it had been a shed; now it was a home. The broad leaves of a wide-spreading cottonwood sheltered the sunken roof of weathered boards. Like an Indian hut, it had one floor. Round about it were a few scanty rows of vegetables, such as the hand of a weak woman had time and strength to cultivate. This little dwelling-place was just outside the village limits, and the widow who lived there had to carry her water from the nearest irrigation ditch. As Jane Withersteen entered the unfenced yard a child saw her, shrieked with joy, and came tearing toward her with curls flying. This child was a little girl of four called Fay. Her name suited her, for she was an elf, a sprite, a creature so fairy-like and beautiful that she seemed unearthly.

"Muvver sended for oo," cried Fay, as Jane kissed her, "an' oo never tome."

"I didn't know, Fay; but I've come now."

Fay was a child of outdoors, of the garden and ditch and field, and she was dirty and ragged. But rags and dirt did not hide her beauty. The one thin little bedraggled garment she wore half covered her fine, slim body. Red as cherries were her cheeks and lips; her eyes were violet blue, and the crown of her childish loveliness was the curling golden hair. All the children of Cottonwoods were Jane Withersteen's friends; she loved them all. But Fay was dearest to her. Fay had few playmates, for among the Gentile children there were none near her age, and the Mormon children were forbidden to play with her. So she was a shy, wild, lonely child.

"Muvver's sick," said Fay, leading Jane toward the door of the hut.

Jane went in. There was only one room, rather dark and bare, but it was clean and neat. A woman lay upon a bed.

"Mrs. Larkin, how are you?" asked Jane, anxiously.

"I've been pretty bad for a week, but I'm better now."

"You haven't been here all alone—with no one to wait on you?"

"Oh no! My women neighbors are kind. They take turns coming in."

"Did you send for me?"

"Yes, several times."

"But I had no word—no messages ever got to me."

"I sent the boys, and they left word with your women that I was ill and would you please come."

A sudden deadly sickness seized Jane, She fought the weakness, as she fought to be above suspicious thoughts, and it passed, leaving her conscious of her utter impotence. That, too, passed as her spirit rebounded. But she had again caught a glimpse of dark underhand domination, running its secret lines this time into her own household. Like a spider in the blackness of night an unseen hand had begun to run these dark lines, to turn and twist them about her life, to plait and weave a web. Jane Withersteen knew it now, and in the realization further coolness and sureness came to her, and the fighting courage of her ancestors.

"Mrs. Larkin, you're better, and I'm so glad," said Jane. "But may I not do something for you—a turn at nursing, or send you things, or take care of Fay?"

"You're so good. Since my husband's been gone what would have become of Fay and me but for you? It was about Fay that I wanted to speak to you. This time I thought surely I'd die, and I was worried about Fay. Well, I'll be around all right shortly, but my strength's gone and I won't live long. So I may as well speak now. You remember you've been asking me to let you take Fay and bring her up as your daughter?"

"Indeed yes, I remember. I'll be happy to have her. But I hope the day—"

"Never mind that. The day 'll come—sooner or later. I refused your offer, and now I'll tell you why."

"I know why," interposed Jane. "It's because you don't want her brought up as a Mormon."

"No, it wasn't altogether that." Mrs. Larkin raised her thin hand and laid it appealingly on Jane's. "I don't like to tell you. But—it's this: I told all my friends what you wanted. They know you, care for you, and they said for me to trust Fay to you. Women will talk, you know. It got to the ears of Mormons—gossip of your love for Fay and your wanting her. And it came straight back to me, in jealousy, perhaps, that you wouldn't take Fay as much for love of her as because of your religious duty to bring up another girl for some Mormon to marry."

"That's a damnable lie!" cried Jane Withersteen.

"It was what made me hesitate," went on Mrs. Larkin, "but I never believed it at heart. And now I guess I'll let you—"

"Wait! Mrs. Larkin, I may have told little white lies in my life, but never a lie that mattered, that hurt any one. Now believe me. I love little Fay. If I had her near me I'd grow to worship her. When I asked for her I thought only of that love. . . . Let me prove this. You and Fay come to live with me. I've such a big house, and I'm so lonely. I'll help nurse you, take care of you. When you're better you can work for me. I'll keep little Fay and bring her up—without Mormon teaching. When she's grown, if she should want to leave me, I'll send her, and not empty-handed, back to Illinois where you came from. I promise you."

"I knew it was a lie," replied the mother, and she sank back upon her pillow with something of peace in her white, worn face. "Jane Withersteen, may Heaven bless you! I've been deeply grateful to you. But because you're a Mormon I never felt close to you till now. I don't know much about religion as religion, but your God and my God are the same."

CHAPTER VIII

SURPRISE VALLEY

BACK in that strange cañon, which Venters had found indeed a valley of surprises, the wounded girl's whispered appeal, almost a prayer, not to take her back to the rustlers crowned the events of the last few days with a confounding climax. That she should not want to return to them staggered Venters. Presently, as logical thought returned, her appeal confirmed his first impression—that she was more unfortunate than bad—and he experienced a sensation of gladness. If he had known before that Oldring's Masked Rider was a woman his opinion would have been formed and he would have considered her abandoned. But his first knowledge had come when he lifted a white face quivering in a convulsion of agony; he had heard God's name whispered by blood-stained lips; through her solemn and awful eyes he had caught a glimpse of her soul. And just now had come the entreaty to him, "Don't—take—me—back—there!"

Once for all Venters's quick mind formed a permanent conception of this poor girl. He based it, not upon what the chances of life had made her, but upon the revelation of dark eyes that pierced the infinite, upon a few pitiful, halting words that betrayed failure and wrong and misery, yet breathed the truth of a tragic fate rather than a natural leaning to evil.

"What's your name?" he inquired

"Bess," she answered.

"Bess what?"

"That's enough—just Bess."

The red that deepened in her cheeks was not all the flush of fever. Venters marveled anew, and this time at the tint of shame in her face, at the momentary drooping of long lashes. She might be a rustler's girl, but she was still capable of shame; she might be dying, but she still clung to some little remnant of honor.

"Very well, Bess. It doesn't matter," he said. "But this matters—what shall I do with you?"

"Are—you—a rider?" she whispered.

"Not now. I was once. I drove the Withersteen herds. But I lost my place—lost all I owned—and now I'm—I'm a sort of outcast. My name's Bern Venters."

"You won't—take me—to Cottonwoods—or Glaze? I'd be—hanged."

"No, indeed. But I must do something with you. For it's not safe for me here. I shot that rustler who was with you. Sooner or later he'll be found, and then my tracks. I must find a safer hiding-place where I can't be trailed."

"Leave me—here."

"Alone—to die!"

"Yes."

"I will not." Venters spoke shortly with a kind of ring in his voice.

"What—do you want—to do—with me?" Her whispering grew difficult, so low and faint that Venters had to stoop to hear her.

"Why, let's see," he replied, slowly. "I'd like to take you some place where I could watch by you, nurse you, till you're all right again."

"And—then?"

"Well, it 'll be time to think of that when you're cured of your wound. It's a bad one. And—Bess, if you don't want to live—if you don't fight for life—you'll never—"

"Oh! I want—to live! I'm afraid—to die. But I'd rather—die—than go back—to—to—"

"To Oldring?" asked Venters, interrupting her in turn.

Her lips moved in an affirmative.

"I promise not to take you back to him or to Cottonwoods or to Glaze."

The mournful earnestness of her gaze suddenly shone with unutterable gratitude and wonder. And as suddenly Venters found her eyes beautiful as he had never seen or felt beauty. They were as dark blue as the sky at night. Then the flashing changed to a long, thoughtful look, in which there was wistful, unconscious searching of his face, a look that trembled on the verge of hope and trust.

"I'll try—to live," she said. The broken whisper just reached his ears. "Do what—you want—with me."

"Rest then—don't worry—sleep," he replied.

Abruptly he arose, as if her words had been decision for him, and with a sharp command to the dogs he strode from the camp. Venters was conscious of an indefinite conflict of change within him. It seemed to be a vague passing of old moods, a dim coalescing of new forces, a moment of inexplicable transition. He was both cast down and uplifted. He wanted to think and think of the meaning, but he resolutely dispelled emotion. His imperative need at present was to find a safe retreat, and this called for action.

So he set out. It still wanted several hours before dark. This trip he turned to the left and wended his skulking way southward a mile or more to the opening of the valley, where lay the strange scrawled rocks. He did not, however, venture boldly out into the open sage, but clung to the right-hand wall and went along that till its perpendicular line broke into the long incline of bare stone.

Before proceeding farther he halted, studying the

strange character of this slope and realizing that a moving black object could be seen far against such background. Before him ascended a gradual swell of smooth stone. It was hard, polished, and full of pockets worn by centuries of eddying rain-water. A hundred yards up began a line of grotesque cedar-trees, and they extended along the slope clear to its most southerly end. Beyond that end Venters wanted to get, and he concluded the cedars, few as they were, would afford some cover.

Therefore he climbed swiftly. The trees were farther up than he had estimated, though he had from long habit made allowance for the deceiving nature of distances in that country. When he gained the cover of cedars he paused to rest and look, and it was then he saw how the trees sprang from holes in the bare rock. Ages of rain had run down the slope, circling, eddying in depressions, wearing deep round holes. There had been dry seasons, accumulations of dust, wind-blown seeds, and cedars rose wonderfully out of solid rock. But these were not beautiful cedars. They were gnarled, twisted into weird contortions, as if growth were torture, dead at the tops, shrunken, gray, and old. Theirs had been a bitter fight, and Venters felt a strange sympathy for them. This country was hard on trees—and men.

He slipped from cedar to cedar, keeping them between him and the open valley. As he progressed, the belt of trees widened, and he kept to its upper margin. He passed shady pockets half full of water, and, as he marked the location for possible future need, he reflected that there had been no rain since the winter snows. From one of these shady holes a rabbit hopped out and squatted down, laying its ears flat.

Venters wanted fresh meat now more than when he had only himself to think of. But it would not do to fire his rifle there. So he broke off a cedar branch and threw it. He crippled the rabbit, which started to flounder up the slope. Venters did not wish to lose the meat, and he never allowed crippled game to escape, to die lingeringly in some covert. So after a careful glance below, and back toward the cañon, he began to chase the rabbit.

The fact that rabbits generally ran uphill was not new to him. But it presently seemed singular why this rabbit, that might have escaped downward, chose to ascend the slope. Venters knew then that it had a burrow higher up. More than once he jerked over to seize it, only in vain, for the rabbit by renewed effort eluded his grasp. Thus the chase continued on up the bare slope. The farther Venters climbed the more determined he grew to catch his quarry. At last, panting and sweating, he captured the rabbit at the foot of a steeper grade. Laying his rifle on the bulge of rising stone, he killed the animal and slung it from his belt.

Before starting down he waited to catch his breath. He had climbed far up that wonderful smooth slope, and had almost reached the base of yellow cliff that rose skyward, a huge scarred and cracked bulk. It frowned down upon him as if to forbid further ascent. Venters bent over for his rifle, and, as he picked it up from where it leaned against the steeper grade, he saw several little nicks cut in the solid stone.

They were only a few inches deep and about a foot apart. Venters began to count them—one—two—three—four—on up to sixteen. That number carried his glance to the top of this first bulging bench of cliff-base. Above, after a more level offset, was still steeper slope, and the line of nicks kept on, to wind round a projecting corner of wall.

A casual glance would have passed by these little dents; if Venters had not known what they signified he would never have bestowed upon them the second glance. But he knew they had been cut there by hand,

and, though age-worn, he recognized them as steps cut in the rock by the cliff-dwellers. With a pulse beginning to beat and hammer away his calmness, he eyed that indistinct line of steps, up to where the buttress of wall hid further sight of them. He knew that behind the corner of stone would be a cave or a crack which could never be suspected from below. Chance, that had sported with him of late, now directed him to a probable hiding-place. Again he laid aside his rifle, and, removing boots and belt, he began to walk up the steps. Like a mountain goat, he was agile, sure-footed, and he mounted the first bench without bending to use his hands. The next ascent took grip of fingers as well as toes, but he climbed steadily, swiftly, to reach the projecting corner, and slipped around it. Here he faced a notch in the cliff. At the apex he turned abruptly into a ragged vent that split the ponderous wall clear to the top, showing a narrow streak of blue sky.

At the base this vent was dark, cool, and smelled of dry, musty dust. It zigzagged so that he could not see ahead more than a few yards at a time. He noticed tracks of wildcats and rabbits in the dusty floor. At every turn he expected to come upon a huge cavern full of little square stone houses, each with a small aperture like a staring dark eye. The passage lightened and widened, and opened at the foot of a narrow, steep, ascending chute.

Venters had a moment's notice of the rock, which was of the same smoothness and hardness as the slope below, before his gaze went irresistibly upward to the precipitous walls of this wide ladder of granite. These were ruined walls of yellow sandstone, and so split and splintered, so overhanging with great sections of balancing rim, so impending with tremendous crumbling crags, that Venters caught his breath sharply, and, appalled, he instinctively recoiled as if a step upward might jar the ponderous cliffs from their foundation. Indeed, it seemed that these ruined cliffs were but awaiting a breath of wind to collapse and come tumbling down. Venters hesitated. It would be a foolhardy man who risked his life under the leaning, waiting avalanches of rock in that gigantic split. Yet how many years had they leaned there without falling! At the bottom of the incline was an immense heap of weathered sandstone all crumbling to dust, but there were no huge rocks as large as houses, such as rested so lightly and frightfully above, waiting patiently and inevitably to crash down. Slowly split from the parent rock by the weathering process, and carved and sculptured by ages of wind and rain, they waited their moment. Venters felt how foolish it was for him to fear these broken walls; to fear that, after they had endured for thousands of years, the moment of his passing should be the one for them to slip. Yet he feared it.

"What a place to hide!" muttered Venters. "I'll climb—I'll see where this thing goes. If only I can find water!"

With teeth tight shut he essayed the incline. And as he climbed he bent his eyes downward. This, however, after a little grew impossible; he had to look to obey his eager, curious mind. He raised his glance and saw light between row on row of shafts and pinnacles and crags that stood out from the main wall. Some leaned against the cliff, others against each other; many stood sheer and alone; all were crumbling, cracked, rotten. It was a place of yellow, ragged ruin. The passage narrowed as he went up; it became a slant, hard for him to stick on; it was smooth as marble. Finally he surmounted it, surprised to find the walls still several hundred feet high, and a narrow gorge leading down on the other side. This was a divide between two inclines, about twenty yards wide. At one side stood an enormous rock. Venters gave it a second glance, because it rested on a pedestal. It attracted closer attention. It was like a colossal pear of stone standing on its stem. Around the bottom were thousands of little nicks just distinguishable to the eye. They were marks of stone hatchets. The cliff-dwellers had chipped and chipped away at this boulder till it rested its tremendous bulk upon a mere pin-point of its surface. Venters pondered. Why had the little stone-men hacked away at that big boulder? It bore no semblance to a statue or an idol or a godhead or a sphinx. Instinctively he put his hands on it and pushed; then his shoulder and heaved. The stone seemed to groan, to stir, to grate, and then to move. It tipped a little downward and hung balancing for a long instant, slowly returned, rocked slightly, groaned, and settled back to its former position.

Venters divined its significance. It had been meant for defense. The cliff-dwellers, driven by dreaded enemies to this last stand, had cunningly cut the rock until it balanced perfectly, ready to be dislodged by strong hands. Just below it leaned a tottering crag that would have toppled, starting an avalanche on an acclivity where no sliding mass could stop. Crags and pinnacles, splintered cliffs, and leaning shafts and monuments, would have thundered down to block forever the outlet to Deception Pass.

"That was a narrow shave for me," said Venters, soberly. "A balancing rock! The cliff-dwellers never had to roll it. They died, vanished, and here the rock stands, probably little changed. . . . But it might serve another lonely dweller of the cliffs. I'll hide up here somewhere, if I can only find water."

He descended the gorge on the other side. The slope was gradual, the space narrow, the course straight for many rods. A gloom hung between the up-sweeping walls. In a turn the passage narrowed to scarce a dozen feet, and here was darkness of night. But light shone ahead; another abrupt turn brought day again, and then wide open space.

SURPRISE VALLEY

Above Venters loomed a wonderful arch of stone bridging the cañon rims, and through the enormous round portal gleamed and glistened a beautiful valley shining under sunset gold reflected by surrounding cliffs. He gave a start of surprise. The valley was a cove a mile long, half that wide, and its enclosing walls were smooth and stained, and curved inward, forming great caves. He decided that its floor was far higher than the level of Deception Pass and the intersecting cañons. No purple sage colored this valley floor. Instead there were the white of aspens, streaks of branch and slender trunk glistening from the green of leaves, and the darker green of oaks, and through the middle of this forest, from wall to wall, ran a winding line of brilliant green which marked the course of cottonwoods and willows.

"There's water here—and this is the place for me," said Venters. "Only birds can peep over those walls. I've gone Oldring one better."

Venters waited no longer, and turned swiftly to retrace his steps. He named the cañon Surprise Valley and the huge boulder that guarded the outlet Balancing Rock. Going down he did not find himself attended by such fears as had beset him in the climb; still, he was not easy in mind and could not occupy himself with plans of moving the girl and his outfit until he had descended to the notch. There he rested a moment and looked about him. The pass was darkening with the approach of night. At the corner of the wall, where the stone steps turned, he saw a spur of rock that would serve to hold the noose of a lasso. He needed no more aid to scale that place. As he intended to make the move under cover of darkness, he wanted most to be able to tell where to climb up. So, taking several small stones with him, he stepped and slid down to the edge of the slope where he had left his rifle and boots. Here he placed the stones some yards apart. He left the rabbit lying upon the bench where the steps began.

Then he addressed a keen-sighted, remembering gaze to the rim-wall above. It was serrated, and between two spears of rock, directly in line with his position, showed a zigzag crack that at night would let through the gleam of sky. This settled, he put on his belt and boots and prepared to descend. Some consideration was necessary to decide whether or not to leave his rifle there. On the return, carrying the girl and a pack, it would be added encumbrance; and after debating the matter he left the rifle leaning against the bench. As he went straight down the slope he halted every few rods to look up at his mark on the rim. It changed, but he fixed each change in his memory. When he reached the first cedar-tree, he tied his scarf upon a dead branch, and then hurried toward camp, having no more concern about finding his trail upon the return trip.

Darkness soon emboldened and lent him greater speed. It occurred to him, as he glided into the grassy glade near camp and heard the whinny of a horse, that he had forgotten Wrangle. The big sorrel could not be gotten into Surprise Valley. He would have to be left here.

Venters determined at once to lead the other horses out through the thicket and turn them loose. The farther they wandered from this cañon the better it would suit him. He easily descried Wrangle through the gloom, but the others were not in sight. Venters whistled low for the dogs, and when they came trotting to him he sent them out to search for the horses, and followed. It soon developed that they were not in the glade nor the thicket Venters grew cold and rigid at the thought of rustlers having entered his retreat. But the thought passed, for the demeanor of Ring and Whitie reassured him. The horses had wandered away.

Under the clump of silver spruces hung a denser mantle of darkness, yet not so thick that Venters's night-practiced eyes could not catch the white oval of a still face. He bent over it with a slight suspension of breath that was both caution lest he frighten her and chill uncertainty of feeling lest he find her dead. But she slept, and he arose to renewed activity.

He packed his saddle-bags. The dogs were hungry, they whined about him and nosed his busy hands; but he took no time to feed them nor to satisfy his own hunger. He slung the saddle-bags over his shoulders and made them secure with his lasso. Then he wrapped the blankets closer about the girl and lifted her in his arms. Wrangle whinnied and thumped the ground as Venters passed him with the dogs. The sorrel knew he was being left behind, and was not sure whether he liked it or not. Venters went on and entered the thicket. Here he had to feel his way in pitch blackness and to wedge his progress between the close saplings. Time meant little to him now that he had started, and he edged along with slow side movement till he got clear of the thicket. Ring and Whitie stood waiting for him. Taking to the open aisles and patches of the sage, he walked guardedly, careful not to stumble or step in dust or strike against spreading sage-branches.

If he were burdened he did not feel it. From time to time, when he passed out of the black lines of shade into the wan starlight, he glanced at the white face of the girl lying in his arms. She had not awakened from her sleep or stupor. He did not rest until he cleared the black gate of the cañon. Then he leaned against a stone breast-high to him and gently released the girl from his hold. His brow and hair and the palms of his hands were wet, and there was a kind of nervous contraction of his muscles. They seemed to ripple and string tense. He had a desire to hurry and no sense of fatigue. A wind blew the scent of sage in his face. The first early blackness of night passed with the brightening of the stars. Somewhere back on his trail a coyote yelped, splitting the dead silence. Venters's faculties seemed singularly acute.

He lifted the girl again and pressed on. The valley afforded better traveling than the cañon. It was lighter, freer of sage, and there were no rocks. Soon, out of the pale gloom shone a still paler thing, and that was the low swell of slope. Venters mounted it, and his dogs walked beside him. Once upon the stone he slowed to snail pace, straining his sight to avoid the pockets and holes. Foot by foot he went up. The weird cedars, like great demons and witches chained to the rock and writhing in silent anguish, loomed up with wide and twisting naked arms. Venters crossed this belt of cedars, skirted the upper border, and recognized the tree he had marked, even before he saw his waving scarf.

Here he knelt and deposited the girl gently, feet first, and slowly laid her out full length. What he feared was to reopen one of her wounds. If he gave her a violent jar, or slipped and fell! But the supreme confidence so strangely felt that night admitted of no such blunders.

The slope before him seemed to swell into obscurity, to lose its definite outline in a misty, opaque cloud that shaded into the over-shadowing wall. He scanned the rim where the serrated points speared the sky, and he found the zigzag crack. It was dim, only a shade lighter than the dark ramparts; but he distinguished it, and that served.

Lifting the girl, he stepped upward, closely attending to the nature of the path under his feet. After a few steps he stopped to mark his line with the crack in the rim. The dogs clung closer to him. While chasing the rabbit this slope had appeared interminable to him; now, burdened as he was, he did not think of length or height or toil. He remembered only to avoid a misstep and to keep his direction. He climbed on, with frequent stops to watch the rim, and before he dreamed of gaining the bench he bumped his knees into it, and saw, in the dim gray light, his rifle and the rabbit. He had come straight up without mishap or swerving off his course, and his shut teeth unlocked.

As he laid the girl down in the shallow hollow of the little ridge, with her white face upturned, she opened her eyes. Wide, staring, black, at once like both the night and the stars, they made her face seem still whiter.

"Is—it—you?" she asked, faintly.

"Yes," replied Venters.

"Oh! Where—are we?"

"I'm taking you to a safe place where no one will ever find you. I must climb a little here and call the dogs. Don't be afraid. I'll soon come for you."

She said no more. Her eyes watched him steadily for a moment and then closed. Venters pulled off his boots and then felt for the little steps in the rock. The shade of the cliff above obscured the point he wanted to gain, but he could see dimly a few feet before him. What he had attempted with care he now went at with surpassing lightness. Buoyant, rapid, sure, he attained the corner of wall and slipped around it. Here he could not see a hand before his face, so he groped along, found a little flat space, and there removed the saddle-bags. The lasso he took back with him to the corner and looped the noose over the spur of rock.

"Ring—Whitie—come," he called, softly.

Low whines came up from below

"Here! Come, Whitie—Ring," he repeated, this time sharply.

Then followed scraping of claws and pattering of feet; and out of the gray gloom below him swiftly climbed the dogs to reach his side and pass beyond.

Venters descended, holding to the lasso. He tested its strength by throwing all his weight upon it. Then he gathered the girl up, and, holding her securely in his left arm, he began to climb, at every few steps jerking his right hand upward along the lasso. It sagged at each forward movements he made, but he balanced himself lightly during the interval when he lacked the support of a taut rope. He climbed as if he had wings, the strength of a giant, and knew not the sense of fear. The sharp corner of cliff seemed to cut out of the darkness. He reached it and the protruding shelf, and then, entering the black shade of the notch, he moved blindly but surely to the place where he had left the saddlebags. He heard the dogs, though he could not see them. Once more he carefully placed the girl at his feet. Then, on hands and knees, he went over the little flat space, feeling for stones. He removed a number, and, scraping the deep dust into a heap, he unfolded the outer blanket from around the girl and laid her upon this bed. Then he went down the slope again for his boots, rifle, and the rabbit, and, bringing also his lasso with him, he made short work of that trip.

"Are—you—there?" The girl's voice came low from the blackness.

"Yes," he replied, and was conscious that his laboring breast made speech difficult.

"Are we—in a cave?"

"Yes."

"Oh, listen! . . . The waterfall! . . . I hear it! You've brought me back!"

Venters heard a murmuring moan that one moment swelled to a pitch almost softly shrill and the next lulled to a low, almost inaudible sigh.

"That's—wind blowing—in the—cliffs," he panted. "You're far—from Oodring's—cañon."

The effort it cost him to speak made him conscious of extreme lassitude following upon great exertion. It seemed that when he lay down and drew his blanket over him the action was the last before utter prostration. He stretched inert, wet, hot, his body one great strife of throbbing, stinging nerves and bursting veins. And there he lay for a long while before he felt that he had begun to rest.

Rest came to him that night, but no sleep. Sleep he did not want. The hours of strained effort were now as if they had never been, and he wanted to think. Earlier in the day he had dismissed an inexplicable feeling of change; but now, when there was no longer demand on his cunning and strength and he ha l time to think, he could not catch the illusive thing that had sadly perplexed as well as elevated his spirit.

Above him, through a V-shaped cleft in the dark rim of the cliff, shone the lustrous stars that had been his lonely accusers for a long, long year. To-night they were different. He studied them. Larger, whiter, more radiant they seemed; but that was not the difference he meant. Gradully it came to him that the distinction was not one he saw, but one he felt. In this he divined as much of the baffling change as he thought would be revealed to him then. And as he lay there, with the singing of the cliff-winds in his ears, the white stars above the dark, bold vent, the difference which he felt was that he was no longer alone.

CHAPTER IX

SILVER SPRUCE AND ASPENS

THE rest of that night seemed to Venters only a few moments of starlight, a dark overcasting of sky, an hour or so of gray gloom, and then the lighting of dawn.

When he had bestirred himself, feeding the hungry dogs and breaking his long fast, and had repacked his saddle-bags, it was clear daylight, though the sun had not tipped the yellow wall in the east. He concluded to make the climb and descent into Surprise Valley in one trip. To that end he tied his blanket upon Ring and gave Whitie the extra lasso and the rabbit to carry. Then, with the rifle and saddle-bags slung upon his back, he took up the girl. She did not awaken from heavy slumber.

That climb up under the rugged, menacing brows of the broken cliffs, in the face of a grim, leaning boulder that seemed to be weary of its age-long wavering, was a tax on strength and nerve that Venters felt equally with something sweet and strangely exulting in its accomplishment. He did not pause until he gained the narrow divide and there he rested. Balancing Rock loomed huge, cold in the gray light of dawn, a thing without life, yet it spoke silently to Venters: "I am waiting to plunge down, to shatter and crash, roar and boom, to bury your trail, and close forever the outlet to Deception Pass!"

On the descent of the other side Venters had easy going, but was somewhat concerned because Whitie appeared to have succumbed to temptation, and while carrying the rabbit was also chewing on it. And Ring evidently regarded this as an injury to himself, especially as he had carried the heavier load. Presently he snapped at one end of the rabbit and refused to let go. But his action prevented Whitie from further misdoing, and then the two dogs pattered down, carrying the rabbit between them.

Venters turned out of the gorge, and suddenly paused stock-still, astounded at the scene before him. The curve of the great stone bridge had caught the sunrise, and through the magnificent arch burst a glorious stream of gold that shone with a long slant down into the center of Surprise Valley. Only through the arch did any sunlight pass, so that all the rest of the valley lay still asleep, dark green, mysterious, shadowy, merging its level into walls as misty and soft as morning clouds.

Venters then descended, passing through the arch, looking up at its tremendous height and sweep. It spanned the opening to Surprise Valley, stretching in almost perfect curve from rim to rim. Even in his hurry and concern Venters could not but feel its majesty, and the thought came to him that the cliff-dwellers must have regarded it as an object of worship.

Down, down, down Venters strode, more and more feeling the weight of his burden as he descended, and still the valley lay below him. As all other cañons and coves and valleys had deceived him, so had this deep, nestling oval. At length he passed beyond the slope of weathered stone that spread fan-shape from the arch, and encountered a grassy terrace running to the right and about on a level with the tips of the oaks and cottonwoods below. Scattered here and there upon this shelf were clumps of aspens, and he walked through them into a glade that surpassed, in beauty and adaptability for a wild home, any place he had ever seen.

Silver spruces bordered the base of a precipitous wall that rose loftily. Caves indented its surface, and there were no detached ledges or weathered sections that might dislodge a stone. The level ground, beyond the spruces, dropped down into a little ravine. This was one dense line of slender aspens from which came the low splashing of water. And the terrace, lying open to the west, afforded unobstructed view of the valley of green tree-tops.

For his camp Venters chose a shady, grassy plot between the silver spruces and the cliff. Here, in the stone wall, had been wonderfully carved by wind or washed by water several deep caves above the level of the terrace. They were clean, dry, roomy. He cut spruce boughs and made a bed in the largest cave and laid the girl there. The first intimation that he had of her being aroused from sleep or lethargy was a low call for water.

He hurried down into the ravine with his canteen. It was a shallow, grass-green place with aspens growing up everywhere. To his delight he found a tiny brook of swift-running water. Its faint tinge of amber reminded him of the spring at Cottonwoods, and the thought gave him a little shock. The water was so cold it made his fingers tingle as he dipped the canteen. Having returned to the cave, he was glad to see the girl drink thirstily. This time he noted that she could raise her head slightly without his help.

"You were thirsty," he said. "It's good water. I've found a fine place. Tell me—how do you feel?"

"There's pain—here," she replied, and moved her hand to her left side.

"Why, that's strange! Your wounds are on your right side. I believe you're hungry. Is the pain a kind of dull ache—a gnawing?"

"It's like—that."

"Then it's hunger." Venters laughed, and suddenly

HE DID NOT PAUSE UNTIL HE GAINED THE NARROW DIVIDE

caught himself with a quick breath and felt again the little shock. When had he laughed? "It's hunger," he went on. "I've had that gnaw many a time. I've got it now. But you mustn't eat. You can have all the water you want, but no food just yet."

"Won't I—starve?"

"No, people don't starve easily. I've discovered that. You must lie perfectly still and rest and sleep—for days."

"My hands—are dirty; my face feels—so hot and sticky; my boots hurt." It was her longest speech as yet, and it trailed off in a whisper.

"Well, I'm a fine nurse!"

It annoyed him that he had never thought of these things. But then, awaiting her death and thinking of her comfort were vastly different matters. He unwrapped the blanket which covered her. What a slender girl she was! No wonder he had been able to carry her miles and pack her up that slippery ladder of stone. Her boots were of soft, fine leather, reaching clear to her knees. He recognized the make as one of a bootmaker in Sterling. Her spurs that he had stupidly neglected to remove, consisted of silver frames and gold chains, and the rowels, large as silver dollars, were fancifully engraved. The boots slipped off rather hard. She wore heavy woollen rider's stockings, half length, and these were pulled up over the ends of her short trousers. Venters took off the stockings to note her little feet were red and swollen. He bathed them. Then he removed his scarf and bathed her face and hands.

"I must see your wounds now," he said, gently.

She made no reply, but watched him steadily as he opened her blouse and untied the bandage. His strong fingers trembled a little as he removed it. If the wounds had reopened! A chill struck him as he saw the angry red bullet-mark, and a tiny stream of blood winding from it down her white breast. Very carefully he lifted her to see that the wound in her back had closed perfectly. Then he washed the blood from her breast, bathed the wound, and left it unbandaged, open to the air.

Her eyes thanked him.

"Listen," he said, earnestly. "I've had some wounds, and I've seen many. I know a little about them. The hole in your back has closed. If you lie still three days the one in your breast will close and you'll be safe. The danger from hemorrhage will be over."

He had spoken with earnest sincerity, almost eagerness.

"Why—do you—want me—to get well?" she asked, wonderingly.

The simple question seemed unanswerable except on grounds of humanity. But the circumstances under which he had shot this strange girl, the shock and realization, the waiting for death, the hope, had resulted in a condition of mind wherein Venters wanted her to live more than he had ever wanted anything. Yet he could not tell why. He believed the killing of the rustler and the subsequent excitement had disturbed him. For how else could he explain the throbbing of his brain, the heat of his blood, the undefined sense of full hours, charged, vibrant with pulsating mystery where once they had dragged in loneliness?

"I shot you," he said, slowly, "and I want you to get well so I shall not have killed a woman. But—for your own sake, too—"

A terrible bitterness darkened her eyes, and her lips quivered.

"Hush," said Venters. "You've talked too much already."

In her unutterable bitterness he saw a darkness of mood that could not have been caused by her present weak and feverish state. She hated the life she had led, that she probably had been compelled to lead. She had suffered some unforgivable wrong at the hands of Oldring. With that conviction Venters felt a flame throughout his body, and it marked the rekindling of fierce anger and ruthlessness. In the past long year he had nursed resentment. He had hated the wilderness—the loneliness of the uplands. He had waited for something to come to pass. It had come. Like an Indian stealing horses he had skulked into the recesses of the cañons. He had found Oldring's retreat; he had killed a rustler; he had shot an unfortunate girl, then had saved her from this unwitting act, and he meant to save her from the consequent wasting of blood, from fever and weakness. Starvation he had to fight for her and for himself. Where he had been sick at the letting of blood, now he remembered it in grim, cold calm. And as he lost that softness of nature, so he lost his fear of men. He would watch for Oldring, biding his time, and he would kill this great black-bearded rustler who had held a girl in bondage, who had used her to his infamous ends.

Venters surmised this much of the change in him—idleness had passed; keen, fierce vigor flooded his mind and body; all that had happened to him at Cottonwoods seemed remote and hard to recall; the difficulties and perils of the present absorbed him, held him in a kind of spell.

First, then, he fitted up the little cave adjoining the girl's room for his own comfort and use. His next work was to build a fireplace of stones and to gather a store of wood. That done, he spilled the contents of his saddle-bags upon the grass and took stock. His outfit consisted of a small-handled axe, a hunting-knife, a large number of cartridges for rifle or revolver, a tin plate, a cup, and a fork and spoon, a quantity of dried beef and dried fruits, and small canvas bags containing tea, sugar, salt, and pepper. For him alone this supply would have been bountiful to begin a sojourn in the wilderness, but he was no longer alone. Starvation in the uplands was not an unheard-of thing; he did not, however, worry at all on that score, and feared only his possible inability to supply the needs of a woman in a weakened and extremely delicate condition

If there was no game in the valley—a contingency he doubted—it would not be a great task for him to go by night to Oldring's herd and pack out a calf. The exigency of the moment was to ascertain if there were game in Surprise Valley. Whitie still guarded the dilapidated rabbit, and Ring slept near by under a spruce. Venters called Ring and went to the edge of the terrace, and there halted to survey the valley.

He was prepared to find it larger than his unstudied glances had made it appear; for more than a casual idea of dimensions and a hasty conception of oval shape and singular beauty he had not had time. Again the felicity of the name he had given the valley struck him forcibly. Around the red perpendicular walls, except under the great arc of stone, ran a terrace fringed at the cliff-base by silver spruces; below that first terrace sloped another wider one densely overgrown with aspens, and the center of the valley was a level circle of oaks and alders, with the glittering green line of willows and cottonwood dividing it in half. Venters saw a number and variety of birds flitting among the trees. To his left, facing the stone bridge, an enormous cavern opened in the wall; and low down, just above the tree-tops, he made out a long shelf of cliff-dwellings, with little black, staring windows or doors. Like eyes they were, and seemed to watch him. The few cliff-dwellings he had seen—all ruins—had left him with haunting memory of age and solitude and of something past. He had come, in a way, to be a cliff-dweller himself, and those silent eyes would look down upon him, as if in surprise that after thousands of years a man had invaded the valley.

Venters felt sure that he was the only white man who had ever walked under the shadow of the wonderful stone bridge, down into that wonderful valley with its circle of caves and its terraced rings of silver spruce and aspens.

The dog growled below and rushed into the forest. Venters ran down the declivity to enter a zone of light shade streaked with sunshine. The oak-trees were slender, none more than half a foot thick, and they grew close together, intermingling their branches. Ring came running back with a rabbit in his mouth. Venters took the rabbit and, holding the dog near him, stole softly on. There were fluttering of wings among the branches and quick bird-notes, and rustling of dead leaves and rapid patterings. Venters crossed well-worn trails marked with fresh tracks; and when he had stolen on a little farther he saw many birds and running quail, and more rabbits than he could count. He had not penetrated the forest of oaks for a hundred yards, had not approached anywhere near the line of willows and cottonwoods which he knew grew along a stream. But he had seen enough to know that Surprise Valley was the home of many wild creatures.

Venters returned to camp. He skinned the rabbits, and gave the dogs the one they had quarreled over, and the skin of this he dressed and hung up to dry, feeling that he would like to keep it. It was a particularly rich, furry pelt with a beautiful white tail. Venters remembered that but for the bobbing of that white tail catching his eye he would not have espied the rabbit, and he would never have discovered Surprise Valley. Little incidents of chance like this had turned him here and there in Deception Pass; and now they had assumed to him the significance and direction of destiny.

His good fortune in the matter of game at hand brought to his mind the necessity of keeping it in the valley. Therefore he took the axe and cut bundles of aspens and willows, and packed them up under the bridge to the narrow outlet of the gorge. Here he began fashioning a fence, by driving aspens into the ground and lacing them fast with willows. Trip after trip he made down for more building material, and the afternoon had passed when he finished the work to his satisfaction. Wildcats might scale the fence, but no coyote could come in to search for prey, and no rabbits or other small game could escape from the valley.

Upon returning to camp he set about getting his supper at ease, around a fine fire, without hurry or fear of discovery. After hard work that had definite purpose, this freedom and comfort gave him peculiar satisfaction. He caught himself often, as he kept busy round the camp-fire, stopping to glance at the quiet form in the cave, and at the dogs stretched cozily near him, and then out across the beautiful valley. The present was not yet real to him.

While he ate, the sun set beyond a dip in the rim of the curved wall. As the morning sun burst wondrously through a grand arch into this valley, in a golden, slanting shaft, so the evening sun, at the moment of setting, shone through a gap of cliffs, sending down a broad red burst to brighten the oval with a blaze of fire. To Venters both sunrise and sunset were unreal.

A cool wind blew across the oval, waving the tips of oaks, and, while the light lasted, fluttering the aspen leaves into millions of facets of red, and sweeping the graceful spruces. Then with the wind soon came a shade and a darkening, and suddenly the valley was gray. Night came there quickly after the sinking of the sun. Venters went softly to look at the girl. She slept, and her breathing was quiet and slow. He lifted Ring into the cave, with stern whisper for him to stay there on guard. Then he drew the blanket carefully over her and returned to the camp-fire.

Though exceedingly tired, he was yet loath to yield

to lassitude, but this night it was not from listening, watchful vigilance; it was from a desire to realize his position. The details of his wild environment seemed the only substance of a strange dream. He saw the darkening rims, the gray oval turning black, the undulating surface of forest, like a rippling lake, and the spear-pointed spruces. He heard the flutter of aspen-leaves and the soft, continuous splash of falling water. The melancholy note of a cañon bird broke clear and lonely from the high cliffs. Venters had no name for this night singer, and he had never seen one; but the few notes, always pealing out just at darkness, were as familiar to him as the cañon silence. Then they ceased, and the rustle of leaves and the murmur of water hushed in a growing sound that Venters fancied was not of earth. Neither had he a name for this, only it was inexpressibly wild and sweet. The thought came that it might be a moan of the girl in her last outcry of life, and he felt a tremor shake him. But no! This sound was not human, though it was like despair. He began to doubt his sensitive perceptions, to believe that he half-dreamed what he thought he heard. Then the sound swelled with the strengthening of the breeze, and he realized it was the singing of the wind in the cliffs.

By and by a drowsiness overcame him, and Venters began to nod, half asleep, with his back against a spruce. Rousing himself and calling Whitie, he went to the cave. The girl lay barely visible in the dimness. Ring crouched beside her, and the patting of his tail on the stone assured Venters that the dog was awake and faithful to his duty. Venters sought his own bed of fragrant boughs; and as he lay back, somehow grateful for the comfort and safety, the night seemed to steal away from him and he sank softly into intangible space and rest and slumber.

Venters awakened to the sound of melody that he imagined was only the haunting echo of dream music.

He opened his eyes to another surprise of this valley of beautiful surprises. Out of his cave he saw the exquisitely fine foliage of the silver spruces crossing a round space of blue morning sky; and in this lacy leafage fluttered a number of gray birds with black and white stripes and long tails. They were mocking-birds, and they were singing as if they wanted to burst their throats. Venters listened. One long, silver-tipped branch drooped almost to his cave, and upon it, within a few yards of him, sat one of the graceful birds. Venters saw the swelling and quivering of its throat in song. He arose, and when he slid down out of his cave the birds fluttered and flew farther away.

Venters stepped before the opening of the other cave and looked in. The girl was awake, with wide eyes and listening look, and she had a hand on Ring's neck.

"Mocking-birds!" she said.

"Yes," replied Venters, "and I believe they like our company."

"Where are we?"

"Never mind now. After a little I'll tell you."

"The birds woke me. When I heard them—and saw the shiny trees—and the blue sky—and then a blaze of gold dropping down—I wondered—"

She did not complete her fancy, but Venters imagined he understood her meaning. She appeared to be wandering in mind. Venters felt her face and hands and found them burning with fever. He went for water, and was glad to find it almost as cold as if flowing from ice. That water was the only medicine he had, and he put faith in it. She did not want to drink, but he made her swallow, and then he bathed her face and head and cooled her wrists.

The day began with a heightening of the fever. Venters spent the time reducing her temperature, cooling her hot cheeks and temples. He kept close watch over her, and at the least indication of restlessness, that he knew led to tossing and rolling of the body, he held her tightly, so no violent move could reopen her wounds. Hour after hour she babbled and laughed and cried and moaned in delirium; but whatever her secret was she did not reveal it. Attended by something somber for Venters, the day passed. At night in the cool winds the fever abated and she slept.

The second day was a repetition of the first. On the third he seemed to see her wither and waste away before his eyes. That day he scarcely went from her side for a moment, except to run for fresh, cool water; and he did not eat. The fever broke on the fourth day and left her spent and shrunken, a slip of a girl with life only in her eyes. They hung upon Venters with a mute observance, and he found hope in that.

To rekindle the spark that had nearly flickered out, to nourish the little life and vitality that remained in her, was Venters's problem. But he had little resource other than the meat of the rabbits and quail; and from these he made broths and soups as best he could, and fed her with a spoon. It came to him that the human body, like the human soul, was a strange thing and capable of recovering from terrible shocks. For almost immediately she showed faint signs of gathering strength. There was one more waiting day, in which he doubted, and spent long hours by her side as she slept, and watched the gentle swell of her breast rise and fall in breathing, and the wind stir the tangled chestnut curls. On the next day he knew that she would live.

Upon realizing it he abruptly left the cave and sought his accustomed seat against the trunk of a big spruce, where once more he let his glance stray along the sloping terraces. She would live, and the somber gloom lifted out of the valley, and he felt relief that was pain. Then he roused to the call of action, to the many things he needed to do in the way of making camp fixtures and utensils, to the necessity of hunting food, and the desire to explore the valley.

But he decided to wait a few more days before going far from camp, because he fancied that the girl rested easier when she could see him near at hand. And on the first day her languor appeared to leave her in a renewed grip of life. She awoke stronger from each short slumber; she ate greedily, and she moved about in her bed of boughs; and always, it seemed to Venters, her eyes followed him He knew now that her recovery would be rapid. She talked about the dogs, about the caves, the valley, about how hungry she was, till Venters silenced her, asking her to put off further talk till another time. She obeyed, but she sat up in her bed, and her eyes roved to and fro, and always back to him.

Upon the second morning she sat up when he awakened her, and would not permit him to bathe her face and feed her, which actions she performed for herself. She spoke little, however, and Venters was quick to catch in her the first intimations of thoughtfulness and curiosity and appreciation of her situation. He left camp and took Whitie out to hunt for rabbits. Upon his return he was amazed and somewhat anxiously concerned to see his invalid sitting with her back to a corner of the cave and her bare feet swinging out. Hurriedly he approached, intending to advise her to lie down again, to tell her that perhaps she might overtax her strength. The sun shone upon her, glinting on the little head with its tangle of bright hair and the small, oval face with its pallor, and dark-blue eyes underlined by dark-blue circles. She looked at him and he looked at her. In that exchange of glances he imagined each saw the other in some different guise. It seemed impossible to Venters that this frail girl could be Oldring's Masked Rider. It flashed over him that he had made a mistake which presently she would explain.

"Help me down," she said.

"But—are you well enough?" he protested. "Wait—a little longer."

"I'm weak—dizzy. But I want to get down."

He lifted her—what a light burden now!—and stood her upright beside him, and supported her as she essayed to walk with halting steps. She was like a stripling of a boy; the bright, small head scarcely reached his shoulder. But now, as she clung to his arm, the rider's costume she wore did not contradict, as it had done at first, his feeling of her femininity. She might be the famous Masked Rider of the uplands, she might resemble a boy; but her outline, her little hands and feet, her hair, her big eyes and tremulous lips, and especially a something that Venters felt as a subtle essence rather than what he saw, proclaimed her sex.

She soon tired. He arranged a comfortable seat for her under the spruce that overspread the camp-fire.

"Now tell me—everything," she said.

He recounted all that had happened from the time of his discovery of the rustlers in the cañon up to the present moment.

"You shot me—and now you've saved my life?"

"Yes. After almost killing you I've pulled you through."

"Are you glad?"

"I should say so!"

Her eyes were unusually expressive, and they regarded him steadily; she was unconscious of that mirroring of her emotions, and they shone with gratefulness and interest and wonder and sadness.

"Tell me—about yourself?" she asked.

He made this a briefer story, telling of his coming to Utah, his various occupations till he became a rider, and then how the Mormons had practically driven him out of Cottonwoods, an outcast.

Then, no longer able to withstand his own burning curiosity, he questioned her in turn.

"Are you Oldring's Masked Rider?"

"Yes," she replied, and dropped her eyes.

"I knew it—I recognized your figure—and mask, for I saw you once. Yet I can't believe it! . . . But you never *were* really that rustler, as we riders knew him? A thief—a marauder—a kidnapper of women—a murderer of sleeping riders!"

"No! I never stole—or harmed any one—in all my life. I only rode and rode—"

"But why—why?" he burst out. "Why the name? I understand Oldring made you ride. But the black mask—the mystery—the things laid to your hands—the threats in your infamous name—the night-riding credited to you—the evil deeds deliberately blamed on you and acknowledged by rustlers—even Oldring himself! Why? Tell me why?"

"I never knew that," she answered low. Her drooping head straightened, and the large eyes, larger now and darker, met Venters's with a clear, steadfast gaze in which he read truth. It verified his own conviction.

"Never knew? That's strange! Are you a Mormon?"

"No."

"Is Oldring a Mormon?"

"No."

"Do you—care for him?"

"Yes. I hate his men—his life—sometimes I almost hate him!"

Venters paused in his rapid-fire questioning, as if to brace himself to ask for a truth that would be abhorrent for him to confirm, but which he seemed driven to hear.

"What are—what *were* you to Oldring?"

Like some delicate thing suddenly exposed to blasting heat, the girl wilted; her head dropped, and into her white, wasted cheeks crept the red of shame.

Venters would have given anything to recall that question. It seemed so different—his thought when spoken. Yet her shame established in his mind something akin to the respect he had strangely been hungering to feel for her.

"D—n that question!—forget it!" he cried, in a passion of pain for her and anger at himself. "But once and for all—tell me—I know it, yet I want to hear you say so—you couldn't help yourself?"

"Oh no."

"Well, that makes it all right with me," he went on, honestly. "I—I want you to feel that . . . you see—we've been thrown together—and—and I want to help you—not hurt you. I thought life had been cruel to me, but when I think of yours I feel mean and little for my complaining. Anyway, I was a lonely outcast. And now! . . . I don't see very clearly what it all means. Only we are here—together. We've got to stay here, for long, surely till you are well. But you'll never go back to Oldring. And I'm sure helping you will help me, for I was sick in mind. There's something now for me to do. And if I can win back your strength—then get you away, out of this wild country—help you somehow to a happier life—just think how good that 'll be for me!"

CHAPTER X

LOVE

DURING all these waiting days Venters, with the exception of the afternoon when he had built the gate in the gorge, had scarcely gone out of sight of camp and never out of hearing. His desire to explore Surprise Valley was keen, and on the morning after his long talk with the girl he took his rifle and, calling Ring, made a move to start. The girl lay back in a rude chair of boughs he had put together for her. She had been watching him, and when he picked up the gun and called the dog Venters thought she gave a nervous start.

"I'm only going to look over the valley," he said.

"Will you be gone long?"

"No," he replied, and started off. The incident set him thinking of his former impression that, after her recovery from fever, she did not seem at ease unless he was close at hand. It was fear of being alone, due, he concluded, most likely to her weakened condition. He must not leave her much alone.

As he strode down the sloping terrace, rabbits scampered before him, and the beautiful valley quail, as purple in color as the sage on the uplands, ran fleetly along the ground into the forest. It was pleasant under the trees, in the gold-flecked shade, with the whistle of quail and twittering of birds everywhere. Soon he had passed the limit of his former excursions and entered new territory. Here the woods began to show open glades and brooks running down from the slope, and presently he emerged from shade into the sunshine of a meadow. The shaking of the high grass told him of the running of animals, what species he could not tell, but from Ring's manifest desire to have a chase they were evidently some kind wilder than rabbits. Venters approached the willow and cottonwood belt that he had observed from the height of slope. He penetrated it to find a considerable stream of water and great half-submerged mounds of brush and sticks, and all about him were old and new gnawed circles at the base of the cottonwoods.

"Beaver!" he exclaimed. "By all that's lucky! The meadow's full of beaver! How did they ever get here?"

Beaver had not found a way into the valley by the trail of the cliff-dwellers, of that he was certain; and he began to have more than curiosity as to the outlet or inlet of the stream. When he passed some dead water, which he noted was held by a beaver-dam, there was a current in the stream, and it flowed west. Following its course, he soon entered the oak forest again, and passed through to find himself before massed and jumbled ruins of cliff-wall. There were tangled thickets of wild plum-trees and other thorny growths that made passage extremely laborsome. He found innumerable tracks of wildcats and foxes. Rustlings in the thick undergrowth told him of stealthy movements of these animals. At length his further advance appeared futile, for the reason that the stream disappeared in a split at the base of immense rocks over which he could not climb. To his relief he concluded that though beaver might work their way up the narrow chasm where the water rushed, it would be impossible for men to enter the valley there.

This western curve was the only part of the valley where the walls had been split asunder, and it was a wildly rough and inaccessible corner. Going back a little way, he leaped the stream and headed toward the southern wall. Once out of the oaks he found again the low terrace of aspens, and above that the wide, open terrace fringed by silver spruces. This side of the valley contained the wind or water worn caves. As he pressed on, keeping to the upper terrace, cave after cave opened out of the cliff; now a large one, now a small one. Then yawned, quite suddenly and wonderfully above him, the great cavern of the cliff-dwellers.

It was still a goodly distance, and he tried to imagine, if it appeared so huge from where he stood, what it would be when he got there. He climbed the terrace and then faced a long, gradual ascent of weathered rock and dust, which made climbing too difficult for attention to anything else. At length he entered a zone of shade, and looked up. He stood just within the hollow of a cavern so immense that he had no conception of its real dimensions. The curved roof, stained by ages of leakage, with buff and black and rust-colored streaks, swept up and loomed higher and seemed to soar to the rim of the cliff. Here again was a magnificent arch, such as formed the grand gateway to the valley, only in this instance it formed the dome of a cave instead of the span of a bridge.

Venters passed onward and upward. The stones he dislodged rolled down with strange, hollow crack and roar. He had climbed a hundred rods inward, and yet he had not reached the base of the shelf where the cliff-dwellings rested, a long half-circle of connected stone house, with little dark holes that he had fancied were eyes. At length he gained the base of the shelf, and here found steps cut in the rock. These facilitated climbing, and as he went up he thought how easily this vanished race of men might once have held that stronghold against an army. There was only one possible place to ascend, and this was narrow and steep.

Venters had visited cliff-dwellings before, and they had been in ruins, and of no great character or size but this place was of proportions that stunned him, and it had not been desecrated by the hand of man, nor had it been crumbled by the hand of time. It was a stupendous tomb. It had been a city. It was just as it had been left by its builders. The little houses were there, the smoke-blackened stains of fires, the pieces of pottery scattered about cold hearths, the stone hatchets; and stone pestles and mealing-stones lay beside round holes polished by years of grinding maize—lay there as if they had been carelessly dropped yesterday. But the cliff-dwellers were gone!

Dust! They were dust on the floor or at the foot of the shelf, and their habitations and utensils endured. Venters felt the sublimity of that marvelous vaulted arch, and it seemed to gleam with a glory of something that was gone. How many years had passed since the cliff-dwellers gazed out across the beautiful valley as he was gazing now? How long had it been since women ground grain in those polished holes? What time had rolled by since men of an unknown race lived, loved, fought, and died there? Had an enemy destroyed them? Had disease destroyed them, or only that greatest destroyer—time? Venters saw a long line of blood-red hands painted low down upon the yellow roof of stone. Here was strange portent, if not an answer to his queries. The place oppressed him. It was light, but full of a transparent gloom. It smelled of dust and musty stone, of age and disuse. It was sad. It was solemn. It had the look of a place where silence had become master and was now irrevocable and terrible and could not be broken. Yet, at the moment, from high up in the carved crevices of the arch, floated down the low, strange wail of wind—a knell indeed for all that had gone.

Venters, sighing, gathered up an armful of pottery, such pieces as he thought strong enough and suitable for his own use, and bent his steps toward camp. He mounted the terrace at an opposite point to which he had left. He saw the girl looking in the direction he had gone. His footsteps made no sound in the deep grass, and he approached close without her being aware of his presence. Whitie lay on the ground near where she sat, and he manifested the usual actions of welcome, but the girl did not notice them. She seemed to be oblivious to everything near at hand. She made a pathetic figure drooping there, with her sunny hair contrasting so markedly with her white, wasted cheeks and her hands listlessly clasped and her little bare feet propped in the framework of the rude seat. Venters could have sworn and laughed in one breath at the idea of the connection between this girl and Oldring's Masked Rider. She was the victim of more than accident of fate—a victim to some deep plot the mystery of which burned him. As he stepped forward with a half-formed thought that she was absorbed in watching for his return, she turned her head and saw him. A swift start, a change rather than rush of blood under her white cheeks, a flashing of big eyes that fixed their glance upon him, transformed her face in that single instant of turning; and he knew she had been watching for him, that his return was the one thing in her mind. She did not smile; she did not flush; she did not look glad. All these would have meant little compared to her indefinite expression. Venters grasped the peculiar, vivid, vital something that leaped from her face. It was as if she had been in a dead, hopeless clamp of inaction and feeling, and had been suddenly shot through and through with quivering animation. Almost it was as if she had returned to life.

And Venters thought with lightning swiftness, "I've saved her—I've unlinked her from that old life—she was watching as if I were all she had left on earth—she belongs to me!" The thought was startlingly new. Like a blow it was in an unprepared moment. The cheery salutation he had ready for her died unborn, and he tumbled the pieces of pottery awkwardly on the grass, while some unfamiliar, deep-seated emotion, mixed with pity and glad assurance of his power to succor her, held him dumb.

"What a load you had!" she said. "Why, they're pots and crocks! Where did you get them?"

Venters laid down his rifle, and, filling one of the pots from his canteen, he placed it on the smoldering camp-fire.

"Hope it 'll hold water," he said, presently. "Why, there's an enormous cliff-dwelling just across here. I got the pottery there. Don't you think we needed something? That tin cup of mine has served to make tea, broth, soup—everything."

"I noticed we hadn't a great deal to cook in."

She laughed. It was the first time. He liked that laugh, and though he was tempted to look at her, he did not want to show his surprise or his pleasure.

"Will you take me over there, and all around in the valley—pretty soon when I'm well?" she added.

"Indeed I shall. It's a wonderful place. Rabbits so thick you can't step without kicking one out. And quail, beaver, foxes, wildcats. We're in a regular den. But—haven't you ever seen a cliff-dwelling?"

"No. I've heard about them, though. The—the men say the Pass is full of old houses and ruins."

"Why, I should think you'd have run across one in all your riding around," said Venters. He spoke slowly, choosing his words carefully, and he essayed a perfectly casual manner, and pretended to be busy assorting pieces of pottery. She must have no cause again to suffer shame for curiosity of his. Yet never in all his days had he been so eager to hear the details of any-one's life.

"When I rode—I rode like the wind," she replied, "and never had time to stop for anything."

"I remember that day I—I met you in the Pass—how dusty you were, how tired your horse looked. Were you always riding?"

"Oh, no. Sometimes not for months, when I was shut up in the cabin."

Venters tried to subdue a hot tingling.

"You were shut up, then?" he asked, carelessly.

"When Oldring went away on his long trips—he was gone for months sometimes—he shut me up in the cabin."

"What for?"

"Perhaps to keep me from running away. I always threatened that. Mostly, though, because the men got drunk at the villages. But they were always good to me. I wasn't afraid."

"A prisoner! That must have been hard on you?"

"I liked that. As long as I can remember I've been locked up there at times, and those times were the only happy ones I ever had. It's a big cabin, high up on a cliff, and I could look out. Then I had dogs and pets I had tamed, and books. There was a spring inside, and food stored, and the men brought me fresh meat. Once I was there one whole winter."

It now required deliberation on Venters's part to persist in his unconcern and to keep at work. He wanted to look at her, to volley questions at her.

"As long as you can remember—you've lived in Deception Pass?" he went on.

"I've a dim memory of some other place, and women and children; but I can't make anything of it. Sometimes I think till I'm weary."

"Then you can read—you have books?"

"Oh yes, I can read, and write, too, pretty well. Oldring is educated. He taught me, and years ago an old rustler lived with us, and he had been something different once. He was always teaching me."

"So Oldring takes long trips," mused Venters. "Do you know where he goes?"

"No. Every year he drives cattle north of Sterling—then does not return for months. I heard him accused once of living two lives—and he killed the man. That was at Stone Bridge."

Venters dropped his apparent task and looked up with an eagerness he no longer strove to hide.

"Bess," he said, using her name for the first time, "I suspected Oldring was something besides a rustler. Tell me, what's his purpose here in the Pass? I believe much that he has done was to hide his real work here."

"You're right. He's more than a rustler. In fact, as the men say, his rustling cattle is now only a bluff. There's gold in the cañons!"

"Ah!"

"Yes, there's gold, not in great quantities, but gold enough for him and his men. They wash for gold week in and week out. Then they drive a few cattle and go into the villages to drink and shoot and kill—to bluff the riders."

"Drive a few cattle! But, Bess, the Withersteen herd, the red herd—twenty-five hundred head! That's not a few. And I tracked them into a valley near here."

"Oldring never stole the red herd. He made a deal with Mormons. The riders were to be called in, and Oldring was to drive the herd and keep it till a certain time—I don't know when—then drive it back to the range. What his share was I didn't hear."

"Did you hear *why* that deal was made?" queried Venters.

"No. But it was a trick of Mormons. They're full of tricks. I've heard Oldring's men tell about Mormons. Maybe the Withersteen woman wasn't minding her halter! I saw the man who made the deal. He was a little, queer-shaped man, all humped up. He sat his horse well. I heard one of our men say afterward there was no better rider on the sage than this fellow. What was the name? I forget."

"Jerry Card?" suggested Venters.

"That's it. I remember—it's a name easy to remember—and Jerry Card appeared to be on fair terms with Oldring's men."

"I shouldn't wonder," replied Venters, thoughtfully. Verification of his suspicions in regard to Tull's underhand work—for the deal with Oldring made by Jerry Card assuredly had its inception in the Mormon Elder's brain, and had been accomplished through his orders—revived in Venters a memory of hatred that had been smothered by press of other emotions. Only a few days had elapsed since the hour of his encounter with Tull, yet they had been forgotten and now seemed far off, and the interval one that now appeared large and profound with incalculable change in his feelings. Hatred of Tull still existed in his heart; but it had lost its white heat. His affection for Jane Withersteen had not changed in the least; nevertheless, he seemed to view it from another angle and see it as another thing—what, he could not exactly define. The recalling of these two feelings was to Venters like getting glimpses into a self that was gone; and the wonder of them—perhaps the change which was too illusive for him—was the fact that a strange irritation accompanied the memory and a desire to dismiss it from mind. And straightway he did dismiss it, to return to thoughts of his significant present.

"Bess, tell me one more thing," he said. "Haven't you known any women—any young people?"

"Sometimes there were women with the men; but Oldring never let me know them. And all the young people I ever saw in my life was when I rode fast through the villages."

Perhaps that was the most puzzling and thought-provoking thing she had yet said to Venters. He pondered, more curious the more he learned, but he curbed his inquisitive desires, for he saw her shrinking on the verge of that shame, the causing of which had occasioned him such self-reproach. He would ask no more. Still he had to think, and he found it difficult to think clearly. This sad-eyed girl was so utterly different from what it would have been reason to believe such a remarkable life would have made her. On this day he had found her simple and frank, as natural as any girl he had ever known. About her there was something sweet. Her voice was low and well modulated. He could not look into her face, meet her steady, unabashed, yet wistful eyes, and think of her as the woman she had confessed herself. Oldring's Masked Rider sat before him, a girl dressed as a man. She had been made to ride at the head of infamous forays and drives. She had been imprisoned for many months of her life in an obscure cabin. At times the most vicious of men had been her companions; and the vilest of women, if they had not been permitted to approach her, had, at least, cast their shadows over her. But—but in spite of all this—there thundered at Venters some truth that lifted its voice higher than the clamoring facts of dishonor, some truth that was the very life of her beautiful eyes; and it was innocence.

In the days that followed, Venters balanced perpetually in mind this haunting conception of innocence over against the cold and sickening fact of an unintentional yet actual gift. How could it be possible for the two things to be true? He believed the latter to be true, and he would not relinquish his conviction of the former; and these conflicting thoughts augmented the mystery that appeared to be a part of Bess. In those ensuing days, however, it became clear as clearest light that Bess was rapidly regaining strength; that, unless reminded of her long association with Oldring, she seemed to have forgotten it; that, like an Indian who lives solely from moment to moment, she was utterly absorbed in the present.

Day by day Venters watched the white of her face slowly change to brown, and the wasted cheeks fill out by imperceptible degrees. There came a time when he could just trace the line of demarcation between the part of her face once hidden by a mask and that left exposed to wind and sun. When that line disappeared in clear bronze tan it was as if she had been washed clean of the stigma of Oldring's Masked Rider. The suggestion of the mask always made Venters remember; now that it was gone he seldom thought of her past. Occasionally he tried to piece together the several stages of strange experience and to make a whole. He had shot a masked outlaw the very sight of whom had been ill omen to riders; he had carried off a wounded woman whose bloody lips quivered in prayer; he had nursed what seemed a frail, shrunken boy; and now he watched a girl whose face had become strangely sweet, whose dark-blue eyes were ever upon him without boldness, without shyness, but with a steady, grave, and growing light. Many times Venters found the clear gaze embarrassing to him, yet, like wine, it had an exhilarating effect. What did she think when she looked at him so? Almost he believed she had no thought at all. All about her and the present there in Surprise Valley, and the dim yet subtly impending future, fascinated Venters and made him thoughtful as all his lonely vigils in the sage had not.

Chiefly it was the present that he wished to dwell upon; but it was the call of the future which stirred him to action. No idea had he of what that future had in store for Bess and him. He began to think of improving Surprise Valley as a place to live in, for there was no telling how long they would be compelled to stay there. Venters stubbornly resisted the entering into his mind of an insistent thought that, clearly realized, might have made it plain to him that he did not want to leave Surprise Valley at all. But it was imperative that he consider practical matters; and whether or not he was destined to stay long there, he felt the immediate need of a change of diet. It would be necessary for him to go farther afield for a variety of meat, and also that he soon visit Cottonwoods for a supply of food.

It occurred again to Venters that he could go to the cañon where Oldring kept his cattle, and at little risk he could pack out some beef. He wished to do this, however, without letting Bess know of it till after he had made the trip. Presently he hit upon the plan of going while she was asleep.

That very night he stole out of camp, climbed up under the stone bridge, and entered the outlet to the Pass. The gorge was full of luminous gloom. Balancing Rock loomed dark and leaned over the pale descent. Transformed in the shadowy light, it took shape and dimensions of a spectral god waiting—waiting for the moment to hurl himself down upon the tottering walls and close forever the outlet to Deception Pass. At night more than by day Venters felt something fearful and fateful in that rock, and that it had leaned and waited through a thousand years to have somehow to deal with his destiny.

"Old man, if you must roll, wait till I get back to the girl, and then roll!" he said, aloud, as if the stones were indeed a god.

And those spoken words, in their grim note to his ear, as well as contents to his mind, told Venters that he was all but drifting on a current which he had not power nor wish to stem.

Venters exercised his usual care in the matter of hiding tracks from the outlet, yet it took him scarcely an hour to reach Oldring's cattle. Here sight of many calves changed his original intention, and instead of packing out meat he decided to take a calf out alive. He roped one, securely tied its feet, and swung it up over his shoulder. Here was an exceedingly heavy burden, but Venters was powerful—he could take up a sack of grain and with ease pitch it over a pack-saddle—and he made long distance without resting. The hardest work came in the climb up to the outlet and on through to the valley. When he had accomplished it, he became fired with another idea that again changed his intention. He would not kill the calf, but keep it alive. He would go back to Oldring's herd and pack out more calves. Thereupon he secured the calf in the best available spot for the moment and turned to make a second trip.

When Venters got back to the valley with another calf, it was close upon daybreak. He crawled into his cave and slept late. Bess had no inkling that he had been absent from camp nearly all night, and only remarked solicitously that he appeared to be more tired than usual, and more in the need of sleep. In the afternoon Venters built a gate across a small ravine near camp, and here corralled the calves; and he succeeded in completing his task without Bess being any the wiser.

That night he made two more trips to Oldring's range, and again on the following night, and yet another on the next. With eight calves in his corral, he concluded that he had enough; but it dawned upon him then that he did not want to kill one. "I've rustled Oldring's cattle," he said, and laughed. He noted then that all the calves were red. "Red!" he exclaimed. "From the red herd. I've stolen Jane Withersteen's cattle! . . . That's about the strangest thing yet."

One more trip he undertook to Oldring's valley, and this time he roped a yearling steer and killed it and cut out a small quarter of beef. The howling of coyotes told him he need have no apprehension that the work of his knife would be discovered. He packed the beef back to camp and hung it upon a spruce-tree. Then he sought his bed.

On the morrow he was up bright and early, glad that he had a surprise for Bess. He could hardly wait for her to come out. Presently she appeared and walked under the spruce. Then she approached the camp-fire. There was a tinge of healthy red in the bronze of her cheeks, and her slender form had begun to round out in graceful lines.

"Bess, didn't you say you were tired of rabbit?" inquired Venters. "And quail and beaver?"

"Indeed I did."

"What would you like?"

"I'm tired of meat, but if we have to live on it I'd like some beef."

"Well, how does that strike you?" Venters pointed to the quarter hanging from the spruce-tree. "We'll have fresh beef for a few days, then we'll cut the rest into strips and dry it."

"Where did you get that?" asked Bess, slowly.

"I stole that from Oldring."

"You went back to the cañon—you risked—" While she hesitated the tinge of bloom faded out of her cheeks.

"It wasn't any risk, but it was hard work."

"I'm sorry I said I was tired of rabbit. Why! How—When did you get that beef?"

"Last night."

"While I was asleep?"

"Yes."

"I woke last night sometime—but I didn't know."

Her eyes were widening, darkening with thought, and whenever they did so the steady, watchful, seeing gaze gave place to the wistful light. In the former she saw as the primitive woman without thought; in the latter she looked inward, and her gaze was the reflection of a troubled mind. For long Venters had not seen that dark change, that deepening of blue, which he thought was beautiful and sad. But now he wanted to make her think.

"I've done more than pack in that beef," he said. "For five nights I've been working while you slept. I've got eight calves corralled near a ravine. Eight calves, all alive and doing fine!"

"You went five nights!"

All that Venters could make of the dilation of her eyes, her slow pallor, and her exclamation, was fear—fear for herself or for him.

"Yes. I didn't tell you, because I knew you were afraid to be left alone."

"Alone?" She echoed his word, but the meaning of it was nothing to her. She had not even thought of being left alone. It was not, then, fear for herself, but for him. This girl, always slow of speech and action, now seemed almost stupid. She put forth a hand that might have indicated the groping of her mind. Suddenly she stepped swiftly to him, with a look and touch that drove from him any doubt of her quick intelligence or feeling.

"Oldring has men watch the herds—they would kill you. You must never go again!"

When she had spoken, the strength and the blaze of her died, and she swayed toward Venters.

"*Bess, I'll not go again,*" he said, catching her.

She leaned against him, and her body was limp and vibrated to a long, wavering tremble. Her face was upturned to his. Woman's face, woman's eyes, woman's lips—all acutely and blindly and sweetly and terribly truthful in their betrayal! But as her fear was instinctive, so was her clinging to this one and only friend.

Venters gently put her from him and steadied her upon her feet; and all the while his blood raced wild, and a thrilling tingle unsteadied his nerve, and something—that he had seen and felt in her—that he could

"BESS, I'LL NOT GO AGAIN"

not understand—seemed very close to him, warm and rich as a fragrant breath, sweet as nothing had ever before been sweet to him.

With all his will Venters strove for calmness and thought and judgment unbiased by pity, and reality unswayed by sentiment. Bess's eyes were still fixed upon him with all her soul bright in that wistful light. Swiftly, resolutely he put out of mind all of her life except what had been spent with him. He scorned himself for the intelligence that made him still doubt. He meant to judge her as she had judged him. He was face to face with the inevitableness of life itself. He saw destiny in the dark, straight path of her wonderful eyes. Here was the simplicity, the sweetness of a girl contending with new and strange and enthralling emotions; here the living truth of innocence; here the blind terror of a woman confronted with the thought of death to her savior and protector. All this Venters saw, but, besides, there was in Bess's eyes a slow-dawning consciousness that seemed about to break out in glorious radiance.

"Bess, are you thinking?" he asked.

"Yes—oh yes!"

"Do you realize we are here alone—man and woman?"

"Yes."

"Have you thought that we may make our way out to civilization, or we may have to stay here—alone—hidden from the world all our lives?"

"I never thought—till now."

"Well, what's your choice—to go—or to stay here—alone with me?"

"Stay!" New-born thought of self, ringing vibrantly in her voice, gave her answer singular power.

Venters trembled, and then swiftly turned his gaze from her face—from her eyes. He knew what she had only half divined—that she loved him.

CHAPTER XI

FAITH AND UNFAITH

AT Jane Withersteen's home the promise made to Mrs. Larkin to care for little Fay had begun to be fulfilled. Like a gleam of sunlight through the cottonwoods was the coming of the child to the gloomy house of Withersteen. The big, silent halls echoed with childish laughter. In the shady court, where Jane spent many of the hot July days, Fay's tiny feet pattered over the stone flags and splashed in the amber stream. She prattled incessantly. What difference, Jane thought, a child made in her home! It had never been a real home, she discovered. Even the tidiness and neatness she had so observed, and upon which she had insisted to her women, became, in the light of Fay's smile, habits that now lost their importance. Fay littered the court with Jane's books and papers, and other toys her fancy improvised, and many a strange craft went floating down the little brook.

And it was owing to Fay's presence that Jane Withersteen came to see more of Lassiter. The rider had for the most part kept to the sage. He rode for her, but he did not seek her except on business; and Jane had to acknowledge in pique that her overtures had been made in vain. Fay, however, captured Lassiter the moment he first laid eyes on her.

Jane was present at the meeting, and there was something about it which dimmed her sight and softened her toward this foe of her people. The rider had clanked into the court, a tired yet wary man, always looking for the attack upon him that was inevitable and might come from any quarter; and he had walked right upon little Fay. The child had been beautiful even in her rags and amid the surroundings of the hovel in the sage, but now, in a pretty white dress, with her shining curls brushed and her face clean and rosy, she was lovely. She left her play and looked up at Lassiter.

If there was not an instinct for all three of them in that meeting, an unreasoning tendency toward a closer intimacy, then Jane Withersteen believed she had been subject to a queer fancy. She imagined any child would have feared Lassiter. And Fay Larkin had been a lonely, a solitary elf of the sage, not at all an ordinary child, and exquisitely shy with strangers. She watched Lassiter with great, round, grave eyes, but showed no fear. The rider gave Jane a favorable report of cattle and horses; and as he took the seat to which she invited him, little Fay edged as much as half an inch nearer. Jane replied to his look of inquiry and told Fay's story. The rider's gray, earnest gaze troubled her. Then he turned to Fay and smiled in a way that made Jane doubt her sense of the true relation of things. How could Lassiter smile so at a child when he had made so many children fatherless? But he did smile, and to the gentleness she had seen a few times he added something that was infinitely sad and sweet. Jane's intuition told her that Lassiter had never been a father; but if life ever so blessed him he would be a good one. Fay, also, must have found that smile singularly winning. For she edged closer and closer, and then, by way of feminine capitulation, went to Jane, from whose side she bent a beautiful glance upon the rider.

Lassiter only smiled at her.

Jane watched them, and realized that now was the moment she should seize, if she was ever to win this man from his hatred. But the step was not easy to take. The more she saw of Lassiter the more she respected him, and the greater her respect the harder it became to lend herself to mere coquetry. Yet as she thought of her great motive, of Tull, and of that other whose name she had schooled herself never to think of in connection with Milly Erne's avenger, she suddenly found she had no choice. And her creed gave her boldness far beyond the limit to which vanity would have led her.

"Lassiter, I see so little of you now," she said, and was conscious of heat in her cheeks.

"I've been ridin' hard," he replied.

"But you can't live in the saddle. You come in sometimes. Won't you come here to see me—oftener?"

"Is that an order?"

"Nonsense! I simply ask you to come to see me when you find time."

"Why?"

The query once heard was not so embarrassing to Jane as she might have imagined. Moreover, it established in her mind a fact that there existed actually other than selfish reasons for her wanting to see him. And as she had been bold, so she determined to be both honest and brave.

"I've reasons—only one of which I need mention," she answered. "If it's possible I want to change you toward my people. And on the moment I can conceive of little I wouldn't do to gain that end."

How much better and freer Jane felt after that confession! She meant to show him that there was one Mormon who could play a game or wage a fight in the open.

"I reckon," said Lassiter, and he laughed.

It was the best in her, if the most irritating, that Lassiter always aroused.

"Will you come?" She looked into his eyes, and for the life of her could not quite subdue an imperiousness that rose with her spirit. "I never asked so much of any man—except Bern Venters."

"'Pears to me that you'd run no risk, or Venters, either. But mebbe that doesn't hold good for me."

"You mean it wouldn't be safe for you to be often here? You look for ambush in the cottonwoods?"

"Not that so much."

At this juncture little Fay sidled over to Lassiter.

"Has oo a little dirl?" she inquired.

"No, lassie," replied the rider.

Whatever Fay seemed to be searching for in Lassiter's sun-reddened face and quiet eyes she evidently found. "Oo tan tum to see me," she added, and with that, shyness gave place to friendly curiosity. First his sombrero with its leather band and silver ornaments commanded her attention; next his quirt, and then the clinking, silver spurs. These held her for some time, but presently, true to childish fickleness, she left off playing with them to look for something else. She laughed in glee as she ran her little hands down the slippery, shiny surface of Lassiter's leather chaps. Soon she discovered one of the hanging gun-sheaths, and she dragged it up and began tugging at the huge black handle of the gun. Jane Withersteen repressed an exclamation. What significance there was to her in the little girl's efforts to dislodge that heavy weapon! Jane Withersteen saw Fay's play and her beauty and her love as most powerful allies to her own woman's part in a game that suddenly had acquired a strange zest and a hint of danger. And as for the rider, he appeared to have forgotten Jane in the wonder of this lovely child playing about him. At first he was much the shyer of the two. Gradually her confidence overcame his backwardness, and he had the temerity to stroke her golden curls with a great hand. Fay rewarded his boldness with a smile, and when he had gone to the extreme of closing that great hand over her little brown one, she said, simply, "I like oo!"

Sight of his face then made Jane oblivious for the

time to his character as a hater of Mormons. Out of the mother longing that swelled her breast she divined the child hunger in Lassiter.

He returned the next day, and the next; and upon the following he came both at morning and at night. Upon the evening of this fourth day Jane seemed to feel the breaking of a brooding struggle in Lassiter. During all these visits he had scarcely a word to say, though he watched her and played absent-mindedly with Fay. Jane had contented herself with silence. Soon little Fay substituted for the expression of regard, "I like oo," a warmer and more generous one, "I love oo."

Thereafter Lassiter came oftener to see Jane and her little protégée. Daily he grew more gentle and kind, and gradually developed a quaintly merry mood. In the morning he lifted Fay upon his horse and let her ride as he walked beside her to the edge of the sage. In the evening he played with the child at an infinite variety of games she invented, and then, oftener than not, he accepted Jane's invitation to supper. No other visitor came to Withersteen House during those days. So that in spite of watchfulness he never forgot, Lassiter began to show he felt at home there. After the meal they walked into the grove of cottonwoods or up by the lakes, and little Fay held Lassiter's hand as much as she held Jane's. Thus a strange relationship was established, and Jane liked it. At twilight they always returned to the house, where Fay kissed them and went in to her mother. Lassiter and Jane were left alone.

Then, if there were anything that a good woman could do to win a man and still preserve her self-respect, it was something which escaped the natural subtlety of a woman determined to allure. Jane's vanity, that after all was not great, was soon satisfied with Lassiter's silent admiration. And her honest desire to lead him from his dark, blood-stained path would never have blinded her to what she owed herself. But the driving passion of her religion, and its call to save Mormons' lives, one life in particular, bore Jane Withersteen close to an infringement of her womanhood. In the beginning she had reasoned that her appeal to Lassiter must be through the senses. With whatever means she possessed in the way of adornment she enhanced her beauty. And she stooped to artifices that she knew were unworthy of her, but which she deliberately chose to employ. She made of herself a girl in every variable mood wherein a girl might be desirable. In those moods she was not above the methods of an inexperienced though natural flirt. She kept close to him whenever opportunity afforded; and she was forever playfully, yet passionately underneath the surface, fighting him for possession of the great black guns. These he would never yield to her. And so in that manner their hands were often and long in contact. The more of simplicity that she sensed in him the greater the advantage she took.

She had a trick of changing—and it was not altogether voluntary—from this gay, thoughtless, girlish coquettishness to the silence and the brooding, burning mystery of a woman's mood. The strength and passion and fire of her were in her eyes, and she so used them that Lassiter had to see this depth in her, this haunting promise more fitted to her years than to the flaunting guise of a wilful girl.

The July days flew by. Jane reasoned that if it were possible for her to be happy during such a time, then she was happy. Little Fay completely filled a long aching void in her heart. In fettering the hands of this Lassiter she was accomplishing the greatest good of her life, and to do good even in a small way rendered happiness to Jane Withersteen. She had attended the regular Sunday services of her church; otherwise she had not gone to the village for weeks. It was unusual that none of her churchmen or friends had called upon her of late; but it was neglect for which she was glad. Judkins and his boy riders had experienced no difficulty in driving the white herd. So these warm July days were free of worry, and soon Jane hoped she had passed the crisis; and for her to hope was presently to trust, and then to believe. She thought often of Venters, but in a dreamy, abstract way. She spent hours teaching and playing with little Fay. And the activity of her mind centered around Lassiter. The direction she had given her will seemed to blunt any branching off of thought from that straight line. The mood came to obsess her.

In the end, when her awakening came, she learned that she had builded better than she knew. Lassiter, though kinder and gentler than ever, had parted with his quaint humor and his coldness and his tranquillity to become a restless and unhappy man. Whatever the power of his deadly intent toward Mormons, that passion now had a rival, and one equally burning and consuming. Jane Withersteen had one moment of exultation before the dawn of a strange uneasiness. What if she had made of herself a lure, at tremendous cost to him and to her, and all in vain!

That night in the moonlit grove she summoned all her courage and, turning suddenly in the path, she faced Lassiter and leaned close to him, so that she touched him and her eyes looked up to his.

"Lassiter! . . . Will you do anything for me?"

In the moonlight she saw his dark, worn face change, and by that change she seemed to feel him immovable as a wall of stone.

Jane slipped her hands down to the swinging gun-sheaths, and when she had locked her fingers around the huge, cold handles of the guns, she trembled as with a chilling ripple over all her body.

"May I take your guns?"

"Why?" he asked, and for the first time to her his voice carried a harsh note. Jane felt his hard, strong hands close round her wrists. It was not wholly with intent that she leaned toward him, for the look of his eyes and the feel of his hands made her weak.

"It's no trifle—no woman's whim—it's deep—as my heart. Let me take them?"

"Why?"

"I want to keep you from killing more men—Mormons. You must let me save you from more wickedness—more wanton bloodshed—" Then the truth forced itself falteringly from her lips. "You must—let—me—help me to keep my vow to Milly Erne. I swore to her—as she lay dying—that if ever any one came here to avenge her—I swore I would stay his hand. Perhaps I—I alone can save the—the man who—who—Oh, Lassiter! . . . I feel that if I can't change you—then soon you'll go out to kill—and you'll kill by instinct—and among the Mormons you kill will be the one—who . . . Lassiter, if you care a little for me—let me—for my sake—let me take your guns!"

As if her hands had been those of a child, he unclasped their clinging grip from the handles of his guns, and, pushing her away, he turned his gray face to her in one look of terrible realization and then strode off into the shadows of the cottonwoods.

When the first shock of her futile appeal to Lassiter had passed, Jane took his cold, silent condemnation and abrupt departure not so much as a refusal to her entreaty as a hurt and stunned bitterness for her attempt at his betrayal. Upon further thought and slow consideration of Lassiter's past actions, she believed he would return and forgive her. The man could not be hard to a woman, and she doubted that he could stay away from her. But at the point where she had hoped to find him vulnerable she now began to fear he was proof against all persuasion. The iron and stone quality that she had early suspected in him had actually cropped out as an impregnable barrier. Nevertheless, if Lassiter remained in Cottonwoods she would never give up her hope and desire to change him. She would change him if she had to sacrifice everything dear to her except hope of heaven. Passionately devoted as she was to her religion, she had yet refused to marry a Mormon. But a situation had developed wherein self paled in the great white light of religious duty of the highest order. That was the leading motive, the divinely spiritual one; but there were other motives, which, like tentacles, aided in drawing her will to the acceptance of a possible abnegation. And through the watches of that sleepless night Jane Withersteen, in fear and sorrow and doubt, came finally to believe that if she must throw herself into Lassiter's arms to make him abide by "Thou shalt not kill!" she would yet do well.

In the morning she expected Lassiter at the usual hour, but she was not able to go at once to the court, so she sent little Fay. Mrs. Larkin was ill and required attention. It appeared that the mother, from the time of her arrival at Withersteen House, had relaxed and was slowly losing her hold on life. Jane had believed that absence of worry and responsibility coupled with good nursing and comfort would mend Mrs. Larkin's broken health. Such, however, was not the case.

When Jane did get out to the court, Fay was there alone, and at the moment embarking on a dubious voyage down the stone-lined amber stream upon a craft of two brooms and a pillow. Fay was as delightfully wet as she could possibly wish to get.

Clatter of hoofs distracted Fay and interrupted the scolding she was gleefully receiving from Jane. The sound was not the light-spirited trot that Bells made when Lassiter rode him into the outer court. This was slower and heavier, and Jane did not recognize in it any of her other horses. The appearance of Bishop

Dyer startled Jane. He dismounted with his rapid, jerky motion, flung the bridle, and, as he turned toward the inner court and stalked up on the stone flags, his boots rang. In his authoritative front, and in the red anger unmistakably flaming in his face, he reminded Jane of her father.

"Is that the Larkin pauper?" he asked, bruskly, without any greeting to Jane.

"It's Mrs. Larkin's little girl," replied Jane, slowly.

"I hear you intend to raise the child?"

"Yes."

"Of course you mean to give her Mormon bringing-up?"

"No!"

His questions had been swift. She was amazed at a feeling that some one else was replying for her.

"I've come to say a few things to you." He stopped to measure her with stern, speculative eye.

Jane Withersteen loved this man. From earliest childhood she had been taught to revere and love bishops of her church. And for ten years Bishop Dyer had been the closest friend and counselor of her father, and for the greater part of that period her own friend and Scriptural teacher. Her interpretation of her creed and her religious activity in fidelity to it, her acceptance of mysterious and holy Mormon truths, were all invested in this Bishop. Bishop Dyer as an entity was next to God. He was God's mouthpiece to the little Mormon community at Cottonwoods. God revealed himself in secret to this mortal.

And Jane Withersteen suddenly suffered a paralyzing affront to her consciousness of reverence by some strange, irresistible twist of thought wherein she saw this Bishop as a man. And the train of thought hurdled the rising, crying protests of that other self whose poise she had lost. It was not her Bishop who eyed her in curious measurement. It was a man who tramped into her presence without removing his hat, who had no greeting for her, who had no semblance of courtesy. In looks, as in action, he made her think of a bull stamping cross-grained into a corral. She had heard of Bishop Dyer forgetting the minister in the fury of a common man, and now she was to feel it. The glance by which she measured him in turn momentarily veiled the divine in the ordinary. He looked a rancher; he was booted, spurred, and covered with dust; he carried a gun at his hip, and she remembered that he had been known to use it. But during the long moment while he watched her there was nothing commonplace in the slow-gathering might of his wrath.

"Brother Tull has talked to me," he began. "It was your father's wish that you marry Tull, and my order. You refused him?"

"Yes."

"You would not give up your friendship with that tramp Venters?"

"No."

"But you'll do as *I* order!" he thundered. "Why, Jane Withersteen, you are in danger of becoming a heretic! You can thank your Gentile friends for that. You face the damning of your soul to perdition."

In the flux and reflux of the whirling torture of Jane's mind, that new, daring spirit of hers vanished in the old habitual order of her life. She was a Mormon, and the Bishop regained ascendance.

"It's well I got you in time, Jane Withersteen. What would your father have said to these goings-on of yours? He would have put you in a stone cage on bread and water. He would have taught you something about Mormonism. Remember, you're a *born* Mormon. There have been Mormons who turned heretic—damn their souls!—but no born Mormon ever left us yet. Ah, I see your shame. Your faith is not shaken. You are only a wild girl." The Bishop's tone softened. "Well, it's enough that I got to you in time. . . . Now tell me about this Lassiter. I hear strange things."

"What do you wish to know?" queried Jane.

"About this man. You hired him?"

"Yes, he's riding for me. When my riders left me I had to have any one I could get."

"Is it true what I hear—that he's a gun-man, a Mormon-hater, steeped in blood?"

"True—terribly true, I fear."

"But what's he doing here in Cottonwoods? This place isn't notorious enough for such a man. Sterling and the villages north, where there's universal gun-packing and fights every day—where there are more men like him, it seems to me they would attract him most. We're only a wild, lonely border settlement. It's only recently that the rustlers have made killings here. Nor have there been saloons till lately, nor the drifting in of outcasts. Has not this gun-man some special mission here?"

Jane maintained silence.

"Tell me," ordered Bishop Dyer, sharply.

"Yes," she replied.

"Do you know what it is?"

"Yes."

"Tell me that."

"Bishop Dyer, I don't want to tell."

He waved his hand in an imperative gesture of command. The red once more leaped to his face, and in his steel-blue eyes glinted a pin-point of curiosity.

"That first day," whispered Jane, "Lassiter said he came here to find—Milly Erne's grave!"

With downcast eyes Jane watched the swift flow of the amber water. She saw it and tried to think of it, of the stones, of the ferns; but, like her body, her mind was in a leaden vise. Only the Bishop's voice could release her. Seemingly there was silence of longer duration than all her former life.

"For what—else?" When Bishop Dyer's voice did cleave the silence it was high, curiously shrill, and on the point of breaking. It released Jane's tongue, but she could not lift her eyes.

"To kill the man who persuaded Milly Erne to abandon her home and her husband—and her God!"

With wonderful distinctness Jane Withersteen heard her own clear voice. She heard the water murmur at her feet and flow on to the sea; she heard the rushing of all the waters in the world. They filled her ears with low, unreal murmurings—these sounds that deadened her brain and yet could not break the long and terrible silence. Then, from somewhere—from an immeasurable distance—came a slow, guarded, clinking, clanking step. Into her it shot electrifying life. It released the weight upon her numbed eyelids. Lifting her eyes she saw—ashen, shaken, stricken—not the Bishop but the man! And beyond him, from round the corner came that soft, silvery step. A long black boot with a gleaming spur swept into sight—and then Lassiter! Bishop Dyer did not see, did not hear: he stared at Jane in the throes of sudden revelation.

"Ah, I understand!" he cried, in hoarse accents. "That's why you made love to this Lassiter—to bind his hands!"

It was Jane's gaze riveted upon the rider that made Bishop Dyer turn. Then clear sight failed her. Dizzily, in a blur, she saw the Bishop's hand jerk to his hip. She saw gleam of blue and spout of red. In her ears burst a thundering report. The court floated in darkening circles around her, and she fell into utter blackness.

The darkness lightened, turned to slow-drifting haze, and lifted. Through a thin film of blue smoke she saw the rough-hewn timbers of the court roof. A cool, damp touch moved across her brow. She smelled powder, and it was that which galvanized her suspended thought. She moved, to see that she lay prone upon

IT WAS JANE'S GAZE RIVETED UPON THE RIDER THAT MADE BISHOP DYER TURN

the stone flags with her head on Lassiter's knee, and he was bathing her brow with water from the stream. The same swift glance, shifting low, brought into range of her sight a smoking gun and splashes of blood.

"*Ah-h!*" she moaned, and was drifting, sinking again into darkness, when Lassiter's voice arrested her.

"It's all right, Jane. It's all right."

"Did—you—kill—him?" she whispered.

"Who? That fat party who was here? No. I didn't kill him."

"Oh! . . . Lassiter!"

"Say! It was queer for you to faint. I thought you were such a strong woman, not faintish like that. You're all right now—only some pale. I thought you'd never come to. But I'm awkward round women folks. I couldn't think of anythin'."

"Lassiter! . . . the gun there! . . . the blood!"

"So that's troublin' you. I reckon it needn't. You see it was this way. I come round the house an' seen that fat party an' heard him talkin' loud. Then he seen me, an' very impolite goes straight for his gun. He oughtn't have tried to throw a gun on me—whatever his reason was. For that's meetin' me on my own grounds. I've seen runnin' molasses that was quicker 'n him. Now I didn't know who he was, visitor or friend or relation of yours, though I seen he was a Mormon all over, an' I couldn't get serious about shootin'. So I winged him—put a bullet through his arm as he was pullin' at his gun. An' he dropped the gun there, an' a little blood. I told him he'd introduced himself sufficient, an' to please move out of my vicinity. An' he went."

Lassiter spoke with slow, cool, soothing voice, in which there was a hint of levity, and his touch, as he continued to bathe her brow, was gentle and steady. His impassive face, and the kind, gray eyes, further stilled her agitation.

"He drew on you first, and you deliberately shot to cripple him—you wouldn't kill him—you—*Lassiter?*"

"That's about the size of it."

Jane kissed his hand.

All that was calm and cool about Lassiter instantly vanished.

"Don't do that! I won't stand it! An' I don't care a d——n who that fat party was."

He helped Jane to her feet and to a chair. Then with the wet scarf he had used to bathe her face he wiped the blood from the stone flags and, picking up the gun, he threw it upon a couch. With that he began to pace the court, and his silver spurs jangled musically, and the great gun-sheaths softly brushed against his leather chaps.

"So—it's true—what I heard him say?" Lassiter asked, presently halting before her. "You made love to me—to bind my hands?"

"Yes," confessed Jane. It took all her woman's courage to meet the gray storm of his glance.

"All these days that you've been so friendly an' like a pardner—all these evenin's that have been so bewilderin' to me—your beauty—an'—an' the way you looked an' came close to me—they were woman's tricks to bind my hands?"

"Yes."

"An' your sweetness that seemed so natural, an' your throwin' little Fay an' me so much together—to make me love the child—all that was for the same reason?"

"Yes."

Lassiter flung his arms—a strange gesture for him.

"Mebbe it wasn't much in your Mormon thinkin', for you to play that game. But to ring the child in—that was hellish!"

Jane's passionate, unheeding zeal began to loom darkly.

"Lassiter, whatever my intention in the beginning,

Fay loves you dearly—and I—I've grown to—to like you."

"That's powerful kind of you, now," he said. Sarcasm and scorn made his voice that of a stranger. "An' you sit there an' look me straight in the eyes! You're a wonderful strange woman, Jane Withersteen."

"I'm not ashamed, Lassiter. I told you I'd try to change you."

"Would you mind tellin' me just what you tried?"

"I tried to make you see beauty in me and be softened by it. I wanted you to care for me so that I could influence you. It wasn't easy. At first you were stone-blind. Then I hoped you'd love little Fay, and through that come to feel the horror of making children fatherless."

"Jane Withersteen, either you're a fool or noble beyond my understandin'. Mebbe you're both. I know you're blind. What you meant is one thing—what you *did* was to make me love you."

"Lassiter!"

"I reckon I'm a human bein', though I never loved any one but my sister, Milly Erne. That was long—"

"Oh, are you Milly's brother?"

"Yes, I was, an' I loved her. There never was any one but her in my life till now. Didn't I tell you that long ago I back-trailed myself from women? I was a Texas ranger till—till Milly left home, an' then I became somethin' else—Lassiter! For years I've been a lonely man set on one thing. I came here an' met you. An' now I'm not the man I was. The change was gradual, an' I took no notice of it. I understand now that never-satisfied longin' to see you, listen to you, watch you, feel you near me. It's plain now why you were never out of my thoughts. I've had no thoughts but of you. I've lived an' breathed for you. An' now when I know what it means—what you've done—I'm burnin' up with hell's fire!"

"Oh, Lassiter—no—no—you don t love me that way!" Jane cried.

"If that's what love is, then I do."

"Forgive me! I didn't mean to make you love me like that. Oh, what a tangle of our lives! You—Milly Erne's brother! And I—heedless, mad to melt your heart toward Mormons. Lassiter, I may be wicked, but not wicked enough to hate. If I couldn't hate Tull, could I hate you?"

"After all, Jane, mebbe you're only blind—Mormon blind. That only can explain what's close to selfishness—"

"I'm not selfish. I despise the very word. If I were free—"

"But you're not free. Not free of Mormonism. An' in playin' this game with me you've been unfaithful."

"Un-faithful!" faltered Jane.

"Yes, I said unfaithful. You're faithful to your Bishop an' unfaithful to yourself. You're false to your womanhood an' true to your religion. But for a savin' innocence you'd have made yourself low an' vile—betrayin' yourself, betrayin' me—all to bind my hands an' keep me from snuffiin' out Mormon life. It's your damned Mormon blindness."

"Is it vile—is it blind—is it only Mormonism to save human life? No, Lassiter, that's God's law, divine, universal for all Christians."

"The blindness I mean is blindness that keeps you from seein' the truth. I've known many good Mormons. But some are blacker than hell. You won't see that even when you know it. Else, why all this blind passion to save the life of that—that. . . ."

Jane shut out the light, and the hands she held over her eyes trembled and quivered against her face.

"Blind—yes, an' let me make it clear an' simple to you," Lassiter went on, his voice losing its tone of anger. "Take, for instance, that idea of yours last night when you wanted my guns. It was good an' beautiful, an' showed your heart—but—why, Jane, it was crazy. Mind I'm assumin' that life to me is as sweet as to any other man. An' to preserve that life is each man's first an' closest thought. Where would any man be on this border without guns? Where, especially, would Lassiter be? Well, I'd be under the sage with thousands of other men now livin' an' sure better men than me. Gun-packin' in the West since the Civil War has growed into a kind of moral law. An' out here on this border it's the difference between a man an' somethin' not a man. Look what your takin' Venters's guns from him all but made him! Why, your churchmen carry guns. Tull has killed a man an' drawed on others. Your Bishop has shot a half dozen men, an' it wasn't through prayers of his that they recovered. An' to-day he'd have shot me if he'd been quick enough on the draw. Could I walk or ride down into Cottonwoods without my guns? This is a wild time, Jane Withersteen, this year of our Lord eighteen seventy-one."

"No time—for a woman!" exclaimed Jane, brokenly. "Oh, Lassiter, I feel helpless—lost—and don't know where to turn. If I *am* blind—then—I need some one —a friend—you, Lassiter—more than ever!"

"Well, I didn't say nothin' about goin' back on you, did I?"

CHAPTER XII

THE INVISIBLE HAND

JANE received a letter from Bishop Dyer, not in his own handwriting, which stated that the abrupt termination of their interview had left him in some doubt as to her future conduct. A slight injury had incapacitated him from seeking another meeting at present, the letter went on to say, and ended with a request which was virtually a command, that she call upon him at once.

The reading of the letter acquainted Jane Withersteen with the fact that something within her had all but changed. She sent no reply to Bishop Dyer nor did she go to see him. On Sunday she remained absent from the service—for the second time in years—and though she did not actually suffer there was a dead-lock of feelings deep within her, and the waiting for a balance to fall on either side was almost as bad as suffering. She had a gloomy expectancy of untoward circumstances, and with it a keen-edged curiosity to watch developments. She had a half-formed conviction that her future conduct—as related to her churchmen—was beyond her control and would be governed by their attitude toward her. Something was changing in her, forming, waiting for decision to make it a real and fixed thing. She had told Lassiter that she felt helpless and lost in the fateful tangle of their lives; and now she feared that she was approaching the same chaotic condition of mind in regard to her religion. It appalled her to find that she questioned phases of that religion. Absolute faith had been her serenity. Though leaving her faith unshaken, her serenity had been disturbed, and now it was broken by open war between her and her ministers. That something within her—a whisper—which she had tried in vain to hush had become a ringing voice, and it called to her to wait. She had transgressed no laws of God. Her churchmen, however invested with the power and the glory of a wonderful creed, however they sat in inexorable judgment of her, must now practice toward her the simple, common, Christian virtue they professed to preach, "Do unto others as you would have others do unto you!"

Jane Withersteen, waiting in darkness of mind, remained faithful still. But it was darkness that must soon be pierced by light. If her faith were justified, if her churchmen were trying only to intimidate her, the fact would soon be manifest, as would their failure, and then she would redouble her zeal toward them and toward what had been the best work of her life—work for the welfare and happiness of those among whom she lived, Mormon and Gentile alike. If that secret, intangible power closed its toils round her again, if that great invisible hand moved here and there and everywhere, slowly paralyzing her with its mystery and its inconceivable sway over her affairs, then she would know beyond doubt that it was not chance, nor jealousy, nor intimidation, nor ministerial wrath at her revolt, but a cold and calculating policy thought out long before she was born, a dark, immutable will of whose empire she and all that was hers was but an atom.

Then might come her ruin. Then might come her fall into black storm. Yet she would rise again, and to the light. God would be merciful to a driven woman who had lost her way.

A week passed. Little Fay played and prattled and pulled at Lassiter's big black guns. The rider came to

Withersteen House oftener than ever. Jane saw a change in him, though it did not relate to his kindness and gentleness. He was quieter and more thoughtful. While playing with Fay or conversing with Jane he seemed to be possessed of another self that watched with cool, roving eyes, that listened, listened always as if the murmuring amber stream brought messages, and the moving leaves whispered something. Lassiter never rode Bells into the court any more, nor did he come by the lane or the paths. When he appeared it was suddenly and noiselessly out of the dark shadow of the grove.

"I left Bells out in the sage," he said, one day at the end of that week. "I must carry water to him."

"Why not let him drink at the trough or here?" asked Jane, quickly.

"I reckon it 'll be safer for me to slip through the grove. I've been watched when I rode in from the sage."

"Watched? By whom?"

"By a man who thought he was well hid. But my eyes are pretty sharp. An', Jane," he went on, almost in a whisper, "I reckon it 'd be a good idea for us to talk low. You're spied on here by your women."

"Lassiter!" she whispered in turn. "That's hard to believe. My women love me."

"What of that?" he asked. "Of course they love you. But they're Mormon women."

Jane's old, rebellious loyalty clashed with her doubt.

"I won't believe it," she replied, stubbornly.

"Well then, just act natural an' talk natural, an' pretty soon—give them time to hear us—pretend to go over there to the table, an' then quick-like make a move for the door an' open it."

"I will," said Jane, with heightened color. Lassiter was right; he never made mistakes; he would not have told her unless he positively knew. Yet Jane was so tenacious of faith that she had to see with her own eyes, and so constituted that to employ even such small deceit toward her women made her ashamed, and angry for her shame as well as theirs. Then a singular thought confronted her that made her hold up this simple ruse—which hurt her, though it was well justified—against the deceit she had wittingly and eagerly used toward Lassiter. The difference was staggering in its suggestion of that blindness of which he had accused her. Fairness and justice and mercy, that she had imagined were anchor-cables to hold fast her soul to righteousness, had not been hers in the strange, biased duty that had so exalted and confounded her.

Presently Jane began to act her little part, to laugh and play with Fay, to talk of horses and cattle to Lassiter. Then she made deliberate mention of a book in which she kept records of all pertaining to her stock, and she walked slowly toward the table, and when near the door she suddenly whirled and thrust it open. Her sharp action nearly knocked down a woman who had undoubtedly been listening.

"Hester," said Jane, sternly, "you may go home, and you need not come back."

Jane shut the door and returned to Lassiter. Standing unsteadily, she put her hand on his arm. She let him see that doubt had gone, and how this stab of disloyalty pained her.

"Spies! My own women! . . . Oh, miserable!" she cried, with flashing, tearful eyes.

"I hate to tell you," he replied. By that she knew he had long spared her. "It's begun again—that work in the dark."

"Nay, Lassiter—it never stopped!"

So bitter certainty claimed her at last, and trust fled Withersteen House and fled forever. The women who owed much to Jane Withersteen changed not in love for her, nor in devotion to their household work, but they poisoned both by a thousand acts of stealth and cunning and duplicity. Jane broke out once and caught them in strange, stone-faced, unhesitating falsehood. Thereafter she broke out no more. She forgave them because they were driven. Poor, fettered, and sealed Hagars, how she pitied them! What terrible thing bound them and locked their lips, when they showed neither consciousness of guilt toward their benefactress nor distress at the slow wearing apart of long-established and dear ties?

"The blindness again!" cried Jane Withersteen. "In my sisters as in me! . . . O God!"

There came a time when no words passed between Jane and her women. Silently they went about their household duties, and secretly they went about the underhand work to which they had been bidden. The gloom of the house and the gloom of its mistress, which darkened even the bright spirit of little Fay, did not pervade these women. Happiness was not among them, but they were aloof from gloom. They spied and listened; they received and sent secret messengers; and they stole Jane's books and records, and finally the papers that were deeds of her possessions. Through it all they were silent, rapt in a kind of trance. Then one by one, without leave or explanation or farewell, they left Withersteen House, and never returned.

Coincident with this disappearance Jane's gardeners and workers in the alfalfa fields and stable men quit her, not even asking for their wages. Of all her Mormon employees about the great ranch only Jerd remained. He went on with his duty, but talked no more of the change than if it had never occurred.

"Jerd," said Jane, "what stock you can't take care of turn out in the sage. Let your first thought be for Black Star and Night. Keep them in perfect condition. Run them every day and watch them always."

Though Jane Withersteen gave with such liberality, she loved her possessions. She loved the rich, green stretches of alfalfa, and the farms, and the grove, and the old stone house, and the beautiful, ever-faithful amber spring, and every one of a myriad of horses and colts and burros and fowls down to the smallest rabbit that nipped her vegetables; but she loved best her noble Arabian steeds. In common with all riders of the upland sage Jane cherished two material things—the cold, sweet, brown water that made life possible in the wilderness and the horses which were a part of that life. When Lassiter asked her what Lassiter would be without his guns he was assuming that his horse was part of himself. So Jane loved Black Star and Night because it was her nature to love all beautiful creatures—perhaps all living things; and then she loved them because she herself was of the sage and in her had been born and bred the rider's instinct to rely on his four-footed brother. And when Jane gave Jerd the order to keep her favorities trained down to the day it was a half-conscious admission that presaged a time when she would need her fleet horses.

Jane had now, however, no leisure to brood over the coils that were closing round her. Mrs. Larkin grew weaker as the August days began; she required constant care; there was little Fay to look after; and such household work as was imperative. Lassiter put Bells in the stable with the other racers, and directed his efforts to a closer attendance upon Jane. She welcomed the change. He was always at hand to help, and it was her fortune to learn that his boast of being awkward around women had its root in humility and was not true.

His great, brown hands were skilled in a multiplicity of ways which a woman might have envied. He shared Jane's work, and was of especial help to her in nursing Mrs. Larkin. The woman suffered most at night, and this often broke Jane's rest. So it came about that Lassiter would stay by Mrs. Larkin during the day, when she needed care, and Jane would make up the sleep she lost in night-watches. Mrs. Larkin at once took kindly to the gentle Lassiter, and, without ever asking who or what he was, praised him to Jane. "He's a good man and loves children," she said. How sad to hear this truth spoken of a man whom Jane thought lost beyond all redemption! Yet ever and ever Lassiter towered above her, and behind or through his black, sinister figure shone something luminous that strangely affected Jane. Good and evil began to seem incomprehensibly blended in her judgment. It was her belief that evil could not come forth from good; yet here was a murderer who dwarfed in gentleness, patience, and love any man she had ever known.

She had almost lost track of her more outside concerns when early one morning Judkins presented himself before her in the courtyard.

Thin, hard, burnt, bearded, with the dust and sage thick on him, with his leather wrist-bands shining from use, and his boots worn through on the stirrup side, he looked the rider of riders. He wore two guns and carried a Winchester.

Jane greeted him with surprise and warmth, set meat and bread and drink before him; and called Lassiter out to see him. The men exchanged glances, and the meaning of Lassiter's keen inquiry and Judkins's bold reply, both unspoken, was not lost upon Jane.

"Where's your hoss?" asked Lassiter, aloud.

"Left him down the slope," answered Judkins. "I footed it in a ways, an' slept last night in the sage. I went to the place you told me you 'most always slept, but didn't strike you."

"I moved up some, near the spring, an' now I go there nights."

"Judkins—the white herd?" queried Jane, hurriedly.

"Miss Withersteen, I make proud to say I've not lost a steer. Fer a good while after thet stampede Lassiter milled we hed no trouble. Why, even the sage dogs left us. But it's begun agin—thet flashin' of lights over ridge tips, an' queer puffin' of smoke, an' then at night strange whistles an' noises. But the herd's acted magnificent. An' my boys, say, Miss Withersteen, they're only kids, but I ask no better riders. I got the laugh in the village fer takin' them out. They're a wild lot, an' you know boys hev more nerve than grown men, because they don't know what danger is. I'm not denyin' there's danger. But they glory in it, an' mebbe I like it myself—anyway, we'll stick. We're goin' to drive the herd on the far side of the first break of Deception Pass. There's a great round valley over there, an' no ridges or piles of rocks to aid these stampeders. The rains are due. We'll hev plenty of water fer a while. An' we can hold thet herd from anybody except Oldrin'. I come in fer supplies. I'll pack a couple of burros an' drive out after dark to-night."

"Judkins, take what you want from the store-room. Lassiter will help you. I—I can't thank you enough . . . but—wait."

Jane went to the room that had once been her father's, and from a secret chamber in the thick stone wall she took a bag of gold, and, carrying it back to the court, she gave it to the rider.

"There, Judkins, and understand that I regard it as little for your loyalty. Give what is fair to your boys, and keep the rest. Hide it. Perhaps that would be wisest."

"Oh . . . Miss Withersteen!" ejaculated the rider. "I couldn't earn so much in—in ten years. It's not right —I oughtn't take it."

"Judkins, you know I'm a rich woman. I tell you I've few faithful friends. I've fallen upon evil days. God only knows what will become of me and mine! So take the gold."

She smiled in understanding of his speechless gratitude, and left him with Lassiter. Presently she heard him speaking low at first, then in louder accents emphasized by the thumping of his rifle on the stones. "As infernal a job as even you, Lassiter, ever heerd of."

"Why, son," was Lassiter's reply, "this breakin' of Miss Withersteen may seem bad to you, but it ain't bad—yet. Some of these wall-eyed fellers who look jest as if they was walkin' in the shadow of Christ himself, right down the sunny road, now they can think of things an' do things that are really hell-bent."

Jane covered her ears and ran to her own room, and there like a caged lioness she paced to and fro till the coming of little Fay reversed her dark thoughts.

The following day, a warm and muggy one threatening rain, while Jane was resting in the court, a horseman clattered through the grove and up to the hitching-rack. He leaped off and approached Jane with the manner of a man determined to execute a difficult mission, yet fearful of its reception. In the gaunt, wiry figure and the lean, brown face Jane recognized one of her Mormon riders, Blake. It was he of whom Judkins had long since spoken. Of all the riders ever in her employ Blake owed her the most, and as he stepped before her, removing his hat and making manly efforts to subdue his emotion, he showed that he remembered.

"Miss Withersteen, mother's dead," he said.

"Oh—Blake!" exclaimed Jane, and she could say no more.

"She died free from pain in the end, and she's buried—resting at last, thank God! . . . I've come to ride for you again, if you'll have me. Don't think I mentioned mother to get your sympathy. When she was living and your riders quit, I had to also. I was afraid of what might be done—said to her. . . . Miss Withersteen, we can't talk of—of what's going on now—"

"Blake, do you know?"

"I know a great deal. You understand, my lips are

shut. But without explanation or excuse I offer my services. I'm a Mormon—I hope a good one. But—there are some things! . . . It's no use, Miss Withersteen, I can't say any more—what I'd like to. But will you take me back?"

"Blake! . . . You know what it means?"

"I don't care. I'm sick of—of—I'll show you a Mormon who'll be true to you!"

"But, Blake—how terribly you might suffer for that!"

"Maybe. Aren't you suffering now?"

"God knows indeed I am!"

"Miss Withersteen, it's a liberty on my part to speak so, but I know you pretty well—know you'll never give in. I wouldn't if I were you. And I—I must— Something makes me tell you the worst is yet to come. That's all. I absolutely can't say more. Will you take me back—let me ride for you—show everybody what I mean?"

"Blake, it makes me happy to hear you. How my riders hurt me when they quit!" Jane felt the hot tears well to her eyes and splash down upon her hands. "I thought so much of them—tried so hard to be good to them. And not one was true. You've made it easy to forgive. Perhaps many of them really feel as you do, but dare not return to me. Still, Blake, I hesitate to take you back. Yet I want you so much."

"Do it, then. If you're going to make your life a lesson to Mormon women, let me make mine a lesson to the men. Right is right. I believe in you, and here's my life to prove it."

"You hint it may mean your life!" said Jane, breathless and low.

"We won't speak of that. I want to come back. I want to do what every rider aches in his secret heart to do for you. . . . Miss Withersteen, I hoped it'd not be necessary to tell you that my mother on her deathbed told me to have courage. She knew how the thing galled me—she told me to come back. . . . Will you take me?"

"God bless you, Blake! Yes, I'll take you back. And will you—will you accept gold from me?"

"Miss Withersteen!"

"I just gave Judkins a bag of gold. I'll give you one. If you will not take it you must not come back. You might ride for me a few months—weeks—days till the storm breaks. Then you'd have nothing, and be in disgrace with your people. We'll forearm you against poverty, and me against endless regret. I'll give you gold which you can hide—till some future time."

"Well, if it pleases you," replied Blake. "But you know I never thought of pay. Now, Miss Withersteen, one thing more. I want to see this man Lassiter. Is he here?"

"Yes, but, Blake—what— Need you see him? Why?" asked Jane, instantly worried. "I can speak to him—tell him about you."

"That won't do. I want to—I've got to tell him myself. Where is he?"

"Lassiter is with Mrs. Larkin. She is ill. I'll call him," answered Jane, and going to the door she softly called for the rider. A faint, musical jingle preceded his step—then his tall form crossed the threshold.

"Lassiter, here's Blake, an old rider of mine. He has come back to me and he wishes to speak to you."

Blake's brown face turned exceedingly pale.

"Yes, I had to speak to you," he said, swiftly. "My name's Blake. I'm a Mormon and a rider. Lately I quit Miss Withersteen. I've come to beg her to take me back. Now I don't know you, but I know—what you are. So I've this to say to your face. It would never occur to this woman to imagine—let alone suspect me to be a spy. She couldn't think it might just be a low plot to come here and shoot you in the back. Jane Withersteen hasn't that kind of a mind. . . . Well, I've not come for that. I want to help her—to pull a bridle along with Judkins and—and you. The thing is—do you believe me?"

"I reckon I do," replied Lassiter. How this slow, cool speech contrasted with Blake's hot, impulsive words! "You might have saved some of your breath. See here, Blake, cinch this in your mind. Lassiter has met some square Mormons! An' mebbe—"

"Blake," interrupted Jane, nervously anxious to terminate a colloquy that she perceived was an ordeal for him. "Go at once and fetch me a report of my horses."

"Miss Withersteen! . . . You mean the big drove—down in the sage-cleared fields?"

"Of course," replied Jane. "My horses are all there, except the blooded stock I keep here."

"Haven't you heard—then?"

"Heard? No! What's happened to them?"

"They're gone, Miss Withersteen, gone these ten days past. Dorn told me, and I rode down to see for myself."

"Lassiter—did you know?" asked Jane, whirling to him.

"I reckon so. . . . But what was the use to tell you?"

It was Lassiter turning away his face and Blake studying the stone flags at his feet that brought Jane to the understanding of what she betrayed. She strove desperately, but she could not rise immediately from such a blow.

"My horses! My horses! What's become of them?"

"Dorn said the riders report another drive by Oldring. . . . And I trailed the horses miles down the slope toward Deception Pass."

"My red herd's gone! My horses gone! The white herd will go next. I can stand that. But if I lost Black Star and Night, it would be like parting with my own flesh and blood. Lassiter—Blake—am I in danger of losing my racers?"

"A rustler—or—or anybody stealin' hosses of yours would most of all want the blacks," said Lassiter. His evasive reply was affirmative enough. The other rider nodded gloomy acquiescence.

"Oh! Oh!" Jane Withersteen choked, with violent utterance.

"Let me take charge of the blacks?" asked Blake. "One more rider won't be any great help to Judkins. But I might hold Black Star and Night, if you put such store on their value."

"Value! Blake, I love my racers. Besides, there's another reason why I mustn't lose them. You go to the stables. Go with Jerd every day when he runs the horses, and don't let them out of your sight. If you would please me—win my gratitude, guard my black racers."

When Blake had mounted and ridden out of the court Lassiter regarded Jane with the smile that was becoming rarer as the days sped by.

"'Pears to me, as Blake says, you do put some store on them hosses. Now I ain't gainsayin' that the Arabians are the handsomest hosses I ever seen. But Bells can beat Night, an' run neck an' neck with Black Star."

"Lassiter, don't tease me now. I'm miserable—sick. Bells is fast, but he can't stay with the blacks, and you know it. Only Wrangle can do that."

"I'll bet that big raw-boned brute can more 'n show his heels to your black racers. Jane, out there in the sage, on a long chase, Wrangle could kill your favorites.

"No, no," replied Jane, impatiently. "Lassiter, why do you say that so often? I know you've teased me at times, and I believe it's only kindness. You're always trying to keep my mind off worry. But you mean more by this repeated mention of my racers?"

"I reckon so." Lassiter paused, and for the thousandth time in her presence moved his black sombrero round and round, as if counting the silver pieces on the band. "Well, Jane, I've sort of read a little that's passin' in your mind."

"You think I might fly from my home—from Cottonwoods—from the Utah border?"

"I reckon. An' if you ever do an' get away with the blacks I wouldn't like to see Wrangle left here on the sage. Wrangle could catch you. I know Venters had him. But you can never tell. Mebbe he hasn't got him now. . . . Besides—things are happenin', an' somethin' of the same queer nature might have happened to Venters."

"God knows you're right! . . . Poor Bern, how long he's gone! In my trouble I've been forgetting him. But, Lassiter, I've little fear for him. I've heard my riders say he's as keen as a wolf. . . . As to your reading my thoughts—well, your suggestion makes an actual thought of what was only one of my dreams. I believe I dreamed of flying from this wild borderland, Lassiter. I've strange dreams. I'm not always practical and thinking of my many duties, as you said once. For instance—if I dared—if I dared I'd ask you to saddle the blacks and ride away with me—and hide me."

"Jane!"

The rider's sunburnt face turned white. A few times Jane had seen Lassiter's cool calm broken—when he had met little Fay, when he had learned how and why he had come to love both child and mistress, when he had stood beside Milly Erne's grave. But one and all they could not be considered in the light of his present agitation. Not only did Lassiter turn white—not only did he grow tense, not only did he lose his coolness, but also he suddenly, violently, hungrily took her into his arms and crushed her to his breast.

"Lassiter!" cried Jane, trembling. It was an action for which she took sole blame. Instantly, as if dazed, weakened, he released her. "Forgive me!" went on

Jane. "I'm always forgetting your—your feelings. I thought of you as my faithful friend. I'm always making you out more than human . . . only, let me say—I meant that—about riding away. I'm wretched, sick of this—this— Oh, something bitter and black grows on my heart!"

"Jane, the hell—of it," he replied, with deep intake of breath, "is you *can't* ride away. Mebbe realizin' it accounts for my grabbin' you—that way, as much as the crazy boy's rapture your words gave me. I don't understand myself. . . . But the hell of this game is—you *can't* ride away."

"Lassiter! . . . What on earth do you mean? I'm an absolutely free woman."

"You ain't absolutely anythin' of the kind. . . . I reckon I've got to tell you!"

"Tell me all. It's uncertainty that makes me a coward. It's faith and hope—blind love, if you will, that makes me miserable. Every day I awake believing—still believing. The day grows, and with it doubts, fears, and that black bat hate that bites hotter and hotter into my heart. Then comes night—I pray—I pray for all, and for myself—I sleep—and I awake free once more, trustful, faithful, to believe—to hope! Then, O my God! I grow and live a thousand years till night again! . . . But if you want to see me a woman, tell me why I can't ride away—tell me what more I'm to lose—tell me the worst."

"Jane, you're watched. There's no single move of yours, except when you're hid in your house, that ain't seen by sharp eyes. The cottonwood grove's full of creepin', crawlin' men. Like Indians in the grass. When you rode, which wasn't often lately, the sage was full of sneakin' men. At night they crawl under your windows, into the court, an' I reckon into the house. Jane Withersteen, you know, never locked a door! This here grove's a hummin' bee-hive of mysterious happenin's. Jane, it ain't so much that these spies keep out of my way as me keepin' out of theirs. They're goin' to try to kill me. That's plain. But mebbe I'm as hard to shoot in the back as in the face. So far I've seen fit to watch only. This all means, Jane, that you're a marked woman. You can't get away—not now. Mebbe later, when you're broken, you might. But that's sure doubtful. Jane, you're to lose the cattle that's left—your home an' ranch—an' Amber Spring. You can't even hide a sack of gold! For it couldn't be slipped out of the house, day or night, an' hid or buried, let alone be rid off with. You may lose all. I'm tellin' you, Jane, hopin' to prepare you, if the worst does come. I told you once before about that strange power I've got to feel things."

"Lassiter, what can I do?"

"Nothin', I reckon, except know what's comin' an' wait an' be game. If you'd let me make a call on Tull, an' a long-deferred call on—"

"Hush! . . . Hush!" she whispered.

"Well, even that wouldn't help you any in the end."

"What does it mean? Oh, what does it mean? I am my father's daughter—a Mormon, yet I can't see! I've not failed in religion—in duty. For years I've given with a free and full heart. When my father died I was rich. If I'm still rich it's because I couldn't find enough ways to become poor. What am I, what are my possessions to set in motion such intensity of secret oppression?"

"Jane, the mind behind it all is an empire builder."

"But, Lassiter, I would give freely—all I own to avert this—this wretched thing. If I gave—that would leave me with faith still. Surely my—my churchmen think of my soul? If I lose my trust in them—"

"Child, be still!" said Lassiter, with a dark dignity that had in it something of pity. "You are a woman, fine an' big an' strong, an' your heart matches your size. But in mind you're a child. I'll say a little more—then I'm done. I'll never mention this again. Among many thousands of women you're one who has bucked against your churchmen. They tried you out, an' failed of persuasion, an' finally of threats. You meet now the cold steel of a will as far from Christlike as the universe is wide. You're to be broken. Your body's to be held, given to some man, made, if possible, to bring children into the world. But your soul? . . . What do they care for your soul?"

CHAPTER XIII

SOLITUDE AND STORM

IN his hidden valley Venters awakened from sleep, and his ears rang with innumerable melodies from full-throated mocking-birds, and his eyes opened wide upon the glorious golden shaft of sunlight shining through the great stone bridge. The circle of cliffs surrounding Surprise Valley lay shrouded in morning mist, a dim blue low down along the terraces, a creamy, moving cloud along the ramparts. The oak forest in the center was a plumed and tufted oval of gold.

He saw Bess under the spruces. Upon her complete recovery of strength she always rose with the dawn. At the moment she was feeding the quail she had tamed. And she had begun to tame the mocking-birds. They fluttered among the branches overhead, and some left off their songs to flit down and shyly hop near the twittering quail. Little gray and white rabbits crouched in the grass, now nibbling, now laying long ears flat and watching the dogs.

Venters's swift glance took in the brightening valley, and Bess and her pets, and Ring and Whitie. It swept over all to return again and rest upon the girl. She had changed. To the dark trousers and blouse she had added moccasins of her own make, but she no longer resembled a boy. No eye could have failed to mark the rounded contours of a woman. The change had been to grace and beauty. A glint of warm gold gleamed from her hair, and a tint of red shone in the clear dark brown of cheeks. The haunting sweetness of her lips and eyes, that earlier had been illusive, a promise, had become a living fact. She fitted harmoniously into that wonderful setting; she was like Surprise Valley—wild and beautiful.

Venters leaped out of his cave to begin the day.

He had postponed his journey to Cottonwoods until after the passing of the summer rains. The rains were due soon. But until their arrival and the necessity for his trip to the village he sequestered in a far corner of mind all thought of peril, of his past life, and almost that of the present. It was enough to live. He did not want to know what lay hidden in the dim and distant future. Surprise Valley had enchanted him. In this home of the cliff-dwellers there were peace and quiet and solitude, and another thing, wondrous as the golden morning shaft of sunlight, that he dared not ponder over long enough to understand.

The solitude he had hated when alone he had now come to love. He was assimilating something from this valley of gleams and shadows. From this strange girl he was assimilating more.

The day at hand resembled many days gone before. As Venters had no tools with which to build, or to till the terraces, he remained idle. Beyond the cooking of the simple fare there were no tasks. And as there were no tasks, there was no system. He and Bess began one thing, to leave it; to begin another, to leave that; and then do nothing but lie under the spruces and watch the great cloud-sails majestically move along the ramparts, and dream and dream. The valley was a golden, sunlit world. It was silent. The sighing wind and the twittering quail and the singing birds, even the rare and seldom-occurring hollow crack of a sliding weathered stone, only thickened and deepened that insulated silence.

Venters and Bess had vagrant minds.

"Bess, did I tell you about my horse Wrangle?" inquired Venters.

"A hundred times," she replied.

"Oh, have I? I'd forgotten. I want you to see him. He'll carry us both."

"I'd like to ride him. Can he run?"

"Run? He's a demon. Swiftest horse on the sage! I hope he'll stay in that cañon."

"He'll stay."

They left camp to wander along the terraces, into the aspen ravines, under the gleaming walls. Ring and Whitie wandered in the fore, often turning, often trotting back, open-mouthed and solemn-eyed and happy. Venters lifted his gaze to the grand archway over the entrance to the valley, and Bess lifted hers to follow his, and both were silent. Sometimes the bridge held their attention for a long time. To-day a soaring eagle attracted them.

"How he sails!" exclaimed Bess. "I wonder where his mate is?"

"She's at the nest. It's on the bridge in a crack near the top. I see her often. She's almost white."

They wandered on down the terrace, into the shady, sun-flecked forest. A brown bird fluttered crying from a bush. Bess peeped into the leaves.

"Look! A nest and four little birds. They're not afraid of us. See how they open their mouths. They're hungry."

Rabbits rustled the dead brush and pattered away. The forest was full of a drowsy hum of insects. Little darts of purple, that were running quail, crossed the glades. And a plaintive, sweet peeping came from the coverts. Bess's soft step disturbed a sleeping lizard that scampered away over the leaves. She gave chase and caught it, a slim creature of nameless color but of exquisite beauty.

"Jewel eyes," she said. "It's like a rabbit—afraid. We won't eat you. There—go."

Murmuring water drew their steps down into a shallow

shaded ravine where a brown brook brawled softly over mossy stones. Multitudes of strange, gray frogs with white spots and black eyes lined the rocky bank and leaped only at close approach. Then Venters's eye descried a very thin, very long green snake coiled round a sapling. They drew closer and closer till they could have touched it. The snake had no fear and watched them with scintillating eyes.

"It's pretty," said Bess. "How tame! I thought snakes always ran."

"No. Even the rabbits didn't run here till the dogs chased them."

On and on they wandered to the wild jumble of massed and broken fragments of cliff at the west end of the valley. The roar of the disappearing stream dinned in their ears. Into this maze of rocks they threaded a tortuous way, climbing, descending, halting to gather wild plums and great lavender lilies, and going on at the will of fancy. Idle and keen perceptions guided them equally.

"Oh, let us climb there!" cried Bess, pointing upward to a small space of terrace left green and shady between huge abutments of broken cliff. And they climbed to the nook and rested and looked out across the valley to the curling column of blue smoke from their campfire. But the cool shade and the rich grass and the fine view were not what they had climbed for. They could not have told, although whatever had drawn them was all-satisfying. Light, sure-footed as a mountain goat, Bess pattered down at Venters's heels; and they went on, calling the dogs, eyes dreamy and wide, listening to the wind and the bees and the crickets and the birds.

Part of the time Ring and Whitie led the way, then Venters, then Bess; and the direction was not an object. They left the sun-streaked shade of the oaks, brushed the long grass of the meadows, entered the green and fragrant swaying willows, to stop, at length, under the huge old cottonwoods where the beavers were busy.

Here they rested and watched. A dam of brush and logs and mud and stones backed the stream into a little lake. The round, rough beaver houses projected from the water. Like the rabbits, the beavers had become shy. Gradually, however, as Venters and Bess knelt low, holding the dogs, the beavers emerged to swim with logs and gnaw at cottonwoods and pat mud walls with their paddle-like tails, and, glossy and shiny in the sun, to go on with their strange, persistent industry. They were the builders. The lake was a mud-hole, and the immediate environment a scarred and dead region, but it was a wonderful home of wonderful animals.

"Look at that one—he puddles in the mud," said Bess. "And there! See him dive! Hear them gnawing! I'd think they'd break their teeth. How's it they can stay out of the water and under the water?"

And she laughed.

Then Venters and Bess wandered farther, and, perhaps not all unconsciously this time, wended their slow steps to the cave of the cliff-dwellers, where she liked best to go.

The tangled thicket and the long slant of dust and little chips of weathered rock and the steep bench of stone and the worn steps all were arduous work for Bess in the climbing. But she gained the shelf, gasping, hot of cheek, glad of eye, with her hand in Venters's. Here they rested. The beautiful valley glittered below with its millions of wind-turned leaves bright-faced in the sun, and the mighty bridge towered heavenward, crowned with blue sky. Bess, however, never rested for long. Soon she was exploring, and Venters followed; she dragged forth from corners and shelves a multitude of crudely fashioned and painted pieces of pottery, and he carried them. They peeped down into the dark holes of the kivas, and Bess gleefully dropped a stone and waited for the long-coming hollow sound to rise. They peeped into the little globular houses, like mud-wasp nests, and wondered if these had been store-places for grain, or baby cribs, or what; and they crawled into the larger houses and laughed when they bumped their heads on the low roofs, and they dug in the dust of the floors. And they brought from dust and darkness armloads of treasure which they carried to the light. Flints and stones and strange curved sticks and pottery they found; and twisted grass rope that crumbled in their hands, and bits of whitish stone which crushed to powder at a touch and seemed to vanish in the air.

"That white stuff was bone," said Venters, slowly. "Bones of a cliff-dweller."

"No!" exclaimed Bess.

"Here's another piece. Look! . . . Whew! dry, powdery smoke! That's bone."

Then it was that Venters's primitive, childlike mood, like a savage's, seeing, yet unthinking, gave way to the encroachment of civilized thought. The world had not been made for a single day's play or fancy or idle watching. The world was old. Nowhere could be gotten a better idea of its age than in this gigantic silent tomb. The gray ashes in Venters's hand had once been bone of a human being like himself. The pale gloom of the cave had shadowed people long ago. He saw that Bess had received the same shock—could not in moments such as this escape her feeling, living, thinking destiny.

"Bern, people have *lived* here," she said, with wide, thoughtful eyes.

"Yes," he replied.

"How long ago?"

"A thousand years and more."

"What were they?"

"Cliff-dwellers. Men who had enemies and made their homes high out of reach."

"They had to fight?"

"Yes."

"They fought for—what?"

"For life. For their homes, food, children, parents—for their women!"

"Has the world changed any in a thousand years?"

"I don't know—perhaps very little."

"Have men?"

"I hope so—I think so."

"Things crowd into my mind," she went on, and the wistful light in her eyes told Venters the truth of her thoughts. "I've ridden the border of Utah. I've seen people—know how they live—but they must be few of all who are living. I had my books and I studied them. But all that doesn't help me any more. I want to go out into the big world and see it. Yet I want to stay here more. What's to become of us? Are we cliff-dwellers? We're alone here. I'm happy when I don't think. These—these bones that fly into dust—they make me sick and a little afraid. Did the people who lived here once have the same feelings as we have? What was the good of their living at all? They're gone! What's the meaning of it all—of us?"

"Bess, you ask more than I can tell. It's beyond me. Only there was laughter here once—and now there's silence. There was life—and now there's death. Men cut these little steps, made these arrow-heads and mealing-stones, plaited the ropes we found, and left their bones to crumble in our fingers. As far as time is concerned it might all have been yesterday. We're here to-day. Maybe we're higher in the scale of human beings—in intelligence. But who knows? We can't be any higher in the things for which life is lived at all."

"What are they?"

"Why—I suppose relationship, friendship—love."

"Love!"

"Yes. Love of man for woman—love of woman for

man. That's the nature, the meaning, the best of life itself."

She said no more. Wistfulness of glance deepened into sadness.

"Come, let us go," said Venters.

Action brightened her. Beside him, holding his hand, she slipped down the shelf, ran down the long, steep slant of sliding stones, out of the cloud of dust, and likewise out of the pale gloom.

"We beat the slide," she cried.

The miniature avalanche cracked and roared, and rattled itself into an inert mass at the base of the incline. Yellow dust like the gloom of the cave, but not so changeless, drifted away on the wind; the roar clapped in echo from the cliff, returned, went back, and came again to die in the hollowness. Down on the sunny terrace there was a different atmosphere. Ring and Whitie leaped around Bess. Once more she was smiling, gay, and thoughtless, with the dream-mood in the shadow of her eyes.

"Bess, I haven't seen that since last summer. Look!" said Venters, pointing to the scalloped edge of rolling purple clouds that peeped over the western wall. "We're in for a storm."

"Oh, I hope not. I'm afraid of storms."

"Are you? Why?"

"Have you ever been down in one of these walled-up pockets in a bad storm?"

"No, now I think of it, I haven't."

"Well, it's terrible. Every summer I get scared to death and hide somewhere in the dark. Storms up on the sage are bad, but nothing to what they are down here in the cañons. And in this little valley—why, echoes can rap back and forth so quick they'll split our ears."

"We're perfectly safe here, Bess."

"I know. But that hasn't anything to do with it.

The truth is I'm afraid of lightning and thunder, and thunder-claps hurt my head. If we have a bad storm, will you stay close by me?"

"Yes."

When they got back to camp the afternoon was closing, and it was exceedingly sultry. Not a breath of air stirred the aspen leaves, and when these did not quiver the air was indeed still. The dark-purple clouds moved almost imperceptibly out of the west.

"What have we for supper?" asked Bess.

"Rabbit."

"Bern, can't you think of another new way to cook rabbit?" went on Bess, with earnestness.

"What do you think I am—a magician?" retorted Venters.

"I wouldn't dare tell you. But, Bern, do you want me to turn into a rabbit?"

There was a dark-blue, merry flashing of eyes and a parting of lips; then she laughed. In that moment she was naïve and wholesome.

"Rabbit seems to agree with you," replied Venters. "You are well and strong—and growing very pretty."

Anything in the nature of compliment he had never before said to her, and just now he responded to a sudden curiosity to see its effect. Bess stared as if she had not heard aright, slowly blushed, and completely lost her poise in happy confusion.

"I'd better go right away," he continued, "and fetch supplies from Cottonwoods."

A startingly swift change in the nature of her agitation made him reproach himself for his abruptness.

"No, no, don't go!" she said. "I didn't mean—that about the rabbit. I—I was only trying to be—funny. Don't leave me all alone!"

"Bess, I must go sometime."

"Wait then. Wait till after the storms."

The purple cloud-bank darkened the lower edge of

the setting sun, crept up and up, obscuring its fiery red heart, and finally passed over the last ruddy crescent of its upper rim.

The intense dead silence awakened to a long, low, rumbling roll of thunder.

"Oh!" cried Bess, nervously.

"We've had big black clouds before this without rain," said Venters. "But there's no doubt about that thunder. The storms are coming. I'm glad. Every rider on the sage will hear that thunder with glad ears."

Venters and Bess finished their simple meal and the few tasks around the camp, then faced the open terrace, the valley, and the west, to watch and await the approaching storm.

It required keen vision to see any movement whatever in the purple clouds. By infinitesimal degrees the dark cloud-line merged upward into the golden-red haze of the afterglow of sunset. A shadow lengthened from under the western wall across the valley. As straight and rigid as steel rose the delicate spear-pointed silver spruces; the aspen leaves, by nature pendant and quivering, hung limp and heavy; no slender blade of grass moved. A gentle plashing of water came from the ravine. Then again from out of the west sounded the low, dull, and rumbling roll of thunder.

A wave, a ripple of light, a trembling and turning of the aspen leaves, like the approach of a breeze on the water, crossed the valley from the west; and the lull and the deadly stillness and the sultry air passed away on a cool wind.

The night bird of the cañon, with his clear and melancholy notes, announced the twilight. And from all along the cliffs rose the faint murmur and moan and mourn of the wind singing in the caves. The bank of clouds now swept hugely out of the western sky. Its front was purple and black, with gray between, a bulging, mushrooming, vast thing instinct with storm. It had

VENTERS AND BESS FINISHED THEIR SIMPLE MEAL—THEN FACED THE OPEN TERRACE, TO WATCH AND AWAIT THE APPROACHING STORM

a dark, angry, threatening aspect. As if all the power of the winds were pushing and piling behind, it rolled ponderously across the sky. A red flare burned out instantaneously, flashed from west to east, and died. Then from the deepest black of the purple cloud burst a boom. It was like the bowling of a huge boulder along the crags and ramparts, and seemed to roll on and fall into the valley to bound and bang and boom from cliff to cliff.

"Oh!" cried Bess, with her hands over her ears. "What did I tell you?"

"Why, Bess, be reasonable!" said Venters.

"I'm a coward."

"Not quite that, I hope. It's strange you're afraid. I love a storm."

"I tell you a storm down in these cañons is an awful thing. I know Oldring hated storms. His men were afraid of them. There was one who went deaf in a bad storm, and never could hear again."

"Maybe I've lots to learn, Bess. I'll lose my guess if this storm isn't bad enough. We're going to have heavy wind first, then lightning and thunder, then the rain. Let's stay out as long as we can."

The tips of the cottonwoods and the oaks waved to the east, and the rings of aspens along the terraces twinkled their myriad of bright faces in fleet and glancing gleam. A low roar rose from the leaves of the forest, and the spruces swished in the rising wind. It came in gusts, with light breezes between. As it increased in strength the lulls shortened in length till there was a strong and steady blow all the time, and violent puffs at intervals, and sudden whirling currents. The clouds spread over the valley, rolling swiftly and low, and twilight faded into a sweeping darkness. Then the singing of the wind in the caves drowned the swift roar of rustling leaves; then the song swelled to a mourning, moaning wail; then with the gathering power of the wind the wail changed to a shriek. Steadily the wind strengthened and constantly the strange sound changed.

The last bit of blue sky yielded to the onsweep of clouds. Like angry surf the pale gleams of gray, amid the purple of that scudding front, swept beyond the eastern rampart of the valley. The purple deepened to black. Broad sheets of lightning flared over the western wall. There were not yet any ropes or zigzag streaks darting down through the gathering darkness. The storm center was still beyond Surprise Valley.

"Listen! . . . Listen!" cried Bess, with her lips close to Venters's ear. "You'll hear Oldring's knell!"

"What's that?"

"Oldring's knell. When the wind blows a gale in the caves it makes what the rustlers call Oldring's knell. They believe it bodes his death. I think he believes so, too. It's not like any sound on earth. . . . It's beginning. Listen!"

The gale swooped down with a hollow unearthly howl. It yelled and pealed and shrilled and shrieked. It was made up of a thousand piercing cries. It was a rising and a moving sound. Beginning at the western break of the valley, it rushed along each gigantic cliff, whistling into the caves and cracks, to mount in power, to bellow a blast through the great stone bridge. Gone, as into an engulfing roar of surging waters, it seemed to shoot back and begin all over again.

It was only wind, thought Venters. Here sped and shrieked the sculptor that carved out the wonderful caves in the cliffs. It was only a gale, but as Venters listened, as his ears became accustomed to the fury and strife, out of it all or through it or above it pealed low and perfectly clear and persistently uniform a strange sound that had no counterpart in all the sounds of the elements. It was not of earth or of life. It was the grief and agony of the gale. A knell of all upon which it blew!

SOLITUDE AND STORM

Black night enfolded the valley. Venters could not see his companion, and knew of her presence only through the tightening hold of her hand on his arm. He felt the dogs huddle closer to him. Suddenly the dense, black vault overhead split asunder to a blue-white, dazzling streak of lightning. The whole valley lay vividly clear and luminously bright in his sight. Upreared, vast and magnificent, the stone bridge glimmered like some grand god of storm in the lightning's fire. Then all flashed black again—blacker than pitch—a thick, impenetrable coal-blackness. And there came a ripping, crashing report. Instantly an echo resounded with clapping crash. The initial report was nothing to the echo. It was a terrible, living, reverberating, detonating crash. The wall threw the sound across, and could have made no greater roar if it had slipped in avalanche. From cliff to cliff the echo went in crashing retort and banged in lessening power, and boomed in thinner volume, and clapped weaker and weaker till a final clap could not reach across to waiting cliff.

In the pitchy darkness Venters led Bess, and, groping his way, by feel of hand found the entrance to her cave and lifted her up. On the instant a blinding flash of lightning illumined the cave and all about him. He saw Bess's face white now, with dark, frightened eyes. He saw the dogs leap up, and he followed suit. The golden glare vanished; all was black; then came the splitting crack and the infernal din of echoes.

Bess shrank closer to him and closer, found his hands, and pressed them tightly over her ears, and dropped her face upon his shoulder, and hid her eyes.

Then the storm burst with a succession of ropes and streaks and shafts of lightning, playing continuously, filling the valley with a broken radiance; and the cracking shots followed each other swiftly till the echoes blended in one fearful, deafening crash.

Venters looked out upon the beautiful valley—beautiful now as never before—mystic in its transparent, luminous gloom, weird in the quivering, golden haze of lightning. The dark spruces were tipped with glimmering lights; the aspens bent low in the winds, as waves in a tempest at sea; the forest of oaks tossed wildly and shone with gleams of fire. Across the valley the huge cavern of the cliff-dwellers yawned in the glare, every little black window as clear as at noonday; but the night and the storm added to their tragedy. Flung arching to the black clouds, the great stone bridge seemed to bear the brunt of the storm. It caught the full fury of the rushing wind. It lifted its noble crown to meet the lightnings. Venters thought of the eagles and their lofty nest in a niche under the arch. A driving pall of rain, black as the clouds, came sweeping on to obscure the bridge and the gleaming walls and the shining valley. The lightning played incessantly, streaking down through opaque darkness of rain. The roar of the wind, with its strange knell and the recrashing echoes, mingled with the roar of the flooding rain, and all seemingly were deadened and drowned in a world of sound.

In the dimming pale light Venters looked down upon the girl. She had sunk into his arms, upon his breast, burying her face. She clung to him. He felt the softness of her, and the warmth, and the quick heave of her breast. He saw the dark, slender, graceful outline of her form. A woman lay in his arms! And he held her closer. He who had been alone in the sad, silent watches of the night was not now and never must be again alone. He who had yearned for the touch of a hand felt the long tremble and the heart-beat of a woman. By what strange chance had she come to love him! By what change—by what marvel had she grown into a treasure!

No more did he listen to the rush and roar of the thunder-storm. For with the touch of clinging hands and the throbbing bosom he grew conscious of an inward storm—the tingling of new chords of thought, strange music of unheard, joyous bells, sad dreams dawning to wakeful delight, dissolving doubt, resurging hope, force, fire, and freedom, unutterable sweetness of desire. A storm in his breast—a storm of real love.

CHAPTER XIV

WEST WIND

WHEN the storm abated Venters sought his own cave, and late in the night, as his blood cooled and the stir and throb and thrill subsided, he fell asleep.

With the breaking of dawn his eyes unclosed. The valley lay drenched and bathed, a burnished oval of glittering green. The rain-washed walls glistened in the morning light. Waterfalls of many forms poured over the rims. One, a broad, lacy sheet, thin as smoke, slid over the western notch and struck a ledge in its downward fall, to bound into broader leap, to burst far below into white and gold and rosy mist.

Venters prepared for the day, knowing himself a different man.

"It's a glorious morning," said Bess, in greeting.

"Yes. After the storm the west wind," he replied.

"Last night was I—very much of a baby?" she asked, watching him.

"Pretty much."

"Oh, I couldn't help it!"

"I'm glad you were afraid."

"Why?" she asked, in slow surprise.

"I'll tell you some day," he answered, soberly. Then around the camp-fire and through the morning meal he was silent; afterward he strolled thoughtfully off alone along the terrace. He climbed a great yellow rock raising its crest among the spruces, and there he sat down to face the valley and the west.

"I love her!"

Aloud he spoke—unburdened his heart—confessed his secret. For an instant the golden valley swam before his eyes, and the walls waved, and all about him whirled with tumult within.

"I love her! . . . I understand now."

Reviving memory of Jane Withersteen and thought of the complications of the present amazed him with proof of how far he had drifted from his old life. He discovered that he hated to take up the broken threads, to delve into dark problems and difficulties. In this beautiful valley he had been living a beautiful dream. Tranquillity had come to him, and the joy of solitude, and interest in all the wild creatures and crannies of this incomparable valley—and love. Under the shadow of the great stone bridge God had revealed Himself to Venters.

"The world seems very far away," he muttered, "but it's there—and I'm not yet done with it. Perhaps I never shall be. . . . Only—how glorious it would be to live here always and never think again!"

Whereupon the resurging reality of the present, as if in irony of his wish, steeped him instantly in contending thought. Out of it all he presently evolved these things: he must go to Cottonwoods; he must bring supplies back to Surprise Valley; he must cultivate the soil and raise corn and stock, and, most imperative of all, he must decide the future of the girl who loved him and whom he loved. The first of these things required tremendous effort, the last one, concerning Bess, seemed simply and naturally easy of accomplishment. He would marry her. Suddenly, as from roots of poisonous fire, flamed up the forgotten truth concerning her. It seemed to wither and shrivel up all his joy on its hot, tearing way to his heart. She had been Oldring's Masked Rider. To Venters's question, "What were you to Oldring?" she had answered with scarlet shame and drooping head.

"What do I care who she is or what she was!" he cried, passionately. And he knew it was not his old self speaking. It was this softer, gentler man who had awakened to new thoughts in the quiet valley. Tenderness, masterful in him now, matched the absence of joy and blunted the knife-edge of entering jealousy. Strong and passionate effort of will, surprising to him, held back the poison from piercing his soul.

"Wait! . . . Wait!" he cried, as if calling. His hand pressed his breast, and he might have called to the pang there. "Wait! It's all so strange—so wonderful. Anything can happen. Who am I to judge her? I'll glory in my love for her. But I can't tell it—can't give up to it."

Certainly he could not then decide her future. Marrying her was impossible in Surprise Valley and in any village south of Sterling. Even without the mask she had once worn she would easily have been recognized as Oldring's Rider. No man who had ever seen her would forget her, regardless of his ignorance as to her sex. Then more poignant than all other argument was the fact that he did not want to take her away from Surprise Valley. He resisted all thought of that. He had brought her to the most beautiful and wildest place of the uplands; he had saved her, nursed her back to strength, watched her bloom as one of the valley lilies; he knew her life there to be pure and sweet—she belonged to him, and he loved her. Still these were not all the reasons why he did not want to take her away. Where could they go? He feared the rustlers—he feared the riders—he feared the Mormons. And if he should ever succeed in getting Bess safely away from these immediate perils, he feared the sharp eyes of women and their tongues, the big outside world with its problems of existence. He must wait to decide her future, which, after all, was deciding his own. But between her future and his something hung impending.

Like Balancing Rock, which waited darkly over the steep gorge, ready to close forever the outlet to Deception Pass, that nameless thing, as certain yet intangible as fate, must fall and close forever all doubts and fears of the future.

"I've dreamed," muttered Venters, as he rose. "Well, why not? . . . To dream is happiness! But let me just once see this clearly, wholly; then I can go on dreaming till the thing falls. I've got to tell Jane Withersteen. I've dangerous trips to take. I've work here to make comfort for this girl. She's mine. I'll fight to keep her safe from that old life. I've already seen her forget it. I love her. And if a beast ever rises in me I'll burn my hand off before I lay it on her with shameful intent. And, by God! sooner or later I'll kill the man who hid her and kept her in Deception Pass!"

As he spoke the west wind softly blew in his face. It seemed to soothe his passion. That west wind was fresh, cool, fragrant, and it carried a sweet, strange burden of far-off things—tidings of life in other climes, of sunshine asleep on other walls—of other places where reigned peace. It carried, too, sad truth of human hearts and mystery—of promise and hope unquenchable. Surprise Valley was only a little niche in the wide world whence blew that burdened wind. Bess was only one of millions at the mercy of unknown motive in nature and life. Content had come to Venters in the valley; happiness had breathed in the slow, warm air; love as bright as light had hovered over the walls and descended to him; and now on the west wind came a whisper of the eternal triumph of faith over doubt.

"How much better I am for what has come to me!" he exclaimed. "I'll let the future take care of itself. Whatever falls, I'll be ready."

Venters retraced his steps along the terrace back to camp, and found Bess in the old familiar seat, waiting and watching for his return.

"I went off by myself to think a little," he explained.

"You never looked that way before. What—what is it? Won't you tell me?"

"Well, Bess, the fact is I've been dreaming a lot. This valley makes a fellow dream. So I forced myself to think. We can't live this way much longer. Soon I'll simply have to go to Cottonwoods. We need a whole pack train of supplies. I can get—"

"Can you go safely?" she interrupted.

"Why, I'm sure of it. I'll ride through the Pass at night. I haven't any fear that Wrangle isn't where I left him. And once on him—Bess, just wait till you see that horse!"

"Oh, I want to see him—to ride him. But—but, Bern, this is what troubles me," she said. "Will—will you come back?"

"Give me four days. If I'm not back in four days you'll know I'm dead. For that only shall keep me."

"Oh!"

"Bess, I'll come back. There's danger—I wouldn't lie to you—but I can take care of myself."

"Bern, I'm sure—oh, I'm sure of it! All my life I've watched hunted men. I can tell what's in them. And I believe you can ride and shoot and see with any rider of the sage. It's not—not that I—fear."

"Well, what is it, then?"

"Why—why—why should you come back at all?"

"I couldn't leave you here alone."

"You might change your mind when you get to the village—among old friends—"

"I won't change my mind. As for old friends—" He uttered a short, expressive laugh.

"Then—there—there must be a—a woman!" Dark red mantled the clear tan of temple and cheek and neck. Her eyes were eyes of shame, upheld a long moment by intense, straining search for the verification of her fear.

Suddenly they drooped, her head fell to her knees, her hands flew to her hot cheeks.

"Bess—look here," said Venters, with a sharpness due to the violence with which he checked his quick, surging emotion.

As if compelled against her will—answering to an irresistible voice—Bess raised her head, looked at him with sad, dark eyes, and tried to whisper with tremulous lips.

"There's no woman," went on Venters, deliberately holding her glance with his. "Nothing on earth, barring the chances of life, can keep me away."

Her face flashed and flushed with the glow of a leaping joy; but like the vanishing of a gleam it disappeared to leave her as he had never beheld her.

"I am nothing—I am lost—I am nameless!"

"Do you *want* me to come back?" he asked, with sudden stern coldness. "Maybe *you* want to go back to Oldring!"

That brought her erect, trembling and ashy pale, with dark, proud eyes and mute lips refuting his insinuation.

"Bess, I beg your pardon. I shouldn't have said that. But you angered me. I intend to work—to make a home for you here—to be a—a brother to you as long as ever you need me. And you must forget what you are—were—I mean, and be happy. When you remember that old life you are bitter, and it hurts me."

"I was happy—I shall be very happy. Oh, you're so good that—that it kills me! If I think, I can't believe it. I grow sick with wondering *why*. I'm only a—*let me say it*—only a lost, nameless—girl of the rustlers. *Oldring's Girl*, they called me. That you should save me—be so good and kind—want to make me happy—why, it's beyond belief. No wonder I'm wretched at the thought of your leaving me. But I'll be wretched and bitter no more. I promise you. If only I could repay you even a little—"

"You've repaid me a hundredfold. Will you believe me?"

"Believe you! I couldn't do else."

"Then listen! . . . Saving you, I saved myself. Living here in this valley with you, I've found myself. I've learned to think while I was dreaming. I never troubled myself about God. But God, or some wonderful spirit, has whispered to me here. I absolutely deny the truth of what you say about yourself. I can't explain it. There are things too deep to tell. Whatever the terrible wrongs you've suffered, God holds you blameless. I see that—feel that in you every moment you are near me. I've a mother and a sister 'way back in Illinois. If I could I'd take you to them—to-morrow."

"*If it were true!* Oh, I might—I might lift my head!" she cried.

"Lift it then—you child. For I swear it's true."

She did lift her head with the singular wild grace always a part of her actions, with that old unconscious intimation of innocence which always tortured Venters, but now with something more—a spirit rising from the depths that linked itself to his brave words.

"I've been thinking—too," she cried, with quivering smile and swelling breast. "I've discovered myself—too. I'm young—I'm alive—I'm so full—oh! I'm a woman!"

"Bess, I believe I can claim credit of that last discovery—before you," Venters said, and laughed.

"Oh, there's more—there's something I must tell you."

"Tell it, then."

"When will you go to Cottonwoods?"

"As soon as the storms are past, or the worst of them."

"I'll tell you before you go. I can't now. I don't know how I shall then. But it must be told. I'd never let you leave me without knowing. For in spite of what you say there's a chance you mightn't come back."

Day after day the west wind blew across the valley. Day after day the clouds clustered gray and purple and black. The cliffs sang and the caves rang with Oldring's knell, and the lightning flashed, the thunder rolled, the echoes crashed and crashed, and the rains flooded the valley. Wild flowers sprang up everywhere, swaying with the lengthening grass on the terraces, smiling wanly from shady nooks, peeping wondrously from year-dry crevices of the walls. The valley bloomed into a paradise. Every single moment, from the breaking of the gold bar through the bridge at dawn on to the reddening of rays over the western wall, was one of colorful change. The valley swam in thick, transparent haze, golden at dawn, warm and white at noon, purple in the twilight. At the end of every storm a rainbow curved down into the leaf-bright forest to shine and fade and leave lingeringly some faint essence of its rosy iris in the air.

Venters walked with Bess, once more in a dream, and watched the lights change on the walls, and faced the wind from out of the west.

Always it brought softly to him strange, sweet tidings of far-off things. It blew from a place that was old and whispered of youth. It blew down the grooves of time. It brought a story of the passing hours. It breathed low of fighting men and praying women. It sang clearly the song of love. That ever was the burden of its tidings —youth in the shady woods, waders through the wet meadows, boy and girl at the hedgerow stile, bathers in the booming surf, sweet, idle hours on grassy, windy hills, long strolls down moonlit lanes—everywhere in far-off lands, fingers locked and bursting hearts and longing lips—from all the world tidings of unquenchable love.

Often, in these hours of dreams he watched the girl, and asked himself of what was she dreaming? For the changing light of the valley reflected its gleam and its color and its meaning in the changing light of her eyes. He saw in them infinitely more then he saw in his dreams. He saw thought and soul and nature—strong vision of life. All tidings the west wind blew from distance and age he found deep in those dark-blue depths, and found them mysteries solved. Under their wistful shadow he softened, and in the softening felt himself grow a sadder, a wiser, and a better man.

While the west wind blew its tidings, filling his heart full, teaching him a man's part, the days passed, the purple clouds changed to white, and the storms were over for that summer.

"I must go now," he said.

"When?" she asked.

"At once—to-night."

"I'm glad the time has come. It dragged at me. Go—for you'll come back the sooner."

Late in the afternoon, as the ruddy sun split its last flame in the ragged notch of the western wall, Bess walked with Venters along the eastern terrace, up the long, weathered slope, under the great stone bridge. They entered the narrow gorge to climb around the fence long before built there by Venters. Farther than this she had never been. Twilight had already fallen in the gorge. It brightened to waning shadow in the wider ascent. He showed her Balancing Rock, of which he had often told her, and explained its sinister leaning over the outlet. Shuddering, she looked down the long, pale incline with its closed-in, toppling walls.

"What an awful trail! Did you carry me up here?"

"I did, surely," replied he.

"It frightens me, somehow. Yet I never was afraid of trails. I'd ride anywhere a horse could go, and climb where he couldn't. But there's something fearful here. I feel as—as if the place was watching me."

"Look at this rock. It's balanced here—balanced

perfectly. You know I told you the cliff-dwellers cut the rock, and why. But they're gone and the rock waits. Can't you see—feel how it waits here? I moved it once, and I'll never dare again. A strong heave would start it. Then it would fall and bang, and smash that crag, and jar the walls, and close forever the outlet to Deception Pass!"

"Ah! When you come back I'll steal up here and push and push with all my might to roll the rock and close forever the outlet to the Pass!" She said it lightly, but in the undercurrent of her voice was a heavier note, a ring deeper than any ever given mere play of words.

"Bess! . . . You can't dare me! Wait till I come back with supplies—then roll the stone."

"I—was—in—fun." Her voice now throbbed low. "Always you must be free to go when you will. Go now . . . this place presses on me—stifles me."

"I'm going—but you had something to tell me?"

"Yes. . . . Will you—come back?"

"I'll come if I live."

"But—but you mightn't come?"

"That's possible, of course. It 'll take a good deal to kill me. A man couldn't have a faster horse or keener dog. And, Bess, I've guns, and I'll use them if I'm pushed. But don't worry."

"I've faith in you. I'll not worry until after four days. Only—because you mightn't come—I *must* tell you—"

She lost her voice. Her pale face, her great, glowing, earnest eyes, seemed to stand alone out of the gloom of the gorge. The dog whined, breaking the silence.

"I *must* tell you—because you mightn't come back," she whispered. "You *must* know what—what I think of your goodness—of you. Always I've been tongue-tied. I seemed not to be grateful. It was deep in my heart. Even now—if I were other than I am—I couldn't tell you. But I'm nothing—only a rustler's girl—nameless—infamous. You've saved me—and I'm—I'm yours to do with as you like. . . . With all my heart and soul—I love you!"

CHAPTER XV

SHADOWS ON THE SAGE-SLOPE

IN the cloudy, threatening, waning summer days shadows lengthened down the sage-slope, and Jane Withersteen likened them to the shadows gathering and closing in around her life.

Mrs. Larkin died, and little Fay was left an orphan with no known relative. Jane's love redoubled. It was the saving brightness of a darkening hour. Fay turned now to Jane in childish worship. And Jane at last found full expression for the mother-longing in her heart. Upon Lassiter, too, Mrs. Larkin's death had some subtle reaction. Before, he had often, without explanation, advised Jane to send Fay back to any Gentile family that would take her in. Passionately and reproachfully and wonderingly Jane had refused even to entertain such an idea. And now Lassiter never advised it again, grew sadder and quieter in his contemplation of the child, and infinitely more gentle and loving. Sometimes Jane had a cold, inexplicable sensation of dread when she saw Lassiter watching Fay. What did the rider see in the future? Why did he, day by day, grow more silent, calmer, cooler, yet sadder in prophetic assurance of something to be?

No doubt, Jane thought, the rider, in his almost superhuman power of foresight, saw behind the horizon the dark, lengthening shadows that were soon to crowd and gloom over him and her and little Fay. Jane Withersteen awaited the long-deferred breaking of the storm with a courage and embittered calm that had come to her in her extremity. Hope had not died. Doubt and fear, subservient to her will, no longer gave her sleepless nights and tortured days. Love remained. All that she had loved she now loved the more. She seemed to feel that she was defiantly flinging the wealth of her love in the face of misfortune and of hate. No day passed but she prayed for all—and most fervently for her enemies. It troubled her that she had lost, or had never gained, the whole control of her mind. In some measure reason and wisdom and decision were locked in a chamber of her brain, awaiting a key. Power to think of some things was taken from her. Meanwhile, abiding a day of judgment, she fought ceaselessly to deny the bitter drops in her cup, to tear back the slow, the intangibly slow growth of a hot, corrosive lichen eating into her heart.

On the morning of August 10th, Jane, while waiting in the court for Lassiter, heard a clear, ringing report of a rifle. It came from the grove, somewhere toward the corrals. Jane glanced out in alarm. The day was dull, windless, soundless. The leaves of the cottonwoods drooped, as if they had foretold the doom of Withersteen House and were now ready to die and drop and decay. Never had Jane seen such shade. She pondered on the meaning of the report. Revolver shots had of late cracked from different parts of the grove—spies taking snap-shots at Lassiter from a cowardly distance! But a rifle report meant more. Riders seldom used rifles. Judkins and Venters were the exceptions she called to mind. Had the men who hounded her hidden in her grove, taken to the rifle to rid her of Lassiter, her last friend? It was probable—it was likely. And she did not share his cool assumption that his death would never come at the hands of a Mormon. Long had she expected it. His constancy to her, his singular reluctance to use the fatal skill for which he was famed—both now plain to all Mormons—laid him open to inevitable assassination. Yet what charm against ambush and aim and enemy he seemed to bear about him! No, Jane reflected, it was not charm; only a wonderful training of eye and ear, and sense of impending peril. Nevertheless that could not forever avail against secret attack.

That moment a rustling of leaves attracted her attention; then the familiar clinking accompaniment of a slow, soft, measured step, and Lassiter walked into the court.

"Jane, there's a fellow out there with a long gun," he said, and, removing his sombrero, showed his head bound in a bloody scarf.

"I heard the shot; I knew it was meant for you. Let me see—you can't be badly injured?"

"I reckon not. But mebbe it wasn't a close call! . . . I'll sit here in this corner where nobody can see me from the grove." He untied the scarf and removed it to show a long, bleeding furrow above his left temple.

"It's only a cut," said Jane. "But how it bleeds! Hold your scarf over it just a moment till I come back."

She ran into the house and returned with bandages; and while she bathed and dressed the wound Lassiter talked.

"That fellow had a good chance to get me. But he must have flinched when he pulled the trigger. As I dodged down I saw him run through the trees. He had a rifle. I've been expectin' that kind of gun play. I reckon now I'll have to keep a little closer hid myself. These fellers all seem to get chilly or shaky when they draw a bead on me, but one of them might jest happen to hit me."

"Won't you go away—leave Cottonwoods as I've begged you to—before some one does happen to hit you?" she appealed to him.

"I reckon I'll stay."

"But, oh, Lassiter—your blood will be on my hands!"

"See here, lady, look at your hands now, right now. Aren't they fine, firm, white hands? Aren't they bloody now? Lassiter's blood! That's a queer thing to stain your beautiful hands. But if you could only see deeper you'd find a redder color of blood. Heart color, Jane!"

"Oh! . . . My friend!"

"No, Jane, I'm not one to quit when the game grows hot, no more than you. This game, though, is new to me, an' I don't know the moves yet, else I wouldn't have stepped in front of that bullet."

"Have you no desire to hunt the man who fired at you—to find him—and—and kill him?"

"Well, I reckon I haven't any great hankerin' for that."

"Oh, the wonder of it! . . . I knew—I prayed—I trusted. Lassiter, I almost gave—all myself to soften you to Mormons. Thank God, and thank you, my friend. . . . But, selfish woman that I am, this is no great test. What's the life of one of those sneaking cowards to such a man as you? I think of your great hate toward him who— I think of your life's implacable purpose. Can it be—"

"Wait! . . . Listen!" he whispered. "I hear a hoss."

He rose noiselessly, with his ear to the breeze. Suddenly he pulled his sombrero down over his bandaged head and, swinging his gun-sheaths round in front, he stepped into the alcove.

"It's a hoss—comin' fast," he added.

Jane's listening ear soon caught a faint, rapid, rhythmic beat of hoofs. It came from the sage. It gave her a thrill that she was at a loss to understand. The sound rose stronger, louder. Then came a clear, sharp difference when the horse passed from the sage trail to the hard-packed ground of the grove. It became a ringing run—swift in its bell-like clatterings, yet singular in longer pause than usual between the hoofbeats of a horse.

"It's Wrangle! . . . It's Wrangle!" cried Jane Withersteen. "I'd know him from a million horses!"

Excitement and thrilling expectancy flooded out all Jane Withersteen's calm. A tight band closed round her breast as she saw the giant sorrel flit in reddish-brown flashes across the openings in the green. Then he was pounding down the lane—thundering into the court—crashing his great iron-shod hoofs on the stone flags. Wrangle it was surely, but shaggy and wild-eyed, and sage-streaked, with dust-caked lather staining his flanks. He reared and crashed down and plunged. The rider leaped off, threw the bridle, and held hard on a lasso looped round Wrangle's head and neck. Jane's heart sank as she tried to recognize Venters in the rider. Something familiar struck her in the lofty stature, in the sweep of powerful shoulders. But this bearded, long-haired, unkempt man, who wore ragged clothes patched with pieces of skin, and boots that showed bare legs and feet—this dusty, dark, and wild rider could not possibly be Venters.

"Whoa, Wrangle, old boy! Come down. Easy now. So—so—so. You're home, old boy, and presently you can have a drink of water you'll remember."

In the voice Jane knew the rider to be Venters. He tied Wrangle to the hitching-rack and turned to the court.

"Oh, Bern! . . . You wild man!" she exclaimed.

"Jane—Jane, it's good to see you! Hello, Lassiter! Yes, it's Venters."

Like rough iron his hard hand crushed Jane's. In it she felt the difference she saw in him. Wild, rugged, unshorn—yet how splendid! He had gone away a boy—he had returned a man. He appeared taller, wider of shoulder, deeper-chested, more powerfully built. But was that only her fancy—he had always been a young giant—was the change one of spirit? He might have been absent for years, proven by fire and steel, grown like Lassiter, strong and cool and sure. His eyes—were they keener, more flashing than before?—met hers with clear, frank, warm regard, in which perplexity was not, nor discontent, nor pain.

"Look at me long as you like," he said, with a laugh. "I'm not much to look at. And, Jane, neither you nor Lassiter, can brag. You're paler than I ever saw you. Lassiter, here, he wears a bloody bandage under his hat. That reminds me. Some one took a flying shot at me down in the sage. It made Wrangle run some. . . . Well, perhaps you've more to tell me than I've got to tell you."

Briefly, in few words, Jane outlined the circumstances of her undoing in the weeks of his absence.

Under his beard and bronze she saw his face whiten in terrible wrath.

"Lassiter—what held you back?"

No time in the long period of fiery moments and sudden shocks had Jane Withersteen ever beheld Lassiter as calm and serene and cool as then.

"Jane had gloom enough without my addin' to it by shootin' up the village," he said.

As strange as Lassiter's coolness was Venters's curious, intent scrutiny of them both, and under it Jane felt a flaming tide wave from bosom to temples.

"Well—you're right," he said, with slow pause. "It surprises me a little, that's all."

Jane sensed then a slight alteration in Venters, and what it was, in her own confusion, she could not tell. It had always been her intention to acquaint him with the deceit she had fallen to in her zeal to move Lassiter. She did not mean to spare herself. Yet now, at the moment, before these riders, it was an impossibility to explain.

Venters was speaking somewhat haltingly, without his former frankness. "I found Oldring's hiding-place and your red herd. I learned—I know—I'm sure there was a deal between Tull and Oldring." He paused and shifted his position and his gaze. He looked as if he wanted to say something that he found beyond him. Sorrow and pity and shame seemed to contend for mastery over him. Then he raised himself and spoke with effort. "Jane, I've cost you too much. You've almost ruined yourself for me. It was wrong, for I'm not worth it. I never deserved such friendship. Well, maybe it's not too late. You must give me up. Mind, I haven't changed. I am just the same as ever. I'll see Tull while I'm here, and tell him to his face."

"Bern, it's too late," said Jane.

"I'll *make* him believe!" cried Venters, violently.

"You ask me to break our friendship?"

"Yes. If you don't, I shall!"

"Forever?"

"Forever!"

Jane sighed. Another shadow had lengthened down the sage-slope to cast further darkness upon her. A melancholy sweetness pervaded her resignation. The boy who had left her had returned a man, nobler, stronger, one in whom she divined something unbending as steel. There might come a moment later when she would wonder why she had not fought against his will, but just now she yielded to it. She liked him as well—nay, more, she thought, only her emotions were deadened by the long, menacing wait for the bursting storm.

Once before she had held out her hand to him—when she gave it; now she stretched it tremblingly forth in acceptance of the decree circumstance had laid upon them. Venters bowed over it, kissed it, pressed it hard, and half stifled a sound very like a sob. Certain it was that when he raised his head tears glistened in his eyes.

"Some—women—have a hard lot," he said, huskily. Then he shook his powerful form, and his rags lashed about him. "I'll say a few things to Tull—when I meet him."

"Bern—you'll not draw on Tull? Oh, that must not be! Promise me—"

"I promise you this," he interrupted, in stern passion that thrilled while it terrorized her. "If you say one more word for that plotter I'll kill him as I would a mad coyote!"

Jane clasped her hands. Was this fire-eyed man the one whom she had once made as wax to her touch? Had Venters become Lassiter and Lassiter Venters?

"I'll—say no more," she faltered.

"Jane, Lassiter once called you blind," said Venters. "It must be true. But I won't upbraid you. Only don't rouse the devil in me by praying for Tull! I'll try to keep cool when I meet him. That's all. Now there's one more thing I want to ask of you—the last. I've found a valley down in the Pass. It's a wonderful place. I intend to stay there. It's so hidden I believe no one can find it. There's good water, and browse, and game. I want to raise corn and stock. I need to take in supplies. Will you give them to me?"

"Assuredly. The more you take the better you'll please me—and perhaps the less my—my enemies will get."

"Venters, I reckon you'll have trouble packin' anythin' away," put in Lassiter.

"I'll go at night."

"Mebbe that wouldn't be best. You'd sure be stopped. You'd better go early in the mornin'—say, just after dawn. That's the safest time to move round here."

"Lassiter, I'll be hard to stop," returned Venters, darkly.

"I reckon so."

"Bern," said Jane, "go first to the riders' quarters and get yourself a complete outfit. You're a—a sight.

Then help yourself to whatever else you need—burros, packs, grain, dried fruits, and meat. You must take coffee and sugar and flour—all kinds of supplies. Don't forget corn and seeds. I remember how you used to starve. Please—please take all you can pack away from here. I'll make a bundle for you, which you mustn't open till you're in your valley. How I'd like to see it! To judge by you and Wrangle, how wild it must be!"

Jane walked down into the outer court and approached the sorrel. Upstarting, he laid back his ears and eyed her.

"Wrangle—dear old Wrangle," she said, and put a caressing hand on his matted mane. "Oh, he's wild, but he knows me! Bern, can he run as fast as ever?"

"Run? Jane, he's done sixty miles since last night at dark, and I could make him kill Black Star right now in a ten-mile race."

"He never could," protested Jane. "He couldn't even if he was fresh."

"I reckon mebbe the best hoss 'll prove himself yet," said Lassiter, "an', Jane, if it ever comes to that race I'd like you to be on Wrangle."

"I'd like that, too," rejoined Venters. "But, Jane, maybe Lassiter's hint is extreme. Bad as your prospects are, you'll surely never come to the running point."

"Who knows!" she replied, with mournful smile.

"No, no, Jane, it can't be so bad as all that. Soon as I see Tull there'll be a change in your fortunes. I'll hurry down to the village. . . . Now don't worry."

Jane retired to the seclusion of her room. Lassiter's subtle forecasting of disaster, Venters's forced optimism, neither remained in mind. Material loss weighed nothing in the balance with other losses she was sustaining. She wondered dully at her sitting there, hands folded listlessly, with a kind of numb deadness to the passing of time and the passing of her riches. She thought of

Venters's friendship. She had not lost that, but she had lost him. Lassiter's friendship—that was more than love—it would endure, but soon he, too, would be gone. Little Fay slept dreamlessly upon the bed, her golden curls streaming over the pillow. Jane had the child's worship. Would she lose that, too? And if she did, what then would be left? Conscience thundered at her that there was left her religion. Conscience thundered that she should be grateful on her knees for this baptism of fire; that through misfortune, sacrifice, and suffering her soul might be fused pure gold. But the old, spontaneous, rapturous spirit no more exalted her. She wanted to be a woman—not a martyr. Like the saint of old who mortified his flesh, Jane Withersteen had in her the temper for heroic martyrdom, if by sacrificing herself she could save the souls of others. But here the damnable verdict blistered her that the more she sacrificed herself the blacker grew the souls of her churchmen. There was something terribly wrong with her soul, something terribly wrong with her churchmen and her religion. In the whirling gulf of her thought there was yet one shining light to guide her, to sustain her in her hope; and it was that, despite her errors and her frailties and her blindness, she had one absolute and unfaltering hold on ultimate and supreme justice. That was love. "Love your enemies as yourself!" was a divine word, entirely free from any church or creed.

Jane's meditations were disturbed by Lassiter's soft, tinkling step in the court. Always he wore the clinking spurs. Always he was in readiness to ride. She passed out and called him into the huge, dim hall.

"I think you'll be safer here. The court is too open," she said.

"I reckon," replied Lassiter. "An' it's cooler here. The day's sure muggy. Well, I went down to the village with Venters."

"Already! Where is he?" queried Jane, in quick amaze.

"He's at the corrals. Blake's helpin' him get the burros an' packs ready. That Blake is a good fellow."

"Did—did Bern meet Tull?"

"I guess he did," answered Lassiter, and he laughed dryly.

"Tell me! Oh, *you* exasperate me! You're so cool, so calm! For Heaven's sake, tell me what happened!"

"First time I've been in the village for weeks," went on Lassiter, mildly. "I reckon there 'ain't been more of a show for a long time. Me an' Venters walkin' down the road! It was funny. I ain't sayin' anybody was particular glad to see us. I'm not much thought of hereabouts, an' Venters he sure looks like what you called him, a wild man. Well, there was some runnin' of folks before we got to the stores. Then everybody vamoosed except some surprised rustlers in front of a saloon. Venters went right in the stores an' saloons, an' of course I went along. I don't know which tickled me the most—the actions of many fellers we met, or Venters's nerve. Jane, I was downright glad to be along. You see *that* sort of thing is my element, an' I've been away from it for a spell. But we didn't find Tull in one of them places. Some Gentile feller at last told Venters he'd find Tull in that long buildin' next to Parsons's store. It's a kind of meetin'-room; and sure enough, when we peeped in, it was half full of men.

"Venters yelled: 'Don't anybody pull guns! We ain't come for that!' Then he tramped in, an' I was some put to keep alongside him. There was a hard, scrapin' sound of feet, a loud cry, an' then some whisperin', an' after that stillness you could cut with a knife. Tull was there, an' that fat party who once tried to throw a gun on me, an' other important-lookin' men, an' that little frog-legged feller who was with Tull the day I rode in here. I wish you could have seen their faces, 'specially Tull's an' the fat party's. But there ain't no use of me tryin' to tell you how they looked.

"Well, Venters an' I stood there in the middle of the room, with that batch of men all in front of us, an' not a blamed one of them winked an eyelash or moved a finger. It was natural, of course, for me to notice many of them packed guns. That's a way of mine, first noticin' them things. Venters spoke up, an' his voice sort of chilled an' cut, an' he told Tull he had a few things to say."

Here Lassiter paused while he turned his sombrero round and round, in his familiar habit, and his eyes had the look of a man seeing over again some thrilling spectacle, and under his red bronze there was strange animation.

"Like a shot, then, Venters told Tull that the friendship between you an' him was all over, an' he was leaving your place. He said you'd both of you broken off in the hope of propitiatin' your people, but you hadn't changed your mind otherwise, an' never would.

"Next he spoke up for you. I ain't goin' to tell you what he said. Only—no other woman who ever lived ever had such tribute! You had a champion, Jane, an' never fear that those thick-skulled men don't know you now. It couldn't be otherwise. He spoke the ringin', lightnin' truth. . . . Then he accused Tull of the underhand, miserable robbery of a helpless woman. He told Tull where the red herd was, of a deal made with Oldrin', that Jerry Card had made the deal. I thought Tull was goin' to drop, an' that little frog-legged cuss, he looked some limp an' white. But Venters's voice would have kept anybody's legs from bucklin'. I was stiff myself. He went on an' called Tull—called him every bad name ever known to a rider, an' then some. He cursed Tull. I never hear a man get such a cursin'. He laughed in scorn at the idea of Tull bein' a minister. He said Tull an' a few more dogs of hell builded their empire out of the hearts of such innocent an' God-fearin' women as Jane Withersteen. He called Tull a binder of women, a callous beast who hid behind a mock mantle of righteousness—an' the last an' lowest coward on the face of the earth. To prey on weak women through their religion—that was the last unspeakable crime!

"Then he finished, an' by this time he'd almost lost his voice. But his whisper was enough. 'Tull,' he said, '*she* begged me not to draw on you to-day. *She* would pray for you if you burned her at the stake. . . . But listen! . . . I swear if you and I ever come face to face again, I'll kill you!'

"We backed out of the door then, an' up the road. But nobody follered us."

Jane found herself weeping passionately. She had not been conscious of it till Lassiter ended his story, and she experienced exquisite pain and relief in shedding tears. Long had her eyes been dry, her grief deep; long had her emotions been dumb. Lassiter's story put her on the rack; the appalling nature of Venters's act and speech had no parallel as an outrage; it was worse than bloodshed. Men like Tull had been shot, but had one ever been so terribly denounced in public? Overmounting her horror, an uncontrollable, quivering passion shook her very soul. It was sheer human glory in the deed of a fearless man. It was hot, primitive instinct to live—to fight. It was a kind of mad joy in Venters's chivalry. It was close to the wrath that had first shaken her in the beginning of this war waged upon her.

"Well, well, Jane, don't take it that way," said Lassiter, in evident distress. "I had to tell you. There's some things a feller jest can't keep. It's strange you give up on hearin' that, when all this long time you've been the gamest woman I ever seen. But I don't know women. Mebbe there's reason for you to cry. I know this—nothin' ever rang in my soul an' so filled it as what Venters did. I'd like to have done it, but—I'm only good for throwin' a gun, an' it seems you hate that. . . . Well, I'll be goin' now."

"Where?"

"Venters took Wrangle to the stable. The sorrel's shy a shoe, an' I've got to help hold the big devil an' put on another."

"Tell Bern to come for the pack I want to give him —and—and to say good-by," called Jane, as Lassiter went out.

Jane passed the rest of that day in a vain endeavor to decide what and what not to put in the pack for Venters. This task was the last she would ever perform for him, and the gifts were the last she would ever make him. So she picked and chose and rejected, and chose again, and often paused in sad revery, and began again, till at length she filled the pack.

It was about sunset, and she and Fay had finished supper and were sitting in the court, when Venters's quick steps rang on the stones. She scarcely knew him, for he had changed the tattered garments, and she missed the dark beard and long hair. Still he was not the Venters of old. As he came up the steps she felt herself pointing to the pack, and heard herself speaking words that were meaningless to her. He said good-by; he kissed her, released her, and turned away. His tall figure blurred in her sight, grew dim through dark, streaked vision, and then he vanished.

Twilight fell around Withersteen House, and dusk and night. Little Fay slept; but Jane lay with strained, aching eyes. She heard the wind moaning in the cottonwoods and mice squeaking in the walls. The night was interminably long, yet she prayed to hold back the dawn. What would another day bring forth? The blackness of her room seemed blacker for the sad, entering gray of morning light. She heard the chirp of awakening birds, and fancied she caught a faint clatter of hoofs. Then low, dull, distant, throbbed a heavy gunshot. She had expected it, was waiting for it; nevertheless, an electric shock checked her heart, froze the very living fiber of her bones. That vise-like hold on her faculties apparently did not relax for a long time, and it was a voice under her window that released her.

"Jane! . . . Jane!" softly called Lassiter.

She answered somehow.

"It's all right. Venters got away. I thought mebbe you'd heard that shot, an' I was worried some."

"What was it—who fired?"

"Well—some fool feller tried to stop Venters out there in the sage—an' he only stopped lead! . . . I think it 'll be all right. I haven't seen or heard of any other fellers round. Venters 'll go through safe. An', Jane, I've got Bells saddled, an' I'm going to trail Venters. Mind, I won't show myself unless he falls foul of somebody an' needs me. I want to see if this place where he's goin' is safe for him. He says nobody can track him there. I never seen the place yet I couldn't track a man to. Now, Jane, you stay indoors while I'm gone, an' keep close watch on Fay. Will you?"

"Yes! Oh yes!"

"An' another thing, Jane," he continued, then paused for long—"another thing—if you ain't here when I come back—if you're *gone*—don't fear, I'll trail you—I'll find you."

"My dear Lassiter, where could I be gone—as you put it?" asked Jane, in curious surprise.

"I reckon you might be somewhere. Mebbe tied in an old barn—or corralled in some gulch—or chained in a cave! *Milly Erne was*—till she give in! Mebbe that's news to you. . . . Well, if you're gone I'll hunt for you."

"No, Lassiter," she replied, sadly and low. "If I'm

gone just forget the unhappy woman whose blinded selfish deceit you repaid with kindness and love."

She heard a deep, muttering curse, under his breath, and then the silvery tinkling of his spurs as he moved away.

Jane entered upon the duties of that day with a settled, gloomy calm. Disaster hung in the dark clouds, in the shade, in the humid west wind. Blake, when he reported, appeared without his usual cheer; and Jerd wore a harassed look of a worn and worried man. And when Judkins put in appearance, riding a lame horse, and dismounted with the cramp of a rider, his dust-covered figure and his darkly grim, almost dazed expression told Jane of dire calamity. She had no need of words.

"Miss Withersteen, I have to report—loss of the—white herd," said Judkins, hoarsely.

"Come, sit down; you look played out," replied Jane, solicitously. She brought him brandy and food, and while he partook of refreshments, of which he appeared badly in need, she asked no questions.

"No one rider—could hev done more—Miss Withersteen," he went on, presently.

"Judkins, don't be distressed. You've done more than any other rider. I've long expected to lose the white herd. It's no surprise. It's in line with other things that are happening. I'm grateful for your service."

"Miss Withersteen, I knew how you'd take it. But if anythin', that makes it harder to tell. You see, a feller wants to do so much fer you, an' I'd got fond of my job. We hed the herd a ways off to the north of the break in the valley. There was a big level an' pools of water an' tip-top browse. But the cattle was in a high nervous condition. Wild—as wild as antelope! You see, they'd been so scared they never slept. I ain't a-goin' to tell you of the many tricks that were pulled off out there in the sage. But there wasn't a day fer weeks thet the herd didn't get started to run. We allus managed to ride 'em close an' drive 'em back an' keep 'em bunched. Honest, Miss Withersteen, them steers was *thin*. They was *thin* when water and grass was everywhere. *Thin* at this season—thet 'll tell you how your steers was pestered. Fer instance, one night a strange runnin' streak of fire run right through the herd. That streak was a coyote—*with an oiled an' blazin' tail!* Fer I shot it an' found out. We hed hell with the herd that night, an' if the sage an' grass hedn't been wet—we, hosses, steers, an' all would hev burned up. But I said I wasn't goin' to tell you any of the tricks. . . . Strange now, Miss Withersteen, when the stampede did come it was from natural cause—jest a whirlin' devil of dust. You've seen the like often. An' this wasn't no big whirl, fer the dust was mostly settled. It had dried out in a little swale, an' ordinarily no steer would ever hev run fer it. But the herd was nervous an' wild. An' jest as Lassiter said, when that bunch of white steers got to movin' they was as bad as buffalo. I've seen some buffalo stampedes back in Nebraska, an' this bolt of the steers was the same kind.

"I tried to mill the herd jest as Lassiter did. But I wasn't equal to it, Miss Withersteen. I don't believe the rider lives who could hev turned thet herd. We kept along of the herd fer miles, an' more 'n one of my boys tried to get the steers a-millin'. It wasn't no use. We got off level ground, goin' down, an' then the steers ran somethin' fierce. We left the little gullies an' washes level-full of dead steers. Finally I saw the herd was makin' to pass a kind of low pocket between ridges. There was a hog-back—as we used to call 'em—a pile of rocks stickin' up, an I saw the herd was goin' to split round it, or swing out to the left. An' I wanted 'em to go to the right so mebbe we'd be able to drive 'em into the pocket. So, with all my boys except three, I rode hard to turn the herd a little to the right. We couldn't budge 'em. They went on an' split round the rocks, an' the most of 'em was turned sharp to the left by a deep wash we hedn't seen—hed no chance to see.

"The other three boys—Jimmy Vail, Joe Willis, an' thet little Cairns boy—a nervy kid! they, with Cairns leadin', tried to buck thet herd round to the pocket. It was a wild, fool idee. I couldn't do nothin'. The boys got hemmed in between the steers an' the wash—thet they hedn't no chance to see, either. Vail an' Wills was run down right before our eyes. An' Cairns, who rode a fine hoss, he did some ridin' I never seen equaled, an' would hev beat the steers if there'd been any room to run in. I was high up an' could see how the steers kept spillin' by twos an' threes over into the wash. Cairns put his hoss to a place thet was too wide fer any hoss, an' broke his neck an' the hoss's too. We found that out after, an' as fer Vail an' Wills—two thousand steers ran over the poor boys. There wasn't much left to pack home fer burying! . . . An', Miss Withersteen, thet all happened yesterday, an' I believe, if the white herd didn't run over the wall of the Pass, it's runnin' yet."

On the morning of the second day after Judkins's recital, during which time Jane remained indoors a prey to regret and sorrow for the boy riders, and a new and now strangely insistent fear for her own person, she again heard what she had missed more than she dared honestly confess—the soft, jingling step of Lassiter. Almost overwhelming relief surged through her, a feeling as akin to joy as any she could have been capable of in those gloomy hours of shadow, and one that suddenly stunned her with the significance of what Lassiter had come to mean to her. She had begged him, for his own sake, to leave Cottonwoods. She might yet beg that, if her weakening courage permitted her to dare absolute loneliness and helplessness, but she realized now that if she were left alone her life would become one long, hideous nightmare.

When his soft steps clinked into the hall, in answer to her greeting, and his tall, black-garbed form filled the door, she felt an inexpressible sense of immediate safety. In his presence she lost her fear of the dim passageways of Withersteen House and of every sound. Always it had been that, when he entered the court or the hall, she had experienced a distinctly sickening but gradually lessening shock at sight of the huge black guns swinging at his sides. This time the sickening shock again visited her, it was, however, because a revealing flash of thought told her that it was not alone Lassiter who was thrillingly welcome, but also his fatal weapons. They meant so much. How she had fallen —how broken and spiritless must she be—to have still the same old horror of Lassiter's guns and his name, yet feel somehow a cold, shrinking protection in their law and might and use.

"Did you trail Venters—find his wonderful valley?" she asked, eagerly.

"Yes, an' I reckon it's sure a wonderful place."

"Is he safe there?"

"That's been botherin' me some. I tracked him an' part of the trail was the hardest I ever tackled. Mebbe there's a rustler or somebody in this country who's as good at trackin' as I am. If that's so Venters ain't safe."

"Well—tell me all about Bern and his valley."

To Jane's surprise Lassiter showed disinclination for further talk about his trip. He appeared to be extremely fatigued. Jane reflected that one hundred and twenty miles, with probably a great deal of climbing on foot, all in three days, was enough to tire any rider. Moreover, it presently developed that Lassiter had returned in a mood of singular sadness and preoccupation. She put it down to a moodiness over the loss of her white herd and the now precarious condition of her fortune.

Several days passed, and, as nothing happened, Jane's spirits began to brighten. Once in her musings she thought that this tendency of hers to rebound was as sad as it was futile. Meanwhile, she had resumed her walks through the grove with little Fay.

One morning she went as far as the sage. She had not seen the slope since the beginning of the rains, and now it bloomed a rich deep purple. There was a high wind blowing, and the sage tossed and waved and colored beautifully from light to dark. Clouds scudded across the sky and their shadows sailed darkly down the sunny slope.

Upon her return toward the house she went by the lane to the stables, and she had scarcely entered the great open space with its corrals and sheds when she saw Lassiter hurriedly approaching. Fay broke from her and, running to a corral fence, began to pat and pull the long, hanging ears of a drowsy burro.

One look at Lassiter armed her for a blow.

Without a word he led her across the wide yard to the rise of the ground upon which the stable stood.

"Jane—look!" he said, and pointed to the ground.

Jane glanced down, and again, and upon steadier vision made out splotches of blood on the stones, and broad, smooth marks in the dust, leading out toward the sage.

"What made these?" she asked.

"I reckon somebody has dragged dead or wounded men out to where there was hosses in the sage."

"Dead—or—wounded—men!"

"I reckon—Jane, are you strong? Can you bear up?"

His hands were gently holding hers, and his eyes—suddenly she could no longer look into them. "Strong?" she echoed, trembling. "I—I will be."

SHADOWS ON THE SAGE-SLOPE

Up on the stone-flag drive, nicked with the marks made by the iron-shod hoofs of her racers, Lassiter led her, his grasp ever growing firmer.

"Where's Blake—and—and Jerd?" she asked, haltingly.

"I don't know where Jerd is. Bolted, most likely," replied Lassiter, as he took her through the stone door. "But Blake—poor Blake! He's gone forever! . . . Be prepared, Jane."

With a cold prickling of her skin, with a queer thrumming in her ears, with fixed and staring eyes, Jane saw a gun lying at her feet with chamber swung and empty, and discharged shells scattered near.

Outstretched upon the stable floor lay Blake, ghastly white—dead—one hand clutching a gun and the other twisted in his bloody blouse.

"Whoever the thieves were, whether your people or rustlers—Blake killed some of them!" said Lassiter.

"Thieves?" whispered Jane.

"I reckon. Hoss-thieves! . . . Look!" Lassiter waved his hand toward the stalls.

The first stall—Bells's stall—was empty. All the stalls were empty. No racer whinnied and stamped greeting to her. Night was gone! Black Star was gone!

CHAPTER XVI

GOLD

AS Lassiter had reported to Jane, Venters "went through" safely, and after a toilsome journey reached the peaceful shelter of Surprise Valley. When finally he lay wearily down under the silver spruces, resting from the strain of dragging packs and burros up the slope and through the entrance to Surprise Valley, he had leisure to think, and a great deal of the time went in regretting that he had not been frank with his loyal friend, Jane Withersteen.

But, he kept continually recalling, when he had stood once more face to face with her and had been shocked at the change in her and had heard the details of her adversity, he had not had the heart to tell her of the closer interest which had entered his life. He had not lied; yet he had kept silence.

Bess was in transports over the stores of supplies and the outfit he had packed from Cottonwoods. He had certainly brought a hundred times more than he had gone for; enough, surely, for years, perhaps to make permanent home in the valley. He saw no reason why he need ever leave there again.

After a day of rest he recovered his strength and shared Bess's pleasure in rummaging over the endless packs, and began to plan for the future. And in this planning, his trip to Cottonwoods, with its revived hate of Tull and consequent unleashing of fierce passions, soon faded out of mind. By slower degrees his friendship for Jane Withersteen and his contrition drifted from the active preoccupation of his present thought to a place in memory, with more and more infrequent recalls.

And as far as the state of his mind was concerned, upon the second day after his return, the valley, with its golden hues and purple shades, the speaking west wind and the cool, silent night, and Bess's watching eyes with their wonderful light, so wrought upon Venters that he might never have left them at all.

That very afternoon he set to work. Only one thing hindered him upon beginning, though it in no wise checked his delight, and that was that in the multiplicity of tasks planned to make a paradise out of the valley he could not choose the one with which to begin. He had to grow into the habit of passing from one dreamy pleasure to another, like a bee going from flower to flower in the valley, and he found this wandering habit likely to extend to his labors. Nevertheless, he made a start.

At the outset he discovered Bess to be both a considerable help in some ways and a very great hindrance in others. Her excitement and joy were spurs, inspirations; but she was utterly impracticable in her ideas, and she flitted from one plan to another with bewildering vacillation. Moreover, he fancied that she grew more eager, youthful, and sweet; and he marked that it was far easier to watch her and listen to her than it was to work. Therefore he gave her tasks that necessitated her going often to the cave where he had stored his packs.

Upon the last of these trips, when he was some distance down the terrace and out of sight of camp, he heard a scream, and then the sharp barking of the dogs.

For an instant he straightened up, amazed. Danger for her had been absolutely out of his mind. She had seen a rattlesnake—or a wildcat. Still she would not have been likely to scream at sight of either; and the barking of the dogs was ominous. Dropping his work, he dashed back along the terrace. Upon breaking through a clump of aspens he saw the dark form of a man in the camp. Cold, then hot, Venters burst into frenzied speed to reach his guns. He was cursing himself for a thoughtless fool when the man's tall form became familiar and he recognized Lassiter. Then the reversal of emotions changed his run to a walk; he tried to call out, but his voice refused to carry; when he reached camp there was Lassiter staring at the white-faced girl. By that time Ring and Whitie had recognized him.

"Hello, Venters! I'm makin' you a visit," said Lassiter, slowly. "An' I'm some surprised to see you've a—a young feller for company."

One glance had sufficed for the keen rider to read Bess's real sex, and for once his cool calm had deserted him. He stared till the white of Bess's cheeks flared into crimson. That, if it were needed, was the concluding evidence of her femininity; for it went fittingly with her sun-tinted hair and darkened, dilated eyes, the sweetness of her mouth. and the striking symmetry of her slender shape.

"Heavens! Lassiter!" panted Venters, when he caught his breath. "What relief—it's only you! How—in the name of all—that's wonderful—did you ever get here?"

"I trailed you. We—I wanted to know where you was, if you had a safe place. So I trailed you."

"Trailed me!" cried Venters, bluntly.

"I reckon. It was some of a job after I got to them smooth rocks. I was all day trackin' you up to them little cut steps in the rock. The rest was easy."

"Where's your hoss? I hope you hid him."

"I tied him in them queer cedars down on the slope. He can't be seen from the valley."

"That's good. Well, well! I'm completely dumfounded. It was my idea that no man could track me in here."

"I reckon. But if there's a tracker in these uplands as good as me he can find you."

"That's bad. That 'll worry me. But, Lassiter, now you're here I'm glad to see you. And—and my companion here is not a young fellow! . . . Bess, this is a friend of mine. He saved my life once."

The embarrassment of the moment did not extend to Lassiter. Almost at once his manner, as he shook hands with Bess, relieved Venters and put the girl at ease. After Venters's words and one quick look at Lassiter, her agitation stilled, and, though she was shy, if she were conscious of anything out of the ordinary in the situation, certainly she did not show it.

"I reckon I'll only stay a little while," Lassiter was saying. "An' if you don't mind troublin', I'm hungry. I fetched some biscuits along, but they're gone. Venters, this place is sure the wonderfullest ever seen. Them cut steps on the slope! That outlet into the gorge! An' it's like climbin' up through hell into heaven to climb through that gorge into this valley! There's a queer-lookin' rock at the top of the passage. I didn't have time to stop. I'm wonderin' how you ever found this place. It's sure interestin'."

During the preparation and eating of dinner Lassiter listened mostly, as was his wont, and occasionally he spoke in his quaint and dry way. Venters noted, however, that the rider showed an increasing interest in Bess. He asked her no questions, and only directed his attention to her while she was occupied and had no opportunity to observe his scrutiny. It seemed to Venters that Lassiter grew more and more absorbed in his study of Bess, and that he lost his coolness in some strange, softening sympathy. Then, quite abruptly, he arose and announced the necessity for his early departure. He said good-by to Bess in a voice gentle and somewhat broken, and turned hurriedly away. Venters accompanied him, and they had traversed the terrace, climbed the weathered slope, and passed under the stone bridge before either spoke again.

Then Lassiter put a great hand on Venters's shoulder and wheeled him to meet a smoldering fire of gray eyes.

"Lassiter, I couldn't tell Jane! I couldn't," burst out Venters, reading his friend's mind. "I tried. But I couldn't. She wouldn't understand, and she has troubles enough. And I love the girl!"

"Venters, I reckon this beats me. I've seen some queer things in my time, too. This girl—who is she?"

"I don't know."

"Don't know! What is she, then?"

"I don't know that, either. Oh, it's the strangest story you ever heard. I must tell you. But you'll never believe."

"Venters, women were always puzzles to me. But for all that, if this girl ain't a child, an' as innocent, I'm no fit person to think of virtue an' goodness in anybody. Are you goin' to be square with her?"

"I am—so help me God!"

"I reckoned so. Mebbe my temper oughtn't led me to make sure. But, man, she's a woman in all but years. She's sweeter 'n the sage."

"Lassiter, I know, I know. And the *hell* of it is that in spite of her innocence and charm she's—she's not what she seems!"

"I wouldn't want to—of course, I couldn't call you a liar, Venters," said the older man.

"What's more, she was Oldring's Masked Rider!"

Venters expected to floor his friend with that statement, but he was not in any way prepared for the shock his words gave. For an instant he was astounded to see Lassiter stunned; then his own passionate eagerness to unbosom himself, to tell the wonderful story, precluded any other thought.

"Son, tell me all about this," presently said Lassiter

as he seated himself on a stone and wiped his moist brow.

Thereupon Venters began his narrative at the point where he had shot the rustler and Oldring's Masked Rider, and he rushed through it, telling all, not holding back even Bess's unreserved avowal of her love or his deepest emotions.

"That's the story," he said, concluding. "I love her, though I've never told her. If I did tell her I'd be ready to marry her, and that seems impossible in this country. I'd be afraid to risk taking her anywhere. So I intend to do the best I can for her here."

"The longer I live the stranger life is," mused Lassiter, with downcast eyes. "I'm reminded of somethin' you once said to Jane about hands in her game of life. There's that unseen hand of power, an' Tull's black hand, an' my red one, an' your indifferent one, an' the girl's little brown, helpless one. An', Venters, there's another one that's all-wise an' all-wonderful. *That's* the hand guidin' Jane Withersteen's game of life! . . . Your story's one to daze a far clearer head than mine. I can't offer no advice, even if you asked for it. Mebbe I can help you. Anyway, I'll hold Oldrin' up when he comes to the village, an' find out about this girl. I knew the rustler years ago. He'll remember me."

"Lassiter, if I ever meet Oldring I'll kill him!" cried Venters, with sudden intensity.

"I reckon that 'd be perfectly natural," replied the rider.

"Make him think Bess is dead—as she is to him and that old life."

"Sure, sure, son. Cool down now. If you're goin' to begin pullin' guns on Tull an' Oldrin' you want to be cool. I reckon, though, you'd better keep hid here. Well, I must be leavin'."

"One thing, Lassiter. You'll not tell Jane about Bess? Please don't!"

"I reckon not. But I wouldn't be afraid to bet that after she'd got over anger at your secrecy—Venters, she'd be furious once in her life!—she'd think more of you. I don't mind sayin' for myself that I think you're a good deal of a man."

In the further ascent Venters halted several times with the intention of saying good-by, yet he changed his mind and kept on climbing till they reached Balancing Rock. Lassiter examined the huge rock, listened to Venters's idea of its position and suggestion, and curiously placed a strong hand upon it.

"Hold on!" cried Venters. "I heaved at it once and have never gotten over my scare."

"Well, you do seem oncommon nervous," replied Lassiter, much amused. "Now, as for me, why I always had the funniest notion to roll stones! When I was a kid I did it, an' the bigger I got the bigger stones I'd roll. Ain't that funny? Honest—even now I often get off my hoss just to tumble a big stone over a precipice, an' watch it drop, an' listen to it bang an' boom. I've started some slides in my time, an' don't you forget it. I never seen a rock I wanted to roll as bad as this one! Wouldn't there jest be roarin', crashin' hell down that trail?"

"You'd close the outlet forever!" exclaimed Venters. "Well, good-by, Lassiter. Keep my secret and don't forget me. And be mighty careful how you get out of the valley below. The rustlers' cañon isn't more than three miles up the Pass. Now you've tracked me here, I'll never feel safe again."

In his descent to the valley, Venters's emotion, roused to stirring pitch by the recital of his love story, quieted gradually, and in its place came a sober, thoughtful mood. All at once he saw that he was serious, because he would never more regain his sense of security while in the valley. What Lassiter could do another skilful cracker might duplicate. Among the many riders with whom Venters had ridden he recalled no one who could have taken his trail at Cottonwoods and have followed it to the edge of the bare slope in the pass, let alone up that glistening smooth stone. Lassiter, however, was not an ordinary rider. Instead of hunting cattle tracks he had likely spent a goodly portion of his life tracking men. It was not improbable that among Oldring's rustlers there was one who shared Lassiter's gift for trailing. And the more Venters dwelt on this possibility the more perturbed he grew.

Lassiter's visit, moreover, had a disquieting effect upon Bess, and Venters fancied that she entertained the same thought as to future seclusion. The breaking of their solitude, though by a well-meaning friend, had not only dispelled all its dream and much of its charm, but had instilled a canker of fear. Both had seen the footprint in the sand.

Venters did no more work that day. Sunset and twilight gave way to night, and the cañon bird whistled its melancholy notes, and the wind sang softly in the cliffs, and the camp-fire blazed and burned down to red embers. To Venters a subtle difference was apparent in all of these, or else the shadowy change had been in him. He hoped that on the morrow this slight depression would have passed away.

In that measure, however, he was doomed to disappointment. Furthermore, Bess reverted to a wistful sadness that he had not observed in her since her recovery. His attempt to cheer her out of it resulted in dismal failure, and consequently in a darkening of his own mood. Hard work relieved him; still, when the day had passed, his unrest returned. Then he set to deliberate thinking, and there came to him the startling conviction that he must leave Surprise Valley and take Bess with him. As a rider he had taken many chances, and as an adventurer in Deception Pass he had unhesitatingly risked his life; but now he would run no preventable hazard of Bess's safety and happiness, and he was too keen not to see that hazard. It gave him a pang to think of leaving the beautiful valley just when he had the means to establish a permanent and delightful home there. One flashing thought tore in hot temptation through his mind—why not climb up into the gorge, roll Balancing Rock down the trail, and close forever the outlet to Deception Pass? "That was the beast in me—showing his teeth!" muttered Venters, scornfully. "I'll just kill him good and quick! I'll be fair to this girl, if it's the last thing I do on earth!"

Another day went by, in which he worked less and pondered more and all the time covertly watched Bess. Her wistfulness had deepened into downright unhappiness, and that made his task to tell her all the harder. He kept the secret another day, hoping by some chance she might grow less moody, and to his exceeding anxiety she fell into far deeper gloom. Out of his own secret and the torment of it he divined that she, too, had a secret and the keeping of it was torturing her. As yet he had no plan thought out in regard to how or when to leave the valley, but he decided to tell her the necessity of it and to persuade her to go. Furthermore, he hoped his speaking out would induce her to unburden her own mind.

"Bess, what's wrong with you?" he asked.

"Nothing," she answered, with averted face.

Venters took hold of her and gently, though masterfully, forced her to meet his eyes.

"You can't look at me and lie," he said. "Now—what's wrong with you? You're keeping something from me. Well, I've got a secret, too, and I intend to tell it presently."

"Oh—I *have* a secret. I was crazy to tell you when you came back. That's why I was so silly about everything. I kept holding my secret back—gloating over it. But when Lassiter came I got an idea—that changed my mind. Then I hated to tell you."

"Are you going to now?"

"Yes—yes. I was coming to it. I tried yesterday, but you were so cold. I was afraid. I couldn't keep it much longer."

"Very well, most mysterious lady, tell your wonderful secret."

"You needn't laugh," she retorted, with a first glimpse of reviving spirit. "I can take the laugh out of you in one second."

"It's a go."

She ran through the spruces to the cave, and returned carrying something which was manifestly heavy. Upon nearer view he saw that whatever she held with such evident importance had been bound up in a black scarf he well remembered. That alone was sufficient to make him tingle with curiosity.

"Have you any idea what I did in your absence?" she asked.

"I imagine you lounged about, waiting and watching for me," he replied, smiling. "I've my share of conceit, you know."

"You're wrong. I worked. Look at my hands." She dropped on her knees close to where he sat, and, carefully depositing the black bundle, she held out her hands. The palms and inside of her fingers were white, puckered, and worn.

"Why, Bess, you've been fooling in the water," he said.

"Fooling? Look here!" With deft fingers she spread open the black scarf, and the bright sun shone upon a dull, glittering heap of gold.

"Gold!" he ejaculated.

"Yes, gold! See, pounds of gold! I found it—washed it out of the stream—picked it out grain by grain, nugget by nugget!"

"Gold!" he cried.

"Yes. Now—now laugh at my secret!"

For a long minute Venters gazed. Then he stretched forth a hand to feel if the gold was real.

"*Gold!*" he almost shouted. "Bess, there are hundreds—thousands of dollars' worth here!"

He leaned over to her, and put his hand, strong and clenching now, on hers.

"Is there more where this came from?" he whispered.

"Plenty of it, all the way up the stream to the cliff. You know I've often washed for gold. Then I've heard the men talk. I think there's no great quantity of gold here, but enough for—for a fortune for *you*."

"That—was—your—secret!"

"Yes. I hate gold. For it makes men mad. I've seen them drunk with joy and dance and fling themselves around. I've seen them curse and rave. I've seen them fight like dogs and roll in the dust. I've seen them kill each other for gold."

"Is that why you hated to tell me?"

"Not—not altogether." Bess lowered her head. "It was because I knew you'd never stay here long after you found gold."

"You were afraid I'd leave you?"

"Yes."

"Listen! . . . You great, simple child! Listen . . . You sweet, wonderful, wild, blued-eyed girl! I was tortured by my secret. It was that I knew we—*we* must leave the valley. We can't stay here much longer. I couldn't think how we'd get away—out of the country—or how we'd live, if we ever got out. I'm a beggar. That's why I kept my secret. I'm poor. It takes money to make way beyond Sterling. We couldn't ride horses or burros or walk forever. So while I knew we must go, I was distracted over how to go and what to do. *Now!* We've gold! Once beyond Sterling, we'll be safe from rustlers. We've no others to fear.

GOLD

"Oh! Listen! Bess!" Venters now heard his voice ringing high and sweet, and he felt Bess's cold hands in in his crushing grasp as she leaned toward him pale, breathless. "This is how much I'd leave you! You made me live again! I'll take you away—far away from this wild country. You'll begin a new life. You'll be happy. You shall see cities, ships, people. You shall have anything your heart craves. All the shame and sorrow of your life shall be forgotten—as if they had never been. This is how much I'd leave you here alone—you sad-eyed girl. I love you! Didn't you know it? How could you fail to know it? I love you! I'm free! I'm a man—a man you've made—no more a beggar! . . . Kiss me! This is how much I'd leave you here alone—you beautiful, strange, unhappy girl. But I'll make you happy. What—what do I care for—your past! I love you! I'll take you home to Illinois—to my mother. Then I'll take you to far places. I'll make up all you've lost. Oh, I know you love me—knew it before you told me. And it changed my life. And you'll go with me, not as my companion as you are here, nor my sister, but, Bess, darling! . . . *As my wife!*"

CHAPTER XVII

WRANGLE'S RACE RUN

THE plan eventually decided upon by the lovers was for Venters to go to the village, secure a horse and some kind of a disguise for Bess, or at least less striking apparel than her present garb, and to return post-haste to the valley. Meanwhile, she would add to their store of gold. Then they would strike the long and perilous trail to ride out of Utah. In the event of his inability to fetch back a horse for her, they intended to make the giant sorrel carry double. The gold, a little food, saddle blankets, and Venters's guns were to compose the light outfit with which they would make the start.

"I love this beautiful place," said Bess. "It's hard to think of leaving it."

"Hard! Well, I should think so," replied Venters. "Maybe—in years—" But he did not complete in words his thought that it might be possible to return after many years of absence and change.

Once again Bess bade Venters farewell under the shadow of Balancing Rock, and this time it was with whispered hope and tenderness and passionate trust. Long after he had left her, all down through the outlet to the Pass, the clinging clasp of her arms, the sweetness of her lips, and the sense of a new and exquisite birth of character in her remained hauntingly and thrillingly in his mind. The girl who had sadly called herself nameless and nothing had been marvelously transformed in the moment of his avowal of love. It was something to think over, something to warm his heart, but for the present it had absolutely to be forgotten so that all his mind could be addressed to the trip so fraught with danger.

He carried only his rifle, revolver, and a small quantity of bread and meat; and thus lightly burdened, he made swift progress down the slope and out into the valley. Darkness was coming on, and he welcomed it. Stars were blinking when he reached his old hiding-place in the split of cañon wall, and by their aid he slipped through the dense thickets to the grassy enclosure. Wrangle stood in the center of it with his head up, and he appeared black and of gigantic proportions in the dim light. Venters whistled softly, began a slow approach, and then called. The horse snorted and, plunging away with dull, heavy sound of hoofs, he disappeared in the gloom. "Wilder than ever!" muttered Venters. He followed the sorrel into the narrowing split between the walls, and presently had to desist because he could not see a foot in advance. As he went back toward the open Wrangle jumped out of an ebony shadow of cliff and like a thunderbolt shot huge and black past him down into the starlit glade. Deciding that all attempts to catch Wrangle at night would be useless, Venters repaired to the shelving rock where he had hidden saddle and blanket, and there went to sleep.

The first peep of day found him stirring, and as soon as it was light enough to distinguish objects, he took his lasso off his saddle and went out to rope the sorrel. He espied Wrangle at the lower end of the cove and approached him in a perfectly natural manner. When he got near enough, Wrangle evidently recognized him, but was too wild to stand. He ran up the glade and on into the narrow lane between the walls. This favored Venters's speedy capture of the horse, so, coiling his noose ready to throw, he hurried on. Wrangle let Venters get to within a hundred feet and then he broke. But as he plunged by, rapidly getting into his stride, Venters made a perfect throw with the rope. He had time to brace himself for the shock; nevertheless, Wrangle threw him and dragged him several yards before halting.

"You wild devil," said Venters, as he slowly pulled Wrangle up. "Don't you know me? Come now—old fellow—so—so—"

Wrangle yielded to the lasso and then to Venters's strong hand. He was as straggly and wild-looking as a horse left to roam free in the sage. He dropped his long ears and stood readily to be saddled and bridled. But he was exceedingly sensitive, and quivered at every touch and sound. Venters led him to the thicket, and, bending the close saplings to let him squeeze through, at length reached the open. Sharp survey in each direction assured him of the usual lonely nature of the cañon; then he was in the saddle, riding south.

Wrangle's long, swinging canter was a wonderful ground-gainer. His stride was almost twice that of an ordinary horse, and his endurance was equally remarkable. Venters pulled him in occasionally, and walked him up the stretches of rising ground and along the soft washes. Wrangle had never yet shown any indication of distress while Venters rode him. Nevertheless, there was now reason to save the horse; therefore Venters did not resort to the hurry that had characterized his former trip. He camped at the last water in the Pass. What distance that was to Cottonwoods he did not know; he calculated, however, that it was in the neighborhood of fifty miles.

Early in the morning he proceeded on his way, and about the middle of the forenoon reached the constricted gap that marked the southerly end of the Pass, and through which led the trail up to the sage-level. He spied out Lassiter's tracks in the dust, but no others, and, dismounting, he straightened out Wrangle's bridle and began to lead him up the trail. The short climb, more severe on beast than on man, necessitated a rest on the level above, and during this he scanned the wide purple reaches of slope.

Wrangle whistled his pleasure at the smell of the sage. Remounting, Venters headed up the white trail with the fragrant wind in his face. He had proceeded for perhaps a couple of miles when Wrangle stopped with a suddenness that threw Venters heavily against the pommel.

"What's wrong, old boy?" called Venters, looking down for a loose shoe or a snake or a foot lamed by a picked-up stone. Unrewarded, he raised himself from his scrutiny. Wrangle stood stiff, head high, with his long ears erect. Thus guided, Venters swiftly gazed ahead to make out a dust-clouded, dark group of horsemen riding down the slope. If they had seen him, it apparently made no difference in their speed or direction.

"Wonder who they are!" exclaimed Venters. He was not disposed to run. His cool mood tightened under grip of excitement as he reflected that, whoever the approaching riders were, they could not be friends. He slipped out of the saddle and led Wrangle behind the tallest sage-brush. It might serve to conceal them until the riders were close enough for him to see who they were; after that he would be indifferent to how soon they discovered him.

After looking to his rifle and ascertaining that it was in working order, he watched, and as he watched, slowly the force of a bitter fierceness, long dormant, gathered ready to flame into life. If those riders were not rustlers he had forgotten how rustlers looked and rode. On they came, a small group, so compact and dark that he could not tell their number. How unusual that their horses did not see Wrangle! But such failure, Venters decided, was owing to the speed with which they were traveling. They moved at a swift canter affected more by rustlers than by riders. Venters grew concerned over the possibility that these horesemen would actually ride down on him before he had a chance to tell what to expect. When they were within three hundred yards he deliberately led Wrangle out into the trail.

Then he heard shouts, and the hard scrape of sliding hoofs, and saw horses rear and plunge back with up-flung heads and flying manes. Several little white puffs of smoke appeared sharply against the black background of riders and horses, and shots rang out. Bullets struck far in front of Venters, and whipped up the dust and then hummed low into the sage. The range was great for revolvers, but whether the shots were meant to kill or merely to check advance, they were enough to fire that waiting ferocity in Venters. Slipping his arm through the bridle, so that Wrangle could not get away, Venters lifted his rifle and pulled the trigger twice.

He saw the first horseman lean sideways and fall. He saw another lurch in his saddle and heard a cry of pain. Then Wrangle, plunging in fright, lifted Venters and nearly threw him. He jerked the horse down with a powerful hand and leaped into the saddle. Wrangle plunged again, dragging his bridle, that Venters had not had time to throw in place. Bending over with a swift movement, he secured it and dropped the loop over the pommel. Then, with grinding teeth, he looked to see what the issue would be.

The band had scattered so as not to afford such a broad mark for bullets. The riders faced Venters, some with red-belching guns. He heard a sharper report, and just as Wrangle plunged again he caught the whizz of a leaden missile that would have hit him but for Wrangle's sudden jump. A swift, hot wave, turning cold, passed over Venters. Deliberately he picked out the one rider with a carbine, and killed him. Wrangle snorted shrilly and bolted into the sage. Venters let him run a few rods, then with iron arm checked him.

Five riders, surely rustlers, were left. One leaped out

JUST AS WRANGLE PLUNGED AGAIN HE CAUGHT THE WHIZZ OF A LEADEN MISSILE

of the saddle to secure his fallen comrade's carbine. A shot from Venters, which missed the man but sent the dust flying over him, made him run back to his horse. Then they separated. The crippled rider went one way; the one frustrated in his attempt to get the carbine rode another; Venters thought he made out a third rider, carrying a strange-appearing bundle and disappearing in the sage. But in the rapidity of action and vision he could not discern what it was. Two riders with three horses swung out to the right. Afraid of the long rifle—a burdensome weapon seldom carried by rustlers or riders—they had been put to rout.

Suddenly Venters discovered that one of the two men last noted was riding Jane Withersteen's horse Bells—the beautiful bay racer she had given to Lassiter. Venters uttered a savage outcry. Then the small, wiry, frog-like shape of the second rider, and the ease and grace of his seat in the saddle—things so strikingly incongruous—grew more and more familiar in Venters's sight.

"*Jerry Card!*" cried Venters.

It was indeed Tull's right-hand man. Such a white-hot wrath inflamed Venters that he fought himself to see with clearer gaze.

"It's Jerry Card!" he exclaimed, instantly. "*And he's riding Black Star and leading Night!*"

The long-kindling, stormy fire in Venters's heart burst into flame. He spurred Wrangle, and as the horse lengthened his stride Venters slipped cartridges into the magazine of his rifle till it was once again full. Card and his companion were now half a mile or more in advance, riding easily down the slope. Venters marked the smooth gait, and understood it when Wrangle galloped out of the sage into the broad cattle trail, down which Venters had once tracked Jane Withersteen's red herd. This hard-packed trail, from years of use, was as clean and smooth as a road. Venters saw Jerry

Card look back over his shoulder; the other rider did likewise. Then the three racers lengthened their stride to the point where the swinging canter was ready to break into a gallop.

"Wrangle, the race's on," said Venters, grimly. "We'll canter with them and gallop with them and run with them. We'll let them set the pace."

Venters knew he bestrode the strongest, swiftest, most tireless horse ever ridden by any rider across the Utah uplands. Recalling Jane Withersteen's devoted assurance that Night could run neck and neck with Wrangle, and Black Star could show his heels to him, Venters wished that Jane were there to see the race to recover her blacks and in the unqualified superiority of the giant sorrel. Then Venters found himself thankful that she was absent, for he meant that race to end in Jerry Card's death. The first flush, the raging of Venters's wrath, passed, to leave him in sullen, almost cold possession of his will. It was a deadly mood, utterly foreign to his nature, engendered, fostered, and released by the wild passions of wild men in a wild country. The strength in him then—the thing rife in him that was not hate, but something as remorseless—might have been the fiery fruition of a whole lifetime of vengeful quest. Nothing could have stopped him.

Venters thought out the race shrewdly. The rider on Bells would probably drop behind and take to the sage. What he did was of little moment to Venters. To stop Jerry Card, his evil, hidden career as well as his present flight, and then to catch the blacks—that was all that concerned Venters. The cattle trail wound for miles and miles down the slope. Venters saw with a rider's keen vision ten, fifteen, twenty miles of clear purple sage. There were no on-coming riders or rustlers to aid Card. His only chance to escape lay in abandoning the stolen horses and creeping away in the sage to hide. In ten miles Wrangle could run Black Star and

Night off their feet, and in fifteen he could kill them outright. So Venters held the sorrel in, letting Card make the running. It was a long race that would save the blacks.

In a few miles of that swinging canter Wrangle had crept appreciably closer to the three horses. Jerry Card turned again, and when he saw how the sorrel had gained, he put Black Star to a gallop. Night and Bells, on either side of him, swept into his stride.

Venters loosened the rein on Wrangle and let him break into a gallop. The sorrel saw the horses ahead and wanted to run. But Venters restrained him. And in the gallop he gained more than in the canter. Bells was fast in that gait, but Black Star and Night had been trained to run. Slowly Wrangle closed the gap down to a quarter of a mile, and crept closer and closer.

Jerry Card wheeled once more. Venters distinctly saw the red flash of his red face. This time he looked long. Venters laughed. He knew what passed in Card's mind. The rider was trying to make out what horse it happened to be that thus gained on Jane Withersteen's peerless racers. Wrangle had so long been away from the village that not improbably Jerry had forgotten. Besides, whatever Jerry's qualifications for his fame as the greatest rider of the sage, certain it was that his best point was not far-sightedness. He had not recognized Wrangle. After what must have been a searching gaze he got his comrade to face about. This action gave Venters amusement. It spoke so surely of the fact that neither Card nor the rustler actually knew their danger. Yet if they kept to the trail—and the last thing such men would do would be to leave it—they were both doomed.

This comrade of Card's whirled far around in his saddle, and he even shaded his eyes from the sun. He, too, looked long. Then, all at once, he faced ahead again and, bending lower in the saddle, began to fling his right arm up and down. That flinging Venters knew to be the lashing of Bells. Jerry also became active. And the three racers lengthened out into a run.

"Now, Wrangle!" cried Venters. "Run, you big devil!" Run!'

Venters laid the reins on Wrangle's neck and dropped the loop over the pommel. The sorrel needed no guiding on that smooth trail. He was surer-footed in a run than at any other fast gait, and his running gave the impression of something devilish. He might now have been actuated by Venters's spirit; undoubtedly his savage running fitted the mood of his rider. Venters bent forward, swinging with the horse, and gripped his rifle. His eye measured the distance between him and Jerry Card.

In less than two miles of running Bells began to drop behind the blacks, and Wrangle began to overhaul him. Venters anticipated that the rustler would soon take to the sage. Yet he did not. Not improbably he reasoned that the powerful sorrel could more easily overtake Bells in the heavier going outside of the trail. Soon only a few hundred yards lay between Bells and Wrangle. Turning in his saddle, the rustler began to shoot, and the bullets beat up little whiffs of dust. Venters raised his rifle, ready to take snap shots, and waited for favorable opportunity when Bells was out of line with the forward horses. Venters had it in him to kill these men as if they were skunk-bitten coyotes, but also he had restraint enough to keep from shooting one of Jane's beloved Arabians.

No great distance was covered, however, before Bells swerved to the left, out of line with Black Star and Night. Then Venters, aiming high and waiting for the pause between Wrangle's great strides, began to take snap shots at the rustler. The fleeing rider presented a broad target for a rifle, but he was moving swiftly forward and bobbing up and down. Moreover, shooting from Wrangle's back was shooting from a thunderbolt. And added to that was the danger of a low-placed bullet taking effect on Bells. Yet, despite these considerations, making the shot exceedingly difficult, Venters's confidence, like his implacability, saw a speedy and fatal termination of that rustler's race. On the sixth shot the rustler threw up his arms and took a flying tumble off his horse. He rolled over and over, hunched himself to a half-erect position, fell, and then dragged himself into the sage. As Venters went thundering by he peered keenly into the sage, but caught no sign of the man. Bells ran a few hundred yards, slowed up, and had stopped when Wrangle passed him.

Again Venters began slipping fresh cartridges into the magazine of his rifle, and his hand was so sure and steady that he did not drop a single cartridge. With the eye of a rider and the judgment of a marksman he once more measured the distance between him and Jerry Card. Wrangle had gained, bringing him into rifle range. Venters was hard put to it now not to shoot, but thought it better to withhold his fire. Jerry, who, in anticipation of a running fusillade, had huddled himself into a little twisted ball on Black Star's neck, now surmising that this pursuer would make sure of not wounding one of the blacks, rose to his natural seat in the saddle.

In his mind perhaps, as certainly as in Venters's, this moment was the beginning of the real race.

Venters leaned forward to put his hand on Wrangle's neck; then backward to put it on his flank. Under the shaggy, dusty hair trembled and vibrated and rippled a wonderful muscular activity. But Wrangle's flesh was still cold. What a cold-blooded brute, thought Venters, and felt in him a love for the horse he had never given to any other. It would not have been humanly possible for any rider, even though clutched by hate or revenge or a passion to save a loved one or fear of his own life, to be astride the sorrel, to swing with his swing, to see his magnificent stride and hear the rapid thunder of his hoofs, to ride him in that race and not glory in the ride.

So, with his passion to kill still keen and unabated, Venters lived out that ride, and drank a rider's sage-sweet cup of wildness to the dregs.

When Wrangle's long mane, lashing in the wind, stung Venters in the cheek, the sting added a beat to his flying pulse. He bent a downward glance to try to see Wrangle's actual stride, and saw only twinkling, darting streaks and the white rush of the trail. He watched the sorrel's savage head, pointed level, his mouth still closed and dry, but his nostrils distended as if he were snorting unseen fire. Wrangle was the horse for a race with death. Upon each side Venters saw the sage merged into a sailing, colorless wall. In front sloped the lay of ground with its purple breadth split by the white trail. The wind, blowing with heavy, steady blast into his face, sickened him with enduring, sweet odor, and filled his ears with a hollow, rushing roar.

Then for the hundredth time he measured the width of space separating him from Jerry Card. Wrangle had ceased to gain. The blacks were proving their fleetness. Venters watched Jerry Card, admiring the little rider's horsemanship. He had the incomparable seat of the upland rider, born in the saddle. It struck Venters that Card had changed his position, or the position of the horses. Presently Venters remembered positively that Jerry had been leading Night on the right-hand side of the trail. The racer was now on the side to the left. No—it was Black Star. But, Venters argued in amaze, Jerry had been mounted on Black Star. Another clearer, keener gaze assured Venters that Black Star was really riderless. Night now carried Jerry Card.

"He's changed from one to the other!" ejaculated Venters, realizing the astounding feat with unstinted admiration. "Changed at full speed! Jerry Card, that's what you've done unless I'm drunk on the smell of sage. But I've got to see the trick before I believe it."

Thenceforth, while Wrangle sped on, Venters glued his eyes to the little rider. Jerry Card rode as only he could ride. Of all the daring horsemen of the uplands, Jerry was the one rider fitted to bring out the greatness of the blacks in that long race. He had them on a dead run, but not yet at the last strained and killing pace. From time to time he glanced backward, as a wise general in retreat calculating his chances and the power and speed of pursuers, and the moment for the last desperate burst. No doubt, Card, with his life at stake, gloried in that race, perhaps more wildly than Venters. For he had been born to the sage and the saddle and the wild. He was more than half horse. Not until the last call—the sudden up-flashing instinct of self-preservation —would he lose his skill and judgment and nerve and the spirit of that race. Venters seemed to read Jerry's mind. That little crime-stained rider was actually thinking of his horses, husbanding their speed, handling them with knowledge of years, glorying in their beautiful, swift, racing stride, and wanting them to win the race when his own life hung suspended in quivering balance. Again Jerry whirled in his saddle and the sun flashed red on his face. Turning, he drew Black Star closer and closer toward Night, till they ran side by side, as one horse. Then Card raised himself in the saddle, slipped out of the stirrups, and, somehow twisting himself, leaped upon Black Star. He did not even lose the swing of the horse. Like a leech he was there in the other saddle, and as the horses separated, his right foot, that had been apparently doubled under him, shot down to catch the stirrup. The grace and dexterity and daring of that rider's act won something more than admiration from Venters.

For the distance of a mile Jerry rode Black Star and then changed back to Night. But all Jerry's skill and the running of the blacks could avail little more against the sorrel.

Venters peered far ahead, studying the lay of the land. Straightaway for five miles the trail stretched, and then it disappeared in hummocky ground. To the right, some few rods, Venters saw a break in the sage, and this was the rim of Deception Pass. Across the dark cleft gleamed the red of the opposite wall. Venters imagined that the trail went down into the Pass somewhere north of those ridges. And he realized that he must and would overtake Jerry Card in this straight course of five miles.

Cruelly he struck his spurs into Wrangle's flanks. A light touch of spur was sufficient to make Wrangle plunge. And now, with a ringing, wild snort, he seemed to double up in muscular convulsions and to shoot forward with an impetus that almost unseated Venters. The sage blurred by, the trail flashed by, and the wind robbed him of breath and hearing. Jerry Card turned once more. And the way he shifted to Black Star showed he had to make his last desperate running. Venters aimed to the side of the trail and sent a bullet puffing the dust beyond Jerry. Venters hoped to frighten the rider and get him to take to the sage. But Jerry returned the shot, and his ball struck dangerously close in the dust at Wrangle's flying feet. Venters held his fire then, while the rider emptied his revolver. For a mile, with Black Star leaving Night behind and doing his utmost, Wrangle did not gain; for another mile he gained little, if at all. In the third he caught up with the now galloping Night and began to gain rapidly on the other black.

Only a hundred yards now stretched between Black

Star and Wrangle. The giant sorrel thundered on—and on—and on. In every yard he gained a foot. He was whistling through his nostrils, wringing wet, flying lather, and as hot as fire. Savage as ever, strong as ever, fast as ever, but each tremendous stride jarred Venters out of the saddle! Wrangle's power and spirit and momentum had begun to run him off his legs. Wrangle's great race was nearly won—and run. Venters seemed to see the expanse before him as a vast, sheeted, purple plain sliding under him. Black Star moved in it as a blur. The rider, Jerry Card, appeared a mere dot bobbing dimly. Wrangle thundered on—on—on! Venters felt the increase in quivering, straining shock after every leap. Flecks of foam flew into Venters's eyes, burning him, making him see all the sage as red. But in that red haze he saw, or seemed to see, Black Star suddenly riderless and with broken gait. Wrangle thundered on to change his pace with a violent break. Then Venters pulled him hard. From run to gallop, gallop to canter, canter to trot, trot to walk, and walk to stop, the great sorrel ended his race.

Venters looked back. Black Star stood riderless in the trail. Jerry Card had taken to the sage. Far up the white trail Night came trotting faithfully down. Venters leaped off, still half blind, reeling dizzily. In a moment he had recovered sufficiently to have a care for Wrangle. Rapidly he took off the saddle and bridle. The sorrel was reeking, heaving, whistling, shaking. But he had still the strength to stand, and for him Venters had no fears.

As Venters ran back to Black Star he saw the horse stagger on shaking legs into the sage and go down in a heap. Upon reaching him Venters removed the saddle and bridle. Black Star had been killed on his legs, Venters thought. He had no hope for the stricken horse. Black Star lay flat, covered with bloody froth, mouth wide, tongue hanging, eyes glaring, and all his beautiful body in convulsions.

Unable to stay there to see Jane's favorite racer die, Venters hurried up the trail to meet the other black. On the way he kept a sharp lookout for Jerry Card. Venters imagined the rider would keep well out of range of the rifle, but, as he would be lost on the sage without a horse, not improbably he would linger in the vicinity on the chance of getting back one of the blacks. Night soon came trotting up, hot and wet and run out. Venters led him down near the others, and, unsaddling him, let him loose to rest. Night wearily lay down in the dust and rolled, proving himself not yet spent.

Then Venters sat down to rest and think. Whatever the risk, he was compelled to stay where he was, or comparatively near, for the night. The horses must rest and drink. He must find water. He was now seventy miles from Cottonwoods, and, he believed, close to the cañon where the cattle trail must surely turn off and go down into the Pass. After a while he rose to survey the valley.

He was very near to the ragged edge of a deep cañon into which the trail turned. The ground lay in uneven ridges divided by washes, and these sloped into the cañon. Following the cañon line, he saw where its rim was broken by other intersecting cañons, and farther down red walls and yellow cliffs leading toward a deep blue cleft that he made sure was Deception Pass. Walking out a few rods to a promontory, he found where the trail went down. The descent was gradual, along a stone-walled trail, and Venters felt sure that this was the place where Oldring drove cattle into the Pass. There was, however, no indication at all that he ever had driven cattle out at this point. Oldring had many holes to his burrow.

In searching round in the little hollows Venters, much to his relief, found water. He composed himself to rest and eat some bread and meat, while he waited for a sufficient time to elapse so that he could safely give the horses a drink. He judged the hour to be somewhere around noon. Wrangle lay down to rest and Night followed suit. So long as they were down Venters intended to make no move. The longer they rested the better, and the safer it would be to give them water. By and by he forced himself to go over to where Black Star lay, expecting to find him dead. Instead he found the racer partially if not wholly recovered. There was recognition, even fire, in his big black eyes. Venters was overjoyed. He sat by the black for a long time. Black Star presently labored to his feet with a heave and a groan, shook himself, and snorted for water. Venters repaired to the little pool he had found, filled his sombrero, and gave the racer a drink. Black Star gulped it at one draught, as if it were but a drop, and pushed his nose into the hat and snorted for more. Venters now led Night down to drink, and after a further time Black Star also. Then the blacks began to graze.

The sorrel had wandered off down the sage between the trail and the cañon. Once or twice he disappeared in little swales. Finally Venters concluded Wrangle had grazed far enough, and, taking his lasso, he went to fetch him back. In crossing from one ridge to another he saw where the horse had made muddy a pool of water. It occurred to Venters then that Wrangle had drunk his fill, and did not seem the worse for it, and might be anything but easy to catch. And, true enough, he could not come within roping reach of the sorrel. He tried for an hour, and gave up in disgust. Wrangle did not seem so wild as simply perverse. In a quandary Venters returned to the other horses, hoping much, yet doubting more, that when Wrangle had grazed to suit himself he might be caught.

As the afternoon wore away Venters's concern diminished, yet he kept close watch on the blacks and the trail and the sage. There was no telling of what Jerry Card might be capable. Venters sullenly acquiesced to the idea that the rider had been too quick and too shrewd for him. Strangely and doggedly, however, Venters clung to his foreboding of Card's downfall.

The wind died away; the red sun topped the far distant western rise of slope; and the long, creeping purple shadows lengthened. The rims of the cañons gleamed crimson and the deep clefts appeared to belch forth blue smoke. Silence enfolded the scene.

It was broken by a horrid, long-drawn scream of a horse and the thudding of heavy hoofs. Venters sprang erect and wheeled south. Along the cañon rim, near the edge, came Wrangle, once more in thundering flight.

Venters gasped in amazement. Had the wild sorrel gone mad? His head was high and twisted, in a most singular position for a running horse. Suddenly Venters descried a frog-like shape clinging to Wrangle's neck. Jerry Card! Somehow he had straddled Wrangle and now stuck like a huge burr. But it was his strange position and the sorrel's wild scream that shook Venters's nerves. Wrangle was pounding toward the turn where the trail went down. He plunged onward like a blind horse. More than one of his leaps took him to the very edge of the precipice.

Jerry Card was bent forward with his teeth fast in the front of Wrangle's nose! Venters saw it, and there flashed over him a memory of this trick of a few desperate riders. He even thought of one rider who had worn off his teeth in this terrible hold to break or control desperate horses. Wrangle had indeed gone mad. The marvel was what guided him. Was it the half-brute, the more than half-horse instinct of Jerry Card? Whatever the mystery, it was true. And in a few more rods Jerry would have the sorrel turning into the trail leading down into the cañon.

"No—Jerry!" whispered Venters, stepping forward

and throwing up the rifle. He tried to catch the little humped, frog-like shape over the sights. It was moving too fast; it was too small. Yet Venters shot once . . . twice . . . the third time . . . four times . . . five! All wasted shots and precious seconds!

With a deep-muttered curse Venters caught Wrangle through the sights and pulled the trigger. Plainly he heard the bullet thud. Wrangle uttered a horrible strangling sound. In swift death action he whirled, and with one last splendid leap he cleared the cañon rim. And he whirled downward with the little frog-like shape clinging to his neck!

There was a pause which seemed never ending, a shock, and an instant's silence.

Then up rolled a heavy crash, a long roar of sliding rocks dying away in distant echo, then silence unbroken.

Wrangle's race was run.

CHAPTER XVIII

OLDRING'S KNELL

SOME forty hours or more later Venters created a commotion in Cottonwoods by riding down the main street on Black Star and leading Bells and Night. He had come upon Bells grazing near the body of a dead rustler, the only incident of his quick ride into the village.

Nothing was farther from Venters's mind than bravado. No thought came to him of the defiance and boldness of riding Jane Withersteen's racers straight into the arch-plotter's stronghold. He wanted men to see the famous Arabians; he wanted men to see them dirty and dusty, bearing all the signs of having been driven to their limit; he wanted men to see and to know that the thieves who had ridden them out into the sage had not ridden them back. Venters had come for that and for more—he wanted to meet Tull face to face; if not Tull, then Dyer; if not Dyer, then anyone in the secret of these master conspirators. Such was Venters's passion. The meeting with the rustlers, the unprovoked attack upon him, the spilling of blood, the recognition of Jerry Card and the horses, the race, and that last plunge of mad Wrangle—all these things, fuel on fuel to the smoldering fire, had kindled and swelled and leaped into living flame. He could have shot Dyer in the midst of his religious services at the altar; he could have killed Tull in front of wives and babes.

He walked the three racers down the broad, green-bordered village road. He heard the murmur of running water from Amber Spring. Bitter waters for Jane Withersteen! Men and women stopped to gaze at him and the horses. All knew him; all knew the blacks and the bay. As well as if it had been spoken, Venters read in the faces of men the intelligence that Jane Withersteen's Arabians had been known to have been stolen. Venters reined in and halted before Dyer's residence. It was a low, long, stone structure resembling Withersteen House. The spacious front yard was green and luxuriant with grass and flowers; gravel walks led to the hugh porch; a well-trimmed hedge of purple sage separated the yard from the church grounds; birds sang in the trees; water flowed musically along the walks; and there were glad, careless shouts of children. For Venters the beauty of this home, and the serenity and its apparent happiness, all turned red and black. For Venters a shade overspread the lawn, the flowers, the old vine-clad stone house. In the music of the singing birds, in the murmur of the running water, he heard an ominous sound. Quiet beauty—sweet music—innocent laughter! By what monstrous abortion of fate did these abide in the shadow of Dyer?

Venters rode on and stopped before Tull's cottage. Women stared at him with white faces and then flew from the porch. Tull himself appeared at the door, bent low, craning his neck. His dark face flashed out of sight; the door banged; a heavy bar dropped with a hollow sound.

Then Venters shook Black Star's bridle, and, sharply trotting, led the other horses to the center of the village. Here at the intersecting streets and in front of the stores he halted once more. The usual lounging atmosphere of that prominent corner was not now in evidence. Riders and ranchers and villagers broke up what must have been absorbing conversation. There was a rush of many feet, and then the walk was lined with faces.

Venters's glance swept down the line of silent stone-faced men. He recognized many riders and villagers, but none of those he had hoped to meet. There was no expression in the faces turned toward him. All of them knew him, most were inimical, but there were few who were not burning with curiosity and wonder in regard to the return of Jane Withersteen's racers. Yet all were silent. Here were the familiar characteristics—masked feeling—strange secretiveness—expressionless expression of mystery and hidden power.

"Has anybody here seen Jerry Card?" queried Venters, in a loud voice.

In reply there came not a word, not a nod or shake of head, not so much as dropping eye or twitching lip—nothing but a quiet, stony stare.

"Been under the knife? You've a fine knife-wielder here—one Tull, I believe! . . . Maybe you've all had your tongues cut out?"

This passionate sarcasm of Venters brought no response, and the stony calm was as oil on the fire within him.

"I see some of you pack guns, too!" he added, in biting scorn. In the long, tense pause, strung keenly as a tight wire, he sat motionless on Black Star. "All right," he went on. "Then let some of you take this message to Tull. Tell him I've seen Jerry Card! . . . Tell him Jerry Card *will never return!*"

Thereupon, in the same dead calm, Venters backed Black Star away from the curb, into the street, and out of range. He was ready now to ride up to Withersteen House and turn the racers over to Jane.

"Hello, Venters!" a familiar voice cried, hoarsely, and he saw a man running toward him. It was the rider Judkins who came up and gripped Venters's hand. "Venters, I could hev dropped when I seen them hosses. But thet sight ain't a marker to the looks of you. What's wrong? Hev you gone crazy? You must be crazy to ride in here this way—with them hosses—talkin' thet way about Tull an' Jerry Card."

"Jud, I'm not crazy—only mad clean through," replied Venters.

"Wal, now, Bern, I'm glad to hear some of your old self in your voice. Fer when you come up you looked like the corpse of a dead rider with fire fer eyes. You hed thet crowd too stiff fer throwin' guns. Come, we've got to hev a talk. Let's go up the lane. We ain't much safe here."

Judkins mounted Bells and rode with Venters up to the cottonwood grove. Here they dismounted and went among the trees.

"Let's hear from you first," said Judkins. "You fetched back them hosses. Thet *is* the trick. An', of course, you got Jerry the same as you got Horne."

"Horne!"

"Sure. He was found dead yesterday all chewed by coyotes, an' he'd been shot plumb center."

"Where was he found?"

"At the split down the trail—you know where Oldrin's cattle trail runs off north from the trail to the pass."

"That's where I met Jerry and the rustlers. What was Horne doing with them? I thought Horne was an honest cattle-man."

"Lord—Bern, don't ask me thet! I'm all muddled now tryin' to figure things."

Venters told of the fight and the race with Jerry Card and its tragic conclusion.

"I knowed it! I knowed all along that Wrangle was the best hoss!" exclaimed Judkins, with his lean face working and his eyes lighting. "Thet was a race! Lord, I'd like to hev seen Wrangle jump the cliff with Jerry. An' thet was good-by to the grandest hoss an' rider ever on the sage! . . . But, Bern, after you got the hosses why'd you want to bolt right in Tull's face?"

"I want him to know. An' if I can get to him I'll—"

"You can't get near Tull," interrupted Judkins. "Thet vigilante bunch hev taken to bein' bodyguard for Tull an' Dyer, too."

"Hasn't Lassiter made a break yet?" inquired Venters, curiously.

"Naw!" replied Judkins, scornfully. "Jane turned his head. He's mad in love over her—follers her like a dog. He ain't no more Lassiter! He's lost his nerve; he doesn't look like the same feller. It's village talk. Everybody knows it. He hasn't thrown a gun, an' he won't!"

"Jud, I'll bet he does," replied Venters, earnestly. "Remember what I say. This Lassiter is something more than a gun-man. Jud, he's big—he's great! . . . I feel that in him. God help Tull and Dyer when Lassiter does go after them. For horses and riders and stone walls won't save them."

"Wal, hev it your way, Bern. I hope you're right. Nat'rully I've been some sore on Lassiter fer gittin' soft. But I ain't denyin' his nerve, or whatever's great in him thet sort of paralyzes people. No later 'n this mornin' I seen him saunterin' down the lane, quiet an' slow. An' like his guns he comes black—*black*, thet's Lassiter. Wal, the crowd on the corner never batted an eye, an' I'll gamble my hoss thet there wasn't one who hed a heartbeat till Lassiter got by. He went in Snell's saloon, an' as there wasn't no gun play I had to go in, too. An' there, darn my pictures, if Lassiter wasn't standin' to the bar, drinkin' an' talkin' with Oldrin'."

"*Oldring!*" whispered Venters. His voice, as all fire and pulse within him, seemed to freeze.

"Let go my arm!" exclaimed Judkins. "Thet's my bad arm. Sure it was Oldrin'. What the hell's wrong with you, anyway? Venters, I tell you somethin's wrong. You're whiter 'n a sheet. You can't be *scared* of the rustler. I don't believe you've got a scare in you. Wal, now, jest let me talk. You know I like to talk, an' if I'm slow I allus git there sometime. As I said, Lassiter was talkin' chummy with Oldrin'. There wasn't no hard feelin's. An' the gang wasn't payin' no pertic'lar attention. But like a cat watchin' a mouse I hed my eyes on them two fellers. It was strange to me, thet confab. I'm gittin' to think a lot, fer a feller who doesn't know much. There's been some queer deals lately an' this seemed to me the queerest. These men stood to the bar alone, an' so close their big gun-hilts butted together. I seen Oldrin' was some surprised at first, an' Lassiter was cool as ice. They talked, an' presently at somethin' Lassiter said the rustler bawled out a curse, an' then he jest fell up against the bar, an' sagged there. The gang in the saloon looked around an' laughed, an' thet's about all. Finally Oldrin' turned, and it was easy to see somethin' hed shook him. Yes, sir, thet big rustler—you know he's as broad as he is long, an' the powerfulest build of a man—yes, sir, the nerve had been taken out of him. Then, after a little, he began to talk an' said a lot to Lassiter, an' by an' by it didn't take much of an eye to see thet Lassiter was gittin' hit hard. I never seen him anyway but cooler 'n ice—till then. He seemed to be hit harder 'n Oldrin', only he didn't roar out thet way. He jest kind of sunk in, an' looked an' looked, an' he didn't see a livin' soul in thet saloon. Then he sort of come to, an' shakin' hands—mind you, *shakin' hands* with Oldrin'—he went out. I couldn't help thinkin' how easy even a boy could hev dropped the great gun-man then! . . . Wal, the rustler stood at the bar fer a long time, an' he was seein' things far off, too; then he come to an' roared fer whisky, an' gulped a drink thet was big enough to drown me."

"Is Oldring here now?" whispered Venters. He could not speak above a whisper. Judkins's story had been meaningless to him.

"He's at Snell's yet. Bern, I hevn't told you yet thet the rustlers hev been raisin' hell. They shot up Stone Bridge an' Glaze, an' fer three days they've been here drinkin' an' gamblin' an' throwin' of gold. These rustlers hev a pile of gold. If it was gold dust or nugget gold I'd hev reason to think, but it's new coin gold, as if it had jest come from the United States treasury. An' the coin's genuine. Thet's all been proved. The truth is Oldrin's on a rampage. A while back he lost his Masked Rider, an' they say he's wild about thet. I'm wonderin' if Lassiter could hev told the rustler anythin' about thet little masked, hard-ridin' devil. Ride! He was most as good as Jerry Card. An', Bern, I've been wonderin' if you know—"

"Judkins, you're a good fellow," interrupted Venters. "Some day I'll tell you a story. I've no time now. Take the horses to Jane."

Judkins stared, and then, muttering to himself, he mounted Bells, and stared again at Venters, and then, leading the other horses, he rode into the grove and disappeared.

Once, long before, on the night Venters had carried Bess through the cañon and up into Surprise Valley, he had experienced the strangeness of faculties singularly, tinglingly acute. And now the same sensation recurred. But it was different in that he felt cold, frozen, mechanical, incapable of free thought, and all about him seemed unreal, aloof, remote. He hid his rifle in the sage, marking its exact location with extreme care. Then he faced down the lane and strode toward the center of the village. Perceptions flashed upon him, the faint, cold touch of the breeze, a cold, silvery tinkle of flowing water, a cold sun shining out of a cold sky, song of birds and laugh of children, coldly distant. Cold and intangible were all things in earth and heaven. Colder and tighter stretched the skin over his face; colder and harder grew the polished butts of his guns;

colder and steadier became his hands as he wiped the clammy sweat from his face or reached low to his gun-sheaths. Men meeting him in the walk gave him wide berth. In front of Bevin's store a crowd melted apart for his passage, and their faces and whispers were faces and whispers of a dream. He turned a corner to meet Tull face to face, eye to eye. As once before he had seen this man pale to a ghastly, livid white, so again he saw the change. Tull stopped in his tracks, with right hand raised and shaking. Suddenly it dropped, and he seemed to glide aside, to pass out of Venters's sight. Next he saw many horses with bridles down—all clean-limbed, dark bays or blacks—rustlers' horses! Loud voices and boisterous laughter, rattle of dice and scrape of chair and clink of gold, burst in mingled din from an open doorway. He stepped inside.

With the sight of smoke-hazed room and drinking, cursing, gambling, dark-visaged men, reality once more dawned upon Venters.

His entrance had been unnoticed, and he bent his gaze upon the drinkers at the bar. Dark-clothed, dark-faced men they all were, burned by the sun, bow-legged as were most riders of the sage, but neither lean nor gaunt. Then Venters's gaze passed to the tables, and swiftly it swept over the hard-featured gamesters, to alight upon the huge, shaggy, black head of the rustler chief.

"*Oldring!*" he cried, and to him his voice seemed to split a bell in his ears.

It stilled the din.

That silence suddenly broke to the scrape and crash of Oldring's chair as he rose; and then, while he passed, a great gloomy figure, again the thronged room stilled in silence yet deeper.

"Oldring, a word with you!" continued Venters.

"Ho! What's this?" boomed Oldring, in frowning scrutiny.

"Come outside, alone. A word for you—*from your Masked Rider!*"

Oldring kicked a chair out of his way and lunged forward with a stamp of heavy boot that jarred the floor. He waved down his muttering, rising men.

Venters backed out of the door and waited, hearing, as no sound had ever before struck into his soul, the rapid, heavy steps of the rustler.

Oldring appeared, and Venters had one glimpse of his great breadth and bulk, his gold-buckled belt with hanging guns, his high-top boots with gold spurs. In that moment Venters had a strange, unintelligible curiosity to see Oldring alive. The rustler's broad brow, his large black eyes, his sweeping beard, as dark as the wing of a raven, his enormous width of shoulder and depth of chest, his whole splendid presence so wonderfully charged with vitality and force and strength, seemed to afford Venters an unutterable fiendish joy because for that magnificent manhood and life he meant cold and sudden death.

"*Oldring, Bess is alive! But she's dead to you—dead to the life you made her lead—dead as you will be in one second!*"

Swift as lightning Venters's glance dropped from Oldring's rolling eyes to his hands. One of them, the right, swept out, then toward his gun—and Venters shot him through the heart.

Slowly Oldring sank to his knees, and the hand, dragging at the gun, fell away. Venters's strangely acute faculties grasped the meaning of that limp arm, of the swaying hulk, of the gasp and heave, of the quivering beard. But was that awful spirit in the black eyes only one of vitality?

"*Man—why—didn't—you—wait? Bess—was—*" Oldring's whisper died under his beard, and with a heavy lurch he fell forward.

Bounding swiftly away, Venters fled around the cor-

AND VENTERS SHOT HIM THROUGH THE HEART

ner, across the street, and, leaping a hedge, he ran through yard, orchard, and garden to the sage. Here, under cover of the tall brush, he turned west and ran on to the place where he had hidden his rifle. Securing that, he again set out into a run, and, circling through the sage, came up behind Jane Withersteen's stable and corrals. With laboring, dripping chest, and pain as of a knife thrust in his side, he stopped to regain his breath, and while resting his eyes roved around in search of a horse. Doors and windows of the stable were open wide and had a deserted look. One dejected, lonely burro stood in the near corral. Strange indeed was the silence brooding over the once happy, noisy home of Jane Withersteen's pets.

He went into the corral, exercising care to leave no tracks, and led the burro to the watering-trough. Venters, though not thirsty, drank till he could drink no more. Then, leading the burro over hard ground, he struck into the sage and down the slope.

He strode swiftly, turning from time to time to scan the slope for riders. His head just topped the level of sage-brush, and the burro could not have been seen at all. Slowly the green of Cottonwoods sank behind the slope, and at last a wavering line of purple sage met the blue of sky.

To avoid being seen, to get away, to hide his trail—these were the sole ideas in his mind as he headed for Deception Pass; and he directed all his acuteness of eye and ear, and the keenness of a rider's judgment for distance and ground, to stern accomplishment of the task. He kept to the sage far to the left of the trail leading into the Pass. He walked ten miles and looked back a thousand times. Always the graceful, purple wave of sage remained wide and lonely, a clear, undotted waste. Coming to a stretch of rocky ground, he took advantage of it to cross the trail and then continued down on the right. At length he persuaded himself that he would be able to see riders mounted on horses before they could see him on the little burro, and he rode bareback.

Hour by hour the tireless burro kept to his faithful, steady trot. The sun sank and the long shadows lengthened down the slope. Moving veils of purple twilight crept out of the hollows and, mustering and forming on the levels, soon merged and shaded into night. Venters guided the burro nearer to the trail, so that he could see its white line from the ridges, and rode on through the hours.

Once down in the Pass without leaving a trail, he would hold himself safe for the time being. When late in the night he reached the break in the sage, he sent the burro down ahead of him, and started an avalanche that all but buried the animal at the bottom of the trail. Bruised and battered as he was, he had a moment's elation, for he had hidden his tracks. Once more he mounted the burro and rode on. The hour was the blackest of the night when he made the thicket which inclosed his old camp. Here he turned the burro loose in the grass near the spring, and then lay down on his old bed of leaves.

He felt only vaguely, as outside things, the ache and burn and throb of the muscles of his body. But a dammed-up torrent of emotion at last burst its bounds, and the hour that saw his release from immediate action was one that confounded him in the reaction of his spirit. He suffered without understanding why. He caught glimpses into himself, into unlit darkness of soul. The fire that had blistered him and the cold which had frozen him now united in one torturing possession of his mind and heart, and like a fiery steed with ice-shod feet, ranged his being, ran rioting through his blood, trampling the resurging good, dragging ever at the evil.

Out of the subsiding chaos came a clear question. What had happened? He had left the valley to go to

Cottonwoods. Why? It seemed that he had gone to kill a man—Oldring! The name riveted his consciousness upon the one man of all men upon earth whom he had wanted to meet. He had met the rustler. Venters recalled the smoky haze of the saloon, the dark-visaged men, the huge Oldring. He saw him step out of the door, a splendid specimen of manhood, a handsome giant with purple-black and sweeping beard. He remembered inquisitive gaze of falcon eyes. He heard himself repeating: "*Oldring, Bess is alive! But she's dead to you,*" and he felt himself jerk, and his ears throbbed to the thunder of a gun, and he saw the giant sink slowly to his knees. Was that only the vitality of him—that awful light in the eyes—only the hard-dying life of a tremendously powerful brute? A broken whisper, strange as death: "*Man—why—didn't—you wait! Bess—was—*" And Oldring plunged face forward, dead.

"I killed him," cried Venters, in remembering shock. "But it wasn't *that*. Ah, the look in his eyes and his whisper!"

Herein lay the secret that had clamored to him through all the tumult and stress of his emotions. What a look in the eyes of a man shot through the heart! It had been neither hate nor ferocity nor fear of men nor fear of death. It had been no passionate, glinting spirit of a fearless foe, willing shot for shot, life for life, but lacking physical power. Distinctly recalled now, never to be forgotten, Venters saw in Oldring's magnificent eyes the rolling of great, glad surprise—softness—love! Then came a shadow and the terrible superhuman striving of his spirit to speak. Oldring, shot through the heart, had fought and forced back death, not for a moment in which to shoot or curse, but to whisper strange words.

What words for a dying man to whisper! Why had not Venters waited? For what? That was no plea for life. It was regret that there was not a moment of life left in which to speak. Bess was— Herein lay renewed torture for Venters. What had Bess been to Oldring? The old question, like a specter, stalked from its grave to haunt him. He had overlooked, he had forgiven, he had loved, and he had forgotten; and now, out of the mystery of a dying man's whisper rose again that perverse, unsatisfied, jealous uncertainty. Bess had loved that splendid, black-crowned giant—by her own confession she had loved him; and in Venters's soul again flamed up the jealous hell. Then into the clamoring hell burst the shot that had killed Oldring, and it rang in a wild, fiendish gladness, a hateful, vengeful joy. That passed to the memory of the love and light in Oldring's eyes and the mystery in his whisper. So the changing, swaying emotions fluctuated in Venters's heart.

This was the climax of his year of suffering and the crucial struggle of his life. And when the gray dawn came he rose, a gloomy, almost heartbroken man, but victor over evil passions. He could not change the past; and, even if he had not loved Bess with all his soul, he had grown into a man who would not change the future he had planned for her. Only, and once for all, he must know the truth, know the worst, stifle all these insistent doubts and subtle hopes and jealous fancies, and kill the past by knowing truly what Bess had been to Oldring. For that matter he knew—he had always known, but he must hear it spoken. Then, when they had safely gotten out of that wild country to take up a new and an absorbing life, she would forget, she would be happy, and through that, in the years to come, he could not but find life worth living.

All day he rode slowly and cautiously up the Pass, taking time to peer around corners, to pick out hard ground and grassy patches, and to make sure there was no one in pursuit. In the night sometime he came to the smooth, scrawled rocks dividing the valley, and here set the burro at liberty. He walked beyond, climbed the slope and the dim, starlit gorge. Then, weary to the point of exhaustion, he crept into a shallow cave and fell asleep.

In the morning, when he descended the trail, he found the sun was pouring a golden stream of light through the arch of the great stone bridge. Surprise Valley, like a valley of dreams, lay mystically soft and beautiful, awakening to the golden flood which was rolling away its slumberous bands of mist, brightening its walled faces.

While yet far off he discerned Bess moving under the silver spruces, and soon the barking of the dogs told him that they had seen him. He heard the mocking-birds singing in the trees, and then the twittering of the quail. Ring and Whitie came bounding toward him, and behind them ran Bess, her hands outstretched.

"Bern! You're back! You're back!" she cried, in a joy that rang of her loneliness.

"Yes, I'm back," he said, as she rushed to meet him.

She had reached out for him when suddenly, as she saw him closely, something checked her, and as quickly all her joy fled, and with it her color, leaving her pale and trembling.

"Oh! What's happened?"

"A good deal has happened, Bess. I don't need to tell you what. And I'm played out. Worn out in mind more than body."

"Dear—you look strange to me!" faltered Bess.

"Never mind that. I'm all right. There's nothing for you to be scared about. Things are going to turn out just as we have planned. As soon as I'm rested we'll make a break to get out of the country. Only now, right now, I must know the truth about you."

"Truth about me?" echoed Bess, shrinkingly. She seemed to be casting back into her mind for a forgotten key. Venters himself, as he saw her, received a pang.

"Yes—the truth. Bess, don't misunderstand. I haven't changed that way. I love you still. I'll love you more afterward. Life will be just as sweet—sweeter to us. We'll be—be married as soon as ever we can. We'll be happy—but there's a devil in me. A perverse, jealous devil! Then I've queer fancies. I forgot for a long time. Now all those fiendish little whispers of doubt and faith and fear and hope come torturing me again. I've got to kill them with the truth."

"I'll tell you anything you want to know," she replied, frankly.

"Then, by Heaven! we'll have it over and done with! . . . Bess—did Oldring love you?"

"Certainly he did."

"Did—did you love him?"

"Of course. I told you so."

"How can you tell it so lightly?" cried Venters, passionately. "Haven't you any sense of—of—" He choked back speech. He felt the rush of pain and passion. He seized her in rude, strong hands and drew her close. He looked straight into her dark-blue eyes. They were shadowing with the old wistful light, but they were as clear as the limpid water of the spring. They were earnest, solemn in unutterable love and faith and abnegation. Venters shivered. He knew he was looking into her soul. He knew she could not lie in that moment; but that she might tell the truth, looking at him with those eyes, almost killed his belief in purity.

"What are—what were you to—to Oldring?" he panted, fiercely.

"I am his daughter," she replied, instantly.

Venters slowly let go of her. There was a violent break in the force of his feeling—then creeping blankness.

"What—was it—you said?" he asked, in a kind of dull wonder.

"I am his daughter."

"Oldring's daughter?" queried Venters, with life gathering in his voice.

"Yes."

With a passionately awakening start he grasped her hands and drew her close.

"All the time—you've been Oldring's daughter?"

"Yes, of course all the time—always."

"But Bess, you told me—you let me think—I made out you were—a—so—so ashamed."

"It is my shame," she said, with voice deep and full, and now the scarlet fired her cheek. "I told you—I'm nothing—nameless—just Bess, Oldring's girl!"

"I know—I remember. But I never thought—" he went on, hurriedly, huskily. "That time—when you lay dying—you prayed—you—somehow I got the idea you were bad."

"Bad?" she asked, with a little laugh.

She looked up with a faint smile of bewilderment and the absolute unconsciousness of a child. Venters gasped in the gathering might of the truth. She did not understand his meaning.

"Bess! Bess!" He clasped her in his arms, hiding her eyes against his breast. She must not see his face in that moment. And he held her while he looked out across the valley. In his dim and blinded sight, in the blur of golden light and moving mist, he saw Oldring. She was the rustler's nameless daughter. Oldring had loved her. He had so guarded her, so kept her from women and men and knowledge of life that her mind was as a child's. That was part of the secret—part of the mystery. That was the wonderful truth. Not only was she not bad, but good, pure, innocent above all innocence in the world—the innocence of lonely girlhood.

He saw Oldring's magnificent eyes, inquisitive, searching—softening. He saw them flare in amaze, in gladness, with love, then suddenly strain in terrible effort of will. He heard Oldring whisper and saw him sway like a log and fall. Then a million bellowing, thundering voices—gunshots of conscience, thunderbolts of remorse—dinned horribly in his ears. He had killed Bess's father. Then a rushing wind filled his ears like the moan of wind in the cliffs, a knell indeed—Oldring's knell.

He dropped to his knees and hid his face against Bess, and grasped her with the hands of a drowning man.

"My God! . . . My God! . . . Oh, Bess! . . . Forgive me! Never mind what I've done—what I've thought. But forgive me. I'll give you my life. I'll live for you. I'll love you. Oh, I do love you as no man ever loved a woman. I want you to know—to remember that I fought a fight for you—however blind I was. I thought—I thought—never mind what I thought—but I loved you—I asked you to marry me. Let that—let me have that to hug to my heart. Oh, Bess, I was driven! And I might have known! I could not rest nor sleep till I had this mystery solved. God! how things work out!"

"Bern, you're weak—trembling—you talk wildly," cried Bess. "You've overdone your strength. There's nothing to forgive. There's no mystery except your love for me. You have come back to me!"

And she clasped his head tenderly in her arms and pressed it closely to her throbbing breast.

CHAPTER XIX

FAY

AT the home of Jane Withersteen Little Fay was climbing Lassiter's knee.

"Does oo love me?" she asked.

Lassiter, who was as serious with Fay as he was gentle and loving, assured her in earnest and elaborate speech that he was her devoted subject. Fay looked thoughtful and appeared to be debating the duplicity of men or searching for a supreme test to prove this cavalier.

"Does oo love my new muvver?" she asked, with bewildering suddenness.

Jane Withersteen laughed, and for the first time in many a day she felt a stir of her pulse and warmth in her cheek.

It was a still drowsy summer of afternoon, and the three were sitting in the shade of the wooded knoll that faced the sage-slope. Little Fay's brief spell of unhappy longing for her mother—the childish, mystic gloom—had passed, and now where Fay was there were prattle and laughter and glee. She had emerged from sorrow to be the incarnation of joy and loveliness. She had grown supernaturally sweet and beautiful. For Jane Withersteen the child was an answer to prayer, a blessing, a possession infinitely more precious than all she had lost. For Lassiter, Jane divined that little Fay had become a religion.

"Does oo love my new muvver?" repeated Fay.

Lassiter's answer to this was a modest and sincere affirmative.

"Why don't oo marry my new muvver an' be my favver?"

Of the thousands of questions put by little Fay to Lassiter that was the first he had been unable to answer.

"Fay—Fay, don't ask questions like that," said Jane.

"Why?"

"Because," replied Jane. And she found it strangely embarrassing to meet the child's gaze. It seemed to her that Fay's violet eyes looked through her with piercing wisdom.

"Oo love him, don't oo?"

"Dear child—run and play," said Jane, "but don't go too far. Don't go from this little hill."

Fay pranced off wildly, joyous over freedom that had not been granted her for weeks.

"Jane, why are children more sincere than grown-up persons?" asked Lassiter.

"Are they?"

"I reckon so. Little Fay there—she sees things as they appear on the face. An Indian does that. So does a dog. An' an Indian an' a dog are most of the time right in what they see. Mebbe a child is always right."

"Well, what does Fay see?" asked Jane.

"I reckon you know. I wonder what goes on in Fay's mind when she sees part of the truth with the wise eyes of a child, an' wantin' to know more, meets with strange falseness from you? Wait! You are false in a way, though you're the best woman I ever knew. What I want to say is this. Fay has taken you're pretendin' to—to care for me for the thing it looks on the face. An' her little formin' mind asks questions. An' the answers she gets are different from the looks of things. So she'll grow up, gradually takin' on that falseness, an' be like the rest of women, an' men, too. An' the truth of this falseness to life is proved by your appearin' to love me when you don't. Things aren't what they seem."

"Lassiter, you're right. A child should be told the absolute truth. But—is that possible? I haven't been able to do it, and all my life I've loved the truth, and I've prided myself upon being truthful. Maybe that was only egotism. I'm learning much, my friend. Some of those blinding scales have fallen from my eyes. And—and as to caring for you, I think I care a great deal. How much, how little, I couldn't say. My heart is almost broken, Lassiter. So now is not a good time to judge of affection. I can still play and be merry with Fay. I can still dream. But when I attempt serious thought I'm dazed. I don't think. I don't care any more. I don't pray! . . . Think of that, my friend! But in spite of my numb feeling I believe I'll rise out of all this dark agony a better woman, with greater love of man and God. I'm on the rack now; I'm senseless to all but pain, and growing dead to that. Sooner or later I shall rise out of this stupor. I'm waiting the hour."

"It 'll soon come, Jane," replied Lassiter, soberly. "Then I'm afraid for you. Years are terrible things, an' for years you've been bound. Habit of years is strong as life itself. Somehow, though, I believe as you—that you'll come out of it all a finer woman. I'm waitin', too. An' I'm wonderin'—I reckon, Jane, that marriage between us is out of all human reason?"

"Lassiter! . . . My dear friend! . . . It's impossible for us to marry."

"Why—as Fay says?" inquired Lassiter, with gentle persistence.

"Why! I never thought why. But it's not possible. I am Jane, daughter of Withersteen. My father would rise out of his grave. I'm of Mormon birth. I'm being broken. But I'm still a Mormon woman. And you—you are Lassiter!"

"Mebbe I'm not so much Lassiter as I used to be."

"What was it you said? Habit of years is strong as life itself! You can't change the one habit—the purpose of your life. For you still pack those black guns! You still nurse your passion for blood."

A smile, like a shadow, flickered across his face.

"No."

"Lassiter, I lied to you. But I beg of you—don't you lie to me. I've great respect for you. I believe you're softened toward most, perhaps all, my people except— But when I speak of your purpose, your hate, your guns, I have only him in mind. I don't believe you've changed.

For answer he unbuckled the heavy cartridge-belt, and laid it with the heavy, swing gun-sheaths in her lap.

"Lassiter!" Jane whispered, as she gazed from him to the black, cold guns. Without them he appeared shorn of strength, defenseless, a smaller man. Was she Delilah? Swiftly, conscious of only one motive—refusal to see this man called craven by his enemies—she rose, and with blundering fingers buckled the belt round his waist where it belonged.

"Lassiter, *I* am the coward."

"Come with me out of Utah—where I can put away my guns an' be a man," he said. "I reckon I'll prove it to you then! Come! You've got Black Star back, an' Night an' Bells. Let's take the racers an' little Fay, an' ride out of Utah. The hosses an' the child are all you have left. Come!"

"No, no, Lassiter. I'll never leave Utah. What would I do in the world with my broken fortunes and my broken heart? I'll never leave these purple slopes I love so well."

"I reckon I ought to 've knowed that. Presently you'll be livin' down here in a hovel, an' presently Jane Withersteen will be a memory. I only wanted to have a chance to show you how a man—*any* man—can be better 'n he was. If we left Utah I could prove—I reckon I could prove this thing you call love. It's strange, an' hell an' heaven at once, Jane Withersteen. 'Pears to me that you've thrown away your big heart on love—love of religion an' duty an' churchmen, an' riders an' poor families an' poor children! Yet you can't see what love is—how it changes a person! . . . Listen, an' in tellin' you Milly Erne's story I'll show you how love changed her.

"Milly an' me was children when our family moved from Missuori to Texas, an' we growed up in Texas ways same as if we'd been born there. We had been poor, an' there we prospered. In time the little village where we went became a town, an' strangers an' new families kept movin' in. Milly was the belle them days. I can see her now, a little girl no bigger 'n a bird, an' as pretty. She had the finest eyes, dark blue-black when she was excited, an' beautiful all the time. You remember Milly's eyes! An' she had light-brown hair with streaks of gold, an' a mouth that every feller wanted to kiss.

"An' about the time Milly was the prettiest an' the sweetest, along came a young minister who began to ride some of a race with the other fellers for Milly. An' he won. Milly had always been strong on religion, an' when she met Frank Erne she went in heart an' soul for the salvation of souls. Fact was, Milly, through study of the Bible an' attendin' church an' revivals, went a little out of her head. It didn't worry the old folks none, an' the only worry to me was Milly's everlastin' prayin' an' workin' to save my soul. She never converted me, but we was the best of comrades, an' I reckon no brother an' sister ever loved each other better. Well, Frank Erne an' me hit up a great friendship. He was a strappin' feller, good to look at, an' had the most pleasin' ways. His religion never bothered me, for he could hunt an' fish an' ride an' be a good feller. After buffalo once, he come pretty near to savin' my life. We got to be thick as brothers, an' he was the only man I ever seen who I thought was good enough for Milly. An' the day they were married I got drunk for the only time in my life.

"Soon after that I left home—it seems Milly was the only one who could keep me home—an' I went to the bad, as to prosperin'. I saw some pretty hard life in the Pan Handle, an' then I went North. In them days Kansas an' Nebraska was as bad, come to think of it, as these days right here on the border of Utah. I got to be pretty handy with guns. An' there wasn't many riders as could beat me ridin'. An' I can say all modest-like that I never seen the white man who could track a hoss or a steer or a man with me. Afore I knowed it two years slipped by, an' all at once I got homesick, an' pulled a bridle south.

"Things at home had changed. I never got over that home-comin'. Mother was dead an' in her grave. Father was a silent, broken man, killed already on his feet. Frank Erne was a ghost of his old self, through with workin', through with preachin', almost through with livin', an' Milly was gone! . . . It was a long time before I got the story. Father had no mind left, an' Frank Erne was *afraid* to talk. So I had to pick up what 'd happened from different people.

"It 'pears that soon after I left home another preacher come to the little town. An' he an' Frank become rivals. This feller was different from Frank. He preached some other kind of religion, and he was quick an' passionate, where Frank was slow an' mild. He went after people, women specially. In looks he couldn't compare to Frank Erne, but he had power over women. He had a voice, an' he talked an' talked an' preached an' preached. Milly fell under his influence. She became mightily interested in his religion. Frank had patience with her, as was his way, an' let her be as interested as she liked. All religions were devoted to one God, he said, an' it wouldn't hurt Milly none to study a different point of view. So the new preacher often called on Milly, an' sometimes in Frank's absence. Frank was a cattle-man between Sundays.

"Along about this time an incident come off that I couldn't get much light on. A stranger come to town, an' was seen with the preacher. This stranger was a big man with an eye like blue ice, an' a beard of gold. He had money, an' he 'peared a man of mystery, an' the town went to buzzin' when he disappeared about the same time as a young woman known to be mightily interested in the new preacher's religion. Then, presently, along comes a man from somewheres in Illinois, an' he up an' spots this preacher as a famous Mormon proselyter. That ri'led Frank Erne as nothin' ever before, an' from rivals they come to be bitter enemies. An' it ended in Frank goin' to the meetin'-house where Milly was listenin', an' before her an' everybody else he called that preacher—called him, well, almost as hard as Venters called Tull here sometime back. An' Frank followed up that call with a hoss-whippin', an' he drove the proselyter out of town.

"People noticed, so 'twas said, that Milly's sweet disposition changed. Some said it was because she would soon become a mother, an' others said she was pinin' after the new religion. An' there was women who said right out that she was pinin' after the Mormon. Anyway, one mornin' Frank rode in from one of his trips, to find Milly gone. He had no real near neighbors—livin' a little out of town—but those who was nearest said a wagon had gone by in the night, an' they thought it stopped at her door. Well, tracks always tell, an' there was the wagon tracks an' hoss tracks an' man tracks. The news spread like wildfire that Milly had run off from her husband. Everybody but Frank believed it, an' wasn't slow in tellin' why she run off. Mother had always hated that strange streak of Milly's, takin' up with the new religion as she had, an' she believed Milly ran off with the Mormon. That hastened mother's death, an' she died unforgivin'. Father wasn't the kind to bow down under disgrace or misfortune, but he had surpassin' love for Milly, an' the loss of her broke him.

"From the minute I heard of Milly's disappearance I never believed she went off of her own free will. I knew Milly, an' I knew she *couldn't* have done that. I stayed at home awhile, tryin' to make Frank Erne talk. But if he knowed anythin' then he wouldn't tell it. So I set out to find Milly. An' I tried to get on the trail of that proselyter. I knew if I ever struck a town he'd visited that I'd get a trail. I knew, too, that nothin' short of hell would stop his proselytin'. An' I rode from town to town. I had a blind faith that somethin' was guidin' me. An' as the weeks an' months went by I growed into a strange sort of a man, I guess. Anyway, people were afraid of me. Two years after that, way over in a corner of Texas, I struck a town where my man had been. He'd jest left. People said he came to that town *without* a woman. I back-trailed my man through Arkansas an' Mississippi, an' the old trail got hot again in Texas. I found the town where he first went after leavin' home. An' here I got track of Milly. I found a cabin where she had given birth to her baby. There was no way to tell whether she'd been kept a prisoner or not. The feller who owned the place was a mean, silent sort of a skunk, an' as I was leavin' I jest took a chance an' left my mark on him. Then I went home again.

"It was to find I hadn't any home, no more. Father had been dead a year. Frank Erne still lived in the house where Milly had left him. I stayed with him awhile, an' I grew old watchin' him. His farm had gone to weed, his cattle had strayed or been rustled, his house weathered till it wouldn't keep out rain nor wind. An' Frank set on the porch and whittled sticks, an' day by day wasted away. There was times when he ranted about like a crazy man, but mostly he was always sittin' an' starin' with eyes that made a man curse. I figured Frank had a secret fear that I needed to know. An' when I told him I'd trailed Milly for near three years an' had got trace of her, an' saw where she'd had her baby, I thought he would drop dead at my feet. An' when he'd come round more natural-like he begged me to *give up* the trail. But he wouldn't explain. So I let him alone, an' watched him day an' night.

"An' I found there was one thing still precious to him, an' it was a little drawer where he kept his papers. This was in the room where he slept. An' it 'peared he seldom slept. But after bein' patient I got the contents of that drawer an' found two letters from Milly. One was a long letter written a few months after her disappearance. She had been bound an' gagged an' dragged away from her home by three men, an' she named them—Hurd, Metzger, Slack. They was strangers to her. She was taken to the little town where I found trace of her two years after. But she didn't send the letter from that town. There she was penned in. 'Peared that the proselyter, who had, of course, come on the scene, was not runnin' any risks of losin' her. She went on to say that for a time she was out of her head, an' when she got right again all that kept her alive was the baby. It was a beautiful baby, she said, an' all she thought an' dreamed of was somehow to get baby back to its father, an' then she'd thankfully lay down and die. An' the letter ended abrupt, in the middle of a sentence, an' it wasn't signed.

"The second letter was written more than two years after the first. It was from Salt Lake City. It simply said that Milly had heard her brother was on her trail. She asked Frank to tell her brother to give up the search because if he didn't she would suffer in a way too horrible to tell. She didn't beg. She just stated a fact an' made the simple request. An' she ended that letter by sayin' she would soon leave Salt Lake City with the man she had come to love, an' would never be heard of again.

"I recognized Milly's handwritin', an' I recognized her way of puttin' things. But that second letter told me of some great change in her. Ponderin' over it, I felt at last she'd either come to love that feller an' his religion, or some terrible fear made her lie an' say so. I couldn't be sure which. But, of course, I meant to find out. I'll say here, if I'd known Mormons then as I do now I'd left Milly to her fate. For mebbe she was right about what she'd suffer if I kept on her trail. But I was young an' wild them days. First I went to the town where she'd first been taken, an' I went to the place where she'd been kept. I got that skunk who owned the place, an' took him out in the woods, an' made him tell all he knowed. That wasn't much as to length, but it was pure hell's-fire in substance. This time I left him some incapacitated for any more skunk work short of hell. Then I hit the trail for Utah.

"That was fourteen years ago. I saw the incomin' of most of the Mormons. It was a wild country an' a wild time. I rode from town to town, village to village, ranch to ranch, camp to camp. I never stayed long in one place. I never had but one idea. I never rested. Four years went by, an' I knowed every trail in northern Utah. I kept on an' as time went by, an' I'd begun to grow old in my search, I had firmer, blinder faith in whatever was guidin' me. Once I read about a feller who sailed the seven seas an' traveled the world, an' he had a story to tell, an' whenever he seen the man to whom he must tell that story he knowed him on sight. I was like that, only I had a question to ask. An' always I knew the man of whom I must ask. So I never really lost the trail, though for years it was the dimmest trail ever followed by any man.

"Then come a change in my luck. Along in Central Utah I rounded up Hurd, an' I whispered somethin' in his ear, an' watched his face, an' then throwed a gun against his bowels. An' he died with his teeth so tight shut I couldn't have pried them open with a knife. Slack an' Metzger that same year both heard me whisper the same question, an' neither would they speak a word when they lay dyin'. Long before I'd learned no man of this breed or class—or God knows what—would give up any secrets! I had to see in a man's fear of death the connections with Milly Erne's fate. An' as the years passed at long intervals I would find such a man.

"So as I drifted on the long trail down into southern Utah my name preceded me, an' I had to meet a people prepared for me, an' ready with guns. They made me a gun-man. An' that suited me. In all this time signs of the proselyter an' the giant with the blue-ice eyes an' the gold beard seemed to fade dimmer out of the trail. Only twice in ten years did I find a trace of that mysterious man who had visited the proselyter at my home village. What he had to do with Milly's fate was beyond all hope for me to learn, unless my guidin' spirit led me to him! As for the other man, I knew, as sure as I breathed an' the stars shone an' the wind blew, that I'd meet him some day.

"Eighteen years I've been on the trail. An' it led me to the last lonely villages of the Utah border. Eighteen years! . . . I feel pretty old now. I was only twenty when I hit that trail. Well, as I told you, back here a ways a Gentile said Jane Withersteen could tell me about Milly Erne an' show me her grave!"

The low voice ceased, and Lassiter slowly turned his sombrero round and round, and appeared to be counting the silver ornaments on the band. Jane leaning toward him, sat as if petrified, listening intently, waiting to hear more. She could have shrieked, but power of tongue and lips were denied her. She saw only this sad, gray, passion-worn man, and she heard only the faint rustling of the leaves.

"Well, I came to Cottonwoods," went on Lassiter, "an' you showed me Milly's grave. An' though your teeth have been shut tighter 'n them of all the dead men lyin' back along that trail, jest the same you told me the secret I've lived these eighteen years to hear! Jane, I said you'd tell me without ever me askin'. I didn't need to ask my question here. The day, you remember, when that fat party throwed a gun on me in your court, an'—"

"Oh! Hush!" whispered Jane, blindly holding up her hands.

"*I seen in your face that Dyer, now a bishop, was the proselyter who ruined Milly Erne!*"

For an instant Jane Withersteen's brain was a whirling chaos, and she recovered to find herself grasping at Lassiter like one drowning. And as if by a lightning stroke she sprang from her dull apathy into exquisite torture.

"*It's a lie!* Lassiter! No, no!" she moaned. "I swear—you're wrong!"

"Stop! You'd perjure yourself! But I'll spare you that. You poor woman! Still blind! Still faithful! . . . Listen. I *know*. Let that settle it. An' I give up my purpose!"

"What is it—you say?"

"I give up my purpose. I've come to see an' feel differently. I can't help poor Milly. An' I've outgrowed revenge. I've come to see I can be no judge for men. I can't kill a man jest for hate. Hate ain't the same with me since I loved you and little Fay."

"Lassiter! You mean you won't kill him?" Jane whispered.

"No."

"For my sake?"

"I reckon. I can't understand, but I'll respect your feelin's."

"Because you—oh, because you love me? . . . Eighteen years! You were that terrible Lassiter! And *now*—because you love me?"

"That's it, Jane."

"Oh, you'll make me love you! How can I help but love you? My heart must be stone. But—oh, Lassiter, wait, wait! Give me time. I'm not what I was. Once it was so easy to love. Now it's easy to hate. Wait! My faith in God—*some* God—still lives. By it I see happier times for you, poor passion-swayed wanderer! For me—a miserable, broken woman. I loved your sister Milly. I *will* love you. I can't have fallen so low—I can't be so abandoned by God—that I've no love left to give you. Wait! Let us forget Milly's sad life. Ah, I knew it as no one else on earth! There's one thing I shall tell you—if you are at my death-bed, but I can't speak now."

"I reckon I don't want to hear no more," said Lassiter.

Jane leaned against him; as if some pent-up force had rent its way out, she fell into a paroxysm of weeping. Lassiter held her in silent sympathy. By degrees she regained composure, and she was rising, sensible of being relieved of a weighty burden, when a sudden start on Lassiter's part alarmed her.

"I heard hosses—hosses with muffled hoofs!" he said; and he got up guardedly.

"Where's Fay?" asked Jane, hurriedly glancing round the shady knoll. The bright-haired child, who had appeared to be close all the time, was not in sight.

"Fay!" called Jane.

No answering shout of glee. No patter of flying feet. Jane saw Lassiter stiffen.

"*Fay—oh—Fay!*" Jane almost screamed.

The leaves quivered and rustled; a lonesome cricket chirped in the grass; a bee hummed by. The silence of the waning afternoon breathed hateful portent. It terrified Jane. When had silence been so infernal?

"She's—only—strayed—out—of earshot," faltered Jane, looking at Lassiter.

Pale, rigid as a statue, the rider stood, not in listening, searching posture, but in one of doomed certainty. Suddenly he grasped Jane with an iron hand, and, turning his face from her gaze, he strode with her from the knoll.

"See—Fay played here last—a house of stones an' sticks. . . . An' here's a corral of pebbles with leaves for hosses," said Lassiter, stridently, and pointed to the ground. "Back an' forth she trailed here. . . . See, she's buried somethin'—a dead grasshopper—there's a tombstone . . . here she went, chasin' a lizard—see the tiny streaked trail . . . she pulled bark off this cottonwood . . . look in the dust of the path—the letters you taught her—she's drawn pictures of birds an' hosses an' people. . . . Look, a cross! Oh, Jane, *your* cross!"

Lassiter dragged Jane on, and as if from a book read the meaning of little Fay's trail. All the way down the knoll, through the shrubbery, round and round a cottonwood, Fay's vagrant fancy left records of her sweet musings and innocent play. Long had she lingered round a bird-nest to leave therein the gaudy wing of a butterfly. Long had she played beside the running stream, sending adrift vessels freighted with pebbly cargo. Then she had wandered through the deep grass, her tiny feet scarcely turning a fragile blade, and she had dreamed beside some old faded flowers. Thus her steps led her into the broad lane. The little dimpled imprints of her bare feet showed clean-cut in the dust; they went a little way down the lane; and then, at a point where they stopped, the great tracks of a man led out from the shrubbery and returned.

CHAPTER XX

LASSITER'S WAY

FOOTPRINTS told the story of little Fay's abduction. In anguish Jane Withersteen turned speechlessly to Lassiter, and, confirming her fears, she saw him gray-faced, aged all in a moment, stricken as if by a mortal blow.

Then all her life seemed to fall about her in wreck and ruin.

"It's all over," she heard her voice whisper. "It's ended. I'm going—I'm going—"

"Where?" demanded Lassiter, suddenly looming darkly over her.

"To—to those cruel men—"

"Speak names!" thundered Lassiter.

"To Bishop Dyer—to Tull," went on Jane, shocked into obedience.

"Well—what for?"

"I want little Fay. I can't live without her. They've stolen her as they stole Milly Erne's child. I must have little Fay. I want only her. I give up. I'll go and tell Bishop Dyer—I'm broken. I'll tell him I'm ready for the yoke—only give me back Fay—and—and I'll marry Tull!"

"*Never!*" hissed Lassiter.

His long arm leaped at her. Almost running, he dragged her under the cottonwoods, across the court, into the huge hall of Withersteen House, and he shut the door with a force that jarred the heavy walls. Black Star and Night and Bells, since their return, had been locked in this hall, and now they stamped on the stone floor.

Lassiter released Jane and like a dizzy man swayed from her with a hoarse cry and leaned shaking against a table where he kept his rider's accoutrements. He began to fumble in his saddle-bags. His action brought a clinking, metallic sound—the rattling of gun-cartridges. His fingers trembled as he slipped cartridges into an extra belt. But as he buckled it over the one he habitually wore his hands became steady. This second belt contained two guns, smaller than the black ones swinging low, and he slipped them round so that his coat hid them. Then he fell to swift action. Jane Withersteen watched him, fascinated but uncomprehending; and she saw him rapidly saddle Black Star and Night. Then he drew her into the light of the huge window, standing over her, gripping her arm with fingers like cold steel.

"Yes, Jane, it's ended—but you're not goin' to Dyer! . . . *I'm goin' instead!*"

Looking at him—he was so terrible of aspect—she could not comprehend his words. Who was this man with the face gray as death, with eyes that would have made her shriek had she the strength, with the strange, ruthlessly bitter lips? Where was the gentle Lassiter? What was this presence in the hall, about him, about her—this cold, invisible presence?

"Yes, it's ended, Jane," he was saying, so awfully quiet and cool and implacable, "an' I'm goin' to make a little call. I'll lock you in here, an' when I get back have the saddle-bags full of meat an' bread. An' be ready to ride!"

"Lassiter!" cried Jane.

Desperately she tried to meet his gray eyes, in vain; desperately she tried again, fought herself as feeling and thought resurged in torment, and she succeeded; and then she knew.

"No—no—no!" she wailed. "You said you'd foregone your vengeance. You promised not to kill Bishop Dyer."

"If you want to talk to me about him—leave off the Bishop. I don't understand that name, or its use."

"Oh, hadn't you foregone your vengeance on—on Dyer?"

"Yes."

"But—your actions—your words—your guns—your terrible looks! . . . They don't seem foregoing vengeance?"

"Jane, now it's justice."

"You'll—kill him?"

"If God lets me live another hour! If not God—then the devil who drives me!"

"You'll kill him—for yourself—for your vengeful hate?"

"No!"

"For Milly Erne's sake?"

"No."

"For little Fay's?"

"No!"

"Oh—for whose?"

"*For yours!*"

"His blood on my soul!" whispered Jane, and she fell to her knees. This was the long-pending hour of fruition. And the habit of years—the religious passion of her life—leaped from lethargy, and the long months of gradual drifting to doubt were as if they had never been. "If you spill his blood it 'll be on my soul—and on my father's. Listen." And she clasped his knees, and clung there as he tried to raise her. "Listen. Am I nothing to you?"

"Woman—don't trifle at words! I love you! An' I'll soon prove it!"

"I'll give myself to you—I'll ride away with you—marry you, if only you'll spare him?"

His answer was a cold, ringing, terrible laugh.

"Lassiter—I'll love you. Spare him!"

"No!"

She sprang up in despairing, breaking spirit, and encircled his neck with her arms, and held him in an embrace that he strove vainly to loosen. "Lassiter, would you kill me? I'm fighting my last fight for the principles of my youth—love of religion, love of father. You don't know—you can't guess the truth, and I can't speak it! I'm losing all. I'm changing. All I've gone through is nothing to this hour. Pity me—help me in my weakness. You're strong again—oh, so cruelly, coldly strong! You're killing me. I see you—feel you as some other Lassiter! My master, be merciful—spare him!"

His answer was a ruthless smile.

She clung the closer to him, and leaned her panting breast on him, and lifted her face to his. "Lassiter, *I do love you!* It's leaped out of my agony. It comes suddenly with a terrible blow of truth. You are a man! I never knew it till now. Some wonderful change came to me when you buckled on these guns and showed that gray, awful face. I loved you then. All my life I've loved, but never as now. No woman can love like a broken woman. If it were not for one thing—just one thing—and yet! I *can't* speak it—I'd glory in your manhood—the lion in you that means to slay for me. Believe me—and spare Dyer. Be merciful—great as it's in you to be great. . . . Oh, listen and believe—I have nothing, but I'm a woman—a beautiful woman, Lassiter—a passionate, loving woman—and I love you! Take me—hide me in some wild place—and love me and mend my broken heart. Spare him and take me away."

She lifted her face closer and closer to his, until their lips nearly touched, and she hung upon his neck, and with strength almost spent pressed and still pressed her palpitating body to his.

"Kiss me!" she whispered, blindly.

"No—not at your price!" he answered. His voice had changed or she had lost clearness of hearing.

"Kiss me! . . . Are you a man? Kiss me and save me!"

"Jane, you never played fair with me. But now you're blisterin' your lips—blackenin' your soul with lies!"

"By the memory of my mother—by my Bible—no! No, I *have* no Bible! But by my hope of heaven I swear I love you!"

Lassiter's gray lips formed soundless words that meant even her love could not avail to bend his will. As if the hold of her arms was that of a child's he loosened it and stepped away.

"Wait! Don't go! Oh, hear a last word! . . . May a more just and merciful God than the God I was taught to worship judge me—forgive me—save me! For I can no longer keep silent! . . . Lassiter, in pleading for Dyer I've been pleading more for my father. My father was a Mormon master, close to the leaders of the church. It was my father who sent Dyer out to proselyte. It was my father who had the blue-ice eye and the beard of gold. It was my father you got trace of in the past years. Truly, Dyer ruined Milly Erne—dragged her from her home—to Utah—to Cottonwoods. *But it was for my father!* If Milly Erne was ever wife of a Mormon that Mormon was my father! I never knew—never will know whether or not she was a wife. Blind I may be, Lassiter—fanatically faithful to a false religion I may have been, but I know justice, and my father is beyond human justice. Surely he is meeting just punishment—somewhere. Always it has appalled me—the thought of your killing Dyer for my father's sins. So I have prayed!"

"Jane, the past is dead. In my love for you I forgot the past. This thing I'm about to do ain't for myself or Milly or Fay. It's not because of anythin' that ever happened in the past, but for what is happenin' right *now. It's for you!* . . . An' listen. Since I was a boy I've never thanked God for anythin'. If there is a God—an' I've come to believe it—I thank Him now for the years that made me Lassiter! . . . I can reach down an' feel these big guns, an' know what I can do with them. An', Jane, only one of the miracles Dyer professes to believe in can save him!"

Again for Jane Withersteen came the spinning of her brain in darkness, and as she whirled in endless chaos she seemed to be falling at the feet of a luminous figure—a man—Lassiter—who had saved her from herself, who could not be changed, who would slay rightfully. Then she slipped into utter blackness.

When she recovered from her faint she became aware that she was lying on a couch near the window in her sitting-room. Her brow felt damp and cold and wet; some one was chafing her hands; she recognized Judkins, and then saw that his lean, hard face wore the hue and look of excessive agitation.

"Judkins!" Her voice broke weakly.

"Aw, Miss Withersteen, you're comin' round fine. Now jest lay still a little. You're all right; everythin's all right."

"Where is—he?"

"Who?"

"Lassiter!"

"You needn't worry none about him."

"Where is he? Tell me—instantly."

"Wal, he's in the other room patchin' up a few triflin' bullet-holes."

"*Ah! . . . Bishop Dyer?*"

"When I seen him last—a matter of half an hour ago, he was on his knees. He was some busy, *but* he wasn't prayin'!"

"How strangely you talk! I'll sit up. I'm—well,

strong again. Tell me. Dyer on his knees! What was he doing?"

"Wal, beggin' your pardon fer blunt talk, Miss Withersteen, Dyer was on his knees an' *not* prayin'. You remember his big, broad hands? You've seen 'em raised in blessin' over old gray men an' little curly-headed children like—like Fay Larkin! Come to think of thet, I disremember ever hearin' of his liftin' his big hands in blessin' over a *woman*. Wal, when I seen him last—jest a little while ago—he was on his knees, *not* prayin', as I remarked—an' he was pressin' his big hands over some bigger wounds."

"Man, you drive me mad! Did Lassiter kill Dyer?"

"Yes."

"Did he kill Tull?"

"No. Tull's out of the village with most of his riders. He's expected back before evenin'. Lassiter will hev to git away before Tull an' his riders come in. It's sure death fer him here. An' wuss fer you, too, Miss Withersteen. There'll be some of an uprisin' when Tull gits back."

"I shall ride away with Lassiter. Judkins, tell me all you saw—all you know about this killing." She realized, without wonder or amaze, how Judkins's one word, affirming the death of Dyer—that the catastrophe had fallen—had completed the change whereby she had been molded or beaten or broken into another woman. She felt calm, slightly cold, strong as she had not been strong since the first shadow fell upon her.

"I jest saw about all of it, Miss Withersteen, an' I'll be glad to tell you if you'll only hev patience with me," said Judkins, earnestly. "You see, I've been pecooliarly interested, an' nat'rully I'm some excited. An' I talk a lot thet mebbe ain't necessary, but I can't help thet.

"I was at the meetin'-house where Dyer was holdin' court. You know he allus acts as magistrate an' judge when Tull's away. An' the trial was fer tryin' what's left of my boy riders—thet helped me hold your cattle—fer a lot of hatched-up things the boys never did. We're used to thet, an' the boys wouldn't hev minded bein' locked up fer a while, or hevin' to dig ditches, or whatever the judge laid down. You see, I divided the gold you give me among all my boys, an' they all hid it, an' they all feel rich. Howsomever, court was adjourned before the judge passed sentence. Yes, ma'm, court was adjourned some strange an' quick, much as if lightnin' hed struck the meetin'-house.

"I hed trouble attendin' the trial, but I got in. There was a good many people there, all my boys, an' Judge Dyer with his several clerks. Also he hed with him the five riders who've been guardin' him pretty close of late. They was Carter, Wright, Jengessen, an' two new riders from Stone Bridge. I didn't hear their names, but I heard they was handy men with guns an' they looked more like rustlers than riders. Anyway, there they was, the five all in a row.

"Judge Dyer was tellin' Willie Kern, one of my best an' steadiest boys—Dyer was tellin' him how there was a ditch opened near Willie's home lettin' water through his lot, where it hadn't ought to go. An' Willie was tryin' to git a word in to prove he wasn't at home all the day it happened—which was true, as I know—but Willie couldn't git a word in, an' then Judge Dyer went on layin' down the law. An' all to onct he happened to look down the long room. An' if ever any man turned to stone he was thet man.

"Nat'rully I looked back to see what hed acted so powerful strange on the judge. An' there, half-way up the room, in the middle of the wide aisle, stood Lassiter! All white an' black he looked, an' I can't think of anythin' he resembled, onless it's death. Venters made thet same room some still an' chilly when he called Tull; but this was different. I give my word, Miss Withersteen, thet I went cold to my very marrow. I don't know why. But Lassiter has a way about him thet's awful. He spoke a word—a name—I couldn't understand it, though he spoke clear as a bell. I was too excited, mebbe. Judge Dyer must hev understood it, an' a lot more thet was mystery to me, fer he pitched forrard out of his chair right onto the platform.

"Then them five riders, Dyer's bodyguards, they jumped up, an' two of them thet I found out afterward were the strangers from Stone Bridge, they piled right out of a winder, so quick you couldn't catch your breath. It was plain they wasn't Mormons.

"Jengessen, Carter, an' Wright eyed Lassiter, for what must hev been a second an' seemed like an hour, an' they went white an' strung. But they didn't weaken nor lose their nerve.

"I hed a good look at Lassiter. He stood sort of stiff, bendin' a little, an' both his arms were crooked, an' his hands looked like a hawk's claws. But there ain't no tellin' how his eyes looked. I know this, though, an' thet is his eyes could read the mind of any man about to throw a gun. An' in watchin' him, of course, I couldn't see the three men go fer their guns. An' though I was lookin' right at Lassiter—lookin' hard—I couldn't see how he drawed. He was quicker 'n eyesight—thet's all. But I seen the red spurtin' of his guns, an' heard his shots jest the very littlest instant before I heard the shots of the riders. An' when I turned, Wright an' Carter was down, an' Jengessen, who's tough like a steer, was pullin' the trigger of a wabblin' gun. But it was plain he was shot through, plumb center. An' sudden he fell with a crash, an' his gun clattered on the floor.

"Then there was a hell of a silence. Nobody breathed. Sartin I didn't, anyway. I saw Lassiter slip a smokin' gun back in a belt. But he hadn't throwed either of the big black guns, an' I thought thet strange. An' all this was happenin' quick—you can't imagine how quick.

"There come a scrapin' on the floor an' Dyer got up, his face like lead. I wanted to watch Lassiter, but Dyer's face, onct I seen it like thet, glued my eyes. I seen him go fer his gun—why, I could hev done better, quicker—an' then there was a thunderin' shot from Lassiter, an' it hit Dyer's right arm, an' his gun went off as it dropped. He looked at Lassiter like a cornered sage-wolf, an' sort of howled, an' reached down fer his gun. He'd jest picked it off the floor an' was raisin' it when another thunderin' shot almost tore thet arm off—so it seemed to me. The gun dropped again an' he went down on his knees, kind of flounderin' after it. It was some strange an' terrible to see his awful earnestness. Why would such a man cling so to life? Anyway, he got the gun with left hand an' was raisin' it, pullin' trigger in his madness, when the third thunderin' shot hit his left arm, an' he dropped the gun again. But thet left arm wasn't useless yet, fer he grabbed up the gun, an' with a shakin' aim thet would hev been pitiful to me—in any other man—he began to shoot. One wild bullet struck a man twenty feet from Lassiter. An' it killed thet man, as I seen afterward. Then come a bunch of thunderin' shots—nine I calkilated after, fer they come so quick I couldn't count them—an' I knew Lassiter hed turned the black guns loose on Dyer.

"I'm tellin' you straight, Miss Withersteen, fer I want you to know. Afterward you'll git over it. I've seen some soul-rackin' scenes on this Utah border, but this was the awfulest. I remember I closed my eyes, an' fer a minute I thought of the strangest things, out of place there, such as you'd never dream would come to mind. I saw the sage, an' runnin' hosses—an' thet's the beautifulest sight to me—an' I saw dim things in the dark, an' there was a kind of hummin' in my ears. An' I remember distinctly—fer it was what made all these things whirl out of my mind an' opened my eyes—I remember distinctly it was the smell of gunpowder.

"The court had about adjourned fer thet judge. He was on his knees, an' he wasn't prayin'. He was gaspin' an' tryin' to press his big, floppin', crippled hands over his body. Lassiter had sent all those last thunderin' shots through his body. Thet was Lassiter's way.

"An' Lassiter spoke, an' if I ever forgit his words I'll never forgit the sound of his voice.

"'*Proselyter*, I reckon you'd better call quick on thet God who reveals Hisself to you on earth, because He won't be visitin' the place you're goin' to!'

"An' then I seen Dyer look at his big, hangin' hands thet wasn't big enough fer the last work he set them to. An' he looked up at Lassiter. An' then he stared horrible at somethin' thet wasn't Lassiter, nor anyone there, nor the room, nor the branches of purple sage peepin' into the winder. Whatever he seen, it was with the look of a man who *discovers* somethin' too late. Thet's a terrible look! . . . An' with a horrible *understandin'* cry he slid forrard on his face."

Judkins paused in his narrative, breathing heavily while he wiped his perspiring brow.

"Thet's about all," he concluded. "Lassiter left the meetin'-house an' I hurried to catch up with him. He was bleedin' from three gunshots, none of them much to bother him. An' we come right up here. I found you layin' in the hall, an' I hed to work some over you."

Jane Withersteen offered up no prayer for Dyer's soul.

Lassiter's step sounded in the hall—the familiar soft, silver-clinking step—and she heard it with thrilling new emotions in which was a vague joy in her very fear of him. The door opened, and she saw him, the old Lassiter, slow, easy, gentle, cool, yet not exactly the same Lassiter. She rose, and for a moment her eyes blurred and swam in tears.

"Are you—all—all right?" she asked, tremulously.

"I reckon."

"Lassiter, I'll ride away with you. Hide me till danger is past—till we are forgotten—then take me where you will. Your people shall be my people, and your God my God!"

He kissed her hand with the quaint grace and courtesy that came to him in rare moments.

"Black Star an' Night are ready," he said, simply.

His quiet mention of the black racers spurred Jane to action. Hurrying to her room, she changed to her rider's suit, packed her jewelry, and the gold that was left, and all the woman's apparel for which there was space in the saddle-bags, and then returned to the hall. Black Star stamped his iron-shod hoofs and tossed his beautiful head, and eyed her with knowing eyes.

"Judkins, I give Bells to you," said Jane. "I hope you will always keep him and be good to him."

Judkins mumbled thanks that he could not speak fluently, and his eyes flashed.

Lassiter strapped Jane's saddle-bags upon Black Star, and led the racers out into the court.

"Judkins, you ride with Jane out into the sage. If you see any riders comin' shout quick twice. An', Jane, *don't look back!* I'll catch up soon. We'll get to the break into the Pass before midnight, an' then wait until mornin' to go down."

Black Star bent his graceful neck and bowed his noble head, and his broad shoulders yielded as he knelt for Jane to mount.

She rode out of the court beside Judkins, through the grove, across the wide lane into the sage, and she realized that she was leaving Withersteen House forever, and she did not look back. A strange, dreamy, calm peace pervaded her soul. Her doom had fallen upon her, but, instead of finding life no longer worth living she found it doubly significant, full of sweetness as the western breeze, beautiful and unknown as the sage-slope stretching

"DONT—LOOK—BACK!"

its purple sunset shadows before her. She became aware of Judkins's hand touching hers; she heard him speak a husky good-by; then into the place of Bells shot the dead-black, keen, racy nose of Night, and she knew Lassiter rode beside her.

"*Don't—look—back!*" he said, and his voice, too, was not clear.

Facing straight ahead, seeing only the waving, shadowy sage, Jane held out her gauntleted hand, to feel it enclosed in strong clasp. So she rode on without a backward glance at the beautiful grove of Cottonwoods. She did not seem to think of the past, of what she left forever, but of the color and mystery and wildness of the sage-slope leading down to Deception Pass, and of the future. She watched the shadows lengthen down the slope; she felt the cool west wind sweeping by from the rear; and she wondered at low, yellow clouds sailing swiftly over her and beyond.

"*Don't—look—back!*" said Lassiter.

Thick-driving belts of smoke traveled by on the wind, and with it came a strong, pungent odor of burning wood.

Lassiter had fired Withersteen House! But Jane did not look back.

A misty veil obscured the clear, searching gaze she had kept steadfastly upon the purple slope and the dim lines of cañons. It passed, as passed the rolling clouds of smoke, and she saw the valley deepening into the shades of twilight. Night came on, swift as the fleet racers, and stars peeped out to brighten and grow, and the huge, windy, eastern heave of sage-level paled under a rising moon and turned to silver. Blanched in moonlight, the sage yet seemed to hold its hue of purple and was infinitely more wild and lonely. So the night hours wore on, and Jane Withersteen never once looked back.

CHAPTER XXI

BLACK STAR AND NIGHT

THE time had come for Venters and Bess to leave their retreat. They were at great pains to choose the few things they would be able to carry with them on the journey out of Utah.

"Bern, whatever kind of a pack's this, anyhow?" questioned Bess, rising from her work with reddened face.

Venters, absorbed in his own task, did not look up at all, and in reply said he had brought so much from Cottonwoods that he did not recollect the half of it.

"A woman packed this!" Bess exclaimed.

He scarcely caught her meaning, but the peculiar tone of her voice caused him instantly to rise, and he saw Bess on her knees before an open pack which he recognized as the one given him by Jane.

"By George!" he ejaculated, guiltily, and then at sight of Bess's face he laughed outright.

"A woman packed this," she repeated, fixing woeful, tragic eyes on him.

"Well, is that a crime?"

"There—there *is* a woman, after all!"

"Now Bess—"

"You've lied to me!"

Then and there Venters found it imperative to postpone work for the present. All her life Bess had been isolated, but she had inherited certain elements of the eternal feminine.

"But there *was* a woman and you *did* lie to me," she kept repeating, after he had explained.

"What of that? Bess, I'll get angry at you in a moment. Remember you've been pent up all your life. I venture to say that if you'd been out in the world you'd have had a dozen sweethearts and have told many a lie before this."

"I wouldn't anything of the kind," declared Bess, indignantly.

"Well—perhaps not lie. But you'd have had the sweethearts. You couldn't have helped that—being so pretty."

This remark appeared to be a very clever and fortunate one; and the work of selecting and then of stowing all the packs in the cave went on without further interruption.

Venters closed up the opening of the cave with a thatch of willows and aspens, so that not even a bird or a rat could get in to the sacks of grain. And this work was in order with the precaution habitually observed by him. He might not be able to get out of Utah, and have to return to the valley. But he owed it to Bess to make the attempt, and in case they were compelled to turn back he wanted to find that fine store of food and grain intact. The outfit of implements and utensils he packed away in another cave.

"Bess, we have enough to live here all our lives," he said once, dreamily.

"Shall I go roll Balancing Rock?" she asked, in light speech, but with deep-blue fire in her eyes.

"No—no."

"Ah, you don't forget the gold and the world," she sighed.

"Child, you forget the beautiful dresses and the travel—and everything."

"Oh, I want to go. But I want to stay!"

"I feel the same way."

They let the eight calves out of the corral, and kept only two of the burros Venters had brought from Cottonwoods. These they intended to hide. Bess freed all her pets—the quail and rabbits and foxes.

The last sunset and twilight and night were both the sweetest and saddest they had ever spent in Surprise Valley. Morning brought keen exhilaration and excitement. When Venters had saddled the two burros, strapped on the light packs and the two canteens, the sunlight was dispersing the lazy shadows from the valley. Taking a last look at the caves and the silver spruces, Venters and Bess made a reluctant start, leading the burros. Ring and Whitie looked keen and knowing. Something seemed to drag at Venters's feet and he noticed Bess lagged behind. Never had the climb from terrace to bridge appeared so long.

Not till they reached the opening of the gorge did they stop to rest and take one last look at the valley. The tremendous arch of stone curved clear and sharp in outline against the morning sky. And through it streaked the golden shaft. The valley seemed an enchanted circle of glorious veils of gold and wraiths of white and silver haze and dim, blue, moving shade—beautiful and wild and unreal as a dream.

"We—we can—th—think of it—always—re—remember," sobbed Bess.

"Hush! Don't cry. Our valley has only fitted us for a better life somewhere. Come!"

They entered the gorge and he closed the willow gate. From rosy, golden morning light they passed into cool, dense gloom. The burros pattered up the trail with little hollow-cracking steps. And the gorge widened to narrow outlet and the gloom lightened to gray. At the divide they halted for another rest. Venters's keen, remembering gaze searched Balancing Rock, and the long incline, and the cracked toppling walls, but failed to note the slightest change.

The dogs led the descent; then came Bess leading her burro; then Venters leading his. Bess kept her eyes bent downward. Venters, however, had an irresistible desire to look upward at Balancing Rock. It had always haunted him, and now he wondered if he were really to get through the outlet before the huge stone thundered down. He fancied that would be a miracle. Every few steps he answered to the strange, nervous fear and turned to make sure the rock still stood like a giant statue. And, as he descended, it grew dimmer in his sight. It changed form; it swayed; it nodded darkly; and at last, in his heightened fancy, he saw it heave and roll. As in a dream when he felt himself falling yet knew he would never fall, so he saw this long-standing thunderbolt of the little stone-men plunge down to close forever the outlet to Deception Pass.

And while he was giving way to unaccountable dread imaginations the descent was accomplished without mishap.

"I'm glad that's over," he said, breathing more freely. "I hope I'm by that hanging rock for good and all. Since almost the moment I first saw it I've had an idea that it was waiting for me. Now, when it does fall, if I'm thousands of miles away, I'll hear it."

With the first glimpses of the smooth slope leading down to the grotesque cedars and out to the Pass, Venters's cool nerve returned. One long survey to the left, then one to the right, satisfied his caution. Leading the burros down to the spur of rock, he halted at the steep incline.

"Bess, here's the bad place, the place I told you about, with the cut steps. You start down, leading your burro. Take your time and hold on to him if you slip. I've got a rope on him and a half-hitch on this point of rock, so I can let him down safely. Coming up here was a killing job. But it 'll be easy going down."

Both burros passed down the difficult stairs cut by the cliff-dwellers, and did it without a misstep. After that the descent down the slope and over the mile of scrawled, ribbed, and ridged rock required only careful guidance, and Venters got the burros to level ground in a condition that caused him to congratulate himself.

"Oh, if we only had Wrangle!" exclaimed Venters. "But we're lucky. That's the worst of our trail passed. We've only men to fear now. If we get up in the sage we can hide and slip along like coyotes."

They mounted and rode west through the valley and entered the cañon. From time to time Venters walked, leading his burro. When they got by all the cañons and gullies opening into the Pass they went faster and with fewer halts. Venters did not confide in Bess the alarming fact that he had seen horses and smoke less than a mile up one of the intersecting cañons. He did not talk at all. And long after he had passed this cañon and felt secure once more in the certainty that they had been unobserved he never relaxed his watchfulness. But he did not walk any more, and he kept the burros at a steady trot. Night fell before they reached the last water in the Pass and they made camp by starlight. Venters did not want the burros to stray, so he tied them with long halters in the grass near the spring. Bess, tired out and silent, laid her head in a saddle and went to sleep between the two dogs. Venters did not close his eyes. The cañon silence appeared full of the low, continuous hum of insects. He listened until the hum grew into a roar, and then, breaking the spell, once more he heard it low and clear. He watched the stars and the moving shadows, and always his glance returned to the girl's dimly pale face. And he remembered how white and still it had once looked in the starlight. And again stern thought fought his strange fancies. Would all his labor and his love be for naught? Would he lose her, after all? What did the dark shadow around her portend? Did calamity lurk on that long upland trail through the sage? Why should his heart swell and throb with nameless fear? He listened to the silence, and told himself that in the broad light of day he could dispel this leaden-weighted dread.

At the first hint of gray over the eastern rim he awoke Bess, saddled the burros, and began the day's travel. He wanted to get out of the Pass before there was any chance of riders coming down. They gained the break as the first red rays of the rising sun colored the rim.

For once, so eager was he to get up to level ground, he did not send Ring or Whitie in advance. Encouraging Bess to hurry, pulling at his patient, plodding burro, he climbed the soft, steep trail.

Brighter and brighter grew the light. He mounted the last broken edge of rim to have the sun-fired, purple sage-slope burst upon him as a glory. Bess panted up to his side, tugging on the halter of her burro.

"We're up!" he cried, joyously. "There's not a dot on the sage. We're safe. We'll not be seen! Oh, Bess—"

Ring growled and sniffed the keen air and bristled. Venters clutched at his rifle. Whitie sometimes made a mistake, but Ring never. The dull thud of hoofs almost deprived Venters of power to turn and see from where disaster threatened. He felt his eyes dilate as he stared at Lassiter leading Black Star and Night out of the sage, with Jane Withersteen, in rider's costume, close beside them.

For an instant Venters felt himself whirl dizzily in the center of vast circles of sage. He recovered partially, enough to see Lassiter standing with a glad smile and Jane riveted in astonishment.

"Why, Bern!" she exclaimed. "How good it is to see you! We're riding away, you see. The storm burst—and I'm a ruined woman! . . . I thought you were alone."

Venters, unable to speak for consternation, and bewildered out of all sense of what he ought or ought not to do, simply stared at Jane.

"Son, where are you bound for?" asked Lassiter.

"Not safe—where I was. I'm—we're going out of Utah—back East," he found tongue to say.

"I reckon this meetin's the luckiest thing that ever happened to you an' to me—an' to Jane—an' to Bess," said Lassiter, coolly.

"*Bess!*" cried Jane, with a sudden leap of blood to her pale cheek.

It was entirely beyond Venters to see any luck in that meeting.

Jane Withersteen took one flashing, woman's glance at Bess's scarlet face, at her slender, shapely form.

"Venters! is this a girl—a woman?" she questioned, in a voice that stung.

"Yes."

"Did you have her in that wonderful valley?"

"Yes, but Jane—"

"All the time you were gone?"

"Yes, but I couldn't tell—"

"Was it for *her* you asked me to give you supplies? Was it for *her* that you wanted to make your valley a paradise?"

"Oh—Jane—"

"Answer me."

"Yes."

"Oh, you liar!" And with these passionate words Jane Withersteen succumbed to fury. For the second time in her life she fell into the ungovernable rage that had been her father's weakness. And it was worse than his, for she was a jealous woman—jealous even of her friends.

As best he could, he bore the brunt of her anger. It was not only his deceit to her that she visited upon him, but her betrayal by religion, by life itself.

Her passion, like fire at white heat, consumed itself in little time. Her physical strength failed, and still her spirit attempted to go on in magnificent denunciation of those who had wronged her. Like a tree cut deep into its roots, she began to quiver and shake, and her anger weakened into despair. And her ringing voice sank into a broken, husky whisper. Then, spent and pitiable, upheld by Lassiter's arm, she turned and hid her face in Black Star's mane.

Numb as Venters was when at length Jane Withersteen lifted her head and looked at him, he yet suffered a pang.

"Jane, the girl is innocent!" he cried.

"Can you expect me to believe that?" she asked, with weary, bitter eyes.

"I'm not that kind of a liar. And you know it. If I lied—if I kept silent when honor should have made me speak, it was to spare you. I came to Cottonwoods to tell you. But I couldn't add to your pain. I intended to tell you I had come to love this girl. But, Jane, I hadn't forgotten how good you were to me. I haven't changed at all toward you. I prize your friendship as I always have. But, however it may look to you—don't be unjust. The girl is innocent. Ask Lassiter."

"Jane, she's jest as sweet an' innocent as little Fay," said Lasiter. There was a faint smile upon his face and a beautiful light.

Venters saw, and knew that Lassiter saw, how Jane Withersteen's tortured soul wrestled with hate and threw it—with scorn, doubt, suspicion, and overcame all.

"Bern, if in my misery I accused you unjustly, I crave forgiveness," she said. "I'm not what I once was. Tell me—who is this girl?"

"Jane, she is Oldring's daughter, and his Masked Rider. Lassiter will tell you how I shot her for a rustler, saved her life—all the story. It's a strange story, Jane, as wild as the sage. But it's true—true as her innocence. That you must believe!"

"Oldring's Masked Rider! Oldring's daughter!" exclaimed Jane. "And she's innocent! You ask me to believe much. If this girl is—is what you say, how could she be going away with the man who killed her father?"

"Why did you tell that?" cried Venters, passionately.

Jane's question had roused Bess out of stupefaction. Her eyes suddenly darkened and dilated. She stepped toward Venters and held up both hands as if to ward off a blow.

"Did—did you kill Oldring?"

"I did, Bess, and I hate myself for it. But you know I never dreamed he was your father. I thought he'd wronged you. I killed him when I was madly jealous."

For a moment Bess was shocked into silence.

"But he was my father!" she broke out, at last. "And now I must go back—I can't go with you. It's all over—that beautiful dream. Oh, I *knew* it couldn't come true. You can't take me now."

"If you forgive me, Bess, it 'll all come right in the end!" implored Venters.

"It can't be right. I'll go back. After all, I loved him. He was good to me. I can't forget that."

"If you go back to Oldring's men I'll follow you, and then they'll kill me," said Venters, hoarsely.

"Oh no, Bern, you'll not come. Let me go. It's best for you to forget me. I've brought you only pain and dishonor.

She did not weep. But the sweet bloom and life died out of her face. She looked haggard and sad, all at once stunted; and her hands dropped listlessly; and her head drooped in slow, final acceptance of a hopeless fate.

"Jane, look there!" cried Venters, in despairing grief. "Need you have told her? Where was all your kindness of heart? This girl has had a wretched, lonely life. And I'd found a way to make her happy. You've killed it. You've killed something sweet and pure and hopeful, just as sure as you breathe."

"Oh, Bern! It was a slip. I never thought—I never thought!" replied Jane. "How could I tell she didn't know?"

Lassiter suddenly moved forward, and with the beautiful light on his face now strangely luminous, he looked at Jane and Venters and then let his soft, bright gaze rest on Bess.

"Well, I reckon you've all had your say, an' now it's Lassiter's turn. Why, I was jest prayin' for this meetin'. Bess, jest look here."

Gently he touched her arm and turned her to face the others, and then outspread his great hand to disclose a shiny, battered gold locket.

"Open it," he said, with a singularly rich voice.

Bess complied, but listlessly.

"Jane—Venters—come closer," went on Lassiter. "Take a look at the picture. Don't you know the woman?"

Jane, after one glance, drew back.

"Milly Erne!" she cried, wonderingly.

Venters, with tingling pulse, with something growing on him, recognized in the faded miniature portrait the eyes of Milly Erne.

"Yes, that's Milly," said Lassiter, softly. "Bess, did you ever see her face—look hard—with all your heart an' soul?"

"The eyes seem to haunt me," whispered Bess. "Oh, I can't remember—they're eyes of my dreams—but—but—"

Lassiter's strong arm went round her and he bent his head.

"Child, I thought you'd remember her eyes. They're the same beautiful eyes you'd see if you looked in a mirror or a clear spring. They're your mother's eyes. You are Milly Erne's child. Your name is Elizabeth Erne. You're not Oldring's daughter. You're the daughter of Frank Erne, a man once my best friend.

Look! Here's his picture beside Milly's. He was handsome, an' as fine an' gallant a Southern gentleman as I ever seen. Frank come of an old family. You come of the best of blood, lass, an' blood tells."

Bess slipped through his arm to her knees and hugged the locket to her bosom, and lifted wonderful, yearning eyes.

"It—can't—be—true!"

"Thank God, lass, it *is* true," replied Lassiter. "Jane an' Bern here—they both recognize Milly. They see Milly in you. They're so knocked out they can't tell you, that's all."

"Who are you?" whispered Bess.

"I reckon I'm Milly's brother an' your uncle! . . . Uncle Jim! Ain't that fine?"

"Oh, I can't believe— Don't raise me! Bern, let me kneel. I see truth in your face—in Miss Withersteen's. But let me hear it all—all on my knees. Tell me *how* it's true!"

"Well, Elizabeth, listen," said Lassiter. "Before you was born your father made a mortal enemy of a Mormon named Dyer. They was both ministers an' come to be rivals. Dyer stole your mother away from her home. She gave birth to you in Texas eighteen years ago. Then she was taken to Utah, from place to place, an' finally to the last border settlement—Cottonwoods. You was about three years old when you was taken away from Milly. She never knew what had become of you. But she lived a good while hopin' and prayin' to have you again. Then she gave up an' died. An' I may as well put in here your father died ten years ago. Well, I spent my time tracin' Milly, an' some months back I landed in Cottonwoods. An' jest lately I learned all about you. I had a talk with Oldrin' an' told him you was dead, an' he told me what I had so long been wantin' to know. It was Dyer, of course, who stole you from Milly. Part reason he was sore because Milly refused to give you Mormon teachin', but mostly he still hated Frank Erne so infernally that he made a deal with Oldrin' to take you an' bring you up as an infamous rustler an' rustler's girl. The idea was to break Frank Erne's heart if he ever came to Utah—to show him his daughter with a band of low rustlers. Well—Oldrin' took you, brought you up from childhood, an' then made you his Masked Rider. He made you infamous. He kept that part of the contract, but he learned to love you as a daughter an' never let any but his own men know you was a girl. I heard him say that with my own ears, an' I saw his big eyes grow dim. He told me how he had guarded you always, kept you locked up in his absence, was always at your side or near you on those rides that made you famous on the sage. He said he an' an old rustler whom he trusted had taught you how to read an' write. They selected the books for you. Dyer had wanted you brought up the vilest of the vile! An' Oldrin' brought you up the innocentest of the innocent. He said you didn't know what vileness was. I can hear his big voice tremble now as he said it. He told me how the men—rustlers an' outlaws—who from time to time tried to approach you familiarly—he told me how he shot them dead. I'm tellin' you this 'specially because you've showed such shame—sayin' you was nameless an' all that. Nothin' on earth can be wronger than that idea of yours. An' the truth of it is here. Oldrin' swore to me that if Dyer died, releasin' the contract, he intended to hunt up your father an' give you back to him. It seems Oldrin' wasn't all bad, an' he sure loved you."

Venters leaned forward in passionate remorse.

"Oh, Bess! I know Lassiter speaks the truth. For when I shot Oldring he dropped to his knees and fought with unearthly power to speak. And he said: 'Man—why—didn't—you—wait? Bess was—' Then he fell dead. And I've been haunted by his look and words.

Oh, Bess, what a strange, splendid thing for Oldring to do! It all seems impossible. But, dear, you really are not what you thought."

"Elizabeth Erne!" cried Jane Withersteen. "I loved your mother and I see her in you!"

What had been incredible from the lips of men became, in the tone, look, and gesture of a woman, a wonderful truth for Bess. With little tremblings of all her slender body she rocked to and fro on her knees. The yearning wistfulness of her eyes changed to solemn splendor of joy. She believed. She was realizing happiness. And as the process of thought was slow, so were the variations of her expression. Her eyes reflected the transformation of her soul. Dark, brooding, hopeless belief—clouds of gloom—drifted, paled, vanished in glorious light. An exquisite rose flush—a glow—shone from her face as she slowly began to rise from her knees. A spirit uplifted her. All that she had held as base dropped from her.

Venters watched her in joy too deep for words. By it he divined something of what Lassiter's revelation meant to Bess, but he knew he could only faintly understand. That moment when she seemed to be lifted by some spiritual transfiguration was the most beautiful moment of his life. She stood with parted, quivering lips, with hands tightly clasping the locket to her heaving breast. A new conscious pride of worth dignified the old wild, free grace and poise.

"Uncle Jim!" she said, tremulously, with a different smile from any Venters had ever seen on her face.

Lassiter took her into his arms.

"I reckon. It's powerful fine to hear that," replied Lassiter, unsteadily.

Venters, feeling his eyes grow hot and wet, turned away, and found himself looking at Jane Withersteen. He had almost forgotten her presence. Tenderness and sympathy were fast hiding traces of her agitation.

Venters read her mind—felt the reaction of her noble heart—saw the joy she was beginning to feel at the happiness of others. And suddenly blinded, choked by his emotions, he turned from her also. He knew what she would do presently; she would make some magnificent amend for her anger; she would give some manifestation of her love; probably all in a moment, as she had loved Milly Erne, so would she love Elizabeth Erne.

"'Pears to me, folks, that we'd better talk a little serious now," remarked Lassiter, at length. "Time flies."

"You're right," replied Venters, instantly. "I'd forgotten time—place—danger. Lassiter, you're riding away. Jane's leaving Withersteen House?"

"Forever," replied Jane.

"I fired Withersteen House," said Lassiter.

"Dyer?" questioned Venters, sharply.

"I reckon where Dyer's gone there won't be any kidnappin' of girls."

"Ah! I knew it. I told Judkins— And Tull?" went on Venters, passionately.

"Tull wasn't around when I broke loose. By now he's likely on our trail with his riders."

"Lassiter, you're going into the Pass to hide till all this storm blows over?"

"I reckon that's Jane's idea. I'm thinkin' the storm 'll be a powerful long time blowin' over. I was comin' to join you in Surprise Valley. You'll go back now with me?"

"No. I want to take Bess out of Utah. Lassiter, Bess found gold in the valley. We've a saddle-bag full of gold. If we can reach Sterling—"

"Man! how 're you ever goin' to do that? Sterlin' is a hundred miles."

"My plan is to ride on, keeping sharp lookout. Somewhere up the trail we'll take to the sage and go round Cottonwoods and then hit the trail again."

"It's a bad plan. You'll kill the burros in two days."

"Then we'll walk."

"That's more bad an' worse. Better go back down the Pass with me."

"Lassiter, this girl has been hidden all her life in that lonely place," went on Venters. "Oldring's men are hunting me. We'd not be safe there any longer. Even if we would be I'd take this chance to get her out. I want to marry her. She shall have some of the pleasures of life—see cities and people. We've gold—we'll be rich. Why, life opens sweet for both of us. And, by Heaven! I'll get her out or lose my life in the attempt!"

"I reckon if you go on with them burros you'll lose your life all right. Tull will have riders all over this sage. You can't get out on them burros. It's a fool idea. That's not doin' best by the girl. Come with me an' take chances on the rustlers."

Lassiter's cool argument made Venters waver, not in determination to go, but in hope of success.

"Bess, I want you to know. Lassiter says the trip's almost useless now. I'm afraid he's right. We've got about one chance in a hundred to go through. Shall we take it? Shall we go on?"

"We'll go on," replied Bess.

"That settles it, Lassiter."

Lassiter spread wide his hands, as if to signify he could do no more, and his face clouded.

Venters felt a touch on his elbow. Jane stood beside him with a hand on his arm. She was smiling. Something radiated from her, and like an electric current accelerated the motion of his blood.

"Bern, you'd be right to die rather than not take Elizabeth out of Utah—out of this wild country. You must do it. You'll show her the great world, with all its wonders. Think how little she has seen! Think what delight is in store for her! You have gold; you will be free; you will make her happy. What a glorious prospect! I share it with you. I'll think of you—dream of you—pray for you."

"Thank you, Jane," replied Venters, trying to steady his voice. "It does look bright. Oh, if we were only across that wide, open waste of sage!"

"Bern, the trip's as good as made. It 'll be safe—easy. It 'll be a glorious ride," she said, softly.

Venters stared. Had Jane's troubles made her insane? Lassiter, too, acted queerly, all at once beginning to turn his sombrero round with hands that actually shook.

"You are a rider. She is a rider. This will be the ride of your lives," added Jane, in that same soft undertone, almost as if she were musing to herself.

"Jane!" he cried.

"I give you Black Star and Night!"

"*Black Star and Night!*" he echoed.

"It's done. Lassiter, put our saddle-bags on the burros."

Only when Lassiter moved swiftly to execute her bidding did Venters's clogged brain grasp at literal meanings. He leaped to catch Lassiter's busy hands.

"No, no! What are you doing?" he demanded, in a kind of fury. "I won't take her racers. What do you think I am? It 'd be monstrous. Lassiter! stop it, I say! . . . You've got her to save. You've miles and miles to go. Tull is trailing you. There are rustlers in the Pass. Give me back that saddle-bag!"

"Son—cool down," returned Lassiter, in a voice he might have used to a child. But the grip with which he tore away Venters's grasping hands was that of a giant. "Listen—you fool boy! Jane's sized up the situation. The burros 'll do for us. We'll sneak along an' hide. I'll take your dogs an' your rifle. Why, it's the trick. The blacks are yours, an' sure as I can throw a gun you're goin' to ride safe out of the sage."

"Jane—stop him—please stop him," gasped Venters.

"I've lost my strength. I can't do—anything. This 's hell for me! Can't you see that? I've ruined you—it was through me you lost all. You've only Black Star and Night left. You love these horses. Oh! I know how you must love them now! And—you're trying to give them to me. To help me out of Utah! To save the girl I love!"

"That will be my glory."

Then in the white, rapt face, in the unfathomable eyes, Venters saw Jane Withersteen in a supreme moment. This moment was one wherein she reached up to the height for which her noble soul had ever yearned. He, after disrupting the calm tenor of her peace, after bringing down on her head the implacable hostility of her churchmen, after teaching her a bitter lesson of life—he was to be her salvation. And he turned away again, this time shaken to the core of his soul. Jane Withersteen was the incarnation of selflessness. He experienced wonder and terror, exquisite pain and rapture. What were all the shocks life had dealt him compared to the thought of such loyal and generous friendship?

And instantly, as if by some divine insight, he knew himself in the remaking—tried, found wanting; but stronger, better, surer—and he wheeled to Jane Withersteen, eager, joyous, passionate, wild, exalted. He bent to her; he left tears and kisses on her hands.

"Jane, I—I can't find words—now," he said. "I'm beyond words. Only—I understand. And I'll take the blacks."

"Don't be losin' no more time," cut in Lassiter. "I ain't certain, but I think I seen a speck up the sage-slope. Mebbe I was mistaken. But, anyway, we must all be movin'. I've shortened the stirrups on Black Star. Put Bess on him."

Jane Withersteen held out her arms.

"Elizabeth Erne!" she cried, and Bess flew to her.

How inconceivably strange and beautiful it was for

Venters to see Bess clasped to Jane Withersteen's breast!

Then he leaped astride Night.

"Venters, ride straight on up the slope," Lassiter was saying, "an' if you don't meet any riders keep on till you're a few miles from the village, then cut off in the sage an' go round to the trail. But you'll most likely meet riders with Tull. Jest keep right on till you're jest out of gunshot an' then make your cut-off into the sage. They'll ride after you, but it won't be no use. You can ride, an' Bess can ride. When you're out of reach turn on round to the west, an' hit the trail somewhere. Save the hosses all you can, but don't be afraid. Black Star and Night are good for a hundred miles before sundown, if you have to push them. You can get to Sterlin' by night if you want. But better make it along about to-morrow mornin'. When you get through the notch on the Glaze trail, swing to the right. You'll be able to see both Glaze an' Stone Bridge. Keep away from them villages. You won't run no risk of meetin' any of Oldrin's rustlers from Sterlin' on. You'll find water in them deep hollows north of the Notch. There's an old trail there, not much used, an' it leads to Sterlin'. That's your trail. An' one thing more. If Tull pushes you—or keeps on persistent-like, for a few miles—jest let the blacks out an' lose him an' his riders."

"Lassiter, may we meet again!" said Venters, in a deep voice.

"Son, it ain't likely—it ain't likely. Well, Bess Oldrin'—Masked Rider—Elizabeth Erne—now you climb on Black Star. I've heard you could ride. Well, every rider loves a good hoss. An', lass, there never was but one that could beat Black Star."

"Ah, Lassiter, there never was any horse that could beat Black Star," said Jane, with the old pride.

"I often wondered—mebbe Venters rode out that race

when he brought back the blacks. Son, was Wrangle the best hoss?"

"No, Lassiter," replied Venters. For this lie he had his reward in Jane's quick smile.

"Well, well, my hoss-sense ain't always right. An' here I'm talkin' a lot, wastin' time. It ain't so easy to find an' lose a pretty niece all in one hour! Elizabeth—good-by!"

"Oh, Uncle Jim! . . . Good-by!"

"Elizabeth Erne, be happy! Good-by," said Jane.

"Good-by—oh—good-by!"

In lithe, supple action Bess swung up to Black Star's saddle.

"Jane Withersteen! . . . Good-by!" called Venters, hoarsely.

"Bern—Bess—riders of the purple sage—good-by!"

CHAPTER XXII

RIDERS OF THE PURPLE SAGE

BLACK STAR and Night, answering to spur, swept swiftly westward along the white, slow-rising, sage-bordered trail. Venters heard a mournful howl from Ring, but Whitie was silent. The blacks settled into their fleet, long-striding gallop. The wind sweetly fanned Venters's hot face. From the summit of the first low-swelling ridge he looked back. Lassiter waved his hand; Jane waved her scarf. Venters replied by standing in his stirrups and holding high his sombrero. Then the dip of the ridge hid them. From the height of the next he turned once more. Lassiter, Jane, and the burros had disappeared. They had gone down into the Pass. Venters felt a sensation of irreparable loss.

"Bern—look!" called Bess, pointing up the long slope.

A small, dark, moving dot split the line where purple sage met blue sky. That dot was a band of riders.

"Pull the black, Bess."

They slowed from gallop to canter, then to trot. The fresh and eager horses did not like the check.

"Bern, Black Star has great eyesight."

"I wonder if they're Tull's riders. They might be rustlers. But it's all the same to us.

The black dot grew to a dark patch moving under low dust-clouds. It grew all the time, though very slowly. There were long periods when it was in plain sight, and intervals when it dropped behind the sage. The blacks trotted for half an hour, for another half-hour, and still the moving patch appeared to stay on the horizon line. Gradually, however, as time passed, it began to enlarge, to creep down the slope, to encroach upon the intervening distance.

"Bess, what do you make them out?" asked Venters. "I don't think they're rustlers."

"They're sage-riders," replied Bess. "I see a white horse and several grays. Rustlers seldom ride any horses but bays and blacks."

"That white horse is Tull's. Pull the black, Bess. I'll get down and cinch up. We're in for some riding. Are you afraid?"

"Not now," answered the girl, smiling.

"You needn't be. Bess, you don't weigh enough to make Black Star know you're on him. I won't be able to stay with you. You'll leave Tull and his riders as if they were standing still."

"How about you?"

"Never fear. If I can't stay with you I can still laugh at Tull."

"Look, Bern! They've stopped on that ridge. They see us."

"Yes. But we're too far yet for them to make out who we are. They'll recognize the blacks first. We've passed most of the ridges and the thickest sage. Now, when I give the word, let Black Star go and ride!"

Venters calculated that a mile or more still intervened between them and the riders. They were approaching at a swift canter. Soon Venters recognized Tull's white horse, and concluded that the riders had likewise recognized Black Star and Night. But it would be impossible for Tull yet to see that the blacks were not ridden by Lassiter and Jane. Venters noted that Tull and the line of horsemen, perhaps ten or twelve in number, stopped several times and evidently looked hard down the slope. It must have been a puzzling circumstance for Tull. Venters laughed grimly at the thought of what Tull's rage would be when he finally discovered the trick. Venters meant to sheer out into the sage before Tull could possibly be sure who rode the blacks.

The gap closed to a distance of half a mile. Tull halted. His riders came up and formed a dark group around him. Venters thought he saw him wave his arms, and was certain of it when the riders dashed into the sage, to right and left of the trail. Tull had anticipated just the move held in mind by Venters.

"Now Bess!" shouted Venters. "Strike north. Go round those riders and turn west."

Black Star sailed over the low sage, and in few leaps got into his stride and was running. Venters spurred Night after him. It was hard going in the sage. The horses could run as well there, but keen eyesight and judgment must constantly be used by the riders in choosing ground. And continuous swerving from aisle to aisle between the brush, and leaping little washes and mounds of the pack-rats, and breaking through sage, made rough riding. When Venters had turned into a long aisle he had time to look up at Tull's riders. They were now strung out into an extended line riding north-east. And, as Venters and Bess were holding due north, this meant, if the horses of Tull and his riders had the speed and the staying power, they would head the blacks and turn them back down the slope. Tull's men were not saving their mounts; they were driving them desperately. Venters feared only an accident to Black Star or Night, and skilful riding would mitigate possibility of that. One glance ahead served to show him that Bess could pick a course through the sage as well as he. She looked neither back nor at the running riders, and bent forward over Black Star's neck and studied the ground ahead.

It struck Venters, presently, after he had glanced up from time to time, that Bess was drawing away from him as he had expected. He had, however, only thought of the light weight Black Star was carrying and of his superior speed; he saw now that the black was being ridden as never before, except when Jerry Card lost the race to Wrangle. How easily, gracefully, naturally, Bess sat her saddle! She could ride! Suddenly Venters remembered she had said she could ride. But he had not dreamed she was capable of such superb horsemanship. Then all at once, flashing over him, thrilling him, came the recollection that Bess was Oldring's Masked Rider.

He forgot Tull—the running riders—the race. He let Night have a free rein and felt him lengthen out to suit himself, knowing he would keep to Black Star's course, knowing that he had been chosen by the best rider now on the upland sage. For Jerry Card was dead. And fame had rivaled him with only one rider, and that was the slender girl who now swung so easily with Black Star's stride. Venters had abhorred her notoriety, but now he took passionate pride in her skill, her daring, her power over a horse. And he delved into his memory, recalling famous rides which he had heard related in the villages and round the camp-fires. Oldring's Masked Rider! Many times this strange rider, at once well known and unknown, had escaped pursuers by matchless riding. He had run the gantlet of vigilantes down the main street of Stone Bridge, leaving dead horses and dead rustlers behind. He had jumped his horse over the Gerber Wash, a deep, wide ravine separating the fields of Glaze from the wild sage. He had been surrounded north of Sterling; and he had broken through the line. How often had been told the story of day stampedes, of night raids, of pursuit, and then how the Masked Rider, swift as the wind, was gone in the sage! A fleet, dark horse—a slender, dark form—a black mask—a driving run down the slope—a dot on the purple sage—a shadowy, muffled steed disappearing in the night!

And this Masked Rider of the uplands had been Elizabeth Erne!

The sweet sage wind rushed in Venters's face and sang a song in his ears. He heard the dull, rapid beat of Night's hoofs; he saw Black Star drawing away, farther and farther. He realized both horses were swinging to the west. Then gunshots in the rear reminded him of Tull. Venters looked back. Far to the side, dropping behind, trooped the riders. They were shooting. Venters saw no puffs of dust, heard no whistling bullets. He was out of range. When he looked back again Tull's riders had given up pursuit. The best they could do, no doubt, had been to get near enough to recognize who really rode the blacks. Venters saw Tull drooping in his saddle.

Then Venters pulled Night out of his running stride. Those few miles had scarcely warmed the black, but Venters wished to save him. Bess turned, and, though she was far away, Venters caught the white glint of her waving hand. He held Night to a trot and rode on, seeing Bess and Black Star, and the sloping upward stretch of sage, and from time to time the receding black riders behind. Soon they disappeared behind a ridge, and he turned no more. They would go back to Lassiter's trail and follow it, and follow in vain. So Venters rode on, with the wind growing sweeter to taste and smell, and the purple sage richer and the sky bluer in his sight; and the song in his ears ringing. By and by Bess halted to wait for him, and he knew she had come to the trail. When he reached her it was to smile at sight of her standing with arms round Black Star's neck.

"Oh, Bern! I love him!" she cried. "He's beautiful; he knows; and how he can run! I've had fast horses. But Black Star! . . . Wrangle never beat him!"

"I'm wondering if I didn't dream that. Bess, the blacks are grand. What it must have cost Jane—ah!—well, when we get out of this wild country with Star and Night, back to my old home in Illinois, we'll buy a beautiful farm with meadows and springs and cool shade. There we'll turn the horses free—free to roam and browse and drink—never to feel a spur again—never to be ridden!"

"I would like that," said Bess.

They rested. Then, mounting, they rode side by side up the white trail. The sun rose higher behind them. Far to the left a low line of green marked the site of Cottonwoods. Venters looked once and looked no more. Bess gazed only straight ahead. They put the blacks to the long, swinging rider's canter, and at times pulled them to a trot, and occasionally to a walk. The hours passed, the miles slipped behind, and the wall of rock loomed in the fore. The Notch opened wide. It was a rugged, stony pass, but with level and open trail, and Venters and Bess ran the blacks through it. An old trail led off to the right, taking the line of the wall, and this Venters knew to be the trail mentioned by Lassiter.

The little hamlet, Glaze, a white and green patch in the vast waste of purple, lay miles down a slope much like the Cottonwoods slope, only this descended to the west. And miles farther west a faint green spot marked the location of Stone Bridge. All the rest of that world was seemingly smooth, undulating sage, with no ragged lines of cañons to accentuate its wildness.

"Bess, we're safe—we're free!" said Venters. "We're alone on the sage. We're half way to Sterling."

"Ah! I wonder how it is with Lassiter and Miss Withersteen."

"Never fear, Bess. He'll outwit Tull. He'll get away and hide her safely. He might climb into Surprise Valley, but I don't think he'll go so far."

"Bern, will we ever find any place like our beautiful valley?"

"No. But, dear, listen. We'll go back some day, after years—ten years. Then we'll be forgotten. And our valley will be just as we left it."

WHEN HE AND BESS RODE UP OUT OF THE HOLLOW THE SUN WAS LOW

"What if Balancing Rock falls and closes the outlet to the Pass?"

"I've thought of that. I'll pack in ropes and ropes. And if the outlet's closed we'll climb up the cliffs and over them to the valley and go down on rope ladders. It could be done. I know just where to make the climb, and I'll never forget."

"Oh yes, let us go back!"

"It's something sweet to look forward to. Bess, it's like all the future looks to me."

"Call me—Elizabeth," she said, shyly.

"Elizabeth Erne! It's a beautiful name. But I'll never forget Bess. Do you know—have you thought that very soon—by this time to-morrow—you will be Elizabeth Venters?"

So they rode on down the old trail. And the sun sloped to the west, and a golden sheen lay on the sage. The hours sped now; the afternoon waned. Often they rested the horses. The glisten of a pool of water in a hollow caught Venters's eye, and here he unsaddled the blacks and let them roll and drink and browse. When he and Bess rode up out of the hollow the sun was low, a crimson ball, and the valley seemed veiled in purple fire and smoke. It was that short time when the sun appeared to rest before setting, and silence, like a cloak of invisible life, lay heavy on all that shimmering world of sage.

They watched the sun begin to bury its red curve under the dark horizon.

"We'll ride on till late," he said. "Then you can sleep a little, while I watch and graze the horses. And we'll ride into Sterling early to-morrow. We'll be married! . . . We'll be in time to catch the stage. We'll tie Black Star and Night behind—and then—for a country not wild and terrible like this!"

"Oh, Bern! . . . But look! The sun is setting on the sage—the last time for us till we dare come again to the Utah border. Ten years! Oh, Bern, look, so you will never forget!"

Slumbering, fading purple fire burned over the undulating sage ridges. Long streaks and bars and shafts and spears fringed the far western slope. Drifting, golden veils mingled with low, purple shadows. Colors and shades changed in slow, wondrous transformation.

Suddenly Venters was startled by a low, rumbling roar —so low that it was like the roar in a sea-shell.

"Bess, did you hear anything?" he whispered.

"No."

"Listen! . . . Maybe I only imagined— *Ah!*"

Out of the east or north, from remote distance, breathed an infinitely low, continuously long sound—deep, weird, detonating, thundering, deadening—dying.

CHAPTER XXIII

THE FALL OF BALANCING ROCK

THROUGH tear-blurred sight Jane Withersteen watched Venters and Elizabeth Erne and the black racers disappear over the ridge of sage.

"They're gone!" said Lassiter. "An' they're safe now. An' there'll never be a day of their comin' happy lives but what they'll remember Jane Withersteen an'—an' Uncle Jim! . . . I reckon, Jane we'd better be on our way."

The burros obediently wheeled and started down the break with little, cautious steps, but Lassiter had to leash the whining dogs and lead them. Jane felt herself bound in a feeling that was neither listlessness nor indifference, yet which rendered her incapable of interest. She was still strong in body, but emotionally tired. That hour at the entrance to Deception Pass had been the climax of her suffering—the flood of her wrath—the last of her sacrifice—the supremity of her love—and the attainment of peace. She thought that if she had little Fay she would not ask any more of life.

Like an automaton she followed Lassiter down the steep trail of dust and bits of weathered stone; and when the little slides moved with her or piled around her knees she experienced no alarm. Vague relief came to her in the sense of being enclosed between dark stone walls, deep hidden from the glare of sun, from the glistening sage. Lassiter lengthened the stirrup straps on one of the burros and bade her mount and ride close to him. She was to keep the burro from cracking his little hard hoofs on stones. Then she was riding on between dark, gleaming walls. There were quiet and rest and coolness in this cañon. She noted indifferently that they passed close under shady, bulging shelves of cliff, through patches of grass and sage and thicket and groves of slender trees, and over white, pebbly washes, and around masses of broken rock. The burros trotted tirelessly; the dogs, once more free, pattered tirelessly; and Lassiter led on with never a stop, and at every open place he looked back. The shade under the walls gave place to sunlight. And presently they came to a dense thicket of slender trees, through which they passed to rich, green grass and water. Here Lassiter rested the burros for a little while, but he was restless, uneasy, silent, always listening, peering under the trees. She dully reflected that enemies were behind them—before them; still the thought awakened no dread or concern or interest.

At his bidding she mounted and rode on close to the heels of his burro. The cañon narrowed; the walls lifted their rugged rims higher; and the sun shone down hot from the center of the blue stream of sky above. Lassiter traveled slower, with more exceeding care as to the ground he chose, and he kept speaking low to the dogs. They were now hunting-dogs—keen, alert, suspicious, sniffing the warm breeze. The monotony of the yellow walls broke in change of color and smooth surface, and the rugged outline of rims grew craggy. Splits appeared in deep breaks, and gorges running at right angles, and then the Pass opened wide at a junction of intersecting cañons.

Lassiter dismounted, led his burro, called the dogs close, and proceeded at snail pace through dark masses of rock and dense thickets under the left wall. Long he watched and listened before venturing to cross the mouths of side cañons. At length he halted, tied his burro, lifted a warning hand to Jane, and then slipped away among the boulders, and, followed by the stealthy dogs, disappeared from sight. The time he remained absent was neither short nor long to Jane Withersteen.

When he reached her side again he was pale, and his lips were set in a hard line, and his gray eyes glittered coldly. Bidding her dismount, he led the burros into a covert of stones and cedars, and tied them.

"Jane, I've run into the fellers I've been lookin' for, an' I'm goin' after them," he said.

"Why?" she asked.

"I reckon I won't take time to tell you."

"Couldn't we slip by without being seen?"

"Likely enough. But that ain't my game. An' I'd like to know, in case I don't come back, what you'll do."

"What can I do?"

"I reckon you can go back to Tull. Or stay in the Pass an' be taken off by rustlers. Which 'll you do?"

"I don't know. I can't think very well. But I believe I'd rather be taken off by rustlers."

Lassiter sat down, put his head in his hands, and remained for a few moments in what appeared to be deep and painful thought. When he lifted his face it was haggard, lined, cold as sculptured marble.

"I'll go. I only mentioned that chance of my not comin' back. I'm pretty sure to come."

"Need you risk so much? Must you fight more? Haven't you shed enough blood?"

"I'd like to tell you why I'm goin'," he continued, in coldness he had seldom used to her. She remarked it, but it was the same to her as if he had spoken with his old gentle warmth. "But I reckon I won't. Only, I'll say that mercy an' goodness, such as is in you, though they're the grand things in human nature, can't be lived up to on this Utah border. Life's hell out here. You think—or you used to think—that your religion made this life heaven. Mebbe them scales on your eyes has dropped now. Jane, I wouldn't have you no different, an' that's why I'm goin' to try to hide you somewhere in this Pass. I'd like to hide many more women, for I've come to see there are more like you among your people. An' I'd like you to see jest how hard an' cruel this border life is. It's bloody. You'd think churches an' churchmen would make it better. They make it worse. You give names to things—bishops, elders, ministers, Mormonism, duty, faith, glory. You dream—or you're driven mad. I'm a man, an' I know. I name fanatics, followers, blind women, oppressors, thieves, ranchers, rustlers, riders. An' we have—what you've lived through these last months. It can't be helped. But it can't last always. An' remember this—some day the border 'll be better, cleaner, for the ways of men like Lassiter!"

She saw him shake his tall form erect, look at her strangely and steadfastly, and then, noiselessly, stealthily slip away amid the rocks and trees. Ring and Whitie, not being bidden to follow, remained with Jane. She felt extreme weariness, yet somehow it did not seem to be of her body. And she sat down in the shade and tried to think. She saw a creeping lizard, cactus flowers, the drooping burros, the resting dogs, an eagle high over a yellow crag. Once the meanest flower, a color, the flight of a bee, or any living thing had given her deepest joy. Lassiter had gone off, yielding to his incurable blood lust, probably to his own death; and she was sorry, but there was no feeling in her sorrow.

Suddenly from the mouth of the cañon just beyond her rang out a clear, sharp report of a rifle. Echoes clapped. Then followed a piercingly high yell of anguish, quickly breaking. Again echoes clapped, in grim imitation. Dull revolver shots—hoarse yells—pound of hoofs—shrill neighs of horses—commingling of echoes—and again silence! Lassiter must be busily engaged, thought Jane, and no chill trembled over her, no blanching tightened her skin. Yes, the border was a bloody place. But life had always been bloody. Men were blood-spillers. Phases of the history of the world flashed through her mind—Greek and Roman wars, dark, mediæval times, the crimes in the name of religion. On sea, on land, everywhere—shooting, stabbing, cursing, clashing, fighting men! Greed, power, oppression, fanaticism, love, hate, revenge, justice, freedom—for these, men killed one another.

She lay there under the cedars, gazing up through the delicate lacelike foliage at the blue sky, and she thought and wondered and did not care.

More rattling shots disturbed the noonday quiet. She heard a sliding of weathered rock, a hoarse shout of warning, a yell of alarm, again the clear, sharp crack of the rifle, and another cry that was a cry of death. Then rifle reports pierced a dull volley of revolver shots. Bullets whizzed over Jane's hiding-place; one struck a stone and whined away in the air. After that, for a time, succeeded desultory shots; and then they ceased under long, thundering fire from heavier guns.

Sooner or later, then, Jane heard the cracking of horses' hoofs on the stones, and tne sound came nearer and nearer. Silence intervened until Lassiter's soft, jingling step assured her of his approach. When he appeared he was covered with blood.

"All right, Jane," he said. "I come back. An' don't worry."

With water from a canteen he washed the blood from his face and hands.

"Jane, hurry now. Tear my scarf in two, an' tie up these places. That hole through my hand is some inconvenient, worse 'n this cut over my ear. There—you're doin' fine! Not a bit nervous—no tremblin'. I reckon I ain't done your courage justice. I'm glad you're brave jest now—you'll need to be. Well, I was hid pretty good, enough to keep them from shootin' me deep, but they was slingin' lead close all the time. I used up all the rifle shells, an' then I went after them. Mebbe you heard. It was then I got hit. I had to use up every shell in my own guns, an' they did, too, as I seen. Rustlers an' Mormons, Jane! An' now I'm packin' five bullet holes in my carcass, an' guns without shells. Hurry, now."

He unstrapped the saddle-bags from the burros, slipped the saddles and let them lie, turned the burros loose, and, calling the dogs, led the way through stones and cedars to an open where two horses stood.

"Jane, are you strong?" he asked.

"I think so. I'm not tired," Jane replied.

"I don't mean that way. Can you bear up?"

"I think I can bear anything."

"I reckon you look a little cold an' thick. So I'm preparin' you."

"For what?"

"I didn't tell you why I jest had to go after them fellers. I couldn't tell you. I believe you'd have died. But I can tell you now—if you'll bear up under a shock?"

"Go on, my friend."

"*I've got little Fay!* Alive—bad hurt—but she'll live!"

Jane Withersteen's dead-locked feeling, rent by Lassiter's deep, quivering voice, leaped into an agony of sensitive life.

"Here," he added, and showed her where little Fay lay on the grass.

Unable to speak, unable to stand, Jane dropped on her knees. By that long, beautiful golden hair Jane recognized the beloved Fay. But Fay's loveliness was gone. Her face was drawn and looked old with grief. But she was not dead—her heart beat—and Jane Withersteen gathered strength and lived again.

"You see I jest had to go after Fay," Lassiter was saying, as he knelt to bathe her little pale face. "But

I reckon I don't want no more choices like the one I had to make. There was a crippled feller in that bunch, Jane. Mebbe Venters crippled him. Anyway, that's why they were holdin' up here. I seen little Fay first thing, an' was hard put to it to figure out a way to get her. An' I wanted hosses, too. I had to take chances. So I crawled close to their camp. One feller jumped a hoss with little Fay, an' when I shot him, of course she dropped. She's stunned an' bruised—she fell right on her head. Jane, she's comin' to! She ain't bad hurt!"

Fay's long lashes fluttered; her eyes opened. At first they seemed glazed over. They looked dazed by pain. Then they quickened, darkened, to shine with intelligence —bewilderment—memory—and sudden wonderful joy.

"Muvver—Jane!" she whispered.

"Oh, little Fay, little Fay!" cried Jane, lifting, clasping the child to her.

"*Now*, we've got to rustle!" said Lassiter, in grim coolness. "Jane, look down the Pass!"

Across the mounds of rock and sage Jane caught sight of a band of riders filing out of the narrow neck of the Pass; and in the lead was a white horse, which, even at a distance of a mile or more, she knew.

"Tull!" she almost screamed.

"I reckon. But, Jane, we've still got the game in our hands. They're ridin' tired hosses. Venters likely give them a chase. He wouldn't forget that. An' we've fresh hosses."

Hurriedly he strapped on the saddle-bags, gave quick glance to girths and cinches and stirrups, then leaped astride.

"Lift little Fay up," he said.

With shaking arms Jane complied.

"Get back your nerve, woman! This is life or death now. Mind that. Climb up! Keep your wits. Stick close to me. Watch where your hoss 's goin' an' ride!"

Somehow Jane mounted; somehow found strength

to hold the reins, to spur, to cling on, to ride. A horrible quaking, craven fear possessed her soul. Lassiter led the swift flight across the wide space, over washes, through sage, into a narrow cañon where the rapid clatter of hoofs rapped sharply from the walls. The wind roared in her ears; the gleaming cliffs swept by; trail and sage and grass moved under her. Lassiter's bandaged, blood-stained face turned to her; he shouted encouragement; he looked back down the Pass; he spurred his horse. Jane clung on, spurring likewise. And the horses settled from hard, furious gallop into a long-striding, driving run. She had never ridden at anything like that pace; desperately she tried to get the swing of the horse, to be of some help to him in that race, to see the best of the ground and guide him into it. But she failed of everything except to keep her seat in the saddle, and to spur and spur. At times she closed her eyes, unable to bear sight of Fay's golden curls streaming in the wind. She could not pray; she could not rail; she no longer cared for herself. All of life, of good, of use in the world, of hope in heaven centered in Lassiter's ride with little Fay to safety. She would have tried to turn the iron-jawed brute she rode; she would have given herself to that relentless, dark-browed Tull. But she knew Lassiter would turn with her, so she rode on and on.

Whether that run was of moments or hours Jane Withersteen could not tell. Lassiter's horse covered her with froth that blew back in white streams. Both horses ran their limit, were allowed to slow down in time to save them, and went on dripping, heaving, staggering.

"Oh, Lassiter, we must run—we must run!"

He looked back, saying nothing. The bandage had blown from his head, and blood trickled down his face. He was bowing under the strain of injuries, of the ride, of his burden. Yet how cool and gray he looked—how intrepid!

FALL OF BALANCING ROCK

The horses walked, trotted, galloped, ran, to fall again to walk. Hours sped or dragged. Time was an instant—an eternity. Jane Withersteen felt hell pursuing her, and dared not look back for fear she would fall from her horse.

"Oh, Lassiter! Is he coming?"

The grim rider looked over his shoulder, but said no word. Little Fay's golden hair floated on the breeze. The sun shone; the walls gleamed; the sage glistened. And then it seemed the sun vanished, the walls shaded, the sage paled. The horses walked—trotted—galloped—ran—to fall again to walk. Shadows gathered under shelving cliffs. The cañon turned, brightened, opened into long, wide, wall-enclosed valley. Again the sun, lowering in the west, reddened the sage. Far ahead round, scrawled stone appeared to block the Pass.

"Bear up, Jane, bear up!" called Lassiter. "It's our game, if you don't weaken."

"Lassiter! Go on—*alone!* Save little Fay!"

"Only with you!"

"Oh!—I'm a coward—a miserable coward! I can't fight or think or hope or pray! I'm lost! Oh, Lassiter, look back! Is he coming? I'll not—hold out—"

"Keep your breath, woman, an' ride not for yourself or for me, but for Fay!"

A last breaking run across the sage brought Lassiter's horse to a walk.

"He's done," said the rider.

"Oh, no—no!" moaned Jane.

"Look back, Jane, look back. Three—four miles we've come across this valley, an' no Tull yet in sight. Only a few more miles!"

Jane looked back over the long stretch of sage, and found the narrow gap in the wall, out of which came a file of dark horses with a white horse in the lead. Sight of the riders acted upon Jane as a stimulant. The weight of cold, horrible terror lessened. And, gazing forward at the dogs, at Lassiter's limping horse, at the blood on his face, at the rocks growing nearer, last at Fay's golden hair, the ice left her veins, and slowly, strangely, she gained hold of strength that she believed would see her to the safety Lassiter promised. And, as she gazed, Lassiter's horse stumbled and fell.

He swung his leg and slipped from the saddle.

"Jane, take the child," he said, and lifted Fay up. Jane clasped her with arms suddenly strong. "They're gainin'," went on Lassiter, as he watched the pursuing riders. "But we'll beat 'em yet."

Turning with Jane's bridle in his hand, he was about to start when he saw the saddle-bag on the fallen horse.

"I've jest about got time," he muttered, and with swift fingers that did not blunder or fumble he loosened the bag and threw it over his shoulder. Then he started to run, leading Jane's horse, and he ran, and trotted, and walked, and ran again. Close ahead now Jane saw a rise of bare rock. Lassiter reached it, searched along the base, and, finding a low place, dragged the weary horse up and over round, smooth stone. Looking backward, Jane saw Tull's white horse not a mile distant, with riders strung out in a long line behind him. Looking forward, she saw more valley to the right, and to the left a towering cliff. Lassiter pulled the horse and kept on.

Little Fay lay in her arms with wide-open eyes—eyes which were still shadowed by pain, but no longer fixed, glazed in terror. The golden curls blew across Jane's lips; the little hands feebly clasped her arm; a ghost of a troubled, trustful smile hovered round the sweet lips. And Jane Withersteen awoke to the spirit of a lioness.

Lassiter was leading the horse up a smooth slope toward cedar-trees of twisted and bleached appearance. Among these he halted.

"Jane, give me the girl an' get down," he said. As if it wrenched him he unbuckled the empty black guns with a strange air of finality. He then received Fay in his arms and stood a moment looking backward. Tull's white horse mounted the ridge of round stone, and several bays or blacks followed. "I wonder what he'll think when he sees them empty guns. Jane, bring your saddle-bag and climb after me."

A glistening, wonderful bare slope, with little holes, swelled up and up to lose itself in a frowning yellow cliff. Jane closely watched her steps and climbed behind Lassiter. He moved slowly. Perhaps he was only husbanding his strength. But she saw drops of blood on the stone, and then she knew. They climbed and climbed without looking back. Her breast labored; she began to feel as if little points of fiery steel were penetrating her side into her lungs. She heard the panting of Lassiter and the quicker panting of the dogs.

"Wait—here," he said.

Before her rose a bulge of stone, nicked with little cut steps, and above that a corner of yellow wall, and overhanging that a vast, ponderous cliff.

The dogs pattered up, disappeared round the corner. Lassiter mounted the steps with Fay, and he swayed like a drunken man, and he too disappeared. But instantly he returned alone, and half ran, half slipped down to her.

Then from below pealed up hoarse shouts of angry men. Tull and several of his riders had reached the spot where Lassiter had parted with his guns.

"You'll need that breath—mebbe!" said Lassiter, facing downward, with glittering eyes.

"Now, Jane, the last pull," he went on. "Walk up them little steps. I'll follow an' steady you. Don't think. Jest go. Little Fay's above. Her eyes are open. She jest said to me, '*Where's muvver Jane?*'"

Without a fear or a tremor or a slip or a touch of Lassiter's hand Jane Withersteen walked up that ladder of cut steps.

He pushed her round the corner of wall. Fay lay, with wide staring eyes, in the shade of a gloomy wall.

The dogs waited. Lassiter picked up the child and turned into a dark cleft. It zigzagged. It widened. It opened. Jane was amazed at a wonderfully smooth and steep incline leading up between ruined, splintered, toppling walls. A red haze from the setting sun filled this passage. Lassiter climbed with slow, measured steps, and blood dripped from him to make splotches on the white stone. Jane tried not to step in his blood, but was compelled, for she found no other footing. The saddle-bag began to drag her down; she gasped for breath; she thought her heart was bursting. Slower, slower yet the rider climbed, whistling as he breathed. The incline widened. Huge pinnacles and monuments of stone stood alone, leaning fearfully. Red sunset haze shone through cracks where the wall had split. Jane did not look high, but she felt the overshadowing of broken rims above. She felt that it was a fearful, menacing place. And she climbed on in heartrending effort. And she fell beside Lassiter and Fay at the top of the incline in a narrow, smooth divide.

He staggered to his feet—staggered to a huge, leaning rock that rested on a small pedestal. He put his hand on it—the hand that had been shot through—and Jane saw blood drip from the ragged hole. Then he fell.

"Jane—I—can't—do—it!" he whispered.

"What?"

"Roll the—stone! . . . All my—life I've loved—to roll stones—an' now I—can't!"

"What of it? You talk strangely. Why roll that stone?"

"I planned to—fetch you here—to roll this stone. See! It 'll smash the crags—loosen the walls—close the outlet!"

As Jane Withersteen gazed down that long incline, walled in by crumbling cliffs, awaiting only the slightest jar to make them fall asunder, she saw Tull appear at the bottom and begin to climb. A rider followed him—another—and another.

FALL OF BALANCING ROCK

"See! Tull! The riders!"

"Yes—they'll get us—now."

"Why? Haven't you strength left to roll the stone?"

"Jane—it ain't that—I've lost my nerve!"

"*You!* . . . Lassiter!"

"I wanted to roll it—meant to—but I—can't. Venters's valley is down behind here. We could—live there. But if I roll the stone—we're shut in for always. I don't dare. I'm thinkin' of you!"

"Lassiter! Roll the stone!" she cried.

He arose, tottering, but with set face, and again he placed the bloody hand on the Balancing Rock. Jane Withersteen gazed from him down the passageway. Tull was climbing. Almost, she thought, she saw his dark, relentless face. Behind him more riders climbed. What did they mean for Fay—for Lassiter—for herself?

"*Roll the stone! . . . Lassiter, I love you!*"

Under all his deathly pallor, and the blood, and the iron of seared cheek and lined brow, worked a great change. He placed both hands on the rock and then leaned his shoulder there and braced his powerful body.

"ROLL THE STONE!"

It stirred, it groaned, it grated, it moved; and with a slow grinding, as of wrathful relief, began to lean. It had waited ages to fall, and now was slow in starting. Then, as if suddenly instinct with life, it leaped hurtlingly down to alight on the steep incline, to bound more swiftly into the air, to gather momentum, to plunge into the lofty leaning crag below. The crag thundered into atoms. A wave of air—a splitting shock! Dust shrouded the sunset red of shaking rims; dust shrouded Tull as he fell on his knees with uplifted arms. Shafts and monuments and sections of wall fell majestically.

From the depths there rose a long-drawn rumbling roar. The outlet to Deception Pass closed forever.

THE END